THE PROPHECY
Copyright © 2024 by Shabucky WinterRose



ISBN 979-8-9891566-4-1

Cover Design by Brittany Evans

Edited by Represent Publishing

# THE PROPHECY

# WAR OF THE REALMS

# THE PROPHECY

## SHABUCKY WINTERROSE

SugarBug,

To the one who made me a mom and showed me the power of love.
Our adventures have only begun, and the opportunity to create a
dynamic and powerful world in your honor has been most rewarding.

Magyieka is here to enhance the world we have and allow us to explore
unlimited possibilities—this created magic world is yours. It's a
reminder to chase your dreams and know that the world is our
playground while our life's light allows us to be here.

Time is a precious and fragile thing; live every moment to the fullest,
and know I will be here to hold you up, watch you bloom, and fuel you
when your resources are low.

Thanks for bringing light to my world.
Love, Mom.

# PROGLOGUE

## Vienna & Logan's
## POV

Vienna tossed as her nightmare progressed. Sweat drenched her body, leaving plastered hair against her temples. Her parents looked on hopelessly, concern consuming them as their daughter trembled. Tate grumbled as he watched Grace try to unsuccessfully soothe their teenage daughter. Vienna shuddered in pain.

Grace closed her teary eyes, squelching the guilt that plagued her. Their only daughter wouldn't be in this situation if she'd done things differently. Pushing the intrusive thoughts aside, Grace hummed Vienna's favorite childhood lullaby. Pulling the cold cloth from the window, she placed it on Vienna's forehead and watched as waves of steam poured off it.

"This is the third night terror this week. What is causing this?" Tate seethed as he paced helplessly. From the moment they found out they were pregnant, they'd done everything in their power to protect their family. And yet, Vienna's powers were calling.

"Her notebooks are full of facts about the Witch Trials. That's the only thing that could have triggered this," she explained. "The notes go beyond what's taught in schools. She's become obsessed with the topic, Tate."

Grace glanced at him for support, and his jaw clenched. He needed reassurance. "It will be all right. She's strong."

"How long before we tell her? It could be the best thing to do now. To arm her with the knowledge we've held all these years."

Grace flinched at the accusation in his tone. He had wanted to tell Vienna everything from the beginning; she'd disagreed, fearing it would jeopardize their safety.

"Not until we know for certain what's happening. If she learns what we've been hiding, it can ignite her power, sending out a wave of electricity alerting the Council that she's not dormant anymore. Her name would be transcribed into the books, and awareness of her existence would become permanent." Her voice wavered.

Tate kneeled beside Grace. "There must be something we can do. Her fever broke 105 tonight; how much more can her body take?"

"All we can do is wait; she's younger than others raised in this realm. There must be a reason for that." Tears dropped from her quivering chin. "We should have had more time. One spark of power and everything changes."

Tate wrapped his arms around her. "We knew this could happen," he whispered. "We'll get through this."

"That damn class changed everything; it wasn't even on her syllabus," Grace vented. "The night sweats, the mood swings, even her struggle to find energy to make it through the day; it began when she started that class. We should have . . ."

Vienna's body seized before crumpling into a weightless heap. A thin curtain danced in the breeze—the smell of the crisp air soothed her parents.

With Vienna's fever broken, Tate released his wife and stood. "Grab the cloth; I'll close the window. She'll be able to sleep for a while now."

"What if she's a Dreamwalker?" Grace tossed the idea.

"Why would you think that?" Tate asked.

"She speaks of her dreams as if they are real. As a child, I heard stories about the Nether Realm. What she describes"—Grace tucked in her daughter—"reminds me of those stories I heard."

"If that's true, we can't leave her there." He stepped closer, his heartbeat increasing at the thought of Vienna being trapped.

"If she is a Dreamwalker, she could be trapped if we try to wake her. She must go through the entire process; she'll explore and then come back when she's ready. I'm probably wrong, anyway. It's an extremely rare ability." She waved her hand, tossing the thought away, then closed the door behind them.

▽△△▽✳

*My parents' muffled voices drift away; I am not in my room. Instead, I'm tossed into a nightmare, with no way to escape until fate releases me or a tie to my realm reconnects me.*

*Warm air wraps around each curve of my body, and I embrace it as my senses clear and the hazy landscape unfolds. Taking in the copper scenery, I shiver, and the warmth shifts to an achy chill, sending a painful shock up my spine.*

*The familiar desert is barren, void of life. No creatures. No plants. No sound. The nothingness overwhelms my senses. I am cemented in place, and panic rises; blood whooshes as adrenaline urges me to flee . . . to scream. Thoughts of my last visit force a pressure onto my chest, and a scream fails to escape into the night. As I claw at my throat and gasp for air, my panic constricts my quivering lungs, and halos cast shadows across my vision.*

*"Tsk, tsk . . . you naïve girl. There's no use fighting this, Ms. Madizza-Corey. You are powerless here. My puppet."*

*That voice. I still, and my shriveling lungs cease to exist as the voice penetrates my awareness. Glancing across the vast, rustic scenery, I search for the middle-aged woman I know looms nearby. To my left, strands of red hair flicker into view as she saunters closer. A velvet black dress hugs her tightly—sharp hip bones threaten to slice* the seams. She tugs on the train of her dress as she circles me like a predator to its prey.

The villain of my dreams since freshman year. Hope that she will cease to exist fades. With each dream getting more realistic and exhaustion growing upon my waking, my ability to fight dwindles. Still, I meet her fiery gaze with my icy glare—determined to hide my fear.

"Eventually, my dear," the woman hisses with a victorious grin, "you will fail, and I will rise. Once I move from the shadows," she grips my chin, sharp nails slicing the skin, "then my reign will begin."

Lack of oxygen forces my eyelids to droop, and my body goes limp. It hangs weightlessly as she squeezes my bloody face. Darkness consumes my vision, and as my heartbeat slows, my panic is replaced with peace. I close my eyes and think about home.

Please don't let her win, I pray, willing somebody to wake me from this horror and release me from paralysis. I think about waking up in my warm bed, comforted by those I love.

A thunderous cackle assaults my ears. "You will never win, child. You can't even speak in this realm. I will always win here. And soon, I will . . ."

## LOGAN

"The Council has summoned you for an update on Vienna." Mr. Humphrey moved purposefully through Onyx Hall.

"How much do I tell them?" Logan followed behind, pulling at his robe.

"As little as possible. Keep it brief and only answer exactly what they ask." His tone was flat.

"When do we tell her about all this?" Logan asked.

"That I can't answer," Mr. Humphrey said.

Logan stopped outside the large black doors. The Council members would be on the other side. He shook his hands, nervous at the thought of the wrong things slipping.

"Focus on her growth, nothing personal." Mr. Humphrey walked through the doors, leaving Logan standing alone.

Ringing filled the hall, the echo jarring Logan into action. He pushed the doors open and moved through the chamber with a confident stride, opposing his internal quaking.

Standing next to Mr. Humphrey, he looked around the six-sided table that held space for twelve council members. Each member wore a black robe with a colored stripe that represented their territory, with two members representing their people. Logan's silver stripe filled him with pride—the Shadow Realm, Shifter Territory was a strong alliance to have. The opportunity to serve was an honor, but it had come at a cost. Her protection outweighed the loss he felt, giving him strength.

"Logan, for years now you've watched over Ms. Madizza-Corey. Yesterday, it was brought to our attention that she continues to struggle with punctuality, academics, and night terrors. What else can you add?" Mr. Humphrey was blunt. His stare was cold. As Head of the Council, his personality was sharper than in other affairs, and it was hard to adjust to the shift.

"Our interactions have been few this year. I did see an increase in research materials regarding witchcraft, elemental manipulation, and philosophy of realms in her possession." Logan nodded at Ms. Blight; she had helped him by presenting this information and worked directly with him as he continued to watch Vienna.

Ms. Blight smiled, glancing around the table. "The Prophecy predicts a change before the Summer Solstice. With less than a semester left in the Human Realm and the increase of early development, it is in our best interest to prepare an early entrance and one mid-year. Since we are a year-long school, the transition will be challenging, but possible."

"Are you not jumping ahead? The girl has yet to show any magic abilities. What I hear are suspicions and nothing more," Mr. Ozul bit out.

"Ever the skeptic." Ms. Kaliese turned to Mr. Audovera. "You have been around for centuries and know much about the Prophecy; what are your thoughts?"

Mr. Audovera straightened his tie and stood. "The mere fact that Ms. Corey is of pure bloodline is becoming rare. But I implore you to delve deeper. Knowledge of what is happening beneath is crucial. Her character has shifted, and she is intrigued by the topic of witchcraft," he said stoically, watching Mr. Ozul.

"A topic common for a young woman nearing adulthood," Mrs. Laveau said. "Of our kind, it's expected. I see no reason to rush into such assumptions foolishly. The belief that she is the one professed to bring peace to our realms is unfounded."

Logan's pulse pounded as he pulled at his neckline. Mr. Humphrey sent him a warning glance, and Logan inhaled. "Graduation is nearing, and Vienna still plans to attend one of the colleges she was accepted to. This shows us that her human life is still most present." Logan cursed inwardly at the slip of colleges.

*As little as possible . . . keep it brief. Damn it!* he chastised himself.

"Tell me, boy, where are the colleges located?" Mr. Ozul demanded.

Mr. Humphrey shook his head, frustration evident. But he nodded, permitting Logan to answer.

"The ones she shared in class are in southern Oregon, Salem, Massachusetts, and London. Years ago, she also mentioned Germany and Hawaii."

Muffled voices filled the room, and the sound of the scriber ceased. Logan shifted his body weight as discomfort and confusion flushed over him.

"It appears a lapse in transparency has become present, for the details you share are of profound importance," the White Queen of the Seelie Court pointed out.

"Agreed." Mrs. Jaheem stood, her gold stripe glistening. "It's time to tease the possibilities. Logan, you will need to ensure you're ready for this. We understand the grief you've endured as you lost her as a friend. This could increase the distance between you or bring you two closer. The goal is to create closeness to ensure transparency, but if she senses this is an act, connection and trust may be lost."

"There is no deceit to be seen. My loyalty lies in protecting her. Not only because the Council ponders her link to the Prophecy but also because she is a dear friend. It has been unbearable to be apart for so long." He stopped, sure his point was clear.

The members debated the next steps as Logan stood there waiting for orders. Fear that she was The Chosen One couldn't be denied. It would be a dangerous journey, but he would take it with her, no matter how catastrophic things became.

The room went silent. Each member wrote their vote before tossing it to the middle of the table. After every paper touched the table, it erupted into flames.

"With our votes in, we will meet thirty moonfalls before the next solstice to gather for a verdict," Ms. Blight offered. "Until then, maintain the course."

The members left without another word.

"I fucked that up so much," Logan fumed.

"You did well, Logan." The deep voice was unexpected.

"Ovr'seer"—he dipped his head in respect—"I wasn't award you'd be joining today."

"It's an important matter. I wanted to be here to collaborate. With the verdict in, you're about to learn more about Vienna and the safety we have provided her."

"Why now?" Logan squashed his irritation, shoving a frustrated hand through his hair.

"Not only were the votes unanimous, but it is evident that Vienna's intuition is growing. And with the mention of her chosen schools, at some point we missed her earlier connection to our realm."

"In what way?" Logan sat on the edge of the table. Arms crossed, he fought the battle to defend her choices and downplay his slip.

"With each location you shared, there is one common aspect." He paused, allowing Logan to speak, but instead, Logan waved him on.

"Each of the locations holds an active portal that leads to Station Isle, giving her easy access directly to Magyieka. See, now we know there are at least some pieces of her that have always been awake, even raised as a Human. This is rare, Logan. Though you may feel you betrayed her, you have protected her."

"Now what?"

"When we gather, we will assess needs. For now, watch for signs of waking power." The Ovr'seer paused. "And if we see nothing before June, we will know it's time to look elsewhere."

Logan stared blankly, trying to process everything he had just learned. Frustrated, the need to escape beckoned. He pulled off his robe and stormed from Onyx Hall.

# CHAPTER ONE

Vienna slapped the alarm several times, then flopped onto her stomach before slipping into slumber. Snuggling into her pillow, she hoped for an extended snooze, but a final penetrating *BEEP* assaulted her. Bolting up, she looked around, blinking several times. Her stomach somersaulted as the blurry neon numbers focused.

Late, again.

"Crap!" She bolted upright, adrenaline propelling her into action. "Not again! Crappity, crap, crap!" Her senior year had not been going as planned. She had already served multiple detentions for constant tardiness, but no matter how hard she tried, she couldn't get up on time. *Damn the nightmares.*

Jumping out of bed, she gasped as her toe connected with her nightstand. "Seriously?" she screeched through gritted teeth. She hopped across the room, holding her throbbing toe. If there was a higher power, she'd do anything to give them a piece of her mind.

Done with the dramatics, she tore through the clothes on the floor until a set passed the sniff test. Pulling them on while awkwardly moving toward the hall, she paused by her vanity, taking in her appearance. With her pants half up and one arm sleeved, she drenched her hand in flowery de-frizz, then ran her fingers through her tangled, long-dark waves of hair. Finished, she buttoned her jeans and trampled down the stairs. Grabbing her backpack and an apple, she rushed toward her 1967 Camaro.

"Morning, Raven." She slid her hand over the top of the car before jiggling the handle.

After tossing her backpack into the passenger seat, she fired up the engine. With a gentle rev, Raven purred, and Vienna smiled as the car vibrated under her body. Working every summer for two years to purchase the beauty was worth every missed party and aching muscle.

"Atta girl." She patted the dashboard and threw the old girl into drive. Leaving a trail of dust as the rear end slid onto the road, Vienna hauled ass to school.

The car screeched as it swung into the closest parking spot she could find. Her anxiety increased and adrenaline fueled her as the final bell rang. Exiting the car, she flinched at the burned tar that Raven left in the rush. "Fuck it." She dismissed the marks and ran toward the building.

Throwing the front door open, she waved at the secretary, who shook her head. Vienna blushed and slowed to a jog. It had become a routine for the two to meet in quick passing: the secretary ignored Vienna's dash through the hall, and Vienna acted as though she didn't know the middle-aged woman was swiping on a dating app during work.

Out of sight now, Vienna sprinted toward her astronomy class.

The ringing faded, and Vienna accepted defeat . . . Tardy again.

Already late, she stopped outside the classroom door and straightened the threads of her ripped black jeans. She wanted to look her best if she had to walk in late.

Looking through the small rectangular window, she waited until her teacher turned toward the whiteboard. Quietly opening the door, she ducked into class, hoping to slide into her desk without notice. As her back leaned against the chair, Mr. Humphrey cleared his throat. A deep reverberation bounced through the room.

Vienna closed her eyes as crimson crawled across her chest. "Dammit," she whispered. She peered through her lashes in time to see Mr. Humphrey step toward her with crossed arms. She waved and sent a smile his way. He shook his head, unamused.

"Miss Corey, do you or do you not know how to tell time?" he asked with pursed lips.

"Yes, I just—"

"Great." He clapped his hands. "Then there is no reason for you to be late. I assume you enjoyed detention so much that you wanted a second round. Arrive at the library on Saturday at 6 am. If you're late, you'll serve an in-school suspension. So, Miss Corey, ensure you do, in fact, know how to use a clock." Done with his tirade, he turned around and finished writing the day's lesson on the board.

Vienna sat in shock. Mr. Humphrey's hostile show was unusual— he was usually discreet when dealing with problem students. As she sat there stewing, she could feel the heat rising to her face. She glanced across the room as the students stared.

Anger washed over her. Shallow breaths preceded her blurred vision, and she squeezed her eyes shut, desperately pushing away the desire to flee class. Inside her, a voice stirred, and she couldn't help but agree with it: This was personal. Mr. Humphrey had targeted her.

A shiver tingled her spine. She glanced around the room, seeking comfort. Logan looked up, and their eyes locked. Once her best friend, he sat there, detached from her pain. Embarrassment swallowed her rage as a fire ignited within her core. Her face twitched as she refrained from lashing out. Instead, she turned back to the board, suppressing tears.

Rubbing a thumb across her teeth, she thought about everything that had just happened and prayed for clarity. Confused, the agitation and anger grew until tears blurred her vision. She looked back at Logan, pleading for him to notice her desperation. She needed a friend, even an old one.

He looked past her, and her heart sank. His lips were pulled tight, flat as his expression. Her nostrils flared as he continued to ignore her. She flipped him off and gasped as a predatory dominance consumed his features. She knew at that moment he was intentionally ignoring her, allowing her to be an isolated target.

Blood rushed to her head as she jumped to her feet. With an unsteady sway, she gripped the desk, balancing herself. *Steady, steady,* she repeated.

Zaps of electricity moved through her as dark halos filled her vision. Within seconds, all color morphed into a hazy gray fog. Fighting the vertigo, she breathed ten counts. Stabilized, she grabbed her bag and tossed it on her back, ready to escape this torture.

Logan sat like a stone with his eyes squeezed shut. For a brief second, her guard lowered at the sight of his pained features. She stood there, the ice in her veins thawing. She stepped toward him and his eyes snapped open. A defiant smirk replaced the tension he once showed. Startled, she bit the inside of her lip, suppressing a scream.

Confused, she moved to the door and turned the knob with trembling hands. The internal war of choosing between walking away or taking a stance paralyzed her.

*Vindication.* The words coaxed her. *You need vindication.* Anger rose as Mr. Humphrey's actions looped through her mind.

With closed eyes, a stream of clipped, unintelligible words rolled from her tongue in a faint whisper. Embracing her fury, Vienna faced the class, and with lifted arms, her movement and chant synchronized.

Static crept into the room, and Mr. Humphrey turned. His rueful smile made Vienna pause as his eyes glimmered with provocation. Vienna moved forward, accepting the challenge. Feet firmly rooted, she held her ground. Unfazed, he motioned with one hand—she had permission to attack.

Game on.

A foreboding eeriness stirred inside her, and her trembling hands tingled. Following Mr. Humphrey's eyes, she watched two bolts of electricity dance across her fingers, rushing from one hand to the other. A hiss escaped as their speed increased with each leap. Analyzing the electricity, she held her hands up as the lines doubled: four violet bolts danced across each finger.

The overhead lights hummed with increasing frequency. The students grabbed their ears as the high pitch intensified, sending shards of glass ricocheting across the room as the fluorescent lights exploded one by one.

"Stop!" she screamed as she willed the nightmares away. Her focus shifted to Mr. Humphrey as she pleaded for help.

Understanding and empathy flashed across his features, but he didn't move. Shocked by his lack of action, her concentration broke. The noise vanished, replaced by a deafening silence. She took in the surrounding scene.

The students were asleep, slumped over their desks. Textbooks floated mid-air, some vibrating in place, the rest frozen. Several pages hovered with burned edges as smoke curled toward the ceiling. The room was shambled and barely visible; the only light came from the windows, and low beams shined around the gray clouds gathering outside; the blue sky from earlier was engulfed by colorless doom. The drastic change was unreal.

Trembling, Vienna couldn't comprehend what had happened. Intending to wake herself, she pinched her arm, yelping as the sting deepened. She rubbed the fiery ache as it lingered. The realization that this wasn't a dream set in.

A flickering light brought her back to the room, and her attention shifted to Mr. Humphrey. "Did I do this?" she asked.

Mr. Humphrey took in the scene; an amused smile distorted his face. Vienna stared at him. Bewildered, a million questions rushed through her head. *He knows something. Otherwise,* she told herself, *he wouldn't be so calm—he would have fled or fallen asleep like the students.*

"What's going on?" Anger competed with internal dread as she held back a sob that threatened to expose her. "Explain this . . . this insanity," she demanded.

"You've woken." His posture softened, and his lips lifted.

Confused at the change, Vienna took a step back.

"Welcome to the other side, Ms. Madizza-Corey. We're pleased to have you." He bowed. With a wave of his hand, papers and books flew to their rightful place. Shards of glass moved backward, rushing piece by piece back to their proper place. The room once again glowed from the fluorescent lights. Students stirred and rubbed their eyes as they woke; yawns spread across the room as they stretched and sat upright. Her peers looked around, unaware of what had just happened. Stunned, Vienna grabbed her bag and ran.

The secretary smiled as Vienna flew through the front door and sprinted into the parking lot. Adrenaline propelled her forward as lava rushed through her veins. Rage and confusion danced within until a scream erupted from her.

She zig-zagged through the last row of the parking lot. Goose-bumps covered her body as she skidded to a stop, her senses on high alert. Someone was watching her. Her eyes skipped across the parking lot as she moved backward.

Peering into the field, she spotted movement in the trees surrounding the school. A cloaked figure stared at her. Her palms began to sweat as she realized she was being hunted.

Holding her breath, Vienna neared Raven. She trembled, afraid to look away from the cloaked figure. Her stomach dropped as a second cloak moved into view, then a third . . . a fourth. Suddenly, there were as many cloaks as trees.

As her hands connected with Raven, her terror eased. She pulled the handle, but it slipped from her fingers. Locked. Cursing under her breath, she dug for her keys, keeping her eyes on the tree line. She shuffled through her bag while watching for movement, but clinking metal broke her focus; the keys hit the pavement and bounced under Raven.

She dropped to her knees and frantically searched for the key, thrashing her hands under the car. Cold metal nipped her fingers, and she secured her grip. "Gotcha." She glanced over her shoulder to find an empty tree line. Hearing nothing but her pounding heart, she failed to notice a shift in the wind.

Her hands trembled, sending the key sliding down the car, scratching the paint instead of penetrating the lock. "Come on, V. Get it together." She glanced back as two figures closed in on her. They were less than five yards away. After a second failed attempt at landing the key, she secured it on the third try. Relief washed over her as the door popped open.

Beginning to enter Raven, her spine went rigid. Warm air tickled the back of her neck. Her nostrils filled with stench from musky breath. Before she could turn around, her eyelids grew heavy, her vision blurred, and the world tilted. Wobbling, she toppled over.

Strong, sweaty hands grasped her waist seconds before she connected with the ground. Her head fell back. Blurring in and out of focus, she made out a strong jaw and dark eyes. Reaching out to touch the stranger, she paused. Bile rose as the sky spun faster and faster. Scooped into lean, muscular arms, her head fell against a warm, sweaty neck. Fresh dirt and pine filled her senses, and the tension in her body faded. Rapidly blinking, a smile swept across her face—peace replaced all traces of fear.

"You . . . " the words come out jumbled. " . . . everything is so . . . "

"It's the . . . the magic . . . trapped . . . you." She couldn't make out all the words as she faded in and out of consciousness.

"Magic?" Her eyes drifted shut, the heaviness overcoming her. Her body shivered as the adrenaline vanished.

Saying nothing, Logan curled her body closer, pressing her head against his neck. His warmth spread over her, easing her shivering body. Butterflies tickled her stomach, and she collapsed into him; with arms wrapped around his neck, she let go.

"Logan, I . . . "

"Shhh!" He soothed her. "We need to get you home. Rest."

"Logan." She tried again, but the darkness consumed her.

With sad eyes, he kissed her forehead. "Forgive me, V."

# CHAPTER TWO

Vienna woke from the three muffled voices coming from the kitchen. The garbled words made no sense as she stumbled, making her way to the others. She leaned against the couch, unaware of the sudden silence.

"You're awake. Wait right there." Her mom moved to her side and handed her a couple of crackers. "This will help with the nausea."

Her mom helped her to the kitchen, and Vienna nibbled on the crackers, thankful for how they settled her stomach. She sat beside her dad and stared at the third person with squinted eyes. Logan sat on the other side of the table, holding back a smile.

"Why is he here?" She flinched at the sharp tone.

"You have every right to be angry," her dad said. "You've been through a lot, and I can only imagine you're confused and want answers."

Vienna nodded, then bit the edge of another cracker. She fired daggers at Logan, who winked in response. Her blood boiled at his coy attitude. Without thinking, she picked up her cup and splashed the liquid on his face.

"You are such an asshole. First, you ignored me through high school as though we weren't best friends most of childhood, then you sit here and act like you can feel my desperation for your help. I call bullshit, Logan." She seethed, but Logan remained unfazed. She looked between her parents as they watched her. "Say something," she demanded.

"What do you want, V? I couldn't stand up and confront something I didn't fully understand in class. And we aren't friends. We haven't been friends in years."

"Whose fault is that?" she bit at him.

"Mine, and I don't regret it. You've done fine without me." He didn't even blink.

"And what? You're ignorant in all this and don't know what's going on?" she asked.

"Sure," he said sarcastically.

"Right. You happened to be there when something was following me outside the school. And . . . " She tripped on her words, unsure how to articulate everything she was feeling. "And you sat there in class while Mr. Humphrey provoked me, acting as if everything was fine." Consumed in her rage, she picked up a fork and threw it.

Without breaking eye contact, Logan caught the fork before it connected with his face. "Quit being childish," he said quietly, setting the fork on the table; their eyes locked.

A tear pulled at the corner of her eye as she thought about running through the forest with him. Memories of their youth carried her away: swimming in lakes and rivers, climbing the tallest trees, daring one another to ask out their crush, him helping her babysit her brothers during the summer, and late nights where they fell asleep on the trampoline under the stars, reading fantasy and paranormal books. Her heart broke all over again. As though he was thinking about those same precious memories, Logan's mask fell, and he looked away just as Vienna watched a frown pull at the corner of his lips.

"I lost more than a friend when you turned your back on me," she whispered.

He didn't respond.

"I know you're hurting and confused. But can you tell us how much you remember from this morning?" her mom asked. Reaching out, she locked fingers with her daughter.

Vienna filled them all in with everything she remembered: Mr. Humphrey targeting her; the depth of her anger; papers and books frozen in the air; electricity dancing across her fingers; running through the school; her inability to open Raven . . . then nothing. She leaned back, waiting for a response. They all sat in silence.

She squirmed in her chair until her patience ran out. "Well?"

"You don't remember anything else?" Logan asked.

Flickering images of cloaks, large dark eyes, gray clouds, and Raven faded in and out. "I remember you carrying me away from my car and someone in a cloak walking with us. Was that real?"

Logan nodded.

"What is going on?" Vienna asked. Her parents exchanged glances. "Mom? Dad?" She looked at Logan with concern. "Logan," she begged. Thoughts of betrayal and the feeling of being hunted overwhelmed her. She shivered at the thought of what could have happened to her. The bloody images flooded her mind, causing nausea. "How can I trust you if you keep me in the dark? Didn't today show you I need to know what's happening?"

"When people from the Magic Realm come to the Human Realm, it allows their offspring to live a normal life. Your father and I moved here while we were pregnant with you. We hoped"—her mom's face reddened as she continued—"the move would keep you safe and subdue any powers you possess." Her voice grew louder and trembled with rage. "Things were going well until you started learning about the Witch Trials. Now, your powers are active . . . Damn that teacher." Her mom's voice broke, and she slammed her fist on the table.

"What are you talking about? Magic Realm?" Vienna shook her head. "Have you lost your mind?"

Her dad continued, "It's a realm where those who can wield power live. The majority of those born to magic families stay there their whole life. It's like the Human Realm, but the people in the Magic Realm have abilities like those seen in supernatural movies."

"Anything made after the 80s," Logan joked. "Most witchcraft movies made in the 90s and the 21st century can teach you a lot. Earth, Air, Fire, and Water"—he uses his hands to list similarities—"groups or covens being more powerful, a leader in most groups; you know, the basics." He stopped, holding up his hands as her parents glared at him.

Vienna sat in silence. Shocked at what she learned, she felt a rush of excitement underneath. She focused on her hands and remembered the electricity that bounced across her fingers that morning. Fear and anticipation coursed through her as she connected to a deep vibration in her core. She couldn't be sure, but she thought it was her magic calling her.

"Do you have any questions?" Logan probed.

Pulled from her thoughts, she balled her hands into fists and ignored the draw. She looked at each of them as they stared at her with anticipation. The urge to laugh was lost to the continued pain of betrayal from the parents she had always trusted and the boy she once believed would always protect her. "I'll assume that there is a reason nobody told me these things, since we have always relied on *the truth* . . . " she scolded. "There are so many questions I don't know where to start."

"First, we did keep this a secret for a reason. Like we said, it was to keep you safe. You have much to learn," her dad said confidently.

"Safe from what?" Vienna asked. "You say that as if there was no other way."

"There wasn't another option. And people afraid of magic, to start," her dad answered.

"So that electricity that danced across my fingers was the beginning of my magic?" she asked skeptically. Memories of childhood popped up, images flashing through her mind of the magic books she hid at school. The times she played pretend with Logan—he was King Arthur and her Merlin. Excitement bubbled in her.

"Yes, but it will take time to learn . . . " her mom began.

Vienna cut her mom off. "This is awesome!" she shrieked. "What can I do? Why couldn't I access my power before now?" She paused. "I'm a freaking *witch!*"

"Whoa, slow down." Her dad chuckled. "First, those from magic families who can access their power are called 'Enchanters'. We avoid using the term witch or warlock. They are terms created by Humans to create fear and segregation. But yes, both sides of our family have a long lineage of Enchanters." He smiled at her mom.

"To answer your other question," he continued, "it's against the rules to disclose to children raised in this realm about anything supernatural. To stay here, we couldn't say anything. It would put us in danger. Besides, we came here to give you a chance at a normal life. One without the burden of magic and all the dangers and rules that come with it."

"What danger and rules?" With piqued curiosity and increasing anger, she stood up, holding the back of her chair for support. "I can't believe they won't let you tell me."

"Slow down," her mom urged. "You will learn many things, but you won't be able to learn them all in one night. Just know that you will learn. All countries have rules; realms are no different. Telling a child they are an Enchanter increases their ability to connect with their power. This realm wasn't created for that. Look at the Witch Trials. Mere accusations resulted in mass murders. Imagine if you had known and displayed an ability to cast spells at school as a child. You would have faced persecution, or you'd have been shipped to the Magic Realm."

"Especially with that mellow temper of yours," Logan mumbled.

"Fair point." Vienna smirked. She was torn between excitement and the anger of her parents' betrayal. Then she thought about Logan. Looking at him, her heart broke, and the kitchen faded away.

*"Let's make a pact." Vienna poked her finger with a needle she brought from home. As the blood appeared, nature voiced its concern. No longer silent, the wind drifted across the hot summer ground.*

*"Are you crazy, V?" Logan's words drifted off into the breeze as the wind howled through the trees.*

*"Give me your hand." Her eyes were wide, eager. He shook his head but delivered his hand. She stabbed his finger, the pain causing his heart to quicken. She watched as his pulse showed in his neck.*

*"It's okay." She soothed him, placing her forehead on his. She watched as his heartbeat left his neck. With a smile, she sat back and pressed their fingers together.*

*"NO matter what, we will always be there for each other. Promise," she demanded.*

*"Of course." He leaned in and pressed his lips to her cheek, his own flushing at the contact. "Why the blood promise?"*

*"Freshman year starts next week. I don't want anything to change." Vienna's whisper was faint.*

*"Nothing will ever take me away from you."*

*"Just promise we'll always be there for each other. That we'll always protect each other." A tear pooled at the corner of her eye.*

*"Always," he promised. "Besides, it's a blood oath. I can't go back now." They both laughed, falling to the earth with childlike glee.*

Vienna looked at Logan, the memory vivid. As though he, too, thought about that moment, he looked away, shame wiping his earlier pride away. She'd do anything to understand how . . . why he went against their blood oath.

The silence thickened as Vienna processed the events at school and what she'd just learned. Soon, she would be eighteen, and she was now learning she knew nothing about herself or who her family was.

"I want to know what's next." She sat back in her chair and turned toward her mom.

"Now you train," Logan blurted out. Vienna looked at him with curiosity as he continued. "You train both for human combat and to control your power. I've been asked to train you in human combat and be by your side until you return to the Magic Realm."

"Why you?" She winced as his features hardened. "I mean, isn't there someone more educated in training?" She didn't care about his training; the thought of getting close to him again hurt.

"I'm well qualified"—he lifted his chin—"and I'm a peer, so training is easier. Plus, we have a history. People might ask questions if someone new showed up and started hanging around."

"Fair point. But at what point do you just shut me out again?" He flinched at her words.

They had known each other since third grade when Logan moved into the house next door. Fast friends, they had spent all their time together until things changed sophomore year. Logan drifted away when he started hanging out with friends from another school district. He remained a loner at their school and shut her out completely.

Vienna broke the silence. "What about leaving the Human Realm?"

"Now that you can access your power, you must attend the highly reputable Sparks Boarding School. You'll learn the history of our realm and many other important aspects of the Magic Realm. And you'll be surrounded by other Enchantresses," her dad explained.

Vienna's eyes filled with tears. Questions continued to plague her, but she couldn't speak. Instead, she sat there as her parents talked about Sparks Boarding School. She learned it was an all-girls school comparable to a community college. Though part of her was excited about this journey, she was also worried.

"How often will I see you guys?" she asked while fidgeting with her sleeve, which was now tear-drenched.

"You'll come home on holiday breaks, and we can visit a couple of times, like on your birthday and for some of the major events the school hosts," her mom assured her.

"What about phone calls and talking online?"

"Technology there is more like it was during the 1900s here. We will send letters, but they will be sent with the Magic Realm's delivery system. There are no phones, no technology at all. Teachers will have some access to modern technology, like what we have here, but it's different. Communication is limited, as the focus is on building relationships and independence," her dad added.

"Makes sense. That's why our family has less technology than anyone else in school. Like no phones." Vienna scoffed, but nobody responded. "I don't like the idea of not being home. Not seeing you guys . . . my brothers. How are they going to handle this? Can they come to visit?"

"They will see you when you come home," her dad answered. "They can't know about any of this. It would put them in danger."

"So, we lie like you guys did to me? What happens if it backfires on them, too?" Her agitated tone caused Logan to shift.

"She has a point," Logan added.

"I don't need you to fight my battles," she said angrily, not once looking at him.

"We have no choice. We can't tell them any of this. The laws are clear in the World of Magyieka," her mom answered.

Vienna shook her head in frustration. "How long before I go?"

"Two or three months. We will know more in time. For now, you'll use the coming months to train and learn the basics you need. You'll be attending with knowledgeable and experienced peers, so it's going to be a crash course. If you had tapped into your power later, you would have taken classes with others raised here. I'm not sure how they will adjust things." Her mom exchanged a worried look with her dad.

"Is this where you've been when you're absent from school . . . which is, you know, a lot," she asked Logan accusingly.

"My school isn't near yours, but yes. That is where I have been. I am a couple of years older than you are. I was held back." He shrugged, but Vienna knew he was withholding information.

Her dad cut them off. "You'll have plenty of time to learn everything. Right now, I think you need some rest. Logan will begin training you in the morning."

Logan sat like a stone, his eyes set on Vienna. Vienna looked around the table, realizing she'd been dismissed. Her shoulders relaxed. She was grateful, as she wanted time alone to think about what she had just learned and process her future. She left the table and silently walked to her room without a word. She could hear them whispering but couldn't make out the words.

Magic was real. For years, she had been obsessed with witchcraft and paranormal shows, and her parents forbade them. Now, she knew why. Sitting on the edge of her bed, she looked down at her hands. A single zap sparkled off her finger. Lying on her bed, she scrunched her face in thrilled anticipation.

"I'm an Enchantress," she whispered, putting the words into the world. Pride filled her heart. She laid back and enthusiastically kicked her arms and legs in the air.

*Everything was going to be different.*

# CHAPTER THREE

## Vienna & Logan's POV

Vienna sat in front of her mirror, brushing her hair mindlessly. Just a week ago, she'd learned about the magic world. When she had time, she tried to research Magyieka. Though few answers were found, she found some books online about the theory of a magic world. Most led her to online gaming worlds, leaving her empty-handed. However, that ended when their search history was flagged, and her mom came to her with orders from the Council to discontinue all research online. Frustrated, she dove deeper into hand-to-hand combat and tried to access her magic.

Vienna had also spent as much time with her brothers as possible. She'd answered questions about her no longer attending school and why she wasn't attending graduation. She lied about early graduation and choosing not to walk with the rest of the class since she was done with school. The lies made her sick, and how they might affect her relationship with her brothers haunted her. Powerlessness by the governing laws in Magyieka kept her quiet. Dinners were a nightmare for the first time in their life, and her relationships felt strained.

She pushed her parents away as she grew closer to her brothers, trying to find a way to forgive and understand the dilemma her parents had faced.

As she brushed her hair, she thought about last night's dinner.

*Kreo pushed his veggies around his plate. "I don't get why I have to go to school if she doesn't."*

*"Maybe it will make you work harder. Then you can graduate early, too," their dad answered half-heartedly.*

Vienna's skin prickled—anger for pushing him when he struggled in school and using her as leverage was out of line.

*"Or he could just drop out," she fired at their dad.*

*"Sounds like a plan to me," Kreo answered.*

*"That's enough, Vienna."*

*"Hey, it's not her fault. You know Kreo sucks at school." Vulcan aligned with Vienna.*

*Their dad stood up and tossed his plate into the sink, then left, slamming the door behind him.*

*"Let's get the kitchen cleaned up and you guys can head out for a few hours," their mom offered as she began clearing the table.*

*All the kids helped clean up, and Vienna washed dishes as her brothers got the bikes ready for a ride. Staring out the window, she pondered their family dynamics and her role.*

*"Mom, why have I had to watch them? I mean, most kids their age don't have babysitters."*

*"Just in case we were detected. Also, you know Vulcan gets into mischief constantly. He can barely go a week without a phone call from the neighbors, school, or law enforcement." Her mom chuckled.*

*"True, but he's never messed up badly. He usually does impulsive things or is just hyper and obnoxious. But the need to watch for people who may find us makes sense now." Vienna placed the last dishes in the cupboard and folded the towel on the*

*counter. "What about when I'm gone? Who's going to watch them?"*

*Her mom stopped wiping the counter. "I hadn't thought about that. I thought we would have more time before we had to worry about these things. But"—she turned to Vienna—"it's not for you to worry about. You spend time having fun with them and keep up on your practices."*

*"What about Dad? He's been stressed . . . a lot," she pointed out.*

*"His baby girl is getting ready to leave home, and he's never liked fast change." They laughed.*

*"That's for sure."*

*An engine fired up, and Vienna watched Kreo put on Vulcan's helmet.*

*"That's my cue." Vienna grabbed her gloves and headed out, turning before she opened the door. "Hey, Mom."*

*"Yes, sweetheart?"*

*"I love you." With that, she took off for a night ride with her brothers.*

## LOGAN

Logan paced the room. Ms. Blight had led him in before she joined the rest of the Council in their chambers. The short wait grew, and more than an hour passed. He replayed the last time they gathered the extra information. Fearful of the consequences, he slammed his fist into the hexagon table.

The verdict was just a technicality now, as Vienna had tapped into her magic. He knew he had overstepped by taking her home and meeting with her parents. But his soft spot for her won over his role in the Council.

The door swung open, and the Council walked to their places at the table. At the end of the line, Elric entered the room. Logan narrowed his eyes on Elric, remaining silent until the Council was ready.

"Logan, after what we learned this morning, we reviewed the verdict and considered the new information. Are you ready for the results?"

Logan's nostrils flared. "Before we begin, I'd like to know why Elric is here." Flashbacks of Elric's callus teaching during his first year in training flooded back. He had made it clear he had no hope for Logan and disagreed with his clearance.

"Ah yes," the White Queen took over. "Elric, as you know from training, is also a Watcher. He has been charged as her Protector since she moved to the Human Realm."

Logan stepped back, not missing the smirk that flashed across Elric's face.

"How can that be," Logan seethed.

"Watch it," Mr. Ozul corrected him.

"Elric is half-Fae. He is over a century old, and his experience is unmatched," the White Queen snapped.

Logan's eyes wandered to Elric, curious about his importance and what he offered that other choices wouldn't.

"Ah yes." Ms. Blight said. "As a half-blood, he has other talents and is one of few who have no official role in one realm but instead is left without category."

Logan pushed aside the annoyance. He hadn't realized he could trust Elric less, but knowing Elric was half-Fae erased any chance of trusting him. He had yet to meet a Fae without a dark motive. And with Elric's Unseelie characteristics, he couldn't fathom anyone would trust him.

"Can we move forward, or do you have an issue? We can replace you if you are unable to come to terms with this." Mr. Audovera was blunt.

Motivation to protect Vienna trumped his ego, and he nodded in cooperation.

"Good. Not only will you be training Vienna, but Elric will be nearby, suppressing her magic. We cannot risk her being tracked by others seeking the one who may be the key to the Prophecy."

Logan looked to the Ovr'seer, angry at this decision, pleading for another option. His face gave nothing away, and he looked back at each member.

"She has already touched her magic, and I am charged to train her. How am I to respond when she realizes she can no longer tap into her abilities?"

"You lie," Elric said flatly.

"That's easy for you to say. That comes naturally for a Fae. But Shifters have higher standards." His voice rose to a roar, his animal instinct kicking in.

"Enough. Elric is well aware of the consequences if our plans fail. Perhaps you need education on the Fae before you can be of assistance," the White Queen said sharply.

"Logan is well equipped and has a relationship we can't replicate with Vienna. His biases against the Fae, whatever they may be, will need to be pushed aside—something he is capable of." Mr. Humphrey's rescue was not unnoticed, and Logan was grateful.

"I apologize. I didn't mean to insult. This is just a shock, and my protection of Vienna feels challenged knowing she has had another Watcher charged over her." Logan nodded with respect, suppressing the bile that threatened to erupt. He had no desire to learn to trust Elric.

"You both bring different advantages. You'd do well to work together for Vienna's benefit," Mr. Audovera said.

"Can we proceed?" Ms. Blight facilitated a transition.

Logan nodded, ignoring Elric.

"You will train her in combat to allow basic defense skills to be built. You will also educate her as minimally as possible of the realms here. The less she knows, the better. Once she arrives, she can learn more without the threat of discovery," Mr. Humphrey instructed.

"Are we sure she is the one?" Logan answered half-heartedly. He continued to hope they were wrong. No one fully knew the Prophecy, but it was well known that it is a dangerous and exhausting role.

"That we are not. But after many centuries, she has come closest to meeting criteria," Mr. Audovera answered.

"Are you clear on your role, Logan?" Ms. Blight asked.

"I am." He looked at Elric, noting the green stripe on his robe. Logan looked at the White Queen, who also wore the Fae Realm's stripe, representing the Seelie Court.

"Then go and begin. Ignore Elric's presence when he is near—and know you often will not know when he is present as he will be masked. Focus on rebuilding the relationship while you train," the Ovr'seer added.

Logan felt his face burning from the anger. He remained there, waiting.

"You're dismissed," Mr. Ozul said flatly.

Logan turned and left. He tossed his robe to the corner of the room before opening the door. Logan roared as he moved through Onyx Hall. His skin lost its luster, and midnight black hair replaced it, the deep blue undercoat radiating as he merged outdoors to the moon's glow. Letting go of all control, he released himself, allowing his inner beast to take control.

# CHAPTER FOUR

R eady for the day, Vienna zipped up her combat boots and tossed her hair into a tight ponytail. Knowing she was an Enchantress had filled her with a sense of meaning, and learning combat with Logan had renewed her motivation and vigor for life.

Logan was right about him being the best choice to train her. They spent a lot of time together now, and with their history, others assumed they had rekindled their friendship. Sometimes, she believed it herself, but then the betrayal and broken promise brought her back to reality and her shield would shoot back up.

Checking the mirror and applying some lip gloss, she was ready for the day. Excited to start her lesson with Logan, she skipped down the stairs.

"Morning!" She kissed her mom and snuck a piece of bacon. "What time do you work today?"

"I'm off for a couple of days. Why?" Her mom finished putting the dishes away and handed Vienna a high-protein blueberry muffin.

"I have practice with Logan soon and wasn't sure if you needed me home to watch the boys later." She looked out the kitchen window as her brothers jumped on the trampoline. She shook her head, promising to make extra time for them before she left. Water pooled at the corner of her eye, and she swatted it away.

"Just come back in one piece," her mom joked.

"No promises." Vienna snatched one last piece of bacon and headed out, welcoming the long trek ahead.

Making her way up the hill toward the designated training grounds, Vienna paused as Logan came into view when she perched atop the final slope—a breath caught in her chest. Moving gracefully across the grove, he blocked invisible attacks and his sword tore through the air. Sweat glistened, a testament to his intense speed. Vienna noted the flashing cobalt blue she saw as he danced between the shadows that loomed from the enormous pine trees.

"Why are you so gorgeous, Logan Artrusha?" she whispered. Visions of his sculpted torso pushing against hers flashed through her mind. His soft lips, brooding stare . . . she shivered. She thought about the flat, skinny belly he had years ago. Training for multiple years looked good on him. Then and now, there was a soft spot for him.

Pushing mischievous thoughts away, she moved toward the clearing. Moving the last brush aside, she entered the clearing. Logan danced with the enormous sword; his face was intense as he shifted quickly from left to right. He was a talented fighter, which made him a tough trainer. She was thankful for his time, but faith in her safety wavered.

*How do you learn to trust someone who once betrayed you?*

Vienna rubbed the scar from their blood oath. She was falling for him back then. She couldn't make that mistake again. Reminding herself that her heart wasn't safe with him, she shut it off, a block of ice replacing the warmth. The pain from him ending their friendship still burned in her heart, and even knowing why, she couldn't forgive him.

"Are you creeping, V?" Logan chuckled.

Vienna flushed. Lost in thought, she hadn't seen him stop and walk toward her.

"Just trying to figure out what girls see in you," she countered, trying to recover.

"Ah, that would be my charming disposition and deep brown eyes." He fluttered his eyelashes.

A muffled snort escaped Vienna's lips, and she shook her head. "Awkward," she sang. Throwing her bag down, she began stretching. "What's the agenda, Teach?" She watched as he twitched his head in annoyance. Slang names were the only way to get back at him for the brutal routines that sent her running to a hot shower each night.

"Hand-to-hand combat, then we'll go from there. Depending on how you hold up."

"Sweet. So, you're getting your ass kicked again. Got it." Her shoulders slumped as she remembered last night's pain. *Please let him be sore, too.*

"Of course!" he deadpanned. "Any nightmares last night?" he asked, pulling on his gloves.

"Nope," she lied.

"Perfect." His face was flat, and she knew she hadn't fooled him. Annoyance traced his features as he tossed something to her. She snatched it from the air.

"Nice. Getting quicker."

A shiver spread across her body the moment she saw what lay in her hand—a blindfold.

"Are you fucking kidding?" Her wide eyes met his. Her chest seized at the thought of darkness. She pleaded with him silently, begging him to notice her fear, too embarrassed to verbalize it.

"It's not a debate, V. Get ready."

Memories of the desolate landscape controlled by the cruel redhead who twisted her peaceful dreams into chilling nightmares assaulted her. Logan knew darkness brought images of the woman's cruelty. Still, he wrote it off as a memory created from fear. She'd told him about her nightmares several times. Each time, he expressed he believed it was from the red cloak she had seen at the school the day she ran from Mr. Humphrey's class. But he was wrong. It was too real.

"Now, Vienna," he demanded mercilessly.

Trembling hands fought to secure the blindfold. She bit her lip, focusing on the pain as she pushed back tears. She savored the metallic taste that overwhelmed her senses—anything to distract her. Securing the cloth, the last thing she saw was Logan's pensive eyes.

*Is that empathy or disappointment?*

After checking the blindfold, Logan moved in, striking the back of her leg seconds before his fist connected with her chest, forcing the air from her lungs. Knocked off kilter, a pressured grunt escaped as the impact of his fist hit her temple. Struggling to balance, a sharp jab clipped her jaw. Seething from nonstop hits, she moved left. Air whooshed past her, caressing her cheek, as she dodged two blows. Her nose tingled as the air shifted.

"Good. Stay focused," he demanded.

His voice broke her concentration, and he landed a hit directly above her heart, knocking her to the ground—the weight of his foot left her chest throbbing. Anger from the failure threw her into action. She flipped, her feet connecting with the ground after pivoting past her head. She brought herself to a firm stance just in time for Logan's foot to connect with her butt. She flew face-first into the dirt. Humiliation erupted from her throat.

"Come on, V. You're not even trying," he chastised.

She ripped off the blindfold in time to see Logan throw his gloves to the ground. He cursed under his breath as his arms vibrated. He turned away, pushing both hands through his sweaty hair. She knew his stance too well: each hit filled him with regret, but he was determined.

"No one else will hit you. That's my job—to make sure I'm the only one to strike you," he told her last week. But no matter how much she practiced, she wasn't advancing quickly enough to make him happy. His disappointment never stopped.

They stared at each other, her eyes daunting and her stubbornness rising. She took another step forward. "I haven't accessed my magic again, and I suck at hand-to-hand combat. What's the point, Logan? To see you stare at me with pity each day? I can't keep doing it." She punched him in the chest. He stood there motionless, and she punched him again . . . and again. Until she sobbed, leaning into his warmth.

"You can, and you will get better. And you won't quit." He pulled her close, running a soft stroke down her back. "Our focus isn't magic. It's combat. Magic isn't always accessible, especially when you first start learning it. So focus on what you can control."

"Quitting may be the best option. My magic was a fluke, or it wouldn't be M.I.A." She sulked.

"You won't quit because I don't work with quitters." He flicked her lip.

"Maybe I'm not ready to attend this damn school, Logan." She smacked his hand and paced.

"Are you done crying like . . . an unfortunate petty child?" he raged.

"Screw you!" she screamed. "I'm not good enough."

"Because you won't let go!" he yelled.

"Go to hell, Logan," she hissed. She stood toe-to-toe with him and trembled with anger.

"I'm already there," he growled.

The words hit hard. Shocked, she walked away as her scream echoed through the forest.

"Quit being afraid to let loose. Embrace who you are," he commanded, his jaw clenched.

She rushed toward him and swung. He dodged and grabbed her hand. Holding it tightly, he refused to let it go. A deep, throaty growl filled his chest.

"I don't know how," she snapped back. "I can't access my powers and feel uncoordinated every time we deviate from what we normally practice," she admitted.

"It's me." He took a step back.

"How do I release my fear and let go?" she asked. "What aren't you telling me?"

"There is no secret. Except you must trust yourself."

"You're lying."

"You have to trust me fully and let go."

"Trust you?" She seethed. Vienna held up her finger. "I trusted you once before. Remember? Or did you forget how that turned out? How you turned your back on me after swearing I could always turn to you."

Vienna watched him rub his thumb against his finger. His eyes grew distant, but he said nothing.

"How can I learn to trust you again?" She leaned against a tree, and its bark jabbed into her back. It relieved her internal pain as she slid to the cool, damp earth. "At what point does that make me a fool?"

The scent of fresh pine softened her frown. Looking at Logan, goosebumps covered her body. She closed her eyes and inhaled deeply. "I know I made things freeze in class, Logan. But I haven't been able to access it again," she said, shaking her hands. "Maybe I need to talk to Mr. Humphrey," she joked.

"Funny." He chuckled. "Trust yourself."

Looking at the bright sky, she thought about all life's changes. "Tell me more about Sparks Boarding School."

"Besides what you already know, it teaches everything from tele-portation to telepathy and telekinesis. It's designed a lot like high school. You'll have several classes and breaks. But you'll also have a lot of downtime," he said pointedly. Logan had warned her about the differences between schools in the Magic Realm, including the importance of finding a group of allies she could trust. "What else would you like to know? We've talked about the school a lot this week."

"Right." She thought for a while, then asked something that had been bugging her. "Is this why it's hard for me to make friends here? I have acquaintances, but I've never fit in, ya know?" She knew he understood because he'd had the same problem.

"Yes. It's hard. We're not the same as others. We think differently, and we don't like surface-level relationships. We don't click with Humans like we can with those from the Magic Realm."

"Makes sense. Okay"—she turned toward him—"why is there such an interest in me since I accessed supernatural abilities before most people raised in this realm?" Vienna asked. "Since those in the Magic Realm are practicing, it doesn't seem important. I mean, Mermaids turn when they're thirteen, you know," she teased.

"Most Enchanters raised here don't access it until their twenty-first birthday, in time for university. Then they go to the Magic Realm. That means you accessed your abilities three years early, V." He watched her intently, curious why she was asking these questions.

"I overheard my parents talking. They said very few people know about me outside the boarding school staff. Do you know why? From my understanding, it's common-ish for Enchanters to bring their kids here, and it's recorded for public knowledge required by the Council."

"I don't. But knowing your parents, I'm sure there is a good reason. Maybe you should ask them. And you're right about people coming here. But you, I believe, wouldn't have accessed anything if Mr. Humphrey hadn't taught you about the Witch Trials in an astronomy class," he said.

"I still think there's more to him. Maybe he's an Enchanter. I mean, think about it. Why was he teaching about Witch Trials? That could have easily been done by our history teacher. Yet he tied in the moon, theories of astronomy, and the stars with accusations of witchcraft?" She used a stick to draw symbols in the dirt.

"I think he's just a weird old man with odd theories. And it makes him seem cool to some of the students. Look how many signed up for his class after he introduced the Witch Trials."

"That's true."

"You sound worried." He moved closer, watching her draw in the dirt.

"A little. When I go, I want to be farther along than I am now." A throaty chuckle caused her to look up.

"You're strong, V, and you're just getting started. When that time comes, you'll be fine," he assured her.

"Fair enough. Besides, I almost took you down the other day. One more hit," she teased. "If these girls weren't more experienced, I'd take them in a heartbeat." For the first time in a long time, she radiated confidence.

"That's my girl." He wiggled his eyebrows, and the tension from their fight earlier faded away, replaced by the butterflies somersaulting in her stomach. *My girl.* She smiled.

Sitting down beside her, he nudged her with his shoulder. The silence felt natural as she thought about August. Right after her eighteenth birthday, she'd be shipped off to a foreign realm where she knew nobody. She'd learn a new way of life while rooming with girls she'd never met. She'd spent most of her life as an outsider at her school and the community. *Would that finally change?*

A stick snapped, and she shifted. Looking up, she saw Logan's firm body leaning over her. His hooded eyes filled with warmth; his hand rested on the tree as he looked down at her. The silence thickened until she cleared her throat anxiously. Logan reached down, offering her a hand, pulling until she teetered on her feet, his strength moving her in a rush until their bodies connected.

Steady on her feet, Logan tucked a loose strand of hair behind her ear. "Sometimes, magic touches people, and they have two choices." Eyes locked, he continued, "They can walk away as though nothing has changed or they can rise to the challenge. You're meant for greatness, V. You'll rise above any obstacle when the time comes."

Her soul stilled at his words, and she studied each of his features. His nose was soft but chiseled, just like his shoulders. High cheekbones highlighted his dark, blazing eyes, and his slick, sun-kissed skin glowed from the sweat of their lesson. He looked . . . inhuman.

She shook her head. "Maybe you're right"—she stepped back—"but what if I fail?"

"Until recently, you didn't know about the world beyond this one." His arm swept out. "Still, you show up every day preparing for the next chapter. That will never result in failure." Lifting her chin, he took away her ability to hide. "Walk away or march forward with courage. What are you going to choose, V?"

Shoulders squared, she answered, "Daylight's fading. Let's practice."

# CHAPTER FIVE

The sunlight bore down, causing fatigue as practice continued. Sick of hand-to-hand combat, Vienna walked to Logan's bag and riffled through the weapons. Picking a dagger, she twirled it, noting how natural it felt. The cool metal was comfortable in her hand.

"Nice choice. I have to warn you, though, if I kicked your ass before, adding a weapon is going to take this to a whole new level."

"Scared?" she teased him, spinning the dagger in her hand. This time, it flew between Logan's feet, landing inches away from his toes, the blade sticking into the ground. Embarrassment consumed her, and Logan laughed.

"Take it easy. And before you start showing off, daggers typically come in pairs. Grab the other one." He pulled the dagger from the dirt and wiped it on his jeans.

With the second dagger in hand, Vienna moved toward Logan, handing him her chosen weapon. "Will you teach me how to use these?"

"Why the daggers?" he asks in earnest.

"They just seem . . . right," she admitted. "Don't laugh," she demanded, unable to tell whether he was amused or judging her.

"No teasing here. Our weapons find us, not the other way around. Watch," he requested as he walked to the bag. A luminous glow poured from the it. He reached in and pulled out the largest sword she'd ever seen. The glowing ceased once it was placed on top of the bag. Logan pulled on leather gloves. The moment his hand connected with the hilt, the cobalt blue light dimmed. She took in the detail of the sword, noting the blue engravings that projected the light.

As though in a trance, Vienna moved forward, touching the blade. "How did you do that?"

"This one called to me the day I started using weapons." He caressed the blade. "It's a claymore; the glow began when I truly started to trust my ability to wield it." They stared at the edge as it pulsed.

"Aren't you afraid someone will see it and ask about the glow?"

"Only Enchanters can see the glow." Pride radiated from him.

"Epic."

"Watch this." Stepping back, he swung the blade rapidly. The blade sang as he sliced the air. The intensity of the glow increased with each swing; he danced rhythmically as though only he and the blade existed.

"Magnificent," she whispered.

Logan breathed deeply, steadying himself as the performance ended. "In time, we become one with our weapons."

Warmth spread from her chest downward, slowly creeping across her body. She felt a tingle caress her inner thighs, and her breath deepened. Tracing his movements, it was as though she had watched two lovers. She wished it was her in his hands.

Uncomfortable with her intimate feelings, Vienna blurted out, "I thought everyone wanted a katana?" She bit her lip, hopeful he didn't hear the heat in her voice.

"I did. As I said, I didn't choose Ghost; she chose me." His voice was matter-of-fact.

"Right." She looked at the daggers. *Did they choose me?* She pondered if she would one day dance with them as Logan danced with Ghost.

"Here, let me show you how to use them."

He secured Ghost and took one dagger. Side by side, they practiced. She mimicked each step, each jab, and every movement he made. Dripping in sweat, arm throbbing with exhaustion, she watched Logan place the dagger in his left hand. Concern washed across her face, and he nodded with encouragement. Reluctantly, she tried to move her right arm, but she winced in pain . . . her right arm was too weak to lift the dagger. With her left hand, she took the dagger from her dominant arm.

Slower than before, they retraced each step they completed with their right side. Focused on precision. Jab, jab, slice. They pivoted left, then right. Jabbing again, then repeated the sequence before moving in reverse. In sync, they move swiftly, accuracy increasing as new muscles were built.

The blade clinked as it hit the soil. Vienna's hand trembled, unable to grab at the hilt. Her fingers froze, refusing to wrap around it. "My arm is toast . . . both of them," she confessed in a rush of air.

"You did good," he admitted.

Vienna lifted her brow, unwilling to accept his compliment. *Don't let him in. That's how he'll hurt you.* She looked away.

Reluctant to leave the dagger lifeless on the ground, she reached out again. Closing his hand around hers, he blocked her from the dagger, and her shoulders dropped in relief—she knew he'd take care of it. Though she didn't want his help, her body left her vulnerable.

As her body shifted, Logan leaned closer and soothed her with a smile, eyes locked; he grabbed the blade with one hand and gently held her hand with the other. She diverted her eyes as crimson warmth flushed her cheeks.

She placed her hand on her lap and shivered as his hand moved across her leg. "Let's get packed and take you home."

Vienna stood, rolling her shoulders and neck. Each movement sent searing pain to her fingertips. Flexing her fists, she felt the faint pull of electricity.

"V," Logan broke her concentration, "while we have a minute, I've been thinking about what you told me last week."

"Which part? We've talked a lot the last week." She chugged a bottle of water.

"About your dreams." She stiffened at the mention.

"We agreed not to talk about them anymore. I told you because you could tell something was wrong. That was supposed to be the end of it." There was no room for argument in her voice, but Logan ignored it.

"I remember. But it's been bothering me."

"What? Why would it bother you? Ya know what, never mind." She waved her hand, dismissing the question. "What do you want to discuss?" she answered sharply.

"Would you consider telling your parents about the woman in your dreams? At least with the ones with Red. That's what you called her, right?" He tiptoed, and she didn't understand why.

"Why is this important to you?"

"With how vividly you describe the dreams and the panic you wake up in, I think it's important for someone to know." She squinted in curiosity. His voice was serious, but his worry was evident.

"Yes," she answers slowly, "but what are they going to do about it? They're just dreams."

Logan tossed the bag over his shoulder, and they headed toward her house. "Call it your superior's intuition," he taunted her.

She looked at him incredulously before she stopped. She placed her hands on her hips, waiting for him to continue.

He took in her stance, knowing too well that she wouldn't move until he answered. "It's just been bugging me that they don't know. Something feels off about the dreams . . . and the redhead. If I wasn't around for whatever reason, I'd feel more comfortable knowing they know the situation."

"I think there's another reason that you're holding back." She followed behind as he guided them out of the clearing, the thin trail growing dark as the sun drifted below the trees. The crickets began to chirp as a sad smile unfolded. *Man, I am going to miss this place.* A chilly breeze nipped at her tender arms, and she folded them, rubbing the rising goosebumps.

"What are the plans for tomorrow?" *Please give me a break.*

"Humm . . . " He stopped and then abruptly turned. "Make you a deal. If you beat me to your yard, you choose how we spend the day. I win, we start at sunrise, and we don't stop until you win a round. I'll even give you a 5-minute head start . . . and I carry the bags."

Contemplating the options, she moved around him, only stopping when they were face to face. With her back to the trail, she blocked his way around her. Tapping her lip, she squinted her eyes. With a sudden mischievous grin, she nodded.

"Game on." She sprinted down the trail. The power in her legs propelled her forward, increasing her momentum. She nearly toppled over, but she recovered. Regaining her balance, she darted between trees, through trickling streams, and across the final thick of the brush before reaching the forest's edge.

Descending the final hill, Vienna spotted someone unfamiliar. She skidded out of control and slid several feet across the damp forest floor as chunks of mud shot around her. Overcorrecting connected her to the ground with a hard thump. Air rushed from her lungs in an explosion. Scrambling to her feet, she summoned all her inner strength, sucking in a shallow breath.

"Who's out there?" she hollered. She turned in circles but found nobody. Taking one step forward, she paused as a rustling caught her attention. Unwilling to run in fear, she waited. "I'm not running. Come out and face me," she dared.

"Feisty, are we?" A breath tickled Vienna's ear.

Anger bubbled at the shrill voice. She turned around to find a perky girl not much older than herself. The girl looked at Vienna with large, judgmental eyes, her sharp chin jutting out.

Observing the hostile sneer, Vienna felt defiant. One thing was sure: they'd never met, and she didn't like her or her cringing better-than-thou face.

"Who are you?" Vienna demanded. The girl didn't answer. "Or you can start by telling me how you moved so quickly."

"You were scared. You probably didn't realize how close I actually was," she said with a shrug, as though nothing strange had happened.

"May I help you?" Vienna bit out with contempt. Something about this girl made her skin crawl.

Squinting her hazel eyes in amusement, the girl smiled, straightening to full height as she sized Vienna up from head to toe like prey. They landed on Vienna's fingers, where her eyes lingered before looking back at her.

"Vienna, is it?" She puckered her full lips, her revulsion evident. "I'm Cosima. A superior from Sparks Boarding School." She held out an envelope. Vienna observed it with curiosity, noting the old-fashioned seal.

Vienna reached for the envelope, pulling back when pain shot up her arm. She gasped as crimson dripped from her hand. The letter dropped, fluttering to the ground. Cosima beamed with satisfaction.

"There is nothing special about you," Cosima taunted and her face contorted in disgust as she wiped blood from her perfectly manicured nails. "Stay out of my way, or you will regret attending Sparks." The last word faded, echoing into the forest.

"Do you need help removing that sti—" Vienna started but stopped when she looked up to find the girl was gone. She let out an irritated scream before picking up the letter. Inspecting it with curiosity, she saw SBS engraved in the wax seal.

Vienna began the short stretch to her home as she turned the envelope in her hand, a million thoughts racing through her mind, pushing all thoughts of her race with Logan aside.

"Guess we start at dawn."

"Eeeek!" she squealed, her hand grabbing her chest. "Dang it," she sighed with a dramatic nod. "The race."

"That memorable, am I?" he joked. "What is that?" He snatched the letter from her hand.

"I'm not sure." She tried to snatch it back, but he dodged her. "Someone just gave it to me, along with this." She held out her hand with a pouty lip. He granted her a rare, authentic laugh before he flicked her lip. His face hardened at the sight of the bleeding cut.

"What was her name?" He tilted his head.

"Cosima?" she mocked.

"Ugh! One of the mean girls." He shook his head. "It didn't ignite anything, like a desire to roast her?"

"No," she laughed, "but it did ignite an instant disdain for her. She disappeared before I could say anything. How is that possible, by the way? To vanish. Will I be able to do that?"

"There are many things we will learn later," he deflected. "Let's get you home."

Logan walked her the rest of the way home in silence. She thought about the turn of events. Vienna glanced at Logan several times before they arrived at her porch, sure she saw shock at the mention of Cosima's name. The jealousy she felt was unexpected, but she wasn't sure how to ask about it.

"Tell me who Cosima is," she demanded.

"I already told you . . . " he began.

"No," she cut him off, "you're hiding something. What is it about her you're hiding?"

"Why do you think I'm always hiding something?" She looked down at him, expecting him to come onto the porch.

"I'm going to assume that's rhetorical." She stepped toward him.

"I know it's only been a week of working together. But eventually, you need to trust me."

"Trust is earned, Logan. I made the mistake of giving it freely once before."

Logan nodded his head mindlessly.

She moved down, standing in front of him. "Answer me. Who is she?"

"She's a girl . . . woman from Magyieka. An Enchantress we can't trust and who I don't like. There is nothing more to say."

"Part of me wants to trust you. I remember our childhood and how close we were." Vienna looked to the sky, the darkness consuming. "I remember the magic we tried to create." She giggled at his amused grunt. "I remember how safe I always felt when you were near."

Logan waited, saying nothing, giving her time to say her piece.

"Then I remember the agonizing pain. The heartbreak felt as though my soul was being ripped from my being." She looked back at him. "You just disappeared at the end of that summer. No messages, no letters. How can I let myself be hurt like that again?"

"If you don't know by now, I had no choice because of the laws and our Council . . . "

"Our connection felt deeper than any law," she answered honestly.

"I would never hurt you if I had a choice," he said flatly. "One day you'll believe—no," he corrected, "one day you will know because everything will be clear."

"Maybe that day I'll be able to trust you again." His flinch at her words didn't go unnoticed, but she held her ground.

"See you at dawn." Logan wobbled at the bottom of the porch.

"What about the interference?" she screeched. *He isn't going to take advantage of this situation, is he?*

"A loss is a loss, and I won. We start at dawn and fight until you win. Or can't you rise to the challenge, my Esteemed Enchantress?" he joked.

Leaning near him, now even in height, Vienna squared her shoulders. She stuck her finger to his chest. "Don't you ever call me that again." She left no room for questions.

Taken aback, he paused, tossing both hands up. "Don't shoot."

His attempted charm didn't work . . . she didn't waver. Ineffective, he leaned closer.

His lips passed hers, moving to her ear. Warm air brushed her earlobe, sending a chill down her spine. "Mine . . . or Enchantress?" he whispered. Moving backward, he nodded farewell before walking away.

Vienna stood on the steps, speechless.

# CHAPTER SIX

## Vienna & Logan's POV

Vienna watched as Logan walked away. The darkness thickened overhead and vanished into the night. Flicking the envelope's edge, she walked toward the front door, unwilling to open anything from the Magic Realm alone.

"Hi, Mom." She forced a smile that quickly became authentic as her mom kissed her head.

"Hey, sweetheart! How was practice?" Her mom darted back to the kitchen—standing still had never been her strength.

"Good." Her shaky voice caught her mom's attention. She stirred a large bowl of potato salad, waiting. Vienna chewed her lip as she held out the letter. "Do you know what this is?"

"An envelope?" Her mom grabbed it.

Turning it over several times, her mom sighed in confusion before tracing a finger over the seal. "SBS," she whispered. "I've never seen a letter like this delivered here." She looked at Vienna with concern. "Who gave it to you?"

"A friendly girl from the school." Sarcasm rang out in her words.

"She said her name is Cosima." Vienna glanced at the cut throbbing on her hand before hiding it under the cuff of her sleeve.

"Did she say anything about it?" Her mom handed it back to Vienna.

"Nope." Vienna placed it on the counter and started setting the dinner table. "The only message she gave me was to steer clear of her," Vienna mocked.

Her mom abruptly dropped the cooking supplies, and the metal spoon rang in retaliation for the harsh release. "Did she say why?"

"Uh, no." Vienna looked at her mom with concern.

"Sorry, I didn't mean to come off so harsh. I'd like to know more about the situation and about this girl."

"She was rude, pretty, tall, brunette . . . did I say rude?" She batted her eyes. "Anyway, I was surprised anyone from the school would send someone so . . . uh . . . warm and inviting," Vienna offered, trying to ease the tension in the room.

Her mom held back a smile and moved dinner to the table; Vienna hopped onto the counter and watched her mom set the table in Mach speed.

"Unfortunately, they probably don't know she's like that. Some girls at the school have different personalities depending on who is nearby. It's the same at any school." Her mom shrugged.

"Should I be worried about her?"

"What do you have to worry about?" her dad asked as he dropped his keys on the counter and hung up his hat. Above the fridge, he keyed in the code for a lockbox and secured his GLOCK 22. As he turned, he took in her mom's concerned features.

"Vienna had a girl from Sparks show up. She left her with a sealed envelope and a notable warning." Her mom raised a knowing eyebrow at Vienna.

*Why did I even try?* Her mom was a personal investigator, and her dad was the police chief; secrets were impossible in this home . . . for the kids, that is.

Her dad hugged his girls and leaned against the fridge with a hot cup of coffee. "That's weird. I've never heard of someone receiving a message that way. Here, anyway."

"That's what Mom said."

"Did you notice anything unusual about her?" he asked.

"She can vanish. She made it clear that we wouldn't be friends. Oh, and she makes the mean girls at my school look like a welcoming party," Vienna replied.

Her mom hugged her. "It's up to you, but we should open it together. Then we can get online and find out who this Cosima is. The more information you have, the more prepared you'll be when you re-encounter her. Clearly, she knows about you. So let's even the playing field."

Her dad nodded in agreement. Before anything else was said, her brothers walked in, and silence fell across the kitchen. Vienna watched them with admiration. At fifteen, Kreo spent the day at an alternative high school learning a variety of trades—a natural at design, mechanics, and creation. Vulcan was only twelve but attended a boot camp that taught youth to harness their natural talents—he displayed exquisite athletic abilities fueled by his volcanic temper. God, her heart ached each time she thought about leaving them.

*Soon,* she reminded herself, *they will learn about my attendance at a boarding school in a different country. For now, normalcy is the goal.*

Light banter flowed with ease through dinner, and tension from the last week faded as they talked about school, work, and the future. With dinner finished and the kitchen cleaned, Kreo and Vulcan rushed outside to enjoy the evening. Out of sight, Vienna tossed the envelope onto the table and sat down. She dropped her head into laced fingers and stared down at the delicate wax that secured the message inside.

"I'm nervous." Her dad rubbed her back. Placing water next to Vienna, her mom sat on the opposite side of her dad—both showing their support.

"Rip the Band-Aid off," her mom suggested.

Vienna broke the seal and pulled out an aged ivory page. The edges were frayed, the ink immaculate, and each letter was perfectly lined.

"Here we go." Vienna handed the letter to her dad, knowing his soothing voice would narrate the message well.

Clearing his voice, he wiggled in his chair to ease the tension. Vienna chuckled. Memories of her childhood eased her fears. With a nod, her dad began:

# SPARKS BOARDING SCHOOL

Ms. Vienna Madizza-Corey,

With great pleasure, we extend this invitation to attend the elite all-girls academy—Sparks Boarding School—to you. Please note that prestigious marks are essential for all first-year students as this ensures continued enrollment. Since high achievement is obligatory in all courses and extracurricular activities, we urge those outside the Magic Realm to heed caution with their time. Late to the crowd yet young for the alignment, we urge you to embrace this honor and rise to the challenge.

We are sure Mr. and Mrs. Corey will provide ample details of lineage, Magyieka History, and basic concepts of powers wielded by Enchanters. The Council has attached suggested and mandatory extra supplements to aid your success.

We will honor student's arrival as the next Blue Moon rises.

Welcome Home,

The Council

Vienna took the letter from her father and looked it over, reading each word carefully. Glancing over the wording one last time, she flipped the paper over. "I don't see a list of mandatory or suggested items." She shook her head with frustration as a list appeared at the bottom of the letter. Books and websites were etched out one by one.

"So cool." She watched intently until the writing stopped.

With the list complete, she lowered the letter as three new books landed in front of her, a cloud of smoke fading.

"Holy crap!" she squealed, sending her chair crashing across the floor. Hands locked behind her neck, she paced, holding her breath, then releasing a long exhale.

"They just . . . " Unable to find the words, she flashed her hands around before finding her bearings. "They just . . . *poofed* onto the table!"

Her mom doubled over and laughed until she wheezed. Several seconds passed before she took in a painful breath. "Your face . . . "— gasp—" . . . you turned red and . . . *bahaha!*" She leaned her head on the table, holding her aching waist with one hand and wiping away a tear with the other. "I'm so sorry. You're just too cute." Vienna stared, unamused.

"You've got to learn to expect the unexpected," her dad piped up before sending a disapproving look to his wife before turning to Vienna.

Sobering a bit, her mom agreed. "Your father's right," she added after a loud hiccup escaped. "You need to prepare for anything . . . and everything." She touched Vienna's cheek and moved her thumb over her prominent chin, then tapped her nose. Comforted, Vienna leaned into her mom's hand, moving it securely against her face.

"To be honest," her dad continued, "we hoped you wouldn't receive this gift." He looks at her mom. "You will have a lot of burdens as a Madizza-Corey."

"I keep hearing Madizza-Corey, but I have no clue what it means. You make it sound like a bad thing." Vienna slid her thumb over her front teeth, a nervous childhood habit.

"Well, guess tonight we start family history as The Council has requested." Her mom grabbed her dad's hand. "Can you get our family chest?"

Without hesitating, he headed to their bedroom and returned with a giant antique chest. Words beyond Vienna's recognition were whispered as her dad touched the front of the chest. The lock popped open. Wide-eyed, Vienna smiled. Stacks of antique documents, family portraits, and bundles of unknown items were stacked to the brim.

A fragile parchment paper dropped to the floor. Picking it up, Vienna looked at her family tree. "Madizza-Corey" was written in bold across the top; it twinkled, and she smiled at the simple beauty. Under her last name, Vienna, Vulcan, and Kreo were in one line— right where two trees merged is a split branch, her parents' names on either side. With certainty, Vienna knew that nothing in her life would ever be the same.

## LOGAN

Looking back, Logan watched Vienna walk into her house. "Elric," he summoned.

"Yes." Elric's voice was flat, annoyance seeping through his calm demeanor as he appeared next to him.

"Why was Cosima here?" Logan turned to him, expecting answers.

"I'm as surprised as you. We need to report this." Disdain seeped through Elric's features moments before he touched Logan's arm.

Logan was unable to prepare for transportation without warning. He landed on his knees outside the Council doors of Onyx Hall.

"Wait here." Elric walked into the chamber.

"As if I have a choice," Logan fumed, knowing he had to wait for permission.

Within minutes, the door opened and Logan entered. Part of the Council was missing, with the Ovr'seer, Ms. Blight, Mr. Humphrey, Mr. O'Cain, and Mr. Audovera being the only ones present.

"Elric has informed us that Cosima delivered the letter but left an unspoken message," Mr. Humphrey announced.

"That's correct," Logan answered bluntly.

"Speak freely," Mr. O'Cain commanded.

Logan hesitated as he took in the members sitting before him. "Why was Cosima sent with the invitation?"

"She is a trustworthy Enchantress," Ms. Blight answered. "As you know, her mother, Agnes Leos, is our stenographer. She transcribes our sessions . . ."

"Except for this one," Logan pointed out. He watched as the Council members looked at one another.

"A complaint was received upon her arrival. As such, we felt it was best for her family to be absent," Mr. Audovera admitted.

"I'd appreciate notice when visits are expected from the magic world," Logan requested.

"Request will be considered." Mr. Audovera nodded.

"We would also like to inform you that we are considering a volunteer to work with you and Vienna in the coming months, especially during times when you may be unavailable," the Ovr'seer admitted.

"Who is this volunteer? With the current dynamics," Logan looked to Elric, "there is already a lot of magic in the Human Realm."

"Is that concern for Vienna, or your stance with her?" Elric cut in.

"Watch it," Logan challenged.

"Check your accusations." Elric smirked.

"If I didn't know better," Logan countered, "I would worry you're projecting your own feelings." Elric's face fell.

"Why don't we worry about what brought us here?" Ms. Bright interjected.

"I agree with another person helping to prepare Vienna for her transition to Sparks." Elric stared at Logan.

"Knowing who would be present is safe, but if this is something we can negotiate and I can learn more about, I'm sure we can make arrangements," Logan answered.

"Great. Then we are set. More details will come as we get them." Ms. Blight stood. "However, it is in Vienna's best interest that you two"—she pointed at Logan and Elric—"learn to work together. Her life could depend on it, and regardless of what either of you feel for her, you are both Watchers. As such, your duty is to protect her, with your life if it comes to that."

"That won't be a problem." Logan rubbed his finger. "In all ways, my duty is to keep her safe and show up for her in whatever form is needed."

"Get some rest, both of you. The morning brings more practice." The Ovr'seer left, and the Council followed closely behind.

With the door closed, Elric turned to Logan. "I agree that Cosima was a poor choice. Though I don't understand their reasoning, we must keep watch of Vienna. You don't need to like me, but know I will protect her with my life."

"That I trust," Logan admitted, "but I see the way you look at her. You're centuries older than her, yet you look at her like you two have a future."

"It wouldn't be the first time a Watcher fell for their Ward and made a life together." Elric's emerald eyes glimmered before he vanished.

"Coward." Logan threw the desk across the room as Ms. Blight walked in. She was dressed in casual wear, her Enchantress robe gone.

"It's hard to be in love with the one you're charged to protect. But sometimes, it means protection is promised, as you'll lay your life down for her." She tilted her head, and he wondered what her point was.

"Perhaps she has two Watchers who love her." Regret of all the lies and secrets filled him as Ms. Blight continued. "You had no choice and did all you could to live up to that blood oath." She nodded to his finger.

He jutted out his jaw, confused.

"Many of us have watched her since childhood. There was something special about her. I remember the day her family came to us and told her they were leaving Magyieka. My magic pulled to hers. I've watched you two grow, and I have no doubt you'll earn her forgiveness. But you can't do that by fighting others for her affection."

"I told my dads the day I saw her that I would do anything for her." He laughed. Putting the table back, he sat on the edge. "As a kid, every morning, I'd rush through my chores so I could get to her. She glowed. I vaguely remember it, but an aura drew me in. The real magic came with her laughter and those stupid daydreams."

"You talk as if you've already lost her, Logan. But I saw you two today. I watched as her heart warmed for you. Why else would she be angry at you? You stop being angry when you stop loving someone. Goodnight, Logan."

Logan thought about Ms. Blight's words and realized it didn't matter if she never loved him. He'd spend his life protecting her and ensuring she was safe and happy. Whether he was there as a friend, lover, or just her Watcher, she'd never be alone again.

# CHAPTER SEVEN

## Vienna & Logan's POV

Vienna sat on the floor, looking into the chest, captivated by the history within her reach. "How old is it?" she asked as she moved to the chair.

"This chest was handed down from your father's great-grandparents, and my family line was added in to make it complete for our children. From their stories, it dates back over a century," her mom answered. "Your entire family history from both sides is here."

Vienna picked up a scroll, rolling it over the table, her name flashing in gold. "Why does it do that? The family tree did the same thing," Vienna says, pointing to her name.

"Do what?" her dad asks.

"The letters in my name are gold. It's like my name is glowing . . . with a pulse," she mused with confusion.

Ignoring her parents' concerned look, Vienna moved the family tree next to the scroll, examining the identical cursive font with curiosity. The words were delicately handwritten, with each letter overemphasized.

"Don't." Her dad grabbed her hand, pulling it away from the letters, urging her not to touch them. "It will compromise the gold."

"The ink's infused with alchemy. Each new member added to the family has their name appear in its rightful place." Her mom smiled at her children's names. "It ensures they're registered in the Magic Realm."

"That reminds me." With her trance broken, Vienna jumped off-topic. She dug under the stacks of paper and pulled out the letter she had received. "Here." She pointed to two different spots. "What is Magyieka and Blue Moon?" she asked with confusion.

"That's a great place to start," her mom decided. "Magyieka is the name of the magic world. It's pronounced M-ah-g-ee-ka." Vienna practiced the odd word as she struggled to articulate the soft "g" with the right accent. "You'll get it," her mom encouraged her.

"Blue Moon is the name of the third full moon of an astronomical season that hosts four full moons. The astronomical season—which is how seasons are gauged in the magic world—are measured by Magyieka's position as it rotates around the sun," her mom explained. "There are four seasons. Unlike here in the states, the season begins at the Summer Solstice, then it's Winter Solstice, Spring Equinox, and Autumnal Equinox. This fall, the Autumnal Equinox has four full moons that fall within it. The third will be a Blue Moon, which symbolizes your first year at Magyieka. The letter lets us know that will be the day you go."

Vienna blinked in confusion. "Say what?"

"It's the third full moon of four this fall," her dad simplified.

Vienna pondered for a second. "I think I get it. Will the Blue Moon start simultaneously with the Magic Realm not being here? It says when the Blue Moon rises." She pointed to the invitation.

Her dad began riffling through the chest until he spotted a bronze velvet tapestry. Tossing it atop the other documents, Vienna saw a detailed breakdown of the astronomical seasons in each realm, each broken down into precise timelines.

"It's small enough to keep it in your books until you learn it. This year, the Blue Moon is at the end of the summer." He moved his hands across the tapestry. "I'd guess the last week of August." Vienna watched him in wonder.

"Did I mention I did well in astronomy and astronomical timing?" he bragged.

"Apparently not." Vienna gave him knuckles. "The Blue Moon hits near my birthday."

"Yes, it does. In fact"—her mom handed her dad the letter and calendar—"you leave at the exact same time you were born."

The silence was deafening. She would turn eighteen the day school started. She'd be leaving the minute she turned eighteen. "That's crap."

"Wow, that was a sudden change," her dad commented.

"First, I was told I had no choice; I was being sent to a Magic Realm. Now, it's on my birthday. Has anyone considered everything I've lost?"

"I guess we haven't talked about that," her dad answered.

"No, we haven't. I haven't even had time to process the grief I feel. I'm too busy learning combat and doing what I'm told." Vienna stood up and tugged at her jacket. She pulled out a large envelope that was folded in her inner pocket. As she returned to the table, she unfolded the envelope and pulled out a stack of papers. She sat down and slid them to her parents.

"I got into my top schools." Her voice broke. "I haven't sent in a denial yet. Part of me keeps thinking I will wake up, and all this will disappear." She picked up an acceptance letter to a local college. She chuckled. "If I could go here and still access magic, ignoring the whole alternative realm, or whatever, that would be my dream. But now it's gone. Along with any choice I have at a normal life as an adult. I'm almost eighteen and feel like I did when I started high school."

"What do you mean?" Vienna's mom took her hands in hers.

"You still have a choice," her dad said. "You go to Sparks

Boarding School, then you choose what you do after that. University, here or there, a career. Family, if you want one."

"You don't get it. My whole life has been a lie. Everyone I've trusted lied to me and is now telling me what I have to do. And who knows if I will have a choice in the future? I accessed my powers early. What else could be in store? The choice is just a dangled carrot to keep me going." Vienna slumped into her chair. "Oh ya, let's not forget. The only friend I had ever trusted even betrayed me." Anger surged and the paper she touched burst into flames.

Her mom grabbed a wet cloth and put the fire out. "Looks like the magic is lurking underneath."

"Why didn't you use your magic?" Numb from anger, she felt no excitement about accessing her own powers. Instead, the realization that she'd never seen her parents use magic was her only thought.

"We're in the Human Realm. It's easier not to use it," her dad answered.

Vienna nodded her head, expecting the answer. "We can toss the rest of these." She pushed the invitations to her parents.

"Whatever you need us to do," her dad offered.

"Can I keep the chest in my room so I can learn as much as possible?" With a flat voice, she forced down a sob.

"I don't see why not. It will need to remain locked, along with your door. We can't chance Kreo and Vulcan catching on to any of this." There was no room for discussion as her dad placed everything back into the chest and sealed it with an odd language before carrying it to Vienna's room.

Once he was out of sight, Vienna asked the one thing that she'd been struggling with. "Mom, why didn't you tell me your maiden name?"

Her mom nodded robotically before answering. "Like your father's last name, Madizza comes from a long line of powerful Enchanters. Madizza is Italian, and Corey is a Salem name—as far as we know. Both family names are prestigious Enchanter bloodlines from powerful and successful families. Until now, a Madizza, who has one of the longest bloodlines known in Enchanter history, has never borne children with another pure bloodline. This means . . ."

Her dad took over as he walked into the kitchen. "It means that with the two bloodlines mixed, you have more than a pure bloodline. You have an Elite Bloodline, which has only happened one time before. That one time, people sought the child who was born; some desired to harm her, others to control her." Worry etched his features and fear replaced Vienna's wonder.

"What happened to her?"

"We'll address that later." Her mom shifted the conversation back to why she hid her last name. "Many families fled the Magic Realm to escape the harsh rules of the Council. Since we aren't allowed to talk about magic outside Magyieka, one spouse typically doesn't have Enchanter lineage. This has resulted in diluted bloodlines for several generations. Those who did stay often had to choose to allow their bloodline to parish, bear children with impure lines, or choose someone from the Human Realm, hoping their children would be gifted Enchanter abilities. To hide the family's purity, we dropped my last name, changing it to Smith to keep us safe."

"With the Witch Trials killing many innocent people, they also killed many Enchanters and their bloodlines. This has made it improbable that superiority could be gained from strong bloodlines. But yours," her dad said with a smile, "is the purest bloodline ever known, as both our families remained in Magyieka. Madizzas as royalty, and the Coreys, their honored Knights, which is why my line is shorter; not many Knights married and carried on their line."

"This means others may see you as a threat, especially since you developed supernatural abilities early," her mom finished. "Though you have a strong bloodline, only a handful know you come from royalty." Sorrowful for the challenges that lie ahead for their daughter, her dad moved behind her mom and embraced her.

Shocked by everything she had just learned, Vienna sat in silence. It all started to make sense: *Cosima's threats. Logan waiting in the Human Realm for her. Early powers. Feeling different since childhood.*

"Why was Logan sent here to protect me? To teach me?" Vienna asked.

"Like your father, his family is full of Knights."

"So, is he a pure bloodline?" She ignored the hope rising.

"No." She noted the short clip of her father's voice. *He's hiding something.*

As though reading her mind, her mom pulled her attention away from Logan. "I say we look into Cosima and see what we find."

Hours of research resulted in more answers than they had expected. Cosima Leos came from a long line of Mediterranean and Greek Enchanters, one of the most powerful bloodlines known in Magyieka. She wasn't, however, of pure blood.

Vienna watched her parents, unsure if they were confused or curious about their findings. "Do you guys know any of these family names?"

"I've heard them both but don't know much about them," her mom answered.

"This is why she finds me threatening; we are very alike."

"But you're kind. From what we just read, Cosima is not," her dad noted. "She has a strong lineage, though, so I'd steer clear. Don't give her any more reason to target you."

"I'm not going to hide from her," Vienna countered.

"I would never ask you to. You can hold your own," her dad responded.

Her mom tucked Vienna's hair behind her ear. "Now you can put her from your mind. Focus on your practice with Logan and learn what you can before the Blue Moon. That's all you need to do right now."

Vienna kissed her parents before heading to bed. Leaving her bedroom door cracked, her brothers' voices drifted through the house. They shared their adventurous night with their parents as Vienna listened. She smiled at the childishness in their voices as they recounted climbing trees, hiding in trenches, and racing through barbaric trails. They were close in age, but Kreo had a youthfulness she never had. She didn't know if it was his carefree attitude or something about his awkward social tendencies, but his voice filled up the house when he was excited, and his focus was on the small joys in life; it warmed her heart.

Clicking the door shut, she tossed a blanket onto the family's chest, her mind wandering to Cosima: president of her class and a star student with high regard from staff and students. But there were escalated accounts of violence and strange events that began after she arrived at Sparks Boarding School. Yet nobody tied them to her. Vienna shivered at the thought of Cosima's violence before pushing the thoughts aside and falling into a deep slumber.

▽△△▽⊕

*The landscape rushes into view, the copper dirt of the rolling hills and bronze trenches announcing I've arrived in Hell. Peering around, the echo of a light breeze is welcoming. Wait! Realizing the void's absence is startling. I've grown accustomed to the games played in this prison. It's different this time.*

*Red hair vanishes beyond a distant pillar.*

*Red.*

*"A beautiful name." Her bony hip scrapes my wrist as she steps into me. "Fitting, too."*

*I hold my breath as she spews dislodged particles from her teeth, several specks connecting with my face. Bile rises as I fight the urge to wipe it from my face.*

*"It's been weeks." She pouts as though her favorite pet wandered from home. "I can't blame you," she eggs me on. "Logan is a handsome young man."*

*My teeth clench, the muscles in my cheeks pulsing with anger. Debate of engaging or remaining silent conflicts within me. My mouth* opens instinctively. I slam it shut, knowing I'll regret any words that escape. Less than a second passes before I open my mouth, the urge to fight winning.

"Why have you been stalking me?"

"Would you expect anything less? After all, how else would you get to know this oasis and your bewitching talents?"

Oasis? Did she call the sauna-filled waste a magical oasis?

"Isn't it? The dark clouds." Where empty skies once loomed, black clouds roll in, and lightning crashes across them. Thunder echoes as the clouds move closer, dropping a tubular cloud that inches to the ground. A large hand constricts at the base of the tunnel. Veins of lightning shoot through the fingers until blue streaks of light flicker through the black tunnel. Hitting down, the ground rumbles; I steady myself as it turns slowly before transforming into an enormous tornado.

My heart stops as another arm shoots to the ground faster than the last. Quickly this time, it begins turning high speed before touchdown. They rush toward me, picking up speed as they suck in the dirt, spinning faster and faster before they move forward, covering the landscape as its velocity tosses grains of sand across the plane. Looking at the twisters, an orange wave pushes out of its base. Fear crawls down my spine as the thought of abrasive sandpaper slicing my skin sends me into a panic. It moves nearer, the distance between us shrinking rapidly.

Sweat gathers across my neck, and I wipe it, the palm of my hand pausing. Turning it over, I see several welts where thickening skin is forming from the hours spent practicing with daggers. Swaying, reality crashes into me. Can this be?

Closing my hands, I meet my nemesis' eyes. Unblinking, I search for understanding, finding an unwelcome answer as her thin lips curve into a snaky grin.

Over a dozen dreams. Over a dozen times I've been stuck under Red's command . . . paralysis holding me captive, and only now, with the use of Logan's name, does it dawn on me.

*"These aren't dreams, are they?"*

*Her baleful laugh dies as she addresses me. "This is the Nether Realm. And I"—she moves toward me—"your welcoming host."*

## LOGAN

"Thanks for meeting us." Mr. Humphrey sat with the rest of the Council. "We have decided that Valda will be attending the training with you."

Logan racked his brain; the name sounded familiar, but he couldn't place it. "Do I know her?"

"She was at Domar's briefly during training the first fall you attended. She's skilled in telepathy and combat, and her magic is enhanced by those she fights with." Mr. Humphrey continued, "Her specialty is rare. As you know, not many females visit Domar, but her uniqueness and rarity made her presence justified."

"The Enlitner," Logan said flatly.

"Yes. Do you have a problem with that?" Ms. Blight asked.

"No. Though I am curious why you chose an Enlitner and one with only moderate experience," he asked.

"You asked for someone we can trust, someone skilled, and she fits both. I am concerned with the way you speak about Enlitners," Mr. Ozul commented.

Logan said nothing. He watched, wondering if they knew the mother who abandoned him was an Enlitner.

"Rare in their abilities, they often make their own way in the magic world. Their fierce combat skills and extra-human strength match their ability to use other Enchanter's magic to boost their own; they are assets to powerful Enchanters. It would be wise to see the benefits in this situation," Mr. Ozul lectured.

"She will arrive for your next session. As you know, Enlitners can connect quickly due to their ability to read emotions and create deep connections from their natural talents. We predict no issues with the transition, as Valda takes over some of the areas you are currently training for." The White Queen watched as Logan seethed.

"Even with all the positive assets the Enlitner will bring, you are uncomfortable," Ms. Blight pointed out.

"I'm struggling with letting go of control." It was only a partial lie. The thought of spending less time with Vienna bothered him.

"A full moon is upon us, requiring your presence in the Shadow Realm. Her comfort with Valda must be established by then," Mr. Audovera reminded him.

"And Elric? Will he be able to stand guard during my absence?" Fire spread in his chest at the thought of Elric watching her in his absence.

"Yes." Logan turned to find Elric behind him. "I'd say we've done well so far. Me in the shadows keeping her magic at bay, you fighting the urge to form a deeper connection."

Logan flinched at the accusation.

"Do we have something to worry about?" the White Queen asked.

"No," Elric answered, "just playful banter."

"When do we allow her to access her magic? Her frustration is growing, and I'm surprised her impatience hasn't won out," Logan said flatly.

"I guess she'll learn more lessons than we planned then, won't she?" Mrs. Jaheem smiled.

"Is there anything else?" Logan asked.

"You're dismissed," Mr. Ozul answered.

Logan pushed past, his shoulder slamming into Elric. The force turned Elric, his eye-widening in anger. Logan did look back, worried his rage would win, with his frustration and fear rising. *How could he protect her when he'd be gone for a week, especially when he couldn't tell her . . . again?*

# CHAPTER EIGHT

R estless sleep taunted Vienna as she woke off and on through the night. Neon numbers flashed at 2 o'clock, and with less than 5 hours of sleep, her annoyance grew. Giving up on sleep, she realized it wouldn't be a people-type day and decided to investigate her family history.

She moved to the floor and uncovered the family's chest. Several attempts lead to success, and the top popped open. Rifling through, she gathered a large stack of documents and scattered them across the floor, determined to learn as much as possible. Journals from the Corey family marked major historical events from the Magic Realm and the Human Realm.

*Magyieka 1650 A.D.*

*Enchanters are fleeing Magyieka in safety after the loss of our Elite Enchantress. With the homeland in fear of ruin, as the Council scrambles to secure our borders, many have* chosen to seek refuge in the Human Realm. As the last remaining Corey who can carry on my name, I have not joined fellow Enchanters in the Human Realm. As a Guard, I stand ready to protect my homeland. Though young, my Corey heart will carry me through, and my bloodline will not cease to exist.

    E. Corey

Salem, MA 1665 A.D.

    The Council has sent me to the Human Realm; Enchanters have chosen to live in the Human Realms for centuries, but not in masses like now, and it's not without consequence. Though my unit started in Europe, we have fled with our people due to the witch hunt that continues. We now reside in Salem, Massachusetts, a small settlement in America founded less than a decade ago.

    I fear we have brought irreversible danger to Humans as they continue to turn on one another; accusations of witchery have ended in thousands of deaths in Europe, and there is talk that it has followed us to the Americas.

    It is best that we're forbidden to share our lineage to those we bear children with outside of Magyieka. This curse may die in time as blood dilutes, eliminating the hatred and reasons to kill the innocent as the hunters seek the Enchanters they call witches.

    E. Corey

Salem, MA 1680 A.D.

    The Council has forbidden discussion and the use of

*power in the Human Realm. Enchanters are outraged and combative as they struggle in this new world. For many, enchantments have brought them success and safety.*

  *E. Corey*

Her intrigue at the connection between the Witch Trials and the Magic Realm grew. Not only had she learned that the trials started before they hit Salem, Massachusetts, as many of her peers in school had thought, but the theory of witchery also dated back before 1300 B.C. Early on, trials were held through church bodies. Controversy about witchcraft being false was debated until proof was built and jurisdiction shifted from church to state. With less widespread panic and fear, the hunts didn't start to spread until the 1500s. In 1542 A.D., the Witchcraft Act was created by English law, making witchcraft punishable by death, and soon after, the Witch Trial slaughters began. Convictions spread across Europe, not ending until the Witchcraft Act ended in 1736 A.D. During this time, in the early 1690s, the witch hunt entered the United States.

She recalled this information and thought about how it fit the family's timelines. Vienna read quickly through the Corey journals; each filled the gaps in her knowledge while adding to her long list of questions.

*Salem, MA 1687 A.D.*

*My request to return home to ensure my bloodline continues within Magyieka comes with terms of returning to the Human Realm if the need arises again during my lifetime. It's agreed that I will continue to serve as a Guard, or what Humans call Knights. The decades spent on Earth have left me full of knowledge and ideas to increase unity in* my homeland. It has also taught me much about hatred and the fear of corruption.

I will miss the friends I made here, but I yearn for home. I shall take leave with Magyieka's war ending and my people safe in America.

E. Corey


Magyieka 1691 A.D.

As the year ends, chatter in the Magic Realm of witch hunts moving to America has increased. I shall leave my new son and wife to protect the Human Realm once more— this time from what we now know we have created. Enchanters continue to use their natural abilities to impress or make a living. Humans face persecution.

The Council will continue to allow Enchanters to live in the Human Realm, but they must keep their abilities secret —even from their children. A prophecy states Enchanter numbers will dwindle through the centuries. Until today, we didn't know how.

How many Enchanters will risk an end to their lineage and stay in the Human Realm?

E. Corey


Salem, MA 1692 A.D.

The curse of magic continues to create tragedy as Humans die on their own; accusing of witchcraft, they drown and hang the innocent. Is it the Enchanters who brought this to the Human Realm, or are Humans crueler than we knew before arriving?

At dawn, we will flee and take our leave west. The Council has increased punishment for any use and speaking of supernatural enchantments when outside the Magic Realm. It is our hope that this will bring with it an end to the bloodshed, so our children may choose to remain in the realm they choose.

E. Corey

West Coast 1730 A.D.

Exploration of the West Coast has proved daunting. Though mid-aged for Enchanters, the Human Realm is progressing my age as I remain here. I hope to return home soon, as we have found a settlement safe and secluded in lands like our own: no Human population has resided nearby; trees reach the skyline; brooks and springs run free and are abundant. We have traveled through intense envi-ronments filled with blazing sun and winters too harsh for civilization. Now we are home. Many have considered naming it after our first home in the United States, though I am not sure the Council will approve. With the struggle for Enchanters to settle this area, we hope many decades will pass before we need to settle with Humans—perhaps then they will be safe.

E. Corey

West Coast 1732 A.D.

My wife and son arrived this morning. With continued safety and our lifestyle here, there is no reason to be apart. Still, they will not stay, for the long winters can be harsh

for a child. They will stay until the Autumn Equinox.
    E. Corey

Oasis 1735 A.D.

Enchanters have been safe from harm, with the witch hunts slowing to a near stop since we fled, and no Humans present in the general area; the Council has granted my return home. I leave before the next full moon. My people will remain in this place we now call Oasis.
    E. Corey

Magyieka 1841 A.D.

Tomorrow, I head back to the Human Realm. After less than a century home, Humans have found Oasis, and we must clear our tracks and hide until they settle the land. My wife and son will join me for a temporary stay. Tanto-rian is excited to see the Human Realm now that he is a young man.
    E. Corey

Salem, Oregon 1842 A.D.

Salem, Oregon is the chosen name of the nearby town where we settled in this Oasis. If not still saddened by the horror of Salem, Massachusetts, it could be amusing that Salem is the chosen name of this town. Perhaps it was destined as Enchanters and settlers shared stories of their time across the Americas.

Before the Winter Solstice, we returned to Magyieka to continue our life. My son and I, as Guards of our Realm;

*his Enchantress wife, whom he met in Salem, will travel with us. The thrill in my wife's eyes as she welcomed our new daughter reminded me of our future together. I welcome the day we watch a grandchild patter across our home; I have many experiences to make up for. I missed many years of Tantorian's childhood.*

*E. Corey*

Vienna stared at the ceiling as the first hint of dawn crept through the window. She soaked in the tranquility, processing everything she'd learned about her family line, Enchanter history, and the differences between the two realms. With magic at their whim, it shocked her that many, like her family, lived without modern technology, but their family chest created a gateway to the knowledge needed. A sense of excitement bloomed at the thought of living as though she stepped back in time—but filled with magic she once thought was a fairy tale.

After reading her family history, she saw how the magic world impacted Humans and why it was important for magic to remain a secret. So much loss happened the last time witchcraft was detected, and Enchanters were allowed to roam freely, using their magic in daily life. With the family journey noting their tragic effect and the loss of Humans and Witches, she hoped one day both realms could live in unity.

Deep in thought, Vienna strummed her fingers across her stomach before her antsy energy became untamable. Exaggerating, she bounced off her bed, threw on her combat gear, and skipped down the stairs, blood rushing as she anticipated her intensive workout.

Grabbing a boiled egg, she slipped out the front door, shutting it slowly, trying not to wake her family. Looking through the window, the house was still, and she smiled as she imagined them sleeping until the sun was bright overhead and the morning chill faded.

"Where ya going?"

Vienna jumped at the deep voice, letting go of the screen door; it closed with a thud. Turning, she found Logan on her porch, bright-eyed and bushy-tailed. *Ugh, why is he always so happy in the morning?* she thought.

"You scared the piss out of me." She pushed his shoulder. "And seriously, put away the Cinderella morning attitude." With the door locked, she turned her full attention to him. "What are you doing here, Logan?"

"We have a lesson," he chirped, rocking from toe to heel. "You didn't forget, did you? You owe me a win?" He pushed off the railing and moved purposefully until he stood inches before her.

"Of course! How could I forget?" She shrugged. Her breath slowed the closer he got.

"Hey." He tapped her forehead. "It's going to be okay, V. I'll be easy on you. I know how much you love mornings." His teasing fell flat when she saw the fear in his eyes. His lip twitched, and warmth spread across her chest as she watched his lips spread to a wide grin.

She pushed past him and galloped down the porch steps, annoyed at falling for his charm. "You seem different today." She looked at him skeptically.

He shrugged. "Every morning is a new beginning. I get to spend the day with a sweet young woman in a beautiful forest."

"Okay . . . you're creeping me out."

"Just looking forward to kicking your ass today."

She scowled at him. "Mark my words, one day you'll underestimate my growth."

"I'm counting on it. Now let's go."

"Can I ask you something?"

"Don't you always?"

"I'm serious." She threw a glare at him.

"So am I." He scoffed.

"Whatever." She paused for a moment, gathering her courage.

"Why do you get to attend school here *and* in the Magic Realm?" She peeked back at him.

"That was just to keep an eye on you," he answered with a sly smile.

Vienna stopped, waiting for an earnest answer.

"Okay. As you know, I'm a couple of years older than you. So I accessed my . . . " he thought momentarily, and she watched as he calculated his words. " . . . skills the summer I left."

"The summer you disappeared," she corrected.

Shaking off her accusation and scorned words, he continued, "The Council came to me after we moved back to Magyieka. With your pure bloodline, they felt it was wise to keep a close eye on you. They offered me the opportunity to attend both schools to watch for any signs of magic or anything off."

"I know a pure bloodline is becoming rare, but enough to have you watch me?"

"Ya. It's that rare, Vienna." The shock at her lack of seriousness in the situation seeped into his tone.

"Okay. That leaves me wondering how it's possible. How do you attend both schools?"

"Time is different in each place, and I don't do extra activities there." He made it sound simple, which made Vienna envious that he had access to both places.

Deep in thought as they wandered toward the forest, she pondered his answer. It made sense the school sent Logan to watch, especially after what she'd learned about her bloodline. Looking up, she caught his content expression as he snapped a twig into several small pieces.

"Do you miss it?" she asked. "Normal life and one school, I mean."

"I did . . . at first." He matched her stride. "Then Domar's Boarding School became like home. That's the boys' school in the Magic Realm," he explained. "The people there are like me. Both my parents went there. They loved it. When my powers showed, they told me everything about the school, their experiences, and how much they loved it there. Neither one had a great home life. Being queer was not accepted back then. So boarding school was an escape for them."

"My parents said boarding school was a great experience, too," she confessed. "Are they accepted now?" She remembered the struggle they had experienced. "I know it wasn't easy for them here, either. They never seemed to let it bother them. I always admired that."

"There are still a lot of challenges, but most of them are with work right now. Living here for so long has left many biases and doubts in their abilities. Sometimes, I think it's a relief to have the focus elsewhere. But the Magyieka is adapting to change and accepting differences every year that goes by."

"I love that for them. I miss your dad's cookies, man."

Logan laughed, the first full laugh she'd heard from him since they started working together. His whole body rocked with his laughter, which infected her.

"Any other questions? We're almost to our spot," he announced.

"Yes, actually!" She came to an abrupt stop and turned on him. "Why is Sparks' location such a secret? How do we get there? I asked my parents, and they refused to tell me?" She jutted her chin out.

Logan chuckled. "Always the patient one."

Vienna turned, her blood boiling.

"Wait up. I'm sorry, V. It's not a secret. It's best not to ruin the surprise," he called.

# CHAPTER NINE

## Vienna & Logan's POV

"I can't believe how much you've improved over the last two weeks," Logan admitted.

His words replayed in her mind, and they danced around the forest. He wasn't able to take her down as quickly as before, but it felt nice. Her arms had grown stronger, and she was more confident. But after several hours of brutal practice, Vienna's back and shoulders burned. Deep breaths eased her swimming head and freed her mind. For the first time all week, she was at ease.

Knuckles cracked against her jaw. A light buzz filled her head, and she swayed—her eyes vibrated, and nausea rose. Blinking rapidly, the three wobbling figures in front of her faded in and out.

"Vienna, can you hear me? Oh, man." He squeezed her shoulders. Logan's voice pulled her attention back. She rubbed her eyes, and the three figures became one.

"Ouch," slipped slowly from her lips. Logan released his grip.

"What the hell, V?" He clenched his jaw.

"What happened?" Vienna barely got the words out.

"We were in combat mode. You were doing well." His voice shook as he slid a hand through his hair. "You dropped your arms in the middle of practice and went blank. I popped you, expecting you to block. It was a hard hit, V." His eyes were wild.

Vienna threw her head back, laughing hysterically. "Oh my God, Logan, I'm so sorry." She caught her breath, wiping a tear from her hysteria. "I was so content during practice." Pulling back, she looked at him. "For the first time since . . . well, since forever, I felt complete." She thought for a moment, searching for the right word. "I felt *free*." Her heart warmed as she smiled at him. With a trembling voice, she admitted, "I felt completely free as all my worries melted away. It was so serene, I just stopped." Something tickled her hand, and she lifted it. A small violet bloomed under her hand. She looked at it curiously, certain she hadn't seen a violet in the area before.

"I know the feeling." Logan brought her out of thought. There was a look in his eyes that Vienna couldn't place, but it sent a shiver down her body.

Vienna rolled onto her back and stared at the sky, pondering if he was safe to reveal all her secrets to. It had been almost a month since they began spending each day together, and the trust was building. She also had nobody else close enough to trust with important secrets. Knowing this was one area she could start to work toward building their relationship, she decided to share what she found that morning. She picked the violet and twirled it as she told him about the family chest.

"There were journals from my family going back centuries. I read through a little bit each morning. They talked about some of the problems the Human Realm has faced because of Enchanters. It was sad but at the same time satisfying to learn about the history of my family."

Logan was quiet as he listened. She looked over to find him gazing at her intently, and a sparkle danced in his eyes. Just inches away from her, hands locked behind his head, he waited.

She shifted, nervous at his intense gaze. "Why are you looking at me like that?" she spit out, harsher than intended. She bit her lip.

"Story of your family and Enchanters." He ignored her question. "Keep going."

She filled him in on everything she read and the excitement she felt. Knowing she would learn more as she dug through her family's chest invigorated her. She rambled on about the possibilities until she ran out of things to say. "I can't help but wonder if I'll learn more about what powers run through our family. What causes the realms to be at odds. How society functions in Magyieka. What myths and magical beings in human mythology and folklore are real. So many things."

He smiled at her eagerness. "I can tell you there are many realms with creatures found in stories of our world, and some never discovered."

Unwilling to ask what creatures she'd learn about, fearing it would ruin the surprise, she smiled at what he offered.

They lay there in silence, enjoying the serenity. Unsure of the time, Vienna looked over and stared at Logan's relaxed face. *You're more than an Enchanter. I know it.* His eyes shifted to her before drifting from one cloud to the next as they embraced the silence. She'd never seen him at peace like he was at that moment. Determined to let him have this moment, she held back the urge to ask about his magic side. Her lips tilted, and she looked back to the sky, finding the form of each cloud: a dove. How ironic.

▽△△▽✺

*The breeze that carries the chirping bird calls drift away. Feelings of the Dream Realm hit me, but it's not copper around me. Instead, a cottage is nestled in a dark enclosure next to a long row of berries. I look around, confused.*

*"Where am I?" I ask aloud, hoping to break the silence.*

*"Where do you think you are?" a small voice asks in return.*

*My heart speeds up. Unfamiliar territory and an unknown voice are both unexpected. But it's not Red. So, I move forward.*

*"Who are you?"*

*"My mom says I can't tell you that." A little girl peeks around the edge of a tree. Her large eyes are colorless as gray shifts over the cottage and surrounding area.*

*"Can you tell me where I am?" Moving closer, I kneel. There are six feet between us. Her features are unfocused, but I can sense her warning.*

*"This is my safe place." A muffled giggle escapes, and she rushes into the woods. Laughter echoes through the trees as her footsteps fade.*

*"Wait," I holler and chase her.*

*"Come play with me, Vienna." I stop at the sound of my name.*

*"How do you know my name?" I ask.*

*Laughter dances through the forest. She's nowhere in sight. Frozen in place, I look through the thick pines. Emerald eyes shine in the distance. Like prey, I don't blink, but the eyes fade to slivers before disappearing.*

*The landscape melts as the world spins around me . . . faster . . . faster . . . faster, like water washing away chalk, and everything fades.*

▽△△▽✳

Vienna's eyes popped open. She blinked at the darkened sky, then launched into an upright position. Owls began to hoot, and darkness pressed upon her . . . hours had passed since her eyes drifted closed. The sky was bright with scattered clouds just minutes ago, yet the brief dream drained hours from her day.

"Time to go, V." Logan buzzed around. He grabbed all the gear before returning to Vienna and holding out his hand. "We can make it to your house in time for dinner."

"So soon? I had a blast today." Stretching out for several minutes, she waited for motivation.

"Come on, V. It's late. We fell asleep, so I guess we can consider this your win," he joked. "You do like your beauty rest."

"Funny." She punched him in the arm.

"Jesus, you're getting strong," he admitted.

She smiled, then looked at the glowing moon. It cast a mesmerizing light across the clearing. It was bewitching. Logan held all the gear, ready to go.

She moved toward him, locking his hand with hers. Deep breaths lifted his chest, and he brushed a loose strand of her hair from her face. She bit her cheek and suppressed a sigh as his tongue grazed across his lower lip. Dropping her guard, she moved closer, and his firm hands wrapped around her waist and pulled her body tight against hers.

"Logan," she breathed.

She watched his neck move as he swallowed. Shifting toward her, his lips neared hers, his breath brushing against her eager lips, but they didn't connect. Heat shot from her stomach to her chest, her heart pounding rapidly. She fought the urge to move in as images of him walking away flooded her. She closed her eyes, a tear gathering in the corner. The heat was doused with memories of the pain he inflicted when she was abandoned.

Logan stepped back, and she opened her eyes, suppressing a desire to be held by him. The heat flickering in his eyes caused her lips to vibrate. She touched them, harnessing the memory of his nearness. She switched gears, anxious to end the tension.

"I had the weirdest dream. There was a little girl and a cottage. She said her mom wouldn't let her tell me who she is." He said nothing, so she continued. "It felt real, like when Red visits me. But this is the first time I've felt that way somewhere besides the deserted plain. It was creepy."

"Sounds like a nightmare to me," he teased.

"Actually, I felt safe with her. It was the green eyes in the forest that caused me discomfort," she admitted.

"Green eyes? Did you see who they belonged to?" Logan's voice was venomous.

"I would have said so, wouldn't I?"

"It sounds like a warning. What else do you remember?"

"She knew my name, and she wanted to play. There was something so familiar about her." Deep in thought, she tried to recall anything important.

"Let's go." He moved forward, and she caught the concern on his face.

"What are you thinking? What kind of warning could this be?" She matched his pace.

"I'm not sure, but we need to get you home."

"Do we have to? We could practice in the dark," she suggested, hopping up and down. "It's enchanting out here—the moon and night sky are so full . . . It's like fuel . . . In fact"—she poked his shoulder—"I think I *could* win a round."

Laughing, he grabbed her hand. "Well, I'd like to stay on your parents' good side. You can *win*," he exaggerated, "tomorrow morning."

"Why does it matter if my parents like you?" Vienna scoffed.

"Ugh, your mom's cooking is epic. Ain't no way I'm missing out on her delicious meals because you're suddenly revived." He grabbed her hand. "Now, let's get home before you wander off in a giddy dance."

"Fine. Ya killjoy. But"—she wrinkled her nose and pulled her hand from his—"only if you can catch me." Before he could answer, she sprinted down the hill, hiding behind trees and boulders.

Logan never caught up, but the woods filled with laughter as he missed her by mere seconds each time he reached for her. Consumed with joy, she realized this game had them acting like they were ten again. All seriousness faded as he chased her through the moonlit woods. For the first time since starting high school, she felt close to Logan.

"Come on, Logan, you can do better! Over here."

"Just wait. You can't keep this up." Laughing, he lunged behind a boulder and then a tree. She was nowhere.

Hiding behind a small bush, she watched him dart through the forest, searching for her. Just a few feet away, excitement bubbled as he got closer. She bit her lips, a smile spreading at his childish grin.

A dark shadow moved over her, and she looked up. Cosima. She let out a dreadful scream.

"Vienna!" Logan growled. She listened as Logan's footsteps rushed toward her. "Where are you?" He moved toward her with predatory speed. His foot connected with Vienna's ribs, and she watched as he froze at the sight of Cosima.

"What do you want?" he demanded.

"I see the rumors are true." Cosima sneered.

Vienna lay on the ground, unmoving. "What did you do to her?" He bent down and checked for a pulse. Thick power wafted off her in dangerous waves. "What's wrong with her?" He seethed.

"She will not make you happy, Logan. I can promise you." Cosima ignored his question.

He pounced, standing toe-to-toe with her. She smiled, and Vienna watched as his body hardened, freezing him in place. Caressing his jaw, she leaned in and kissed him passionately.

Vienna's stomach turned as bile rose; her anger fought with jealousy. Her body quivered and the angrier she grew, the more she tried to stop it. She imagined being doused in water. A drop of water fell from the sky, splattering across Vienna's cheek, cooling her rage.

"Vienna has been my friend since grade school, nothing more. It's my responsibility to prepare her for school. That is the extent of our relationship." Eyes locked, he jutted out his jaw.

Movement behind Cosima startled them. Vienna watched as everyone turned toward the deep forest.

"For her sake, I hope that's true. I have great plans for you, Logan. Do *not* disappoint me." With that, she disappeared, and her spell broke.

Logan kneeled and placed Vienna's head on his lap.

"Come on, V." He shook her.

"Ouch," she groaned.

"You okay?"

"My head is killing me." She couldn't tell him she'd heard every word. With an aching heart, she grabbed her head and curled into Logan's lap.

"Where did this come from?" He wiped the water from her face.

"My head is pounding," she deflected.

Pulling back in confusion, Logan asked, "Why are you ignoring my question?"

She thought for several seconds, then shrugged. Wide-eyed and confused, they locked their eyes. "I remember running from you and then waking up." She left out hearing their conversation, and the raindrop cooling her.

"Fine, let's go."

"You can't expect me to trust you with everything when you don't do the same." She stood her ground.

"Let's get you home and get something for your headache," he said through gritted teeth.

His temples swelled at his impatience. He clenched his jaw, and Vienna watched through squinted eyes as his features shifted. She smirked as he closed his eyes. At ease, he opened his eyes.

"Okay, but we're going to have to go slow. It's pounding."

"You set the pace, V. I'm not going anywhere."

The walk back was long, and Logan spent most of the time guiding Vienna. She kept her eyes closed. When they arrived, her parents were waiting on the front porch. They both rushed down to help Vienna.

"What happened?" her dad demanded.

"I don't know, Dad."

"Sir, Cosima appeared and spelled V."

"*What?*" Her mom gasped. "That's against our code."

"Some people don't follow the code," Logan reminded them.

"Tell us everything."

"She thought we were dating and warned me . . . she has plans for me." He shook his head, disgusted.

"This is absurd! We must report her." Before her mom could make it up the stairs, Vienna stopped her.

"No, Mom. I'll handle this. I'm not going to start the school year off like this. I'll deal with it when I get there. She'll cool down now that she knows we aren't dating." She looked at Logan. "Right?"

"Yes," he said. "This girl is trouble and isn't afraid to do whatever it takes to get what she wants."

"I understand that. But this is my choice. If things get worse, then I'll report it. Until then, we train. Besides, we're just friends; I'm clearly no threat," she said pointedly, suppressing her disappointment.

## LOGAN

Logan burst through the door, the thud causing the Council members to gasp.

"What is going on?" Mr. Humphrey stood at Logan's entrance.

Logan rushed toward them, swiftly dodging around the transcriber.

"Robes must be worn in the chamb . . ."

A deafening growl cut off Mr. Audovera. "Fuck your robe and your rules." Logan twitched as he fought his rage; his body urged to transform. His vision began to blur, and he applied firm pressure to his temples. The heat and pressure from his hands soothed the rage, allowing his focus to return.

"Mr. Artrusha, you will refrain from using profanity and calm yourself or LEAVE." The Ovr'seer nodded to Mr. Humphrey, who sat.

Cosima stood in the back, smiling at him. Next to her was Elric. Logan locked eyes with him, an animalistic hunger rising.

"You purposely dropped the wall, allowing her magic to be accessed." Logan's voice vibrated in his chest, a feline growl cutting off his communication. He leaned on the table; char crumbled the wood beneath his palms. He stared at Elric and Cosima; his eyes were void of compassion. He was ready to kill.

Elric's eyes brightened as he smiled. "Of course, you expect the worst of me. At what point do you learn to trust your fellow Watchers?" Elric's voice showed no remorse or guilt.

Logan charged, fury blinding him as he leaped across the table, lunging toward Elric's jugular. Mid-air, he began to transform. Waves of energy pulsed seconds before his body slammed to the table.

"Enough!" Ms. Blight shrieked as the Seelie Queen's hand hovered in the air. "Release him."

The pressure dissipated, and Logan looked around the room. The Queen sat, her magic no longer holding him down. The rage he felt flickered in waves.

Logan stared at the Queen, then looked at Elric and Cosima. "Tell me what's going on," he demanded.

Ms. Blight touched his arm, his emotions calming. His muscles relaxed and Ms. Blight nodded to the Queen. "Tonight, Elric was found unconscious and brought home safely by Cosima," she said bluntly.

Logan shook his head in disbelief. "That's not possible. He's an Elite Watcher; few things could render him unconscious."

"Precisely," Mrs. Jaheem answered. "Which is why we are gathered here rather than out celebrating."

"Cosima was just telling us what she remembered," Ms. Blight encouraged Cosima to continue.

Logan hopped down and stood near the table, watching Cosima nervously tugging at her hair. "Well?" He seethed.

"I was stopping in to see how her training was. I was curious. There are stories about her, you know." Cosima glanced at her mom as she transcribed. Logan looked between them, noting the cold, blank stare of her mom.

"What did you see?" the Ovr'seer asked. He drummed his finger on the table impatiently.

"I walked around a cluster of trees and saw Elric lying there. I panicked. I didn't see anyone else, just a dark amber glow in the distance. Then I saw Vienna running around with Logan." Her cheeks flushed. "Sparks of magic pulsed around her. I was afraid, so I transported Elric back here."

The room was silent as the Council looked at one another. Logan watched as Cosima held her breath. Annoyed at their silence, he pushed off the wall and took two steps forward before Mr. Humphrey held up his hand, commanding him to stop.

Logan halted and looked around the room. "Something doesn't add up, Cosima." Her name came out harshly. "How were you able to transport there and back? You only transported there before because the Council sent you. It's not something you can do without help."

His accusation hung in the air; the emotions grew heavy. The Council murmured as he stared into Cosima, his distrust causing physical discomfort as she twitched.

"It seems she doesn't remember," Elric said flatly. "Or are we missing something?"

Cosima shook her head but said nothing. Her chin quivered.

"Perhaps she was spelled," Mr. Ozul thought aloud. Logan squinted his eyes. Mr. Ozul was typically harsh and seldom talked, and it was usually to dismiss or evade. So defending was not what he expected from him.

"Elric," the Ovr'seer spoke up, "please escort Cosima to the Healers to erase tonight from her memories. Then take her to Sparks Boarding School. Where she will remain. We will investigate tonight's situation, and if there is something to share, we will call a meeting."

"My pleasure." Elric led Cosima out of the room. She looked back at Logan before the door closed softly in its place.

Logan swore he saw regret in her eyes, but he couldn't be sure. "We're just going to trust they weren't in on this together? She's not powerful enough to . . . "

Mr. Humphrey cut him off. "We know, and we've already questioned them before you arrived. We are aware something is missing."

"The dark amber aura she talks about isn't heard of. I suspect she remembers incorrectly or is hiding something," the Queen added.

"We will need to keep a closer eye on her. We placed her in Ms. Blight's wing at Sparks due to her cruel nature. Perhaps we need to increase our watch of her," Mrs. Jaheem suggested.

"We will ensure we do. And we will need the Transcriber's mind wiped if tonight's events are more personal than usual. Her family is involved, which could increase her mental resilience," the Ovr'seer spoke as he watched the stenographer.

"I foresee a new stenographer in the future. Her mental capacity is reaching its limit faster than historical Transcribers. I fear she may be compromised or struggling in health," Mrs. Jaheem admitted.

"We all want her safety, Logan. Of that, you can be sure." Mr. Audovera stood. "Valda is ready and will join you tomorrow." The rest of the Council followed his lead.

Furious at the clipped response, Logan shook. Anger consumed him as he watched the Council leave the chamber. He exited, eager to escape Onyx Hall. He wasn't satisfied with the outcome, but he knew there was little he could do. He was grateful for Ms. Blight's ability to soothe, as the shift of cosmic energy nearly consumed him, and attacking a fellow Watcher could have resulted in a trial.

Logan stared through the trees, admiring the glowing moonlight.

He shook his head and investigated the Mist of Salvania. The dark and eerie forest was a comfort, and the second moon peaked its face over the grassy earth. Soon, he would be forced to return to the woods, and Vienna's safety would be out of his hands.

# CHAPTER

# TEN

"I must be dreaming." Everything feels unreal except the beads of sweat that drip down my face. Dreams have been realistic the last few months, but this is more intense than normal. I recall the term Dreamwalker: the ability to travel between realms and worlds, often to gain information. Once skilled, a Dreamwalker will know what's happening. No, it's just one of those dreams that feels real. A dream where you wake up on the floor rather than falling to your death from a tall building.

Closing my hands, I kneel and run my fingers through the sand. I can feel each grain. Squeezing my eyes shut, I try to recall more information about dreamwalking. That's when the images of papers from my family's chest come into my vision. Each paper is bright and easy to recall. The words "Dreamwalker" and "family" float from the pages, and I remember the details so vividly I fall to the ground.

"Looks like your time is up."

Peering up, I see Red. Her lips curled in disgust.

"Did you think you could beat us? You're nothing. You never had a chance." Turning with majestic grace, the woman walks away, her long lace dress flowing behind her. She never looks back.

Confused, I look across the landscape but find nobody. This familiar place I have dreamed of so often, usually haunted by the woman who just walked away, is now vacant. Excitement stirs, and I hop up, my desire to explore the landscape masking any fear.

Walking feels like slow lava as it begins to cool. My legs burn; the mental and physical exertion to take each step is excruciating. As though an invisible force pushes against my body, my feet dig into the sand and push slowly with each trembling inch.

Panting, my body leans at an awkward slant, my head surpassing my feet by nearly a foot. I lean down to slow my breath. Looking back, my footsteps trail behind me for miles.

"What the hell!" Confusion swarms me, and I relax. Focusing, I slowly fight to get back to a vertical stance. Though it feels like I've only moved a yard, many more miles of footsteps show how far I've traveled. Time and distance in this place are not linear to reality.

Pushing away my curiosity, I ready myself to continue. But I'm unable to move—my feet stick and I fall flat on my face. Gasping for air, I push my body up, lifting my face to the sky before realizing my body has been captured.

I'm submerged in quicksand the color of hot embers. My body warms as each muscle tenses from the devouring fear consuming me. Pushing my body back and forth, I pull my weak, trembling legs, trying to free myself, fearful this will become my a tomb. Pain shoots to my feet, igniting my determination, and adrenaline takes over. Forcing fear aside before it wins, I focus on the cool breeze that stirs. It is then that I remember this is a dream and that I am in control. I relax each muscle, welcoming the sense of peace that fills my soul. As I take my last breath, the sand engulfs the rest of my body.

▽△△▽✴

Vienna woke with a gasp. Her lungs burned as if they were full of that sand in her dream. She could recall every emotion and every sensation she'd felt as she'd sunk to her death.

Flipping on her lamp, she grabbed her notebook and pen. She wrote every detail she could remember about the dream, including the woman. This wasn't the first nightmare about her death. The redhead was in every one of them, and her goal was always to harm Vienna.

"Who is she?" she asked out loud. Tapping her pen against her cheek, she lost herself in thought, anxious when no answers came. She sketched the woman's face and colored her hair and eyes, the main things that popped out to her.

"You okay, sweetie?"

Vienna jumped out of her bed, dropping her notebook. Loose papers flew everywhere. "Mom, you scared the crap out of me." She and her mom gathered the pages.

Pausing, her mom stared intensely at the drawing she had picked up.

"What is it, Mom?" Vienna reached out and touched her hand.

"Where have you seen this woman . . . and this tree?" Confused, her mom held up the picture for Vienna to see. Vienna didn't remember drawing the tree.

Vienna looked up from the picture and noticed the terror on her mom's face.

"Vienna, tell me where you've seen this!"

Before she could answer, her dad burst through the door, sending it flying; it slammed against the wall and knocked down a shelf of knickknacks. "What's going on?" His eyes searched the room frantically.

"Look at this picture." Her mom jumped up and shoved the drawing in his face.

After several seconds, his head snapped up to Vienna and darted between her and her mom. "Is . . . is this who I think it is?" he asked.

"I'm not certain . . . but I bet it is." Her mom turned to her. "I need you to tell us every detail about this woman and this place. Meet us downstairs."

Vienna cursed herself for not telling them sooner. Logan was right. God, she hated that. She grabbed her robe and tied it around her, blocking out the chill. After gathering the loose pages that ended up under the bed, she moved to the door. She waited, hoping to hear something, but her parents' whispers were quiet.

Mustering her courage, she walked down the stairs. They sat at the table, holding the drawing her mom freaked over. Nervously, Vienna took her seat and put the other drawings in front of her. Months of drawings were stacked. Different yet similar, they all had one thing in common: Red.

"Before we start," her dad started, "tell us what you've learned through the historical documents."

Restless, Vienna shook the table as her leg bounced; her anxiety was rising. Her body warmed as anticipation built. As quickly as possible, she filled her family in on what she'd learned, making sure to point out her confusion about some of the blank pieces on the family tree.

"Can we go back to the pieces that are different? It's like something is missing." She looked between her parents. "There are blank boxes next to your name, Mom. Under your parents' tree. I've been curious why they are blank but can't figure it out."

"When did you discover that?" her dad asked.

"When I woke up a couple of nights ago. I just forgot to bring it up. It's been a busy week."

"Fair enough. You're right," her mom hesitated, looking to Vienna's dad for support. "I have a sister who was removed from the family tree. She left angry and . . . "

"Wait!" Vienna gasped in shock. She held up her hand, requesting a minute to process. "You have a sister? Why hasn't anyone told me I have an aunt?"

"Had, and it's because she's not someone we communicate with."

Her mom was blunt. Vienna's dad nodded, and she hoped it was time to learn more truths about her family.

"Another betrayal, another lie?" Vienna's heart sank. "Has anything been real in this house?"

"Watch it," her dad warned. "If you want answers, we'll give them. Until now . . ."

"I wasn't ready, right?" she finished. "That answer is growing old."

"Let's give you some backstory, shall we?" her mom cut in. Her dad straightened up and took his wife's hand.

"Your aunt and I met first. We became good friends before I met your mother. After a few months, I realized how angry, dark, and spiteful Gwen was. She found joy in very little and competition in everything. We were in a lab together, and I met your mother when I arrived at her house to study for a final exam." They smiled at each other, and he brushed his thumb down his wife's cheek. "I saw a spark in your mother's eyes." Her dad looked back to Vienna and continued. "Gwen spotted that I had taken a liking to Grace. She spent the entire study session telling me everything about your mom. Everything that she felt would dissolve my interest."

"It was apparent to your father," her mom continued, "that your aunt and I didn't get along. We never have. She's hated me since we were children. After your father and I married, she swore she would never let us have happiness. But we haven't seen or heard from her since that day. She just . . . vanished."

There were several moments of silence, and her mom's eyes glazed in thought. "Part of me always hoped she would come back and be part of our family. That she would have grown up . . . grown kinder. Part of me also feared she would show up to exact her revenge on me. Revenge for stealing her love." Her mom finished by squeezing her dad's hand.

"Why didn't you guys tell me about her before?"

"Honestly, I never thought to. I assumed she was lost to the family and wasn't a threat. I figured she was angry and would get over it, if she hadn't already."

"So why me?" Vienna asked, standing to pace the kitchen.

"Well, I'm afraid she's been waiting for our family to become present in the magic world again. You were exposed when your magic started to wake. Once your magic was reported to the Council, she would have your location as your name is entered into the local register."

"I think you're right, Grace," her dad muttered. "With a past of torture and childhood abuse, we know Gwen is jealous and vengeful. We changed Grace's last name when we moved here. Hoping if she did seek us, we wouldn't be easy to find."

"Clearly, what we did was no help, but we were desperate. That's why we chose to move here, too. Many married to another Enchanter stay in the Magic Realm to raise their kids. But we feared the danger." Her mom sat back.

"That redhead is in each nightmare; she's my aunt." She paused, thinking about her latest dream.

"I'm afraid so," her mom answered honestly.

"Every time she's in the dream, it's dark, and I'm so afraid I can't move. As soon as I feel frozen, I'm suddenly stuck." She shook her head. "I'm stuck *in* something. What's weird is that I'm stuck in something different in each nightmare. Tonight, it was quicksand that looked like lava."

For a second, Vienna stopped, looked up at her parents, and used all her strength to avoid crying uncontrollably—relief from finally telling them and the knowledge that these were more than dreams pulled at her emotions. Terror from her dreams surfaced as her parents exchanged glances and then signaled for Vienna to continue.

Vienna's pace sped up, finding her bearings, and she forced herself to breathe. "But the feeling is always the same: it feels like somebody's watching me. My chest is constricted. My stomach doesn't just tighten; I become so vile that I can barely see straight." Her voice went from deep to high and panicked, and her face became slick with sweat. She covered her face to hide her tears. "It feels so real. It always feels so real."

"These dreams sound terrifying," her mom said as she moved around the table. She put her arm around Vienna's shoulders. "To be honest, I think this could be more than a dream. It's possible she's entering your subconscious, or your actual dream."

"I thought the same thing," her dad said as he sipped his coffee.

Skeptical, Vienna looked at the picture. "But why would she be coming to me in my dreams? What would that do for her?"

"I'm not sure," her mom admitted. "Why don't you get ready? You have practice today. We'll try to figure this out later."

▽△△▽✸

Vienna finished the shower in time to hear a knock on the door. Hearing Logan's voice in the kitchen, she rushed through her routine. She rolled on extra deodorant, tossed her hair in a bun, and threw on her last clean sweats after a quick sniff test.

Running down the stairs, she abruptly stopped when she spotted an unfamiliar girl standing beside Logan. She had long blonde hair braided over her right shoulder. She was dressed in tight black leather and had a red-handled knife strapped to her back. During Vienna's examination, she looked determined, but when she laughed, her entire face lit up, and her head fell back. She was thin, but definite muscle lines showed through her clothes. Vienna stood there for several minutes, watching Logan and this girl talk before he noticed her.

A slow smile spread across his face. His eyes sparkled, and Vienna felt weak. Reminding herself to breathe, she closed her eyes, breathed through her nose, and entered the kitchen.

"Hi!" the girl piped up while walking toward Vienna. "I'm Valda. Logan has told me so much about you." Stopping short, she held out her hand to greet Vienna.

Vienna smiled and shook her hand. The instant their hands

connected, Vienna was overcome with feelings of vengeance. She closed her eyes and saw Valda in battle with a person cast in shadow.

Before the vision ended, Valda pulled her hand away and squinted her large hazel eyes. She pulled Vienna into a quick hug. "We'll talk about this later," she whispered in Vienna's ear.

Not sure what she'd experienced, Vienna put on her acting face, grabbed her lunch bag, said goodbye to her parents, and headed out the door.

"What was that?" she asked Valda, as Logan outpaced them.

"You feel other people's emotions, don't you?" Valda returned.

"I've never experienced something like that. This is the first time," Vienna replied. She squinted her eyes, untrusting.

"I, too, am a telepathic empath."

"What is a telepathic empath?" Vienna asked.

"You're serious." Valda took a step back and cocked her head sideways. "We can communicate through body language, emotions, and waves of strong emotions."

Vienna scrunched her nose in annoyance, feeling judged and mocked as Valda moved away from her. She jutted out her jaw to hide her faltering confidence.

"Well, Vienna Madizza-Corey," Valda mused, "it appears we have much more to teach you than I expected."

"How about starting with what it is and how it works?" Vienna suggested.

"Of course." Valda smiled. "When someone near us has a strong reaction, we sense it in our body and can understand it without verbal confirmation. Most people aren't able to feel that I am reading them, which means you may be able to use telepathy yourself."

Vienna thought back to her life but couldn't pinpoint experiencing telepathy before. "I don't think I've experienced this before, honestly."

"You're sure?" Valda asked.

"Pretty sure. Then again, I didn't know I was looking for superhuman abilities until a month ago."

"Guess we just keep an eye on it." As though nothing had changed, Valda walked away, quickly catching up to Logan. Vienna looked on, not knowing what to think. But her skepticism began to shift. Somehow, she trusted Valda.

"Hurry up, V! We haven't got all day," Logan hollered at her.

After several seconds of trying to decide whether this girl was a friend or foe, Vienna snapped out of her thoughts and, with a smile, hollered back, "Yes, we do!" She ran, catching up to the two people she knew would help her discover who she was and what the future would bring.

# CHAPTER ELEVEN

After arriving at their practice spot, Vienna, Valda, and Logan dropped their gear. Without a word, they sat down to hydrate. Vienna was short of breath after carrying more than she usually did. Logan and Valda appeared to be okay as they watched the sun rise.

"Remind me why the load was so heavy this time?" Vienna whined.

"You can't grow if we don't push you," Logan mused.

After she caught her breath, she leaned back. "Okay, soldiers, how long before I rock my way up here unfazed?" Their abilities were shocking; there was no sign of exhaustion.

"That depends on many things. Like your elemental sign, your talents—or gifts, as you call them—and how much you use the energy around you," Valda explained before chugging down half her water. Then, with smooth grace, she grabbed her sword and twirled it in circles like a professional.

"Impressive! Those are movie-grade skills." After admiring Valda's skills, Vienna recalled what she'd said. "Wait, elemental sign?

Talent? Gifts? Explain." She turned abruptly to Valda, who in turn looked at Logan.

"What the hell have you been teaching her, Logan? Does she know *anything*?" Valda snapped.

Logan shrugged. "Look, we just started and—"

Valda cut him off. "No, you've been working with her for weeks. *Weeks*, Logan. She should at least know the basics."

Squelching her urge to defend him, Vienna leaned against a tree with arms crossed and bit her lip as she smiled at the view of Logan being put in his place. Although he looked pissed as Valda laid into him, there was also a sparkle of amusement in his own eyes. So, with her selfish motives noted, Vienna watched as the two squabbled, hoping Valda would prevail and she would learn more than the little drops she was being given. She agreed with Valda; she was unprepared and quickly running out of time.

"Wait a minute," Logan broke the heated banter. He turned red as he stood taller and leaned toward Valda. "I have been doing the best I can. I was told to focus on physical defense and that she would learn the rest in school."

"That's crap, and you know it. Did your mentor only teach you physical defense?" Valda asked, as she propped her hands on her hips.

Logan looked at Vienna, and Vienna waved. Valda looked between them.

"Oh my God," she said, wide-eyed, covering her mouth. "You've fallen for her. Haven't you?"

Vienna pushed off the tree and took a step forward.

Logan shook his head and sighed. "You're right. I should've thought, but I didn't. I've been distracted."

Vienna was confused. *Was Valda right?*

"Mm-hmm." Valda lifted an eyebrow and smirked. "You know nothing can happen between you," she said softly.

Logan walked away without a word, stomping the innocent earth in anger, and grabbed his Kali stick. He walked over to Vienna, who was wide-eyed and blushing. Avoiding eye contact, she looked down at her nails, hiding her amusement and anxiety.

"Pick your weapon, V," Logan demanded. "After practice, we hit the books."

"It's about time." Vienna walked over and grabbed the other Kali stick. Leaving all anxiety behind—she was ready to attack. Valda smirked as she turned into position, locking her eyes with Vienna. She winked, leaving Vienna curious and caught off guard as she took a hit to the jaw. A surge of energy fired through her body, and Vienna launched a graceful and vicious attack.

▽△△▽✴

Several hours of practice passed, and Vienna was drenched in sweat and barely standing. Her exhaustion was earned, and her thighs shook. But the adrenaline roaring through her aches continued to fuel her unmatched spirit. She was impressed with Valda's fighting abilities. At one point, Valda and Logan demonstrated some mad one-on-one skills. It was like being in a front-row seat at a gladiator duel. By the end, it was a tie, and the whole group was laughing.

"That was amazing, you guys. I've never seen a fight like that." Vienna mimicked their moves until she realized she was doing it. "How long have you been fighting, Valda?"

"Ever since I can remember. It's something we learn when we start walking. It's not a big deal." She shrugged, but there was sadness in her eyes.

"Wait." Vienna walked over to Valda. "I was told we couldn't know anything until we discovered our abilities."

"That's technically true. But when you live in the Magic Realm full time, you learn more at a younger age. My guardian works in the other realm, so we live there. It's impossible to hide stuff when you're surrounded by it. So, when I learned to walk, I learned to fight."

"What about magic?"

"We still don't learn anything about sorcery until we display signs of talent—even if we know we have it. It's illegal for anyone to teach—or even talk about—magic to someone without it," Valda explained with another shrug.

"Good to know." With a smile, Vienna helped Logan pick up the supplies that were tossed around during practice.

"Ready to learn something new, V?" Logan flashed her a cocky smile.

"Absolutely! Will I learn my element and talent today?"

Valda and Logan laughed. "No," they said in unison. Logan covered his toothy grin with a fist. Vienna's impatience had always amused him, but his amusement pissed her off today.

"Those answers will come in time," Valda replied. "It's hard to say how long it will take. Could be a week, could be years."

"*Years?* Seriously? That's bull," Vienna huffed and chewed on the nail of her thumb. It felt impossible to have to wait so long.

"Cheer up. Most people find their element and talent within the first year. Let's head back to your house, and we can go over everything there. Maybe your mom will have some of those Monte Cristo sandwiches I love," Logan chimed in. He rubbed his palms together in excitement.

Laughing, Vienna nodded. "I bet she will. She knows they're your favorite."

"Food? I could go for that. Let's go." Valda grabbed the last weapons and dashed to Vienna's house, leaving the other two in her dust.

"Dang, the girl must be hungry. I can't remember the last time I ran that fast," Vienna joked, marveling at Valda's speed.

"Right? Trying to get *you* to jog is like getting a kid to brush his teeth, let alone ru—" Before he could finish, Vienna punched him in the chest.

"I run lots, thank you very much." Vienna's face burned with embarrassment. Did he think so low of her? Just because Valda was freakishly fast didn't mean she never ran.

"V, I was joking. But damn, girl! You have to stop hitting like that.

You're getting strong. I'm gonna bruise." Logan rubbed his chest for several seconds.

"Well, quit being an ass, and I won't hit you anymore," she suggested victoriously. She folded her arms while looking at Logan—his eyes locked with hers and lingered.

Her stomach flopped, and her heartbeat sped up. It felt like a fairy was in her stomach and tickling her heart. *Darn it,* she thought. At every turn, Logan captured part of her heart. It had started to worry her. She knew she was nothing like the girls he could have. But she also knew she was a good catch. *How can I feel so unique yet so inadequate at the same time?*

Logan's lips lifted slightly to the right, turning into a sideways smirk. It was endearing, like he knew what she was thinking. He reached out, brushed his thumb under her chin, and gathered the remaining supplies. Without another word, they headed down the trail to Vienna's house.

▽ ⟁ △ ▽ ✳

"Thanks for the early dinner, Grace." Logan grabbed a cupcake. "I love Monte Cristos. They should be more common around here."

"Yeah." Valda sat back, holding her stomach. "I think I might pop a button. Now I know why Logan can't stop talking about these things." She patted her belly and belched. Covering her mouth, she apologized, but not before pink spread across her cheeks and down her neck.

Hoping to soften Valda's embarrassment, Vienna belched herself. All three began to laugh.

Her mom laughed, too. "Of course. I'm glad you both are working with Vienna. She's got a lot to learn in a short time." She gathered the dishes from the overcrowded table. Their snacks covered every inch of it, and the aroma of maple syrup and cinnamon filled the air.

Vienna and her friends jumped up to help clean.

"Oh, no. Go train, you three. I don't want you fussing over chores when you have more important things to do."

They thanked her mom again and left out the front door. Vienna was happy to get out of her chores. She despised housework and thanked her busy schedule for getting her out of the house. Excitement bubbled with Valda now on board, and she squealed.

"I'm so glad to have you here," she told Valda. "Two brothers and Logan. You're the first female I've got to spend time with," Vienna admitted.

"Don't get too excited. I'm here to train you. Training is brutal, male or female trainer," Valda informed her.

"So, where do we start?" Vienna asked, brushing off the comment, abruptly turning to face the others. She was determined to learn her element and talent as soon as possible. She figured the best way to speed up the process would be to master as many skills as possible during her lessons. "We should start with the basic concepts of sorcery."

Eagerness fueling each movement, she fell down the last two steps of her porch. Logan grabbed her wrist right before she hit the ground.

"Slow down, speedy," he said with a laugh. "First, we need to get Valda home." His eyes sparkled as he pulled Vienna closer to him.

"No worries. I can transport roadrunner fast nowadays. Tell me when you want me back." Valda looked at the two, then began to rub the palm of her hand down her hip repetitively as perspiration dripped down her temple.

"Tomorrow!" Vienna squealed. It was nice having a friendly female face around helped her feel less like an outcast.

"Deal. See you in the morning. 5 o'clock, sharp."

"Wait." Vienna hated being up at five in the morning. *Seriously,* she thought, *only older adults and the military have that type of schedule. Why can't everything start at noon?*

Logan and Valda both bent over, laughing.

"Your . . . face!" Valda fell to the ground and rolled for a moment.

When she sat up again, she said, still chuckling, "I'll be here at eight. See you then." Before Vienna could reply, Valda was gone. Nothing remained but a hint of glimmer that lasted only a second.

Vienna stood, staring at the empty spot. She reached out to touch the glimmer before it faded, but she didn't make it in time.

"Cool, huh? It never gets old." Logan stuck his hands into his front pockets, straight-armed.

"I can't believe this is my new life." She turned to face him. "I keep expecting to wake up." Her delight turned into a charming smile.

"Get used to it. There's no waking up. Soon, you'll be a pro at whatever you're meant for." His eyes sparkled as he smiled at her. "Let's get going."

They walked in silence for half an hour. Honestly, Vienna despised the silence. It made her anxiety more obvious. She worried about fitting in, being attacked, and failing classes. Mostly, she worried about making friends. She'd never been good at meeting new people.

Snapping out of her thoughts, Vienna looked up and saw her school. She hadn't expected to end up there. Logan hadn't told her where they were going or what he had planned for the rest of the day, and she hadn't asked. Anything with Logan was worth it.

"Umm . . ." She frowned. "So, this is unexpected," she exclaimed after several moments of silence. She took a deep breath through her nose and sighed. *How disappointing*, she thought. She had thought she'd be sitting down for coffee and a chat, or at least at a park to be filled in on expectations, rules, future details . . . anywhere. Well, anywhere but this school.

"Relax, V." He strode to the school's back door and pulled with all his weight. It popped open, moaning like a sinking ship. "Voila!" He gestured toward it with a sweep of his hand.

She couldn't help but smile. "Thank you, kind sir." She gave him a pretend curtsy before passing through the door.

"Very funny, princess," he replied with an eye roll.

"Hey now. Better watch it, or this royal highness will have your head." With a sassy smile, she moved forward. The door thudded shut so hard it echoed through the building, and she jumped. "Holy hell! Are you trying to make me pee myself?" Her hand rested over her pounding heart. "Warn a girl, would you?"

"Sure," he shot back. "I'll let you know every time the door closes. After I open it," he emphasized before he laughed.

"Jerk," she whispered before pushing his shoulder and moving forward.

The area was musty and chilly. There were no lights, but there was visibility from the furnace's fire. All kinds of equipment laid around. They were in the off-limit parts of the school.

They walked forward slowly. Nervous in the dark, Vienna stopped. Panic set in. She wasn't scared of the night, but this was all so eerie. Maybe it was because they were breaking and entering. Or perhaps it was because she could only think of all the horror movies she'd ever watched. The ones where the dummies that went into the dark, forbidden areas vanished or were viciously murdered.

Logan slid in front of her and started moving forward without looking back. Afraid to be left alone, Vienna ran to catch up and walked as close behind him as she could.

# CHAPTER TWELVE

Something was exciting about sneaking around a closed building. Her mind drifted back to Mr. Humphrey. After a month, she still couldn't shake the unease on his face that day in class. The taunting and menace his presence evoked sent a shudder down her spine. The thought of running into him caused a pause. *Would I say something . . . ? Would I ask him questions?* She continued to ponder. *Or would I ignore him, hiding in the shadows, afraid of the answers?*

Vienna's stomach somersaulted as she and Logan entered the boiler room. Her senses were on high alert. The hiss of steam and creaking of old pipes kept her focused as she stayed near Logan.

*Thud!*

Vienna squealed and jumped around to look toward the noise. She stood there for several moments, trying to catch her breath. "What the hell was that?" she hissed.

"It was the metal," Logan said. "The pilot ignited."

She turned to face him, expecting a smug look or a snide

comment about her being jumpy. Instead, he reached out, touched her chin with his index finger, then turned around and continued walking through the room.

She followed, still on high alert. "So . . . what are we doing here again?"

"We need to get a file from the principal's office. It's for your transfer to Sparks. The paper was never sent in, and I figured we might as well do it."

"Wait." She came to an abrupt halt. "You're telling me we just committed a crime to . . . what, send a fax?" She put her hands on her hips.

He shrugged. "Something like that." He exited the closet and headed down the hall.

Running to catch up, Vienna whispered, "Wait, wait, wait, *wait!*" Before he could, though, she heard two voices arguing up ahead.

They froze. Vienna's eyes widened. She stared intensely at Logan, hoping he would understand her telepathic message: *What do we do now?* But he continued walking.

As they inched forward, a door slammed, and whoever was leaving spewed a string of profanities under his breath. Vienna and Logan darted behind the last row of lockers.

Logan tapped her shoulder and pointed up. She followed his finger to find a safety mirror right above them. In the reflection was a dark-haired man with bright eyes. He was tall and slender, but muscular, with a chiseled face. Her chest fluttered, and she glanced at Logan—who stared at the reflection with recognition.

The man turned to scan before he continued on. It looked as though glitter fluttered to the ground.

"It looks like a spell," Logan admitted.

"Who is it?" Vienna asked. "He seems familiar and looks too young to work here."

"Not sure, but I agree."

Once the man turned to walk away, Logan sighed, looking up at the ceiling. Vienna gazed over at him and, staring for a second too long, was caught off-guard when she noticed Logan looking at her. Her face flushed, and she turned away.

Logan chuckled under his breath. "Let's go."

Vienna glanced at the mirror again right as someone else left the office. *The principal!* Before Logan could take one step, she pinned his body against the wall and put one hand over his mouth. She placed her left index finger to her lips before she motioned to the mirror.

The principal looked pissed, and then she disappeared.

"Holy crap!" she exclaimed. "Is sh . . . did you know . . . I mean, what is . . . "

Logan remained silent, so Vienna turned to him. He gaped at the mirror, wide-eyed and stammering.

"You didn't know," Vienna realized. "Which means she's not registered, right?" All Enchanters were supposed to be registered with the authorities. That way, most magical beings could sense each other. But some rebels ignored the registration.

Logan shook his head slowly. "I had no idea. We need to get out of here. Let's get the file before she gets back." He didn't wait for a response; instead, he grabbed her hand and ran for the office.

"Why would she be hiding?" Vienna asked. "Why would *anyone* hide?"

Logan didn't answer, and he didn't stop. As soon as they entered the office, he pulled out all the drawers in the desk and armoire, flinging them across the room. Then he moved on to the bookshelves, tossing all the books.

One book caught Vienna's attention. She picked it up and started flipping through it. Inside were diagrams and phrases she couldn't make out.

Logan started browsing the entire room, running his fingers through his hair. He abruptly stopped, slid the seat out from under the desk, and pulled a latch. There was a slight grinding sound, and then a folder fell from the desk and scattered across the floor.

He grabbed all the papers and shoved them back into the folder. "Got it! Let's go." He jumped up and started moving to the door.

"We need to put the books back. The less obvious we were here, the better." She rushed around the room and started picking up the tossed books.

Logan's eyes fell on the book in Vienna's hands. She held it up. "Check it out. I think it's legit." She passed it to him.

The authentic binding had gold-etched Latin writing. "It looks like a book of spells. Look at the binding." Her voice was quiet, but excitement filled the room as she traced the intricate binding with her fingers.

He took the book from her, and she watched as a spark danced across his palm. "We can't take this with us, V." He returned the text-book to her.

"Did it shock you? I saw a spark when you touched it," she asked, curious why he ignored its effect.

"Put it away and don't touch anything else. You don't want to leave a trace of yourself here for her to sense. She will lock on to you, and I don't know what she's capable of."

"It felt soothing to me, but shocked you. Why?" she asked.

"I'm not sure. Maybe it's spelled for Enchantresses? Do you have your phone?"

"Of course. Why?"

"I need you to take a picture of the book. Then we need to go."

She pulled her phone from her back pocket and took a photo, but the only thing that appeared in the image was the picture on the front of the book. All the words were invisible. "This is all I can get, Logan," she said as she held up her phone to show him.

"It must be spelled, then. Forget it. We need to put everything back and wipe the book down."

Vienna took the book back to the desk, looked at it with longing, then reluctantly put it back on the shelf.

After cleaning up, they snuck back through the school and out the back door.

"Logan . . . " Vienna stopped and looked at Logan, eyes wide and voice quivering. "Is she going to know we touched her book?"

"I'm not sure. She may know someone did, but that doesn't mean she'll know who it was. We wiped it down. We'll need to discuss this with your parents. Maybe they'll know more. Besides, we need to see if they knew she was a part of our world. But we have another stop to make first."

As they ran through the forest, Vienna felt something lurking over them. Hoping to shelter Logan from that feeling, she remained quiet. They silently ran past each moonlit tree, Logan holding Vienna's hand. The fear of stopping propelled her forward.

Entering an unfamiliar neighborhood, Vienna stopped. She grabbed her side and gasped for air. "Where are we?" she asked, confused.

"We have to drop this off with one of my superiors," Logan answered.

"You're not even winded; that's bullshit," she forced out. He acted as though they hadn't just sprinted over a mile.

He shrugged, standing by her until she stood up, her breath slowing.

"Who is this superior?" she questioned, hoping to gain more insight.

"He's called the Ovr'seer. He runs projects in the Human Realm." He started walking toward a house across the street, and Vienna followed.

"That was vague. Anything else I should know about him?"

"He's the one that sent us on this adventure," he teased.

"Clearly," she said, unamused.

Vienna and Logan stopped in front of a small house. She was nervous about meeting this new person.

"Stop fidgeting," Logan snapped. Before she could respond, a powerful voice interrupted them.

"Logan," the voice boomed. "So good to see you. I assume you have the file?"

Logan handed the folder to him while Vienna froze. This man was the broadest and most muscular man she had ever met. He was a prominent Pacific Islander who stood just under seven feet. His black hair was braided and reached the middle of his back.

"Dude, he looks like the Rock," she whispered to Logan, who chuckled at her wide eyes. Fear filled her as she thought about the power of a man of his stature. Then she smiled when an image of him singing in a skirt with dancing tattoos entered her mind.

"You must be Vienna." He held out his hand, unamused by her giggling.

She didn't know why, but didn't want to touch him. She took a step back.

"Don't let his size scare you." Logan nudged her. "He's like a giant teddy bear."

The Ovr'seer looked annoyed. He lifted his eyebrow as his lips thinned. Logan smiled, but the Ovr'seer remained stern. He grunted, then motioned for them to enter his home.

"Take a seat in the front room." His voice bounced off the thin walls. He set the files on an old China hutch. "What has Logan told you?"

"We just needed to make this delivery. What else can you tell us?" She fought her anxiety and stared him in the eyes.

"I'll tell you what I can. The rest you'll need to discover in other ways." His voice was void of emotion.

"Good enough for me," Logan said with a shrug. He sat back. "Ready when you are."

With a nod, the Ovr'seer began. "The leaders of the schools in Magyieka and I were informed that your school's principal had a classified file. We're still unsure who she is, how she got hold of the file, or why she needed it, but we needed it back. I opened an investigation into it."

"Is this file on me and my family?" she asked, pushing down her fear.

"The details inside are classified," he answered.

"Of course they are. Isn't everything?" she snapped.

"You'd do well to learn your place in the order or the hierarchy of Magyieka," he warned.

"Who all knew Logan and I were retrieving this?" She ignored Logan as he shook his head.

"Your parents, the Council, and you two," he answered.

"My parents knew?"

"Yes. I reached out to them early on, Vienna. We needed someone who knew how to investigate properly. Who better than your father—the chief of police? You know he excels at finding information when it's most crucial."

How he responded made her feel naïve, intentional or not, and that bugged her.

Vienna's head bobbed as she tried to understand everything. "Why me and Logan?"

He continued, "I recruited your father and mother to help get as much intel as possible. When I brought them on board, they had the idea to use you and Logan to get the file. What better practice for you than fieldwork? Bonus," he added with a small smile, "it was a good way to gauge your relationship with Logan."

She pursed her lips as she blushed. "We're not a couple. We're not a liability."

The Ovr'seer's smile widened. "We never implied you were either of those. What a curious response."

Beside her, she heard Logan chuckle.

"I asked the Council what they thought, and they agreed to let you both retrieve the file. They were curious how you'd respond to the pressure and how you two would work as a team." The Ovr'seer leaned back in his chair and put his massive hands behind his head.

Vienna grunted and folded her arms. "And that's it?"

"To this point, yes."

*Another secret was kept from me by my parents.* But she was glad she was filled in now. Soon, maybe people would quit hiding things from her. She wanted nothing more than to be helpful.

Vienna couldn't help feeling confused about the secrecy as they left the house. "What are your thoughts on finding someone to talk to about this? I think we're missing some information. But if we ask the wrong person, we could get caught in the middle of something we aren't even aware of."

"I agree." Logan was silent for several moments, pacing and tapping his chin. Vienna stood silent so he could think.

"Okay, what's going on in that brain of yours? I can't wait anymore."

"Always so patient," he laughed. Her heart fluttered as the beautiful sound sliced through the tension surrounding them. "How much do you think your parents know about the files and why we were chosen to get them?"

"I'm not sure, but I think we need to find out," she said.

When they arrived at Vienna's home, her parents said they had suspected the principal for several years. They had already started investigating the principal and her known affiliates, but they had struggled to find anything over the years. With the new information Vienna and Logan found, they decided to try finding information as a team.

After several hours, they were still hitting dead ends. The principal vanished. Vienna's dad thoroughly investigated, but even with his diverse connections, he couldn't find any new information.

The next week, her dad informed them that the principal had ordered an investigation, and the police force searched the school, lockers, classrooms, and everywhere for the stolen property.

"She's looking for the documents we took," Vienna said.

"Yes, and she was livid when nothing was found. School was suspended for the week."

"Do you think the Ovr'seer would give us more information on what was in that file now?" Vienna asked.

Logan turned to her dad and asked, "Can we try and get more answers?"

"Do whatever you need to. Just don't break any more laws." He looked at both of them. Vienna blushed but nodded in agreement.

"Great. He usually gets home around 5 o'clock. If we leave now, we can beat him home."

# CHAPTER THIRTEEN

Before they could knock, the Ovr'seer answered the door. Vienna looked at Logan with surprise, recalling not wanting to make contact with him, and debated expressing her irritation on feeling watched. She glanced around, curious to see if anyone was watching them enter, then she squinted at the Ovr'seer as he closed the door.

"Come on," he said as he sat on his couch.

Vienna and Logan sat across from him, and she frowned when she saw three cups of lemonade and a stack of homemade banana bread.

"You knew we were coming?" she asked.

"I knew you'd want more answers. You"—his eye scrunched—"are a determined young woman. It will serve you well. But watch that temper of yours."

She started to argue, but the anger that ignited at his accusation wasn't going to help her defense. She grabbed a large slice of banana bread and sat there waiting.

"Tell us more about the file we retrieved for you," Logan interrupted.

"The file is a list of other local Enchanters," the Ovr'seer filled them in. "It includes their gifts, which are represented by symbols. Some of those symbols are elemental, but others . . . no one knows what they mean."

"Why was the list important to confiscate?" Vienna inquired.

"Great question. About a month ago, we noticed a trend of attacks on Enchanters. Most weren't serious, but they let us know that someone with access to the list was using it for their own agenda."

"What about the unknown symbols? What could they be?" Logan asked.

"We aren't sure. We have people looking into it, but there are no answers."

Vienna tried to imagine what the symbols might look like. "Have you seen the symbols somewhere else? Somewhere you might be able to use to figure out what they are?" she asked, intrigued.

"Once," he admitted. "There was a book in London. It is filled with symbols from different realms and languages. Many looked like art. Unfortunately, I can't remember what language they belonged to."

"Can we see them?" Logan asked.

"That would be breaking regulations. They need to remain secure in my office. Locked away." After a brief pause, he stared at Vienna pointedly.

Vienna stood up and grabbed Logan's arm. "I have a curfew," she exclaimed.

Logan stared at her, confusion lacing his features. "All right. Yeah, we need to go. Thank you, sir." They headed out before the Ovr'seer could respond. When Vienna turned to wave, she watched as he sat back, the satisfaction of what had just transpired evident in a highly prideful smile.

After the door closed behind them, Vienna turned to Logan. "We're not leaving. We must see those files."

"I had the same thought," he admitted. "I have specific instructions not to look at the file, but now I'm curious."

"Right, and he told us exactly where they are. Tell me that wasn't his way of inviting us to access them." Her voice rose an octave, and her face lit up. "We're doing this."

"What's the plan?"

"That's your job. Let me know when you figure it out." She skipped down the porch steps, moving toward the forest.

Logan smiled and followed her to the nearest section of the woods, where they formed a plan to sneak into the Ovr'seer's home.

▽△△▽✳

"Let's go through the side window. It will drop us off right inside his office." Logan moved to the side of the building.

Vienna shivered behind him, fear and excitement battling as she waited. "That's a long way up. How do we get in there?"

"I'm going to send you up; climb up my back."

"You're fucking with me, right?"

"V, we need this information to find out what's happening. Something is not right, and you know it."

"Fine." She jabbed him in the chest and glared. "If you drop me, I will send you spiraling into the Nether Realm. Got it?"

"Can you do that?" He sounded excited.

"Probably. Piss me off and we'll find out." She shouldered him.

He raised his hands in surrender. "Got it," he said, chuckling quietly. "Now, let's go before we get caught."

Vienna was still jittery as she balanced on Logan's shoulders. The window wasn't secured. "Logan, I think he left it open for us." She popped it open, but the hair on her neck stood. Something was watching them; she could feel it. "Logan . . ."

"I know. I feel it, too. Climb in, then pull me up." A long screech announced the window opening; she froze, glancing around. With nobody near, she pushed it the rest of the way open.

"Got it!" she announced in triumph. Peering down, his proud, cheesy smirk stopped her heart.

Heat bloomed, spreading across her abdomen. She bit her lip, her breathing shallow. Staring down as she felt his breath on her thighs, she shivered . . . his head was inches from connecting with her pubic bone. Her legs trembled.

"We open for business, V?"

"WHAT?" she gasped.

His face crunched in confusion. "Is the window open?"

"Yep, nothing to it." She gulped. "Do I ever fail?" she teased.

"Funny. Get in the window, would you?"

They both got through the window with ease. The moment their feet hit the floor, a ball of light appeared next to Logan. It moved in sync with him.

Vienna's jaw dropped. It was the most incredible thing she'd ever seen. The light flickered enough, illuminating them. It was deep blue in the middle, fading until the outer edges burned white. It was mesmerizing.

"Did you hear me?"

Vienna turned to him. "I'm sorry, what?"

He chuckled. "Okay, first things first. You can't stare at people's magic as it's meant to be entrancing. Time will fly by without you realizing it. Second, we need to hurry. Have you spotted the file?" He grunted. "Never mind. You were distracted."

Vienna's face burned. "How did you do that?"

"It's a simple spell learned in the first year in the Magic Realm."

"Teach me," she demanded.

He said the words and drew a symbol in the air. She followed his guide, and a violet ball of light illuminated from her hands.

"Incredible," she sighed. "I didn't know I could do that yet."

"Neither did I," Logan beamed. "Well done! Looks like your magic is ready. Like you're ready." He smiled.

"It's about damn time!" She shot her hand into the air in victory. "Why are our lights different colors?"

"Each person has a spectrum of their magic color. Mine is blue; as you can tell, it's more of a cobalt blue like Ghost, but it includes all shades of blue." He moved his hand, shifting the ball of light and allowing a variety of shades to peek through. He was right. At its core, the deep blue was the most prominent.

"It allows our magic to be tracked. Others who harness blue energy will appear different than my shade." He wiggled his brows, and Vienna blushed. Her thoughts drifted to his mouth, curious how his lips would feel on hers. The smell of his musky mint breath caused a shudder, and she bit her lip.

She cleared her throat and changed the subject. "What now?"

"You start over there." He motioned with his head. "Look for anything suspicious. I'll look over here."

They explored the office in depth. Each piece of wood was old and engraved with leaves, grapes, and what looked like fairies. Vienna brushed her fingers over the woodwork until she felt something shift. A fairy's wing jiggled a little, like a button. She pressed it firmly and heard a *shhhhh . . . snap.*

"Logan," Vienna whispered, "I think I found something."

He turned to see a drawer floating in mid-air, then walked over and waved his hands in the area behind the drawer. "Weird. There's nothing behind it. I wonder where it came from. How did you find it?"

"Right here." She pointed to the fairy wing she'd pressed.

"Good find, V."

Vienna reached up and put her hand in the drawer. The moment she connected with it, everything went black.

▽△△▽✸

"Where are we?" Vienna walked toward Logan. They were in a wide-open space with a thick white mist circling them.

"I don't know. The last thing I remember was trying to reach into the drawer." He shook his head. "I wonder if this is because of the file."

"You are correct, Mr. Artrusha."

They turned to face the Ovr'seer. He was radiant, glowing white and gold. It was nearly impossible to focus on him without being blinded.

"Where are we? What's going on?" Logan asked, voice level.

"You are in between planes. You are nowhere. You are lost in your mind, like a Dreamwalker traveling across planes. This is possible because of Miss Madizza-Corey's powers." He motioned to her with grace, and Vienna blushed. "The file . . . We knew you would come for it. You are wise, and your intuition is an asset. You were correct in wanting to know more. But discussing it in our realm, where so many are listening and watching, would be dangerous."

"So why not tell us?" Vienna snapped. There were so many secrets and lies, so much deceit. It all made her blood boil.

"We needed to know you could feel its force, that you were ready to know, Miss Madizza-Corey. Your spiritual strength would have been too weak to carry the knowledge without being ready. You could have ceased to exist."

Vienna looked at Logan. It was a test. Of course it was.

"Then what is it we need to know?" Logan asked.

"As Miss Madizza-Corey makes her way through school, she will gain many redeeming qualities. Her power will be desired by those seeking to overtake what we have created." He moved forward and touched Vienna's cheek. "You are critical to our survival. I cannot say much, as you need to make own your way and decisions. All I can tell you is that the file will be of little help. Of most help will be your internal strength as you become one with your destiny. Trust lightly, Miss Madizza-Corey. Know not everyone at Sparks Boarding School will be as they appear."

Vienna felt sick. Survival? Destiny? "But I'm missing so much information and only training right now. How can I make decisions when I don't have everything I need?"

The Ovr'seer gave her a small smile. "May your intuition be true, your fight unwavering, and your heart pure." With that, he was gone.

Vienna was alone with Logan again, feeling empty and cold. She stood frozen like a statue, unable to breathe past her panic. As Logan slid his hand into hers, the mist brightened so much it blinded her. Covering her eyes, she turned to Logan for support. But, just like that, they were gone.

▽△△▽✸

Vienna's eyes opened and locked onto Logan's slumbering body, waking up on the hard, dark floor. He looked peaceful, so peaceful she dared not wake him. She lay there for an hour before his eyes started to flicker, darting under closed lids. Then, with quick blinks, his eyes popped open. But they were black, not dark brown.

Vienna jumped back as his pupils came into view; no irises were left—his eyes were demonic. Her pulse increased, and she remembered about their shift in class. She hadn't been seeing things. Her mind raced. *Is he something else? No,* she thought, *that's impossible.* Dismissing the notion of other creatures—magical creatures—she looked closer, searching for contact. Nothing.

"What's wrong with your eyes, Logan? Do they change when you access magic or something? It's happened before." Her lips shifted sideways.

Stunned and wide-eyed, Vienna bit her lips to silence the scream climbing its way up her throat. She shook her head and told herself it was exhaustion. It was her imagination after many trying events.

He looked down and closed his eyes, breathing deeply. When he opened his eyes again, they were back to dark brown.

"It's a stress response." It wasn't a lie, she could tell. But it wasn't the whole truth. She watched a sadness creep in and decided not to push the subject. Whatever the secret was, it's one that haunted him.

He peeked out the window. "We've lost a lot of time. We need to head back."

"Wait, don't you want to talk about what just happened?" She grabbed his arm, shocked at his dismissal of moving between planes.

"We got knocked out; what else is there to discuss?" He had no idea what she was talking about; she took a step back.

"Nothing. I must have been dreaming," she lied. "Let's go."

"What aren't you telling me, V?"

She ignored him and started walking, shrugging away his question. Her heart raced as she thought about what had just happened. She wanted to tell him, but she still didn't know how to explain everything.

"I hope one day you can trust me."

"Me too." She turned in time to see the pain in his eyes.

Sure enough, the sun was cresting over the mountain when she moved toward the window. *How has so much time passed? Weren't we here right after nightfall?* She shook her head.

Logan jumped up and held his hand down to her. She looked into his dark eyes as the breeze from the window tossed his hair. There was more to Logan than she knew. But how was she supposed to discover all his secrets without him catching on?

Perhaps it was time to work alone with Valda for a while. Then she could get some insight on who the new Logan is. She just needed to time it right.

# CHAPTER FOURTEEN

Vienna sat with Kreo, playing his favorite video game. She watched his hands move around the controller in Mach speed while she fumbled with each button.

"You suck at this," he told her.

"Yep." She laughed. "But you're getting good. You make up for a weak partner. Three kills for you and I'm on a second death."

They played for a while before Vulcan came dashing in. "Hey, let's go ride."

Vienna glanced over at Vulcan as a dooming sound came from the gaming system. "Damn it!" Vienna tossed the controller. "I'm out of lives."

"Finally." Kreo disconnected her controller and kept playing. "Thanks for playing. But next time we should keep to the easy games."

She ruffled his hair, then grabbed her coat. "Well," she told Vulcan, "I thought we were riding."

"Yes," he cheered, pulling his arm in victory. "I thought you'd be too busy. This rocks."

"Slow down, speedy. Grab your helmet."

"Right." Vulcan rushed to his room, coming out with both their helmets, and tossed her one before running out the door.

"Have fun with that," Kreo teased. "He ate an entire bag of candy an hour ago."

Vienna hung her head. "Dammit." She knew that meant he was going to run her ragged. But with the summer flying by, she didn't want to miss the opportunity to spend a lazy Saturday with them.

Kreo was right. Vulcan tore through the forest with little thought to the mere inches he passed by the trees. Her heart hammered as he took each turn without hesitation. At the top of a large hill, he pulled to a stop and killed the engine. She pulled up shortly after and parked next to him. Glancing across the rolling hills, Vienna pulled off her helmet.

"You're fucking crazy, kid." She shook her head at him.

"There's nothing to it when you do it enough." He shrugged.

"Fair enough." She looked over the area, stunned at its beauty. "I haven't been up here in years."

"You've been busy." His voice lowered, "High school must suck."

"It has some perks."

"Then why did you decide to graduate early?" His voice was sad. Vienna needed to proceed with caution.

"I had enough credits. Wasn't too much of a choice," she lied.

"Mom and Dad said we're having a family dinner to talk about this fall. You're leaving." It wasn't a question. She forgot how observant he was, even with his hyperactivity.

"Ya." She didn't know what else to say.

"I knew you'd be going to college. I just thought you'd decide to stay local."

Her stomach soured at the lies. Every part of her wanted to tell him the truth. To take them with her. She watched his blue eyes as he stared out into the forest. Moisture toppled down, and he brushed his cheek on his shoulder, trying to hide the tears. Vienna's heart ached. Of all the family, she would miss him the most. He was the biggest challenge and the brightest joy. Like his name, his volcanic personality could clash with hers. Yet when they were on, there was nobody she'd rather explore with. She followed his eyes and spotted a deer moving over the distant trails.

"I'm going to miss this," she whispered.

"Hey, V?" Vulcan kicked the dirt. She turned at the odd tone in his voice. "Can I tell you something?"

"Always," she answered, squinting at him as he dug his toe in the dirt.

"Do you ever wonder if we're different than other people?" His tone was direct, and Vienna's heart paused.

"What do you mean?" He flinched at the pitch in her tone.

"Sometimes I think we're more than just odd. Mom and Dad talk about us being more energetic and stuff, like because we have a lot of energy and struggle with sitting still. But everyone in school has a close connection and we don't. None of us. Even Mom and Dad don't have friends. Never mind"—he shook his head—"I'm being stupid."

"No you're not." Her response was instant. "I agree. I think we are different. I'm not sure why we struggle socially, but maybe we will know one day." Vienna smiled at his intuition. For such a busy kid who acted on impulse, he sure was perceptive. "Maybe you should talk to Mom and Dad . . ."

"Hell no," he cut her off. "They already think I'm a handful."

"I won't say anything," Vienna promised as a smile crept across her face. "How about I race you home?"

Before he could answer, she had her helmet on and she peeled out on her way home.

▽△△▽✳

"Dinner time," their dad announced.

Her family sat; the quiet was uneasy with the coming news.

"As you know," their mom began, "Vienna is going to college this fall. She decided to study abroad, meaning she won't be local."

Vienna hadn't noticed before, but her mom had a tell when she lied—her lip twitched at the corner, as though fighting a frown or holding in a sob.

"Will we get to visit?" Kreo asked.

"No. But she will come back for Thanksgiving break a couple of months after she leaves." Her dad shoved a spoonful of pasta into his mouth.

"That's several months. That's crap." Vulcan pushed his chair back, his body started to turn pink. "Why can't we visit, and why November? What about Labor Day and birthdays?" He was shaking now.

Vienna's throat began to swell, and her eyes burned. Her chest quivered from the strength it took to hold back her sobs. Her mom's eyes were moist as well. Like a chain reaction, a tear slipped from Vienna.

A door slammed, and Vienna realized Vulcan had left, his helmet no longer on the counter.

"He's right, you know." Kreo put his plate in the sink and went to his room, slamming the door.

"That went well," her dad groaned, sitting back.

Vienna stood; she could barely feel her body. She watched herself as she placed her plate and cup in the sink, then walked to her room. The slam of the door brought her back to the moment, and she looked around her room.

She thought about the weight of the conversation and how it pressed upon her. She slid down her door, looking around her childhood room, and sobbed. Her grief was heavy as memories of her brothers running around in diapers chasing her and the summers they spent inseparably consumed her. Unable to hold anything back, she let all the pain go. In a fetal position, she cried, screaming into the floor until there was nothing left. Lonely tears dripped to the floor as her still body laid there, exhausted. The only comfort was having her back against the door, blocking anyone from finding her as her heart shattered into pieces.

▽ ⟁ △ ▽ ✴

Vienna groaned, grabbing her neck as she stretched it, then rolled it in a circle. The stiffness was intense, and her head pounded. The room was dark, but a clicking came from her window. She got up slowly, making her way across the room, and she looked out the window. Logan and Valda stood below the window, tossing little pebbles up periodically. She smiled at the sight of them.

Moving back to the door, she peeked down the hall. The lights were off, and the house was quiet. She slipped down the stairs and out the front door, cautiously closing the door, preventing the click.

"What are you guys doing here?" She turned around the edge of the house. "It's the middle of the night."

"Actually, it's almost five in the morning," Valda corrected. "You look like shit, by the way."

Vienna popped her neck. "I feel like crap. It was a long night."

"We heard," Logan answered.

"What do you mean?" Vienna looked between them.

"We ran into Vulcan hours ago. He was furious," Logan answered.

"I'd say heartbroken, which caused him to lash out," Valda corrected.

"He lashed out?" Vienna was curious.

"Kid was zooming through the forest like a maniac, and when we ran into him, he went toe to toe with me. Ripped my ass for being the reason you're leaving. I think he's just angry about me leaving all of you. Then I come back into the picture, and everything starts to change," Logan guessed.

"That sounds pretty accurate," Vienna agreed. "So, why are you guys here?"

"I've been called back to Magyieka, so I won't be here to train you for a couple days. Valda's going to take over while I'm gone." Logan looked between Vienna and Valda. "We wanted to let you know and see if you needed anything before I go."

"Works for me." Relieved she didn't need to find a way to ask for more time with Valda and a break from Logan, she thanked the universe. "So just me and Valda," Vienna clarified.

Logan nodded. "For a couple days, then I'll be back."

"Okay. I don't think I need anything." She looked around, sensing an onlooker. Chills trickled down her arms, but she brushed them off.

"Are you okay?" Logan looked around.

"I'm fine," she lied. Switching topics, she asked, "Can you tell me where you're going and why?"

"Unfortunately not." He moved toward her. "You going to miss me, V?" he teased.

"Figured." She looked at him, putting up a front and suppressing her sorrow. She lifted her chin. "And no. I could use a break."

"Ouch," Valda laughed. "Then we will meet around eight and start our first lesson with just the two of us."

Vienna and Logan stared at each other. Vienna sensed a shift; her chest warmed as a ball of heat radiated down to her stomach. From the side of her eye, Vienna watched as Valda inched away, giving them some privacy. Vienna breathed in her nose slowly, calming her nerves as she stared into Logan's eyes. There was a kindness she rarely saw. Mindlessly, she took a step toward him.

"You're giving me notice this time." Vienna's voice was soft and quiet.

"I'm allowed to this time." He stepped closer. "I'm going to miss watching you whine about my lessons."

"You're going to miss my sassy-ass mouth," she corrected him. Feeling overwhelmed by his closeness, she took a half a step back. Logan smiled at the movement.

The silence grew as Vienna took in his features. The breeze

tossed his soft hair and his eyes blazed with passion. Her heart raced faster and faster as each second passed.

Logan reached out and tucked a strand of hair behind her ear. Vienna didn't know how, but they were inches from each other. His musky scent was strong tonight. A shiver ran down her neck, not stopping until goosebumps covered most of her body and her nipples tingled. The reaction to his presence was feral; she wanted to wrap her legs around him.

The heat from his breath caressed her, and she closed her eyes. A soft groan escaped as she inhaled his scent. She knew before her eyes opened. "Logan?" she whispered. He was gone. The heat was replaced with cold night air and his smell vanished.

Vienna's eyes skipped through the forest. Logan was gone, but someone stood beyond the trees. It looked like a man, closer to Logan's age, but larger. Curious, Vienna moved closer, stopping when Valda stepped beside her.

"There's someone watching us," Vienna told her.

"There always is," Valda answered honestly. "And with Logan gone, I wouldn't be surprised if the Council sends more than one person to watch over you."

"Do we know who?" Vienna wasn't sure if she should feel safe.

"Most likely a Watcher."

"A what?" Vienna asked.

"How much do you know about the realms and functions of the magic world?" Valda asked.

"Not much," Vienna admitted.

"How would you feel about a crash course?" Valda smiled.

"I think it's past due."

"Let's go. It's early, so we'll start with what we can use in your home." Valda walked to the porch and made her way in. Vienna followed, impressed with how quickly Valda moved forward with taking the lead on lessons now that Logan was out of the picture. There was zero hesitation—Valda's confidence was solid.

Moving through the house, Vienna grabbed a stack of papers

from her parents' desk that they had looked through when searching Cosima. When they made it to her room, she waited until Valda went to the bathroom before she slipped the blankets off her family chest and opened it up. She pulled a stack of papers she had in her to-do pile and pulled them out, leaving behind her family tree and journals.

"I was thinking, if you have a computer, we would start there," Valda announced as she entered the room.

Vienna tossed the blanket on the chest, closed the closet, and moved to the bed.

"We have a family computer, but we don't have access to much. Most things are blocked to prevent people from locating us." Vienna recited what she'd always been told.

"I expected." Valda pulled a small tablet out of the bag she had carried and opened it.

"You have your own?" Vienna sat on her bed, crossing her legs.

"It's Logan's. He left it so we could access what we needed."

Shocked, Vienna shook her head. "Why would he do that? He's been adamant about being by the book." Vienna couldn't hide her confusion.

"I don't have the same orders as him. We found some flexibility. He wants you to know the basics of the magic world, but I think we need to go farther than that."

"Where do we start?" Vienna asked.

Valda pulled up a picture of a map with multiple lands and handed it to Vienna. Their names were hard to pronounce, so she skipped over them and focused on the geography.

"Is this Magyieka?" she asked. Valda nodded. "It's a picture I haven't seen. But I know most of the information in our world isn't online. I've tried to find it before," Vienna admitted.

"You sound shocked." Valda observed.

"My parents told me that they didn't use technology, but I doubted it. I'm so used to the way this world works," she admitted.

"What are these wavy lines around each body of land?" Vienna traced them with her fingers.

"Magic barriers that keep others out. This one"—Valda pointed to a smaller landmass—"is Arcadia, the Magic Realm. It's the land of Enchanters and where Sparks Boarding School is."

"What about this larger landmass?" Vienna noted the dark outline that contrasted the light lines of the Magic Realm.

"The Shadow Realm. It's larger because the population is greater and the area has a lot of aspects, including zones that are unlivable." Valda pointed out a small landmass between the two. It didn't connect to either, but colorful swirls were located on several corners of the odd island. "This is where we arrive from the Human Realm. From here, we are taken to one of the connecting portals that will send us to the realm we are assigned or needing to visit."

"This is incredible." She looked at the names again, curious of their pronunciation. "Nocshedu—that's the name of the Shadow Realm?"

"Yes. That's where Watchers train," Valda added.

"What is a Watcher?" She thought about the man in the forest.

"There are trained soldiers who are assigned to protect Enchanters," Valda answered.

"That seems vague." Vienna was disappointed, longing for more.

"There isn't a lot known about them. They are rare, and only Enchanters with rare abilities or in a high role in our society are assigned one."

"So he's assigned because Logan is gone and I'm unable to leave the Human Realm until the Blue Moon," Vienna guessed.

"Exactly." Valda shuffled through several pages from Vienna's pile.

"Why is part of the map cut off?" Vienna handed Valda the tablet.

Vienna watched as Valda tried to zoom out. "I don't know. Maybe that's all he wanted you to learn about?"

"What else can I learn, then?"

Valda handed her two pages from the stack. "Have you looked at these before?" she asked.

"No, they aren't normally left out. But the desk was unlocked."

"This one is a list of different kinds of Enchanters." Valda moved next to Vienna and went down the list. "Earth, Air, Fire, Water, and Spirit, as you know. But these ones are the dark side. They often end up in the Shadow Realm or Nether Realm. They use the elements but pull on dark energy. Often using life sources until they die, or ancient black magic, casting summoning power from what some refer to as in-between or nowhere.

"The best way to explain it is that we pull from the astral energy. This is where all magic comes from. A pure or positive soul will access power using their element and with a desire to do good. Though dark magic comes from the same place, a dark soul and hateful acts create dark magic. This can seep into the caster's soul, creating callousness in the crimes they commit."

"So good magic comes from the Magic Realm, and those who choose to use dark magic end up moving to the Shadow Realm, where it's less frowned upon," Vienna clarified.

"Simplified, yes." Valda laughed.

"How often do people use dark magic?"

"It's not common, and some use it just enough to avoid detection and remain in the Magic Realm among Light Enchanters."

"Man, this is complicated." Vienna sat back, looking to the ceiling.

"It gets easier. Separating the dark and light is the fastest way to start."

"So we have Dark and Light Enchanters, and each use different elements." Vienna paused until Valda nodded. "Then we have Watchers, who look over Elite or powerful Enchanters."

"You got it."

"How do Watchers help their Enchanters?" Vienna imagined someone like the Ovr'seer, who brought the physical power.

"They are able to mimic their Ward's magic." Valda paused. "You looked confused."

"A little. How do they use their power, and do they have their own? Are they Enchanters themselves?"

"They don't have their own magic. Instead, they are able to mimic the power of the person they are charged to protect." Vienna shook her head, signaling confusion. "Okay"—she moved closer—"if I was a Watcher, and you were my Ward, and your ability was . . . " She thought for a minute, "Air. You with me?" she asked. Vienna nodded. "Okay. If this was the case, if we were in a situation where I needed to protect you, not only would I have combat skills, but I could pull your connection to Air and create a lightning storm or tornado."

"That's badass," Vienna admitted. "So why are Watchers so rare?"

"They are a rare combination of magic beings and Shadowwalkers."

"What is a Shadowwalker?"

"Shadowwalkers have the ability to walk between realms and worlds, some or all, depending on their strength."

"Like a Dreamwalker?" Vienna's frustration rose.

"No. Dreamwalkers are those who are able to enter another person's dreams. Shadowwalkers can travel to other realms while asleep or awake, as a Dreamwalker can dreams."

"I get it. But when I talked about my dreams, how do we know those were in a Dream Realm and not any other realm? I can't imagine the scene of someone's dreams being so similar to Hell," Vienna confessed.

"For some, their dreams are. Anything else you want to learn about before everyone wakes?" Valda asked. "You look overwhelmed."

"I think I learned plenty. But I am curious. With Watchers being rare, how many are females?"

"Great question." Valda looked shocked at the forethought. "They are only males. A female has never existed."

"Oh, I actually thought you might be one," she admitted.

Valda laughed. "I wish. They are badass. But, no. I'm just good at combat."

Vienna looked out the window. For the first time, she realized the sun was rising. "I think Logan's a Watcher, but I'm not sure."

"Maybe you should ask him next time he's around," Valda offered.

"He doesn't answer my questions." Her voice was laced with frustration.

"When he's allowed to, he will." Valda sounded certain and Vienna admired that.

"I'm going to head out before everyone wakes. Meet me at noon and we'll work on some combat. Maybe we'll be able to start some magic training, too."

Valda didn't wait for a response. She took the tablet and left, closing the door behind her. Vienna gathered the papers and looked through them one last time, hoping to find more on the Magic and Shadow Realm, or anything on Watchers, Wards, or Enchanters. But there was nothing useful.

She skipped down the steps and slid the papers back into their rightful place, turning around in time to see her mom leaning against the wall behind her.

"Long night?" her mom asked.

"Very." Vienna met her stare. "Valda came over for some tutoring and Logan will be gone for a while."

"I see. Anything else?" Her mom handed her a cup of orange juice.

"I learned a little more about Magyieka, but not a lot."

"Good. If you have time later this week, your father and I have been given permission to also give you more details." She turned toward the kitchen. "Cereal for breakfast. Your brothers will be leaving for camp in a couple of hours, and then I'm heading to work. Do you need anything before I go?"

"I'm good." She sipped the orange juice and smiled. It was the first conversation she didn't feel like a child. It was a nice change.

# CHAPTER FIFTEEN

Vienna closed her eyes, thinking about the last two sessions. Valda spent an entire session teaching her to feel the connection to her power. Sometimes she could feel the slightest burn, as though a ball of electricity vibrated just under the surface. But no matter how often she tried, the magic fizzled out, as if someone doused it with water. There was no doubting it; she was quickly progressing with Valda's teachings. Now, they were on the final stretch, and Valda would be done training her after this week.

"Remember, today's goal is to create one intentional spark," Valda reminded her.

Vienna searched inward, looking for the glow within. A tickle of something nipped at her as she focused on the veins in her arms. She centered there, listening to the faintest hiss. Harnessing all her energy, she reached toward its source. A vision of a florescent fuchsia ball of energy came to her mind, and she began to tremble. She slowly reached toward it, imagining her hand moving around its soft edge. With a sharp snap, electricity raced through her arm. Her palm faced the sky as the energy pulled at the tip of her fingers and moved outward. With lightning speed, Vienna flicked her wrist and an extension of herself propelled before fizzling out. Her fist connected with Valda, sending her flying backward.

Valda fell in the middle of a muddy puddle, panting. "Hold up!" She held up a hand in defeat.

"I felt something surging in me," Vienna admitted. "It felt like a calm electricity flowing through my body, but it fizzled out before I connected with you."

"That's great. But you're killing me, kid." They both laughed at the comment.

Over the last week, Vienna's training had started to pay off. She knew from watching Logan spar with her that Valda wasn't used to being knocked around, yet Vienna managed to knock her down so hard she looked like her head was spinning. She beamed with pride.

"Sorry." Vienna sat down next to Valda, out of the mud but close enough that Valda could feel her energy.

"Oh, I'm not mad. I'm proud." Valda wiped her forehead, leaving behind a streak of dirt. "I just don't know how you got so good so fast," she said triumphantly. "How has studying been going?"

"It's been fine. I can't seem to find much to help me. I still haven't talked to Logan since he left. I still keep thinking about that file we took; I spaced, asking him more about it. Besides that, everything is advancing. My skills are improving, and I am connected to the energy within. I feel satisfied with where we are at in the training," Vienna answered.

Valda smiled, but it didn't feel earnest. Vienna felt conflicted about her reaction, like there was something bothering her. She decided not to pry.

"I've been dreaming a lot lately, too," Vienna continued. "But it's always the same dream. There's a swirl and I feel as though I'm transported out of my body. The swirl is alluring, with violet and gold dancing rhythmically, calming my soul. The violet color always surrounds me like an aura. Almost like the Ovr'seer I told you about. His aura was gold, though. I'm violet with a few sparks of gold."

"What are your dreams about? Just the colors?" Valda leaned forward with wide eyes. Maybe Vienna was developing some talents after all. And so soon!

Vienna twisted her lips to the side as she remembered the Ovr'seer's admonition. How much could she trust Valda, really? She pondered all their interactions so far and remembered Valda telling her about the Magic and Shadow Realm, and their initial meeting with the instant connection. How transparent Valda seemed to be. Heeding the warning from her parents on the need to build relationships and trust, she chose this moment to gauge Valda. Focusing on her body, emotions, and physical reactions while she spoke, she opened up.

"It's always different. Usually, someone's after me. A woman. And she's often talking to me. I can never see her, though. She talks about how we will work together and how things will improve because we'll be stronger together. Then she told me about her plan to take over the world." She shrugged. "Anyway, I would always run away when I first started having the dream. Now, I sit and listen to her story. She told me how evil magic users have become and how they have turned their backs on our transition. She wants to help people find the old ways and make them the norm again. Honestly, it's creepy. I always will myself to leave, but I can't leave until she permits me."

Valda's eyes narrowed as she hummed. "That's odd. Does she know you want to help her?"

"Absolutely not. Red creeps me out, like . . . bad! I always wake up with goosebumps and turn all the lights on to feel safe."

"Oh. Do you go anywhere else or only to Ms. Red? I'm a Dreamwalker, remember? This sounds like what I've experienced. Only, it was just the one time." Valda looked down and scowled.

"You've dreamwalked one time?" Vienna asked in surprise. "I

thought all Dreamwalkers walk nearly every night as they get stronger."

"It doesn't matter," Valda muttered. "We all develop differently. I'm a slow bloomer in that way. But my fighting skills came naturally." She looked up, holding back tears.

Vienna didn't know what to say. She wanted to soothe her, but she didn't know how. So she sat with Valda in silence for several minutes.

"Why are you so upset?" Vienna asked.

"My guardian . . . well, she wants me to become superior at dreamwalking. I guess we're supposed to be able to select where we go. We can even kill people in the Nether Realm once we are strong enough. I don't get how you're getting so good already. I've been practicing for years." She shot a look of jealousy at Vienna, but it was gone as quickly as it had come.

Vienna rubbed her thumb over her teeth. "Are we good, Valda?" Fear of Valda leaving flooded Vienna.

"Of course. Why wouldn't we be?"

"No reason. You seem down after talking about my advancement."

"Oh no, just interested." Valda smiled and smacked Vienna's hand. "I'm not going to abandon you." Valda rose her eyebrows.

"Are you a mind reader now?" Vienna laughed uncomfortably.

"Just reading your emotions," Valda answered earnestly. "You ready?"

In agreement, both girls stood up and wiped the mud from their clothes.

Vienna expressed her only theory. "Maybe it's about not trying so hard?"

Valda snorted. "Not likely." Her syllables were short and sharp.

Vienna did her best to ignore the chills Valda's tone sent up her back.

"Anyway, it doesn't matter. It's getting dark. Let's get you home." Valda's tone was chipper again, like she hadn't spit venom at Vienna.

Vienna was confused, but she didn't want to start a fight. After all, this was the first girl she met on this new adventure.

As Vienna's house came into view, she realized the whole walk had been quiet. "Are you . . . are you staying for dinner?" she asked. Over the last week, Valda had stayed with Vienna quite often. Vienna and her parents felt she didn't like her guardian that much. She never spoke of them and always deflected when the topic was discussed. So, they let her stay as long as she wanted.

"Not tonight. I have plans. But thanks. What are you going to be doing over the next week? You leave in twelve days." She looked at Vienna with sad eyes.

Vienna shrugged. "I'll be spending most of my time with family. I'm going to miss them a lot." She sighed. "I can't believe it's so close. Will you be going with me?" She stopped and turned to Valda. They'd never discussed whether Valda attended Sparks.

Valda smiled. "I'm not sure, but I assume so. Why do you think they sent me to train you? Plus, would they let you go half-cocked and half-trained? I don't think so. *Someone* will have to teach you how to not stand out like a sore thumb!" She laughed.

"Ha-ha, very funny," Vienna deadpanned. "I'm glad you'll be there." She twirled a string from her clothes around her index finger. "Is Logan going to be there?"

"It's a girls' school, remember? He'll be at Domar's Boarding School, which is equivalent, but it's not very close to us."

Vienna smacked her forehead. "Right, I forgot. Man, that is going to suck! No boys at all?"

"Nope. Well . . . there are some pretty cute teachers?" she joked.

"Gross!" Vienna giggled.

"Seriously, some aren't that much older than we are. You'll see. The history teacher last year. O.M.G.! He was *so* cute."

"Wait, you went last year?"

"Oh yeah. Since I was born and raised in the Magic Realm, I have studied in the Magic Realm since preschool. Sparks is for nineteen- and twenty-year-olds. But they have a separate class that includes the young adults raised there. You'll be in year nineteen. Think of it like freshman year in college. The other students will be one year older than you, but much more experienced. They spent their high school years in a school designed for Enchanters, where they learned everything about our world. But don't worry, you catch on so fast I don't think it'll be an issue."

"So, you'll be in the same year as me even though I'm younger?"

"Yep, if I go! I'd be year nineteen, too. But like I said, I don't know if I'm going for sure."

"Why wouldn't you?"

"We have some family stuff going on. Anyway, the school year is from January to December. If you turn seventeen that year, you are in year seventeen." Valda must have spotted confusion on Vienna's face because she continued. "Okay, so in the Human Realm, you have a high school for people who are fifteen to eighteen, and then they attend college. In Magyieka, at nineteen and twenty, you attend boarding school before university, where you are sent based on your talents." She smiled as Vienna's face lit up.

"Okay, I get that. I'm really curious about you not attending."

"We were planning on me attending. There is a small change I have to wait for. But I can't say much." She cast her eyes down, and Vienna sensed embarrassment, so she didn't interrogate her. She felt a tension in her chest.

"So technically, I'm so smart that I got jumped a grade." She smiled with pride—the desire to bring comfort back to Valda.

"Something like that," Valda responded flatly. Vienna brushed it off as exhaustion.

"Thanks for helping me understand. It's going to be so different. Are classes set up the same?"

"I think so. You'll have six 45-minute classes a day, a 45-minute lunch break, and then study time for an hour. That's not a class, but it is a requirement. You study in the library or the yard. Oh, and in the physical fitness class, you'll do sports to stay active, but they often let you use magic to some degree."

"That's not what it's like here. We have eight classes a day that are 45 minutes each. And then lunch is only 30 minutes, and we get 3 minutes between classes." Vienna scowled.

"That's the most ridiculous thing I've ever heard! We have 10 minutes between classes. Why do you take so many classes in one day?"

"We have a lot to learn." Vienna used her fingers to count them off. "We have English, math, science, an elective, a fitness class, another elective, government or history, and advisory. I think that's all." She stared at the sky, trying to remember.

"Wow! We have the following depending on the semester: English or writing, math or science, history or government, a health class, and then a spell casting class." Valda laughed when Vienna whistled. "Pretty cool compared to your setup. I don't know how you guys get so much work done. That's a heavy load."

"Tell me about it. It felt like all I did was eat, sleep, do homework, and feel exhausted. So how do they train you for a career there?"

"In year twenty, you pick a class you're interested in, like psychology, law, medicine, or even a trade, like blacksmithing or plumbing. It helps you understand whether you are a natural at it or not. In Magyieka, we also have other areas like Magic Law, herbology specialist, and many other unique fields Enchanters go into."

"Oh my *gosh*! I am so excited to go now!" Vienna squealed, jumping up and down.

"It's still a lot of work, you know."

"I know, but it sounds like so much fun." She clapped her hands and continued bouncing.

Valda laughed again. "I guess after hearing your routine, I can understand your perspective. Let's get you home." Valda shot forward to exit trees, which Vienna knew was the final challenge of the night. Who could finish the last mile first?

▽△△▽✸

Arriving at Vienna's home, both girls fought to catch their breath. Sprinting had drained their energy and lungs. Bending over, Vienna focused on her breath for several seconds.

Vienna gasped out, "You . . . such . . . I don't know . . . how you do . . . so fast!"

"You'll get used to it," Valda said before taking a deep breath. "Our health classes are very intense. At least 15 minutes of the class is developed to push yourself as much as physically possible."

"Good . . . to know."

It took several minutes for Vienna to catch her breath and meet Valda at her front door. She was always behind in that race and felt like puking. But she was getting quicker.

The front door opened. Her parents stood there with worried looks on their faces. "Girls, can you come in here, please?" Her mom smiled weakly.

Vienna and Valda shared an anxious look. Then, they headed into the house.

"What's going on, Mom?" Vienna whispered.

"I can't tell you anything. Just answer questions to the point." She walked ahead and smiled at a tall, gangly man with a stern face. He was dressed in a navy-blue suit and a bowtie. He held a fedora in his hand that had a symbol indicating he was a police officer from the Magic Realm.

"Hello, ladies," the officer said politely. "It has been brought to my attention that a document was taken from the school here in the Human Realm. It happened sometime in the last couple of weeks. This document has some critical information in it. It's most pressing that we find this document and return it to the original owner."

Both girls answered at the same time. "I have no idea where it is."

"I see. For precautionary purposes, we search for each person's memories as we look to find the person responsible for the theft. With your parents' permission, I, with my partner"—a short chubby man with a cookie in his mouth moved from the kitchen to the living room and waved—"will place our hands on your heads and search your memories. We will only look for anything regarding this document. Nothing else will be searched." They began to move toward Vienna.

She stepped back and put a hand out. "Wait! How do I know you won't search for other things, do something to my memory, or plant something there?" Her heart pounded. They were going to discover the document. What would they do to her?

"If we tried, we would lose our place on the Council and be removed from office, as that would infringe on your rights, young girl."

*Young girl?!* Vienna narrowed her eyes at the tone of his voice.

"You can explore my mind first so Vienna can see there's no harm." Valda stepped forward, and both men smiled down at her.

"Excellent." They placed their hands on her head and were done in less than a second. "Good, good. Nothing to see at all. Just school documents in that pretty brain of yours. Now"—he turned to Vienna —"are you ready?"

She wiped her sweaty palms on her dress and moved toward them.

As soon as they placed their hands on her head, they began to dig for answers. It was as if time stood still. She could feel a force digging through her brain.

*Relax,* she heard a voice say in her head. *Let us have access. Trust us.*

She blocked the request with all the strength she could muster.

They repeated the request, chanting in her head. She felt her resolve weakened and sent a surge of power to block them. The room was silent, but her mind held their voices, demanding information she couldn't give. She decided to make it a game. For each word that requested access for sensitive information, she blocked it with an image from childhood. Within minutes, her eyes flew open, staring at the ceiling. She felt something tickling her nose, and she wiped at it. On the back of her hand was a long line of blood. Her mother crouched over her and put a tissue on her nose. She leaned down as if to kiss her cheek but whispered in her ear, "You did good."

She could hear her parents talking, but couldn't make out the words. She listened to the front door close, and soon after, her parents moved her to the couch. She sat up at the sound of Valda's voice.

"You're awake," Valda cheered. "That was *amazing*. You threw them out of your mind. Seconds after holding their hands on your head, they flew backward, slamming into the wall. I didn't know that was possible."

Vienna sat up. "They had no right to intrude like that. Will they come back?"

"No," her mother answered. "But this is a unique ability. What other things have you discovered lately?"

"Vienna is a Dreamwalker, and she's picked up all the paranormal and combat skills I've been teaching her. And now this." Valda looked at Vienna's parents and took a deep breath. "She also said she's dreamed of a spiral and being hued in violet."

"Are you sure it was violet?" her dad asked.

Everyone looked at Vienna. Staring at Valda, she was torn between throwing up a wall and trusting Valda's reason for telling them. A soothing sensation caressed Vienna's soul, and she relaxed. She reminded herself why she'd felt safe with Valda and all she'd helped her with. She leaned into the calm that spread across her.

"Yes"—she jutted out her chin—"in these dreams, I'm often surrounded in a violet shield when dreams are threatening."

Her parents looked at each other.

"Could her element be Spirit?" her mom asked.

Shifting her eyes between her three onlookers, Vienna asked the only thing she could, "What is Spirit?"

# CHAPTER SIXTEEN

Vienna's mom placed a steaming cup of hot chocolate on the table. She unwrapped a candy cane, put it in the cup, and smiled at Vienna. A smile that didn't reach her eyes. Instead, fear traced her features.

Vienna breathed in the fresh aroma as the steam rose, warming her nose. Her favorite. She inhaled deeply as she took her first sip. The thick, warm chocolate warmed her throat. She licked her lips, satisfied.

"Explain everything to me. I need to know what you guys are talking about."

After several heartbeats, her mother began. "Let's start with the elements. As you've learned through studies and movies, those with magical abilities can access Earth, Air, Fire, or Water. But then there is Spirit, which is also known as Ether. Of all the elements, the Spirit is the only one that isn't earthbound, and it is a spiritual place where the divine resides."

"Wait," Vienna cut her mom off, "this sounds like a

Dreamwalker."

"Not quite," Valda corrected.

"Dreamwalkers can travel through planes and project their soul or essence into other realms and worlds, like the Nether Realm. But Spirit is even more rare than a Dreamwalker. When someone wields the power of Spirit, they are a bridge between the physical and spiritual. As such, they are able to transfer between the celestial and physical world. Unlike when one is in another realm in their dream, Spirits move their entire being to any realm and world they desire."

"That's incredible?" Vienna sat back in shock. Memories of the Ovr'seer's house and being transported to "nowhere" due to her powers, as they were told in the in-between, came flooding back. "Oh my God," she gasped.

"What is it?" her mom asked.

Vienna thought for a moment before opting out of telling her parents. They were starting to tell her the things she needed to know; she wasn't going to jeopardize that.

"Nothing. I just don't know why this is all so important."

Her dad continued, "We'll get to that. But do you understand this so far?"

"I think so. Dreamwalkers move to realms in their dreams, like going to the Nether Realm. Spirits can go to any realm or world. But does their body go with them?"

"It can, or they can choose to go without it," her mom answered.

"Grace," Valda interrupted, "you're saying you think Vienna's element is Spirit because of her aura. It may also make sense as electricity ran through her the day she tapped into her magic at school. Books floated in the air, and Vienna said the sky was cast with dark clouds. That's two elements, at least."

"Some of the books' pages were also on fire, Mom," Vienna reminded her.

"My God," her mom gasped.

"If we're right, you will be able to wield all elements and

strengthen the power of those who can access other elements, much like a life source," Valda explained.

"With your experiences in school and now hearing this, we need to find out if this could be true. As it is rare for one to have Spirit as their element," her dad informed them.

"Could this also mean she is the Quintessence?" Valda asked. Vienna swore she saw a sparkle of defiance in her eyes.

Her mom glared at Valda, who met her intensity.

"Grace," her dad offered, "Valda has a point."

"What is Quintessence?" Vienna asked.

They stared at Vienna but didn't answer.

"What is the Quintessence and what else do I need to know? I'm done being kept in the dark." Vienna demanded, "NOW!" She slammed her fist on the table. The house shook, and her eyes burned.

"Your eyes." Valda pointed.

"Dear Gods," her dad whispered.

Seeing their fear, Vienna rushed to a mirror. Her eyes were a radiant violet, with sparks of silver dotted around her pupil. Fearful, she closed her eyes and held her breath. Once her emotions slowed, she looked back into the mirror, where green eyes stared back.

"It's time for transparency." She tuned to the table. "Who wants to start?"

With a long sigh, Valda began. "Quintessence is Latin for Spirit as it means the fifth element. But it goes beyond that."

"Quintessence," her dad interjected, "is like the element Spirit. The difference is that Spirit wielders are rare, as it is the fifth element. But the Quintessence is the purest of all Spirits."

"Just how rare is a Quintessence?" Vienna asked.

"There has only been one supreme Spirit, but there has never been a Quintessence," her mom answered.

"All Spirits have greatness destined, and she was no exception." Valda shifted topics. "She was the one who created the bridge between the Human and Magic Realm."

"Since I can barely access my powers, I'm not the Quintessence," Vienna told Valda.

"I agree. Though your aura is violet like the last Pure Spirit," her mom admitted, "which means you will be a target at school and for anyone who learns of your abilities."

"I can hide my abilities, right?" Vienna asked.

"Yes," her dad continued. "Historically, only those who wielded Spirit were slain by our own, as they are powerful, so choosing one element to access will be crucial."

"Tell me more about the Spirit who created the bridge," Vienna requested.

"The last Pure Spirit was Lavinia. She was the niece of Queen Thalma, the ruler of the Enchanters. Lavinia created the bridge that connected the Magic Realm to the Human Realm."

"Lavinia was the only other Elite Enchantress to walk among us. Her time was so brief that nobody knew much about her. But her ability to create that bridge invoked fear for anyone wielding Spirit," Valda explained. "Which means this is something you must hide."

"Valda is right. You can't let anyone know," her dad said.

"Why?" Vienna's asked.

"Lavinia prophesied that there would be another like her, but more powerful. Which the Council and other Enchanters don't want. It could threaten their power," Valda added.

"You don't let them know. You forget this ever happened and move on. When you determine your element, you choose the one you connect to most. Most won't pay attention enough to know something is going on," her dad explained, trying to offer hope.

"I can do that. We don't even know if any of this is true. It's not likely, anyway," Vienna admitted. "What are the odds I am truly Spirit, let alone a threat to anyone," she scoffed.

Her parents looked at her. "We don't know for certain. But be cautious with your magic use," her mom quipped. "Too much power or use of multiple elements will make people fear you because you're different. It may also make you a stronger Dreamwalker. You may have more elemental strength when walking into different realms and people's dreams. Meaning you must be careful. Other than that, you have nothing to worry about. They will believe you can block people from your mind, which some Dreamwalkers do. Not many, though."

"With the violet aura, our lineage, and your ability to dreamwalk, the odds of you being an Elite Spirit are high. I suggest you inform your parents and nobody else if more abilities unfold," Valda offered.

"How do you know so much about this, Valda?" her mom asked. Vienna watched as her mom moved herself physically away from Valda, as though her depth of information caused discomfort. Curious, Vienna leaned forward, watching their bodies. She recalled Valda's admission to being a telepathic empath. Was she using her ability to calm the room? Could her mom feel it?

Vienna looked at Valda. "I'm curious as well," she said.

"My guardian told me stories. She was a great fan and prayed I would have the same talents. I was told about the rarity of some auras and the importance of Dreamwalkers." Embarrassment flushed her features. "I assure you, I'm not a fan girl," she teased, but it fell flat.

"That makes sense. It's rare to see someone of your age, what early twenties," her mom guessed, "having such deep knowledge."

"I spent my entire life in the Magyieka. I've known nothing else." Valda's voice was laced with sadness. "With my guardian's desire to have a unique and talented Enchantress, I was trained to look for uniqueness in myself."

"Be happy you don't. I feel like I have a target on my head," Vienna mused, hoping to lighten the mood.

"You don't. Not yet, anyway," her mom said as she looked at her husband. "And I hope, somehow, the lack of evidence otherwise is in our favor." She put her forehead to her daughter's, and a single tear fell from her eyes.

At that moment, Vienna knew her mom wasn't being candid. Wielding Spirit meant being a target. Others could easily put it all together with her being a Dreamwalker and accessing her powers early for an Enchanter raised in the Human Realm. Determination to dig deeper into her training filled Vienna with energy. She would not be weak if she became the one Magyieka waited for.

"Valda, would you mind staying the night?" her mom asked.

"She has plans, Mom," Vienna answered.

"I might be able to make some arrangements. If that's okay with you, Vienna." Valda's voice rose an octave, her face mimicking an eager child.

"If that's possible," Vienna answered skeptically.

"Let me make a phone call. Your mom has a cellphone, right?" Vienna nodded. Her mom gave Valda her phone, and Valda moved swiftly from the house but wasn't gone long before she came back and let Vienna's mom know she could stay the night.

Vienna hadn't had a sleepover in years and was thrilled. When she and Valda got to her room, they pulled out a cot. "Have you had a sleepover before?" Vienna asked curiously. "You seemed . . . "

"Excited," Valda laughed. "I am. And no, I haven't had a sleepover before. Sounds like you have?"

"Yes. Logan, actually. As kids, we would spend most of the summer at my house sleeping on the trampoline, camping in the backyard, or camping near the beach."

"Wow. Your parents allowed that?"

"Of course. He was like family." Her voice died off. She flinched at the warmth of Valda's hand on her arm.

Valda stood next to her. "You miss him," Valda pointed out.

"I miss the old him," she responded flatly.

"He's the same person. He just got pulled into the deception required by our elders and the ruling government. The Council isn't forgiving of rule breaking. You need to separate Logan from the role he's taken."

"You make it sound easy." Vienna sat on the side of her bed.

"When we realize we are bound by law and code, the reasoning outweighs the pain." Valda sat next to her. "I remember growing up and being confused by the rules that hurt people. When I learned the consequences of breaking those rules could be harsher than enduring the betrayal, the pain changed."

"Maybe one day that will change, and we won't have to choose between two poor choices."

"That I could get on board with," Valda agreed.

Once they were both ready for bed, they chatted briefly about their school, future goals, and life currently. It eased Vienna's nerves, giving her the courage to ask Valda what she'd longed to know.

"Can you tell me about being a Dreamwalker? I know we've talked about it briefly, and you've talked about how you and I both can sometimes see things before they happen. But what exactly is a Dreamwalker?" Vienna desperately wanted to know more.

"It's the ability to travel between realms and worlds, often to gain information. Once skilled, a Dreamwalker will know what's happening." She expanded on the basic knowledge Vienna had, and it floored her.

"So, if I chose to use this power, I'd just fall asleep and imagine being where I wanted?"

"Yes. Once a Dreamwalker learns how to harness the ability, they can use it as a tool however they want. For example"—Valda propped herself on her arm—"if you wanted to talk to me while I was away, you'd enter my dreams and talk with me. Or, if you wanted to venture into other realms, you could do so. It depends on your level of power and ability. Some become diverse enough they can walk among all realms. But most are stuck walking in the dreamscape of chosen targets." There was sadness in her voice as she talked about the special abilities a Dreamwalker holds.

"Have you ever met someone who is Spirit and a Dreamwalker?" Vienna asked, ignoring Valda's sadness.

"You," Valda said flatly.

Vienna didn't know how to respond. There was no concrete evidence she was either, let alone both; she refused to believe it was possible for her to wield two powers. She watched as Valda picked at the feather that had fallen from her pillow.

"Do you believe I am both?" she finally asked.

"I don't know what else it would be. What you thought were dreams aren't. You can block others in a way that most trained Enchanters can't. There are so many things," she admitted. "If nothing else, you're in the making to be a powerful Enchantress."

Speechless, Vienna pondered her comment. She'd once been told that with greatness comes great responsibility. She hoped she was ready to live up to the potential others seemed to see in her.

With the silence thick, Vienna wished Valda goodnight and fell into a quick slumber.

# CHAPTER SEVENTEEN

## Vienna & Logan's POV

Time passed quickly as Vienna studied as much as she could about Spirit. Between asking Valda and her parents and looking into family journals, she grasped the complexity, uniqueness, and power that came with Spirit. She felt better knowing it wasn't precisely an omen of death like she'd suspected, but it was something to be cautious of, just like her parents said. As usual, she felt overly dramatic.

In the field, Vienna closed her eyes and imagined the wind rustling the trees. The slightest breeze kicked up, cooling her down. She smiled, pleased with her ability.

"Well done." Valda walked by and placed a tin in the center of a tree trunk. "Try and move it."

Vienna strained, concentrating on the power she felt flickering in along her nerves. The can rattled and then fell over. "Damn it, why is moving this so hard?"

"You tap into your magic best when you're angry. Try focusing on Logan and the fact he hasn't tried to reach out to you."

Vienna had reached out to Logan several times by sending messages with Valda. After several letters, she gave up. Even with her last letter begging him to come visit or send a response. Nothing. He'd said he'd be gone for a couple of days, but it had been weeks. Vienna wondered if being cold had bothered him more than she realized. Thoughts of the excruciating pain she'd experienced when he'd left her surfaced. Focusing on the heartache, she refused to feel bad for her behavior. Grief was a bitch, and he was the one who had abandoned her. Having an oath or not, the pain it caused was the same. Regulations and rules be damned. She would never have let him think she was done with their relationship had the roles been reversed. Sadly, as the time from their last meeting grew longer, her reason for keeping him at a distance was reinforced.

Her nostrils flared, and she pushed energy from her, hurling it toward the can. The can ripped through the air, combusting into flames before landing several feet away. "Well, if I need to make someone explode, I'll be fine. Is accidental homicide overlooked in the Magic Realm? For beginners, I mean." She batted her lashes at Valda, who laughed.

"Don't think so." Both girls laughed at the comment.

"Vienna, you've done exceptionally well during your training. You've tapped into your magic in a few different ways. That's a good thing. How about trying each element today? You just nailed Fire. Let's try Wind."

Vienna agreed and imagined creating a dirt-devil. She moved her hands in small circles, increasing their speed.

"Look!!" Valda's voice was filled with excitement, and Vienna opened her eyes. In front of them was a four-foot tunnel of dirt.

"Hell ya!" Vienna cheered.

"That was incredible. You're evolving quickly." Vienna caught a flash of fear in Valda's face but said nothing.

"Now what?"

"You've tapped into each element. I'm curious if you've been able to access any Spirit abilities besides wielding each element?"

"What would I be looking for?" Vienna asked.

"Energy shifting, moving to different realms, healing, to name a few."

"Wow. What about actual shifting? Are there Shifters?" Vienna asked.

"Why do you ask that, of all things?" Valda cocked her head and squinted her eyes.

"I had a dream the other night about werewolves and vampires. I wasn't sure if it was my intuition or just the fantasy world here in the Human Realm that caused the dreams." Vienna laughed, "That's just crazy."

"No worries. Hey, how are things coming along for tonight's party?" Valda asked.

"Good, I guess. My family has invited some people they know and a few acquaintances from school. I honestly would rather not have a party to celebrate my leaving. Everyone thinks it's for my birthday, and in some ways, it is. I'm just not close to the people coming. I do get to wear a nice dress and eat lots of food, though," Vienna bragged.

"Ooh, what kind of food?" Valda was wide-eyed with excitement. "I love your mom's cooking."

Laughing, Vienna answered, "Logan too. I think that's why he stayed around so much as a kid." They both laughed.

"I can totally see that. The boy can eat!"

"How about we head back?" Vienna's heart sank at the thought of Logan. She missed him, and the heaviness of his absence was increasing. She'd be leaving the Human Realm tomorrow and didn't know when she'd see him again.

"Sure. If you're done for the day. We do have time for a round of combat," Valda offered. "No magic." She pointed at her.

"One time. I hit you with magic one time and you'll never let it go."

"Actually, I'm drained after the magic we did. Let's head back and start getting ready."

"Fair enough."

The walk was short, and when they arrived at the house, everyone was busy rushing around. Vienna wanted nothing more than to relax and talk with her family, but she knew the celebration was important to them. At midnight, she would officially be an adult. She felt like the same girl she had always been, but she wasn't. Over the course of the summer, while her peers in the Human Realm had been relaxing, she had been through a roller-coaster of emotions and adventures. Tonight, that all changed. No longer would she have time to prepare. It was time to start living the life she had learned about.

"You're home. Why don't you go relax and then get ready for dinner?" Her mom rushed around preparing several dishes of food.

"How many people did you invite?" Vienna counted twelve dishes of salads, meats, and appetizers.

"A few. Now go."

Vienna groaned. "Fine."

Halfway up the stairs, she turned back. "Do you know if Logan will be here?"

Her mom's pitying look said more than words could.

"Right, we don't know. I'll be down later. Valda said she didn't know if she'd make it, but she would try."

The walk to her room seemed to take longer than normal. She slipped into her room and closed it. As her body slid down the floor, she was swarmed with emotions. Calling the last bit of strength she had, she summoned her magic as she tried to pull her family chest to her. It stopped two feet in front of her. Her magic was tapped out. She manually pulled it the rest of the way and began digging for anything that would trigger motivation.

Pulling out the family tree, she studied it then placed it aside. Underneath was a scroll filled with symbols she learned early that week. Each symbol of the elements was listed, but there was no Spirit. She placed it on the family tree, and it began to glow.

"What do we have here?" she asked. She picked them up together and the two pages combined. Her entire family line shifted.

Next to each person was their elemental symbol. For the first time since she learned about this, she wondered what her parents' magic was. Next to her mom's name, several white lines formed into a gust of wind. By her father's was a stone, the lines a metallic brown. Tracking up the tree, she saw a variety of elements. The most common were Water and Earth, followed by Air and then Fire.

"With as hot headed as we all are, how is there not more Fire?" she asked herself. Realizing she had gone into the past family tree, she moved in the opposite direction. Locating her siblings and herself, she found no symbols. More confused, she dug deeper into the chest, pulling out anything that looked important. Nothing noted anything about Spirit, or indicated when someone would have their sign etched into the documents.

A light knock at the door pulled her from her thoughts. "Who is it?"

"Me," Valda's voice answered.

Vienna scrambled to get all the papers put back into place, then urged the chest back to its place. Silently, it slid back to the base of her bed, and several blankets fell on top.

"Come in," she answered as she scooted aside.

Valda walked in with a plate full of food. "Your mom needed a taste tester." She smiled. "I thought you were supposed to be getting ready?"

"I am. Are you staying long?" she deflected.

"No, I was just coming to let you know I'm going. I'll try to come back tonight, but there are no guarantees." She moved across the room and stood over the chest. "Where did this come from? I don't remember it being here the other night?"

"It was in my closet. It's just for . . . " she hesitated, "spare blankets and stuff."

"It looks like an old family chest." Valda looked at her with accusation.

"It is," she admitted.

"Anything good?"

"Nope. Mainly confusing charts and lots of family journals."

"Bummer. Anyway"—she turned back to Vienna—"Grace said you need to get some rest and have plenty of time to sleep, shower, and get dressed. Kind of bossy when she's frazzled, huh?"

"You have no idea." Vienna shook her head. "Hey"—Valda stopped a few inches from the door—"thanks for all your help. I'm kind of a badass now."

"You better be; you had the best teacher in many realms," she said sarcastically.

Vienna tossed a pillow at her and rolled her eyes.

"I hope Logan shows up." With that, Valda left.

Vienna flopped down on her bed. "Me too." Ready to relax, she fell into a deep sleep. The exhaustion from practicing fading away.

## LOGAN

"Logan, report to the Ovr'seer." Logan turned to see the Captain of the Watchers. He stood on the field holding a parchment paper.

"Does it say why?" Logan asked. He'd requested leave a week ago to see Vienna before she was transported to the Magic Realm, but he hadn't heard back.

"Your request for leave has been granted. That's all I know. Now go," the Captain bit out. The Captain was training the active Watchers and his blunt unwelcoming tone never wavered.

Logan shook his head, annoyed at the Captain's demeanor, but didn't need convincing. He dropped his gear and headed toward Onyx Hall.

As he entered the building, the entire Council sat at the table. Faint murmurs he couldn't understand caused his pulse to quicken. He approached the table and cleared his throat. "You requested to see me." Logan placed his hands behind his back and avoided eye contact, looking at the back wall, anxiously waiting.

"Ah, yes. Mr. Artrusha," Mr. Ozul said, "we received your request. Come, take a seat."

Logan sat next to Mr. Humphrey and looked at the members of the Council. The stenographer stood, leaving the room without a word. The silence thickened as they sat there, waiting. Logan pulled at his sweaty combat clothes, the need to itch rising.

"The Council will permit you to visit Vienna for 2 hours. You are to be back in the Shadow Realm before midnight in the Human Realm," Mr. Humphrey informed him.

"Be conscientious of the time required to transport between realms," Mrs. Jaheem added.

"We urge you to be mindful of our interactions during the moon's current phase and consider its effects on your urges," Mr. Audovera warned.

Ms. Blight cut him off, her tone was sharp. "We have seen your shortened patience during these phases, but there is no doubt"—she glanced at Mr. Audovera—"that with your connection to Vienna and her family, you'll be able to remain balanced and in control."

"If there is nothing else, I would like to have time to get ready." Logan's tone was flat, contradicting the excitement he felt at being granted permission to visit Vienna. Pushing away a smile, he masked any emotions the Council could see as a weakness.

"Of course." The Ovr'seer stood and walked toward the door. Logan followed the urge to talk with the man, pulling him forward.

The Ovr'seer opened the door and gestured for Logan to exit the chamber. "Let's head to toward your room."

Logan did as instructed, glancing back as the feeling of being watched increased. He tracked a small bug flying nearby and ignored it until it came near enough to make out a clear definition.

Logan froze, stunned at what he saw. "What is that?" Logan asked the Ovr'seer. He pointed to where the apple-sized black Dragon once flapped and hovered, but the area was empty. "What the hell," he whispered under his breath.

"It seems like the moon is still causing some discomfort and possible hallucinations." He looked down at Logan with concern.

"I'm fine." Logan looked back and watched as green specks of light fell to the floor. There was nothing there, and the light of the specks died before hitting the ground. He shook his head.

"I wanted to talk to you about your visit." The Ovr'seer walked toward the front doors of Onyx Hall without waiting for Logan.

Rushing to catch up, he slipped through the closing door and waited for him to continue. He matched his step as they walked into the dark, misty forest, heading to his cabin. Sounds of happy forest creatures filled the night, the croaking of frogs the loudest of all the sounds. Logan smiled as he thought about the fat toad he'd found in the forest behind Vienna's house as a child. He'd kept it alive all day, and when his parents got home, he rushed over to Vienna's, showing her his epic find. He thrust it into her face, and she shrieked, falling down the stairs. That didn't phase her. She jumped up and took off running. Clueless at the terror of the giant toad and the stories about kissing a toad to find your prince, Logan chased her through the forest, trying to get her to calm down. They ran until Vienna collapsed and moaned. She was too exhausted to fight, but she cried and cried and cried. Finally, when she was finished, her rage took over. He'd gotten the first lecture in his life from a female figure, and it scared the shit out of him. Her face was purple, and all he remembered was her saying it scared her and the feelings of shame and sorrow he felt. Everything else was a blur until she wrapped her arms around his waist and buried her face into his chest, sobbing.

"Keep up, boy."

Logan didn't realize he had stopped. He looked up at the Ovr'seer, his eyes wide with awareness. His heart warmed, and he held his breath. After all these years, he realized that moment he had fallen in love with his fiery best friend. It was more than a deep connection or a devoted duty to protect someone important to him. He loved her in a way he hadn't loved anyone.

"The smallest thing can trigger a memory that we failed to realize impacted us so deeply." Logan watched as the Ovr'seer picked up a toad that had burrowed in the muddy road.

"How did I forget that memory?"

"As we age, we forget many things, making room for what our brain believes is more important, until something triggers that moment. Part of it is the training Watchers also go through. Of all the things I've learned through my life, love is the one thing that will always find a way back to us." The Ovr'seer placed the toad off the path and moved forward. "As you continue to protect Vienna, you need to remember the important role she may play in the magic world. Love must not come before our people."

"I understand." Logan clenched his jaw, knowing if it came down to protecting Vienna or his people, Vienna would always be his priority. That's why he had put distance between them regardless of the pain it caused her. "You don't stay nearby for no reason. What is your purpose of walking with me tonight?"

The Ovr'seer nodded at Logan, a smile forming. "You are wise beyond your years."

"Please don't deflect. Answer my question," Logan demanded.

"Tonight will be the last time you will have quality time with Vienna for a while. She has grown fond of you over the course of her training, and we can't have her distracted. She has all the signs of Spirit, and as we wait to see if she holds the qualities of the Quintessence, we can't have her distracted. You need to find a way to create some closure without breaking her trust while you are visiting."

Logan stood in silence. Rage boiled as he processed the command he was given. His nostrils flared as he blinked rapidly at the Ovr'seer, trying to formulate a full sentence.

"You can be angry. You were required to get close to her, and now you're being ordered to keep your distance. But if you act on your anger or break your order, you will lose your status as her Watcher, and it will be given to someone else. Neither of us wants that. So choose wisely and get your emotions in order before you leave tonight." The Ovr'seer's lips thinned, and he moved toward Logan. Seething, Logan took a step back.

"I'm sorry, Logan. I wish there were another way."

"You allowed that memory of the toad to seep through on purpose. Why?"

"So you could remember just how important she is to you. That way, you can prioritize her needs above your desires." He placed a hand on Logan's shoulder. "As a Watcher, your duty is to protect and lay down your life. Your needs and wants do not matter. She is your Ward, and there is nobody who will protect her like you will. Your love for her is powerful; with that, I know the connection is deep enough. You will always know when you're needed."

The Ovr'seer snapped his fingers and vanished, leaving Logan to figure out his emotions. Flooded with anger and feeling sorry for himself, he could only stand there as a single tear fell down his face. He looked out into the dark, misty forest, wishing, not for the first time, that he was nothing more than an Enchanter.

# CHAPTER EIGHTEEN

"Time for dinner," her mom hollered up the stairs.

Vienna sat at her vanity for several minutes, thinking about her last night at home. Excitement and sorrow battled, neither one pulling ahead. With her hair and makeup done, she walked to her closet and pulled out a tiny royal blue homecoming dress. *The sparkles would be vibrant under the blue moon,* she thought.

Pulling on the dress, she looked in the mirror. Her arms and legs were more defined from all the practice. She felt pride in her strength, and the stunning blue made her feel like a princess. The soft belly no longer bothered her. She felt like a woman and loved that her strength hadn't changed her completely. Sitting at her vanity, she secured her shoes, then turned to take one last look at her hair.

"Vienna, it's dinner time. What's taking you so long?" Her mom knocked on the door and then walked in as Vienna put one last splash of perfume on her chest.

"Wow," her mom said as she leaned against the door. "Are you dressing up to hide your emotions or to feel less depressed?" She slowly walked over and adjusted one of the pins in Vienna's fancy hairdo. Vienna smiled, thankful for the last-minute help in securing the masterpiece.

"Both . . . " Vienna choked out. She closed her eyes and took a deep breath to keep the tears from falling. "I'll be gone for several months. It's going to be weird. I've never been away from the family. I also keep thinking about the schools I would have been going to. I'm still angry, even with the excitement of learning more about Magyieka."

"Shhhh . . . " Her mom kissed the top of her head. "Everything will work out."

"Will it? What if something happens to the boys? I'm not going to be minutes away or a flight away, Mom. I'm going to be a world away, literally." She sniffled and looked in the mirror, putting one more sprinkle of glitter on her cheeks.

"Always worrying about others. Vienna, this is about *you*. Not us. And if things get too rough, we can come to visit. Or you can call me. Come on." She nudged her with a big smile. "Dinner's getting cold." Before she left, she looked down. "Are you wearing those flats all night? It's a good idea."

"The heels are pretty, but they hurt. Why be in pain for family dinner?" Vienna laughed.

Her mother grinned back. "Okay, see you in a minute."

Vienna was ready to head downstairs, but as she took the first step, she looked down and changed her mind. She rushed to her closet and found her black heels. One last look in the mirror, she said, "Now I'm ready."

She descended the stairs and saw her parents and brothers waiting at the bottom. They were all dressed more formally than usual for the family dinner. Even her dad was wearing a nice shirt.

"Wow, you guys look awesome," she admitted.

"*Us?* You look like a Barbie," her brothers said in unison, then laughed.

"Yeah, well, you guys look like a couple of penguins," she shot back.

"Boys, we talked about this," her mom corrected sternly.

"You look like a princess, V." Her dad kissed her cheek. "We made your favorite for dinner."

"Chocolate?" she joked.

"Maybe for dessert, weirdo," he replied, winking.

"Sounds good to me," Kreo agreed.

Vulcan piped up. "How about gummy worms . . . No, wait, cookies . . . No!" His volume went up. "A candy buffet! Yes. That's what we need."

"How about spaghetti, lasagna, and homemade garlic bread?" her mom countered.

"You made homemade bread? I can't remember the last time you did that." Vienna was shocked. It was one of her favorites. The pasta was perfect comfort food. Mix it with homemade garlic bread and you have an excellent dinner!

"Of course! This is a special night."

They all gathered at the table to enjoy their last family dinner until Thanksgiving break.

"Are you excited about leaving?" Kreo asked as he shoveled food in his face.

"Absolutely! The adventures, new people," she lied, forcing down the guilt. She averted her eyes, hoping Kreo and Vulcan couldn't read her agony and lie.

"That would be so cool. I'd go to"—he glared at his parents—"but they said I can't."

Vienna laughed. "I'd take you with me too."

"What do you think it's going to be like?" Vulcan asked excitedly.

"I don't know," Vienna looked at her parents. "What is it like?"

"It's warm and more tropical feeling than here. But not too different from most schools," her dad said.

"So, the girls are probably hot," Kreo said with a smile.

"Those hot girls wouldn't know what hit them if I showed up with you." Vulcan nodded.

"You might have to remove the food from your face first." Kreo tossed him a napkin, which hit Vulcan on the face.

"At least they might look at me instead of running away." Vulcan laughed so loud that soda foamed from his nose, and the entire family started to laugh.

"Any girl would be lucky to have either of you," her mom told them.

"Just make sure their maturity matches yours," Vienna teased them.

"Well, if we go off that, you're going to have to start looking at the junior high," Kreo teased Vienna.

"If her humor has any indication, I'd say that's about right," her dad added, and Vienna blushed.

The banter continued as they teased each other and discussed the possibilities of Vienna's adventure.

At the end of dinner, they all groaned in pain.

"That was so good. Thanks, Mom," Vienna said as she leaned her head on her mom's shoulder.

"Glad you liked it. Now," her mom said, getting up, "leave the mess. I set up the projector out back for a family movie."

"Cool!" the boys said, dashing toward the back door. "What movie are we watching?"

"It's a surprise!" her dad replied. He turned down the lights on the back porch.

The porch was set up like a prom. There were lights overhead and a table with tons of different treats. *Candy buffet,* Vienna thought, then she laughed.

"This is perfect." She hugged her parents.

She filled her plate and looked up to see Logan and Valda. There was a line of other people behind them. The few acquaintances she liked from school had shown up to celebrate, too.

At that moment, one of her favorite songs came on. She smiled as she swayed to the soothing tone of the song.

"May I have this dance?" Logan asked, standing with his arm behind his back. He looked like a prince asking a princess to dance.

Vienna blushed. "If we must," she teased, "but only if you promise to tell me where you've been."

"Ah, you missed me," he teased smugly while his right hand remained extended. His arm slowly fell as tears pooled in Vienna's eyes. All his smugness disappeared as he moved toward her.

She took one step back, breathing hard and fast through the pain and panic. "Like a wart on my toes," she countered. "Where have you been?" she asked again.

"I'm sorry, V. If I could have contacted you while I was away, I would have. I was put into intense training with no choice or way to reach out. Even now, I only have 2 hours to get back home."

"Did you get any of my letters?" Vienna asked flatly. Her emotions ran wild inside, fear of the answer and hope for answers from the letters.

Confusion consumed his features. "Letters?"

"I sent you several letters. Valda said she delivered them." The air between them thickened as they stood staring at one another.

"She must have dropped them with my unit leader. But I didn't get them." A sadness flashed across his features. "Tell me what was in them." A slow, roguish smile pulled at his lips.

Vienna studied him for a moment before begrudgingly admitting she believed him. She wiped a tear, ignoring his request to tell him what was in the letters. "You could have sent me a message. I thought you'd died, then who would I annoy?" she deadpanned.

"Actually, I couldn't, V. We barely had time to sleep. This practice was brutal."

Vienna watched as sorrow and pain washed over his features. "Do you want to talk about it?" She took a step closer.

He shook his head, and she spotted a scab under his chin. "Does practice get that serious?" Vienna reached out and touched his face.

"That it does." He took her hand, and she smiled at the warmth. His hands were soft and hot . . . hotter than normal.

"Logan?" Vienna moved toward him, their bodies touching, and looked up into his dark eyes. "I know you're more than an Enchanter."

Vienna watched as his body tensed and his shoulders shot to his ears. No longer smiling, he looked down at her. "Because I am, V. And I'm not an Enchanter. There are many things in the world of Magyieka besides Enchanters."

"Will you tell me what you are?" Vienna's excitement rose, a warm, childlike air flowed over her. Thoughts of Vampires, Werewolves, Trolls, and Mermaids filled her thoughts.

Logan raised his right hand again and slightly bowed. With a smile, she took his hand, and they began to dance. As they swayed to the music, their eyes were locked. Vienna noted fear and confusion in Logan's eyes.

"Valda has taught me a lot and I know there is still more to learn. I've known you since childhood. If you're not an Enchanter"—a chill prickled its way down her back—"then I want to know what you are."

Logan placed his forehead on Vienna's. "I don't know what she's taught you, but you'll be learning it all at Sparks, anyway." He released a sigh and moved back a step, looking into Vienna's eyes. "Within Magyieka, there are multiple realms. The one I in at most is the Shadow Realm. It is most common for those who train for battle and protect the border of our land. Each realm is designed like a continent and is protected by some form of magic border. Sparks Boarding School is in the Magic Realm, or Enchanters' Realm, as some call it. But because it is the home base for magic schools and Enchanter families, it's called the Magic Realm."

Logan paused, and Vienna thought about what he'd said. "This makes sense. I like the idea of realms being like continents. How do people get from one to the other?"

"Depends on the realm, but typically portals."

"As an Enchantress, I'll be in the Magic Realm and attending Sparks Boarding School. I assumed you would be at Domar's Boarding School for boys. Is that in the Magic Realm?" she asked with confusion.

"That is where I started. But after showing some of my abilities, I was transferred to the Shadow Realm and enrolled at Domar's training school, Radorkamp Academy. The education is like the boarding school, but there is a high focus on combat skills. It's similar to a university where you choose a focus."

Vienna knew he was leaving something out. "Give me the crash course about Radorkamp Academy?"

Their rhythm slowed as the music ended, but they stood face to face. She watched as his Adam's apple bobbed as he gulped. "It teaches warriors of different breeds and hereditary lines how to be in control while mastering their skills to become part of Magyieka's Armed Forces, or one of the two prominent houses that protect powerful Enchanters and other important figures in our world."

Vienna dropped his hands and took a step back. She thought about what he had just said. "You're a warrior."

Logan nodded. "In a way, yes."

"Like the army or something in the Human Realm?"

"Yes . . . " Logan looked confused.

"But there is something else. What makes you different, Logan? The dark eyes. The magic you used." She took a step closer. "You can trust me. I know there is more. No more lies."

Logan tucked a strand of loose hair behind Vienna's ear. "I don't have permission to tell you yet. But you just highlighted so many things, V. You should know the answer by now." A small growl vibrated his chest, and Vienna's eyes flew open in shock.

"You're a Shifter." The world around Vienna vanished as she stood there in shock. "I'd thought about it before, but thought I was going crazy." She met his eyes, and a warm smile greeted her. "If you're in this combat school and we will be in different realms, how will I see you? I was just starting to trust you again."

Logan laughed, the sound erupting. "You find out I'm a Shifter and all you can worry about is how we'll see each other?"

Vienna felt the warmth of her anger spread across her chest.

"Because of the design of Radorkamp Academy, I will attend events at Sparks Boarding School when Domar is invited. They are run by the same company and those who transferred to the academy are still considered students of Domar Boarding School. Which means we will see each other during dances, and possibly holidays. My parents still own their house here. But you are going to a boarding school for girls and will be learning a lot. You won't have a lot of spare time, either, V."

They walked to the edge of the yard and stared into the night.

"What kind of Shifter are you?" Before he could answer, her parents walked up behind them and invited them to a toast.

Vienna watched Logan as her parents talked about her. Vienna blushed at their retelling of her childhood.

As the toast came to an end, Logan smiled and sent a single nod before he tipped his glass. Following suit, Vienna drank her sparkling cider, smacking her tongue at the sweet flavor. When she looked up, Logan was gone.

Vienna looked for him for only a brief moment. She knew he had left since he was given a short window. Still, her heart ached at another missed goodbye. Frustration over not having an answer fell aside as she mingled with her family.

The rest of the party went smoothly, and Vienna was filled with joy as she realized how loved she was. When the party was over, it was time to head to her room. She had only a few hours left—plenty of time for a nap.

▽△△▽✳

*"Good evening, Vienna."*

*I turn on high alert as my heart gallops, stilling my breath.*

*A gorgeous man stands within reach, an amused smile growing in the silence. I look him over, confused. He's tall and broad, at least a few years older. His eyes are kind but mischievous. Thick black hair sits perfectly atop his head. I take in each feature, and though he feels familiar, I don't recognize him.*

*"Do I know you?" I straighten to let him know I'm not afraid.*

*"We have not met"—he takes a step closer—"but I know you."*

*"That's not comforting." I fight the urge to step back, unwilling to show him weakness.*

*The landscape is different, and the blackening night is heavy. Ebony sand at our feet melts into a deep blue sky that fades into a dense gray.*

*"Tell me where we are," I demand.*

*"We're in my dreamscape." He smiles and moves closer. Our bodies are inches apart, and I feel a pull to him, the need for connection winning.*

*Fear of how I got here and how I can leave consumes me until I'm brought out of my trance by the warmth of his hand on my cheek. I don't pull away. I lean in, my head resting against his hand.*

*"You look confused by our connection." It's not a question. He laces his fingers through mine, and I allow it.*

*I look down and watch as his hands transform, scales replacing skin. I rub my thumb over the scales and watch as claws elongate, replacing his finely polished nails. Following the trail of thick teardrop armor, it consumes his arm, and no skin remains.*

*Slowly, the scales move toward his neck, and I'm transfixed as his eyes brighten to an illuminating, vibrant green.*

*"You're not afraid?" he growls, his mouth unmoving. "It's a pleasure to meet you."*

*His large eyes burn my soul as he looks at me from head to toe. His lust is obvious as he smiles and moves closer.*

*"Why do I keep feeling like we have met before?" A small breath catches in my throat.*

*"We haven't formally met. This is the first, I assure you."*

*His husky breath meets mine, and he leans down. My heart*

*pounds, fear urging me to flee, but I push it away, curious about what this creature wants. His velvet lips brush mine, soft and quick. Dazed, I open my eyes, taking in his gentle smile. Motionless, I watch through fuzzy eyes.*

*Sweet honeysuckle fills my mouth as my tongue touches my lip. I suck in my lip with confusion; the taste opposing his hardened exterior. As he moves away, my desire to return the kiss pulls me toward him. Our bodies are molded together, but I pause before our lips connect. It feels so natural to be in his presence, but a warning keeps me from pursuing him.*

*"What was that for?" I ask in a daze.*

*"I've been watching you for a lifetime." He smiles at me. "I'll see you soon."*

*Before I can respond, everything vanishes.*

▽ △ △ ▽ ✳

"Rise and shine!" Her parents were sitting on the edge of Vienna's bed.

"What time is it?" Vienna rubbed her eyes, grabbed her comforter, and rolled back over.

"Nearing midnight. It's time." Her mom held Vienna's hand and smiled.

Vienna groaned and rolled toward her parents. Her mom gently moved Vienna's hair off her face.

"I'm scared, Mom."

"I know, but that's normal. This is all so new. You're going to do amazing! You always do."

"You're biased," she teased.

"Maybe," her mom laughed.

"But I'm not. I have proof," her dad interrupted.

"Oh yeah?" Vienna yawned. "How so?"

"Because you're your mother's daughter." Without a response, he left. "Get up! We leave in 15 minutes!" he yelled over his shoulder.

"See you downstairs." Her mom squeezed her shoulder.

"Hey, Mom?"

"Yeah?"

"Thank you."

Her mom smiled and quietly closed the door.

"Heavens, please give me strength." She threw on her favorite black ripped jeans and hoodie and quickly brushed her hair. She snuck into her brothers' rooms, leaving them a note and kissing them each. She closed the last door and held back her grief. "I'll see you guys soon."

Downstairs, her parents packed bags into the car.

After her stuff was loaded, she waited in the car. She couldn't help but be annoyed that her parents still hadn't told her where they were heading or how they'd enter the Magic Realm. Yes, she was excited to see this "cool" way of getting there. But she also hated . . . no, she *despised* surprises.

Mid-thought, both parents got into the car.

"Got everything?" her dad asked.

"Yes, let's go." She folded her arms and looked out the window.

"All right. It'll be a bit of a drive, but it shouldn't be too long," her mom said. "Get some sleep."

Vienna leaned back and closed her eyes. She grew dizzy and decided to stare out the window until they arrived.

Before she knew it, they were in Eugene, Oregon. Not too far from home, but the drive felt like it was dragging on. Vienna's ears plugged as they crossed a covered bridge. She grabbed her ears, fake yawning so they would pop. When she opened her eyes, they were no longer on that bridge.

"Wow!" she exclaimed.

Both parents smiled at her. The area was darker due to cloud coverage, but it was Brookings, Oregon. She knew it when she spotted the trail that led to Secret Beach.

"How did that happen?"

"Magic," her dad replied.

"Well, yeah. But how?" she asked again.

"Once you've gained trust in the Magic Realm, you receive the words needed to use all portals in the Human Realm. This one is in the middle of the bridge, but each has its own unique location. But all bring you to the same destination. Secret Beach," her mom explained.

"Do people see us . . . disappear?" Vienna leaned forward, curious.

"No, most people can't mentally process magic. Onlookers may know something happened but aren't sure what it was," her mom answered.

"So why Brookings?" Of all places, Vienna never felt Brookings was anything special. Maybe she was wrong. She had always been partial to Salem.

"The founding families didn't want a direct portal, so they agreed to put one portal in each state that comes to Brookings. Brookings wasn't as busy back then, and people avoided it since it's a long hike to get to the coast. And the gap between realms was always narrow here. The magic pulsed there, even before the bridge was built. So, Lavinia decided it was destined to host the bridge to Magyieka."

"Okay, I can understand that. But how do people going to another school get there from Brookings?"

"You end up in a central transportation station to all realms," her dad jumped in. "Now, back to how to get to your school." He looked at Vienna through the rearview mirror. "There are a lot of things that will be different, but most things are the same as here. When you learn about the realms, laws, and about magic, so many things will begin to make sense."

"But most of the traveling is through portals that Humans can't see?" Vienna asked.

"That's right," her mom answered.

"That's incredible." Vienna paused. "Wait, why are you telling me now?"

"You already have an idea after the bridge, right?" her mom looked at her.

"Absolutely," Vienna said eagerly.

"The next portals are a little harder. They can make you sick, create vertigo, or even leave you tired. We wanted you to know. But we also wanted you to experience the first transport without knowing the details. It's a tradition, I suppose." Her mom looked at her dad, who smirked.

"I agree. I don't know anyone who was aware of the details before they experienced their first portal. It's fun for the parents and usually exciting for their kids. A lot like the magic of Christmas," he explained with pride.

"So, one day, I will do the same thing with my kids?" Vienna smiled. "I like that."

"Yes, but in the *far* future." Her dad knit his brows.

"I know, I know. Jeez." She held up her hand in surrender, then laughed.

"We're here," her mom announced.

Vienna's stomach dropped, and she suddenly felt nauseous. She must have looked like she had just got off a roller coaster because her parents looked at her wide-eyed.

"Breathe. We still have a hike to get through," her mom reminded her.

"Right," Vienna said without conviction. She shook her head enthusiastically.

$$\triangledown \,\triangle \,\triangle \,\triangledown \,\circledast$$

The hike was gorgeous. Vienna hadn't remembered nature's beauty being so captivating. Something about the dark forest was invigorating. The black and purple hues of the shadows felt comforting. Even though the view was mesmerizing, the hike was grueling. With the luggage slowing them down and adding extra hurdles, she felt guilty for packing so much. She'd never heard her dad use so many cuss words. Mom . . . always. But not her dad.

They sat on a rock centered in the sand. Nobody said a word.

Vienna didn't know where the portal was yet, but she didn't want to ask.

"How are we on time?" Her dad broke the silence.

"Less than an hour to go," her mom replied flatly. Her eyes began to fill, and she sniffled. Her dad put his hand on her mom's back and leaned in. She pulled Vienna over, and they stayed there while comforting each other.

Vienna broke the silence several minutes later. "This place is heavenly. Why haven't we come here more?"

"We were afraid the otherworldly electricity in the area would stir your power." Her mom laughed hysterically. "Oh man, here we are, years early anyway." She wiped a tear from her eye. And they all shared a much-needed laugh before her dad started gathering her bags.

Looking at the ocean, her mom started moving toward it. "See the indent right there?" She pointed it out. "You'll walk through the portal and arrive at the station."

"Wait, you're not coming?" Vienna asked.

"Nope. This is all you," her dad answered.

"How will I know where to go?" Her heart began to race, and her hands were sweaty.

"You'll arrive in the middle of Station Isle, which holds all portals needed to travel. You'll see other girls your age and a bit older lined up. You'll load what looks like a trolley, called a Mystickart. It will look like a bus but runs magically. All students will load it and take it to Sparks as a group," her mom explained.

"That bites," Vienna replied. "How much longer before I go?"

"Now." Sorrow echoed in her dad's voice as a tear rolled down his cheek. He pulled his only daughter into a comforting embrace. "God, I love you, kiddo."

Then her mom lost it, bawling as she wrapped her arms around Vienna.

"The Blue Moon is at its peak, Grace. She has to go."

Vienna looked to the sky. The moon was bright, appearing inches from water due to the size; it consumed the sky unlike anything she'd seen before. She stared at it for several seconds, then turned to her parents.

"I love you guys." Vienna's voice cracked. "Remind Vulcan and Kreo how much I love them," she choked.

She grabbed her bags, and with a heavy heart, she squared her shoulders and walked to the rocks. With one backward glance, she watched her dad hold her sobbing mom as they stood on the empty beach. Before she could give a final wave, there was a snap. Vienna jumped, her heart racing at the unexpected sound. Looking into the rock, she watched as the blackness cleared to a dark gray. A loud hiss assaulted her ears and then a sizzle, like lightening kissing the water, sent a wave of energy through her. Within seconds, all colors of the rainbow flashed by her in streams of electricity. Then, everything went black.

# CHAPTER NINETEEN

Vienna wobbled as her ears rang. She stood in a daze as she remembered walking to the cliff and standing by the rock where the water had eroded. The next thing she knew, she was standing in Station Isle. A large sign welcomed her as she waited for her senses to clear.

Unexpectedly, there was no transportation waiting, and nearly fifty girls, who appeared at least two years older, stood waiting. Nobody turned to her, spoke, or even acted surprised that she was suddenly there.

Once the dizziness stopped, she looked around. The station resembled an underground mall—several shops lined the street. She scanned the area and noticed a pale blonde, nearly white-haired girl, standing alone. She was taller than most of her peers, twitching nervously while looking at a group of girls that stood around her. Vienna walked toward the girl but paused as a *hiss* and then a *creak* assaulted her ears. The Mystickart appeared in front of them seconds later. Vienna gasped at the beauty of the warm, vibrant colors under the gold- and silver-etched metal.

Vienna's stomach flipped as she moved toward the door. Everyone piled on, pushing Vienna to the back—she loaded last. She closed her eyes to control the anxiety that crept up. With straight shoulders, she smiled and focused on each step . . . 1 . . . 2 . . . 3. There were just two spots left: with the beautiful girl she saw earlier, who also looked a little lonely, or with a grumpy-looking girl with black hair. *Crap!* She walked over to the pale blonde.

"Hey, can I sit with you?" Vienna asked as she nervously twirled a strand of hair.

"Of course! Here." She looked energetic and elegant as she reached out, grabbed Vienna's bag, and shoved it under the seat.

Vienna noticed her eyes were a pale baby blue. She also had the most petite, sharp nose she'd ever seen.

"I'm Celine. Celine Castro." She held out her hand.

Vienna shook it lightly. Pride from her research swelled in her. In the Magic Realm, it was common practice for people to use their surname to alert status. Vienna thought about the name Castro and recalled its origin. Castro was Galician and came from one of the longest and most well-known families in Magyieka. A large portion of their ancestors now resided in the Human Realm, but the majority had stayed in Magyieka and married into elite, royal, or well-to-do families. Vienna looked at Celine. She'd expected someone of her lineage to be less pleasant.

"Are you okay?" Celine asked. She tilted her head toward Vienna and smiled. "Your cheeks are gossiping." Celine giggled before she leaned back.

"Vienna." She relaxed her shoulders, trying to hide the embarrassment that crept up her cheeks. Celine still looked at her like she was waiting for more information. After several moments of awkward silence, Vienna stared out the window.

"So," Celine prodded, "what year are you?"

"Nineteen. You?"

"Same. Are you excited? I am *so* excited!" she admitted.

Vienna shrugged. "Nervous. It's my first semester."

"First semester?" Celine questioned her. Before Vienna could answer, she watched Celine's eyes widen. "You're from the Human Realm."

"Yes." Vienna held up her chin and suppressed the shame that began working its way in. She was speaking to royalty, or at the very least someone of high status, and here she was, from the Human Realm, knowing very little about the world she was now a part of.

"Well, at least we get to attend together. Do you know anyone yet?" Celine asked.

"Nope."

"I was nervous when I first attended, too. Are you rooming with anyone, or did your parents get you your own room?"

Vienna hadn't thought about any of that. "I don't know."

"Oh, well, some of us had to change rooms after the break. We got a written notice. Perhaps yours is on your schedule."

"I haven't gotten my schedule yet. I didn't know others had." Vienna looked around, curious if anyone had a similar story to hers.

"It's probably a mistake. We've all had the same classes since the start of the year. They'll take care of it when you get there today. We have classes after the porters take our bags. You'll need to see the secretary. Anyway . . . " Celine straightened and sat with a tall back; it matched her proper tone. "Tell me about yourself, Vienna."

"I have two amazing little brothers, and my parents both work full-time jobs." She wasn't sure what would interest someone like Celine, so she told her about her family and how schools were structured back home. "School sounds different here." Vienna motioned around. "Ya know, I just found out about all of this a few months ago."

"I'm sorry. That is one rule I will never understand."

"Me neither. I lied to my brothers about going to a college that I'd always dreamed about, and instead, I was transported to a different world. It's crap!"

"On a positive note, the Human Realm seems so weird, and we have wonderful things here in Magyieka." Celine scrunched her nose and twisted her hair.

"I don't get why they call it a realm instead of the Human World." Vienna thought out loud.

"That's a good point. It's part of our world, in a sense. We have access to it. Any realm or area we can access is considered part of Magyieka, even if it isn't." Celine waited.

"So, it's like the capital of the United States, not technically part of it, but it is, and that's where our government gathers." Vienna smiled at Celine's confusion. "Celine"—Vienna turned toward her— "I looked up some things about the Magic Realm while preparing to come here. Your last name stood out when you introduced yourself."

Celine jutted out her chin, and her mouth moved to a straight line. "Do you have a question?"

"I'm just curious what it means." Nervous, Vienna began to ramble. "I know it's an elite name, and that's about it. I do know people use their surnames here a lot, which is weird, but now I'm curious why you used it if you don't want people to mention it."

Celine sighed. "It's not that." She rubbed her hands nervously, but it was so quiet that Vienna almost didn't notice. "I've had people try to befriend me only based on who I am. I want people to accept me for who I am as a person, not because of my family."

"Who is your family? Like, where are you from?" Vienna sat back, excited to learn about Celine after getting to share parts of herself.

"How much do you know about the different realms?" Celine asked.

"I know about the Magic Realm, which holds Sparks and is the home base of Enchanters. I also know a little about the Shadow Realm and the school that trains warriors there. That's about it." Vienna shrugged.

"So not much." Celine thought for a while. "My family is royalty.

I've spent my life in a castle on hundreds of acres filled with magical forests and creatures." Celine looked at Vienna.

"Well," Vienna gulped, "we definitely came from different backgrounds." Vienna laughed. "I was raised near a forest, but the most magical part was when we got snow or when creatures were born."

"That sounds lovely. What about your home?"

"A small four-bedroom home that my family remodeled. Nothing fancy, but very comfortable."

"How magical. We have many rooms, but I have no siblings and no family who live nearby. My family is always busy running our kingdom, so I spent most of my time alone practicing magic and talking with the creatures of our world." Celine crossed her legs and turned toward Vienna. She reached over and took Vienna's hands in hers.

"Vienna, your energy is soothing but strong. Even with your magic being new, I believe you have a purpose for being here with us. I can see you're younger than most who come here from the Human Realm, but your soul is wise and aged." Vienna sat unmoving. She suppressed an eeriness as she shifted in discomfort and wondered if this girl was off or had a talent for reading people.

Vienna physically moved away as she took in Celine, realizing the girl's eyes were unfocused. Shaking her head, Vienna gulped, then changed the conversation.

"Are there a lot of girls at the boarding school that are from the Human Realm?" Vienna asked.

"No. It's becoming very rare as time goes on. Less pure lines marry. I think you're the only one in a long time. Even ones with some magic are dormant until late life, or it's so minor that they live in the Human Realm if their families tell them." Celine was nonchalant about the statement.

"Wait." Vienna looked at Celine in shock. "How did you know I'm of a pure line?"

"I perceive it," Celine admitted.

Vienna watched Celine, noting no sign she was lying. Deciding to accept her reason, she relaxed.

"It makes me sad to think there are less pure lines and an increase in dormant magic." Vienna leaned into the seat. "I wonder if my brothers will come into magic."

"If you did, the odds are high."

"Maybe things will be different one day, and we won't have to hide anymore." Vienna looked at Celine and noted the spark in her eyes.

"One day, we will be able to make any changes we desire. We are the next generation, after all." Celine tightened her grip on Vienna's hands before she let go. "We have a little more time before we arrive."

They spent the ride chatting about interests and telling each other small life stories. Vienna couldn't believe how close she felt to Celine.

When they arrived, Vienna gasped as she took in the grand boarding school. It must have been on at least fifty acres of land, and the school was a castle. The soft cream stones stood in contrast to the vibrant colors of the bright landscape. In the center of the driveway, a large fountain spewed water that glistened off lush vines wrapped around a curvy, majestic woman made of ivory. She stood in the fountain's center and reached toward the heavens with soft, welcoming features. It was breathtaking.

As the girls unloaded their bags, Vienna and Celine waited. Vienna wasn't eager to rush into the moving herd, but somehow, she and Celine still got separated. Vienna stood at the front of the building, contemplating not going in.

"Hello, Miss Madizza-Corey."

Vienna spun toward the deep voice. It was a man, maybe ten years older than she.

"Hi," she said automatically. "Do I know you?"

"Of course not," he answered, then slowly approached, "but I know you—no need to fear. My name is Mr. Dařeek Audovera."

His name was one she had never heard. *Dar-rrr-eek.* She practiced rolling the *r* from the tip of her tongue, and even though it didn't sound quite the same, it was close. *What an interesting name,* she thought.

"I'm the professor of history," he continued, breaking her out of her trance. "I learn of all the first-year students before term starts. It is an honor to meet you, Vienna." His smile was so slight that she thought she'd imagined it. "I look forward to working with you. For now, how about I walk you to the front office? Nervousness can be hell when you start a new school, no?" He put a hand on his chest. "I speak from experience."

"Oh?" she replied, still struck by his well-poised demeanor and clothing from the 17th century. The silk-green Victorian suit, with the laced cuff, fit his personality well.

After walking a while, he stopped abruptly. "Here we are. Ms. Blight will be your counselor, but Mrs. Murphy will help you get your schedule. See you in class." Just like that, he was gone.

Mrs. Murphy looked up from her work. "Have a seat, please." Her name tag was crooked and dirty.

Mrs. Murphy was an overly happy middle-aged woman with graying hair. She barely stood taller than the counter and used a stepladder for everything in the office. But she did it with a hum and smile. She was sweet, but she had no organizational skills. She rushed around the office frantically, so Vienna took a seat. Being in her presence eased Vienna's nerves a little. Her mind began to run wild as she watched the middle-aged lady dart around the room, mumbling to herself.

Waiting to enroll in a new school created an eruption of emotions. Sitting in the office meant students who came through might stare at her and give her a look of acceptance, curiosity, or discomfort. Vienna was getting the "what a freak" look more than anything. Several students entered the office to grab supplies or talk to Mrs. Murphy. They would look at Vienna distastefully, then laugh as they whispered. Vienna squirmed in her seat, warmth coating her body like a blanket as she tried to ignore anyone coming in. Vienna paced at one point, but when Cosima walked in with another student at her side, she sat down and her stomach rolled from the fluttering butterflies that rose to the top.

Cosima's face distorted, making her disdain for Vienna obvious before she cleared her throat at Mrs. Murphy, who looked terrified at the sight of Cosima.

"Miss Leos, how can I serve you?" She looked down to the floor while addressing Cosima, and Vienna blanched at the act.

Confused by Mrs. Murphy's actions, she watched as they interacted.

"It appears a mistake has been made. I have a student assigned to my room who was not listed last semester"—Cosima tossed a stack of papers onto the floor as she watched Mrs. Murphy—"and I am not pleased with this. It needs to be addressed immediately." Cosima's voice was icy and sharp, causing the poor secretary to tremble.

"I'm so ve . . . ver . . . " Mrs. Murphy stuttered, " . . . very sorry, but each room has an equal number of students right now, and I am unable to assist with this matter. I can put a note in for you." Mrs. Murphy's voice cut off as Cosima tsked at her.

"Now, Mrs. Murphy," Cosima replied sweetly, lifting Mrs. Murphy's chin with a sharp, well-polished nail. "I know you're not that worthless. I will expect a change in this"—she paused as disgust filled her features—"burdensome situation with the cocoa peasant. I'm sure you can find a more fitting room." She glanced at Vienna. "Perhaps with other outcasts we have tarnishing the school." Cosima dropped Mrs. Murphy's chin and left.

Vienna gripped the arms of the chair as the words hit her like a ton of bricks. Not only was Cosima a judgmental bully, but she was also racist and cruel. She fought the urge to follow Cosima and defend whoever this student was, but refused to interfere on her first day. She could feel Cosima's magic—it was strong—and the fear she caused created unease in Vienna. Shaking her head, Vienna couldn't believe a place with such a long history could still face racism and power dynamics that directly affected its people.

Vienna heard a sniffle and looked up to find Mrs. Murphy swatting a tear away. Then, as though nothing had happened, the secretary started rushing back and forth across the office. She watched her for a while and felt a sense of pride in the woman's determination. But as time passed, she started to feel more restless and annoyed at the opportunity it gave her to think about where she was and what she was missing out on in life.

As hard as she tried to ignore the jitters, she couldn't. More than ever, Vienna *felt* like a freak. Her peers back home were preparing for college while she was enrolling in a particular school for people from magical lineage. The last three months had been hell. It seemed like her life had turned upside down ages ago. She'd done all she could to be optimistic, but the last half-hour of waiting and being stared at had her feeling more pessimistic than she'd felt over the previous months.

Snapping out of her reflection, Vienna realized the office was quiet—just her and the secretary. The halls were empty. This meant one thing: she was late to class and still hadn't received a final schedule. Vienna's leg bounced uncontrollably as her panic increased.

"Miss Madizza-Corey, your schedule is ready. You'll meet with the guidance counselor before attending classes," Mrs. Murphy said.

Vienna absently looked around for the guidance counselor. After the tardy bell rang, a beautiful young lady walked in with radiating confidence Vienna had seldom seen. She was stunning and had a sparkle in her eye.

"Hi, you must be Vienna. I'm Echo Blight. I'll be your guidance counselor for the next two years." She held out her hand.

Vienna stood up and shook Ms. Blight's hand. As she let go, she stood there, focusing on her pounding heart and trying not to look so awkward.

"Follow me. Today will be bland, I'm afraid. It's all about learning about Sparks Boarding School, or SBS, as most girls call it." Ms. Blight twirled around without missing a beat and glided through the narrow hallway.

As she followed Ms. Blight, Vienna was mesmerized by her grace.

She was slender and tall, with sandy blonde hair that reached the top of her lower back. It was straighter and shinier than any hair Vienna had ever seen.

Ms. Blight snuck a glance to ensure Vienna followed and flashed her a pearly white smile. Her baby blue eyes sparkled against her soft, pale features.

"Valda filled you in on some of the school's history. Is that correct?" She opened the door to a small but elegantly decorated office and motioned for Vienna to sit.

"Um, yes, a little." Vienna tripped on her words as she took in the office's soft seafoam green and all the miniature woodwork on shelves.

"That's fantastic! Tell me what you know, and then I will know what to tell you more about," Ms. Blight said with a wide grin.

After Vienna finished what she had learned from her parents, Logan, and Valda, Ms. Blight began giving Vienna more details. She itched to look down and search her schedule for information on her room, roommates, and classes, but she resisted.

"Most of the important information sounds like it's been told to you. The boundaries are important for safety measures, so magic locks down the school during night hours. While you're here, you'll learn about all the realms, as you have only heard about some of them. Meals and study halls are required. Though each can be flexible depending on your needs and how things are going. If there are any issues and I am not around, you can also report to any of your teachers. Whoever you feel most comfortable with." Ms. Blight waited.

Vienna sat in wonder with some of the key points Ms. Blight told her. Though she knew some of them, the parts of how the Council created the curriculum and major events, like restructuring through major milestones, fascinated her. Learning how wars on different key topics shifted who could attend Sparks and Domar's was something new. Until now, she thought only Enchantresses attended Sparks, but she now knew it was a stepping stone to choosing a more focused route of magic. Those who are from Magyieka could attend even if they weren't Enchantresses or hadn't come into their magic.

"Vienna?"

Vienna looked up, and Ms. Blight was staring at her with concern. "What?"

"Do you have any questions?"

"The wars you speak of, were there any due to race or anything like that?"

Ms. Blight cocked her head. "We haven't had an issue with race. The wars were mostly about class and the inclusion of people from different economic backgrounds. It took centuries for people who were born into royalty or wealthy families to be able to attend." Ms. Blight paused. "Why do you ask?"

"I heard something in the office today. Someone is unhappy with a roommate, and I think it's due to their race."

Ms. Blight thought for a moment. "Race as in the magic background or more regarding race issues from the Human Realm?" Concern was evident as she waited for an answer.

"Like the Human Realm," Vienna answered flatly, trying to hide her anger.

"I see." She nodded, and Vienna didn't miss the sadness that washed over Ms. Blight's face. "Unfortunately, we do have this issue pop up occasionally. It's important if you spot any issues that may become problematic that you share so we can ensure everyone is safe at the school."

Vienna nodded in agreement and vowed to keep an eye out for Cosima.

"Would you like me to show you to your classes and then take you to your room?"

"Yes, of course. Could you also walk to them in order? Make it less challenging?"

"Of course. Give me 15 minutes, okay?" Ms. Blight got up, tucked her chair in, straightened her blouse, and left the room.

Vienna quickly grabbed her schedule as the door clicked shut. Excitement filled her as she prepared to see what courses she would take.

# *Sparks Boarding School Class Schedule*

**Corey, Vienna**—Year Nineteen—Advanced Entry
**Age:** Eighteen
**Guidance Counselor:** Ms. Blight, Echo
**Home Room:** Mr. Audovera, Dařeek

## *Semester 1*

Breakfast starts at 7:30 am—please be prompt.
School will start at 8:00 am and go until 3:45 pm.
Dinner will start at 6:00 pm—please be prompt.
Lights out and campus lockdown will occur at 9:00 pm.

| **Class** | **Professor** | **Time** |
|---|---|---|
| English: 1500-1900s | Ms. Lefèvre, Amiea | 8:00 am–8:45 am |
| Science: Astronomy | Mrs. Markeive, Elizabeth | 8:55 am–9:40 am |
| History: Witch Trials | Mr. Audovera, Dařeek | 9:50 am–10:35 am |
| Math: Calculus | Ms. Croati, Dinah | 10:45 am–11:30 am |
| *Lunch* | | 11:30 am–1:40 pm |
| The Craft of Spells | Mrs. Jaheem, Aadya | 1:50 pm–2:35 pm |
| Combat Basics | Mr. Malkayz, Josiah | 2:45 pm–3:45 pm |
| Study Hall | Any Student Commons Room | 3:55 pm–5:00 pm |

*We're happy to have you at Sparks Boarding School.*

*Welcome Aboard!*

"I'm screwed!" Vienna dropped the paper and covered her face. Even with the fear and thoughts of failure, hope and excitement rose. She focused on her conversation with Valda about Year Twenty, how she'd choose a focus and hold on to that, and the fact she had a spells class.

Ms. Blight opened the door and put a hand on Vienna's shoulder. "We will have none of that, my dear. It's always overwhelming at first, but you'll do wonderfully." Ms. Blight was very matter-of-fact; it almost helped ease Vienna's fear.

Almost. "You don't understand . . . "

"I do, Miss Madizza-Corey. I was selected as your guidance counselor because your parents know me. Well, your mother does. See," she continued as she pulled her seat over and sat by Vienna, "I was also your mother's guidance counselor. She felt you needed someone on your side." She leaned over to whisper, "But we must not speak out loud regarding why you are nervous." She straightened back up. "Remember, I am here for you, and you can come to me for anything."

"Wow . . . you look so young." Vienna took in her features, wide-eyed with shock. Ms. Blight blinked with a mysterious smile, then pivoted to leave.

Before Vienna could speak, Ms. Blight was at the door, gesturing it was time to go. "Shall we?"

Vienna was filled with questions, but it wasn't the time. She picked up her stuff and headed out to explore her new school.

# CHAPTER TWENTY

Although it took 2 hours, Vienna enjoyed the tour that showed the students the five corridors—the place they would call home. The students were split into groups of twenty and assigned in a specific wing. Until now, Vienna had no clue the school was so small. She had assumed it would consist of several hundred students, but she was wrong. Since the fifth wing was for the school staff to ensure they were always accessible to the students, that meant there were only around eighty students.

The whole building's design was precise. The Founders—the families that had established the Magyieka—had put a lot of thought into designing the perfect school. The school resembled the different elements of the magic system.

After the tour, Ms. Blight took Vienna to the west wing—where Vienna would spend the year. "The west wing is called *Winderaia*, meaning kind one, in Elvish," Ms. Blight explained.

"Wait, so we are automatically placed into a wing, and each wing's name is . . . descriptive?" Vienna had stopped at the base of the west staircase. It looked like a hole in the wall, save for the fancy gold border that resembled waves created by harsh wind. The gold was thin, light, and inviting.

"Excellent, Vienna. Occasionally, it seems the sorting places students in wings that do not fit them. But typically, the sorting places a student in a spot that helps her blossom. The technology includes data, like the student's personal qualities, interests, strengths, and weaknesses. It's very advanced." Ms. Blight smiled down at Vienna before starting up the staircase.

Vienna followed. The stairwell wasn't as dark and gloomy as she'd expected. The entire wall was a window overlooking the garden to the west. She admired how bright the stars were. And everything was so green; there were flowers and trees everywhere. In the center of the yard was a large fountain. The basin underneath was shaped like a W. Seeing the fountain filling the W with bright blue water was mystical. All around were small trails—not sidewalks—with an occasional bench or picnic table.

"This is beautiful. Does each wing have the same design?" she asked.

"Yes, although each, as you probably can guess, has a unique water fountain design into which the fountain flows." Ms. Blight paused beside Vienna to admire the landscape.

Past the yard were shadows of mountains, dark in contrast, almost as if they were cursed. Vienna didn't inquire about it. Something told her she wasn't quite ready to hear the story.

"That range is Schaduw, which is Dutch for shadow. This describes the outer and darker limits of the Magic Realm. You see, we are in . . . Well, I guess the best description would be a supernatural bubble. Outside of it, things are darker and less kind. You'll learn more about it in history." Vienna was unprepared for the warning in her tone, so when Ms. Blight started ascending the stairs, she quickly followed, praying it would ease her pounding heart.

Once they hit the common room at the top of the stairs, Vienna knew she could be happy in this place. There was another large window overlooking the west yard. On the other side of the room was an elegant white sectional, large enough to seat most of the students in the west wing. There was also a sizable red mahogany bookshelf, a marble fireplace, two large gold-encased glass coffee tables, and a painting of the front of the school. After hearing a quiet jingle, Vienna looked up. Above the center of the room was a massive, intricate crystal chandelier that scattered rainbows into the high circular ceiling. The room's shape caused the chandelier's jingle to echo for an extended time, filling the room with comfort.

"This is incredible! Are all the wings like this?" Vienna whispered in awe.

"No," Ms. Blight replied. "They all have a unique color theme, though the setup is the same, as is the painting and window. But each wing has a design of its own. We describe this one as wintry." She beamed.

"Were you in this wing?"

"I was. Each wing has an assigned guidance counselor—typically one who knows everything about the wing. It helps when you've spent time there yourself. It's a good system." Vienna watched as Ms. Blight went into the room with pride.

"Can I ask you something?" Vienna asked.

"Anything, Miss Madizza-Corey."

"Please call me Vienna." She smiled. "I noticed only a couple of male teachers, and most of the teachers are Ms. Very few are Mrs. Why is that?"

"A little off topic, but a good question," Ms. Blight said with a smirk. "It's hard to get a position here if you're married, which means single people are hired. It's not that they won't hire you if you're married; it's more that it's hard to be here full time if you need to go home. It's a boarding school, so most teachers live here. Some of the teachers are married, but most are single or widowed. The married ones are granted permission to be home at night if we have enough staff to keep the students safe. Or they have spouses on the Council, so they stay busy, or are in other careers that keep them away from home as well. Per your reference to men"—she looked at her with sadness—"unfortunately, it also doesn't pay equivalent to many more prestigious lines of work. Most teachers are women. Many of the men tend to move to supervisors or administrators. It's not much different from the Human Realm."

"Some things are problematic in most places, it seems." Vienna walked to the window and surveyed its natural beauty.

"You're holding back. What else would you like to know?" Ms. Blight watched her intensely.

"Why *exactly* are we locked down at night?" Vienna turned to see Ms. Blight's face.

Ms. Blight's smile faded. "There is danger in every world, Vienna. We need to keep you all safe. Wandering around could endanger you or other students. Think about the dangers of walking around some of the most crime-ridden cities in the Human Realm, then magnify that with magic."

"Got it," Vienna replied. She shivered at the thought of the most atrocious crimes in the Human Realm and what they would be like with magic.

Shaking the thoughts away, she bounced from her heels to her toes, feeling awkward in the silence. She looked at Ms. Blight with curiosity. The beauty reminded her of the student she'd met earlier that day. The pale hair, blue eyes, and the elegance. Before she could ask if there was any relation, Vienna heard a lot of shuffling, footsteps, giggling, and talking. She froze.

"It's okay. I'll be making a speech before I leave. You can sit now or wait."

Without waiting, Vienna rushed to the couch and sat down. Standing next to the guidance counselor, she wasn't about to meet all the other girls. It was bad enough that she wasn't in the mass.

*I'm going to freak out,* she thought as she started to break into a sweat. *Why am I so nervous?* Suddenly, her anxiety disappeared, replaced with excitement and energy. She looked up in time for the other girls to walk in and for Ms. Blight to wink at her.

"Thank you," she mouthed at Ms. Blight. Vienna wondered how many tricks she had up her sleeve. For now, she was thankful for the vanishing anxiety.

The girls listened as Ms. Blight discussed the rules, consequences, and expectations. Grumbling rattled the walls when she told them that if they weren't in bed by curfew, they were locked out of their wing and had to request access from a school counselor or a staff member on duty that night.

When the speech ended, each girl went to find her room. They were automatically placed in a room labeled with name tags on the side of the door. Apparently, spaces were based on similar interests and lifestyles, though Vienna doubted she'd have much in common when she was raised elsewhere.

As the final girl left the sitting room, Vienna watched them all scatter, dreading finding her room. There were so many girls! She was afraid she would end up with a mean girl. She'd known many girls back home who people thought were sweet, kind, and inviting but turned out to be cruel, callus, and deceitful. She refused to look around for familiar faces, hoping to calm her anxiety.

"Might as well be on your way. Sitting here will only delay the inevitable," Ms. Blight chirped right before she gracefully turned and exited without waiting for a reply.

"Right," Vienna responded under her breath. She stood up and walked down the hall. The area was much larger than she'd expected. After checking each door, she finally spotted her name on the top of a list of four:

***Vienna Madizza-Corey***
***Celine Castro***
***Iris Ulfred***
***Nessa Flint***

*Celine Castro. Why does that name sound familiar?* she thought. Then, she heard a high-pitched squeal, *"EEK!"* Before she could cover her ears, she was engulfed in an embrace, and all she saw was a glance of almost white hair. Celine. The beautiful blonde from the Mystickart.

"It's like destiny," Celine said before letting Vienna go. "Seriously, what else can it be?" Without missing a beat, she walked into the room and gasped. "This is *beautiful* . . . What bed do you want?" she asked as she twirled around.

"Um . . . bottom bunk? I get up a lot through the night."

"Done! I like to be up high." Celine smiled.

"What about the rest of us?" Vienna turned toward the new voice. A girl with long brown hair, large brown eyes, and light olive skin stood at the door. She was slender but not skinny. Her presence demanded attention, but she had an air of kindness. Right now, she had her hands folded near her hips. As Vienna took in the sight of the girl, she felt an instant connection.

"Sorry, we were tossing ideas around," Celine answered.

"What ideas are you tossing around?" asked a soft, sweet voice. A tall redhead peeked around the brunette.

"We're talking about beds. There are two bunk beds, and those"—the brunette pointed at the one farthest away—"are available and look perfect."

"Sounds good to me. I'll take whatever you don't." The redhead grinned widely at everyone in turn. "I'm Nessa. What are your names?"

"I'm Iris, and I'll take the bottom bunk," the brunette responded with a tight smile. She turned to Vienna and Celine. "And you are?"

"I'm Celine, and this is Vienna. We met on the way here. Isn't that great?" Her enthusiasm oozed.

"It's nice to meet you guys." Iris yawned as she stretched. "Sorry if I came off moody. It's been a long day."

Before anyone could respond, a loud *thump* and then an argument echoed through the hall. The four girls looked at each other and ran to the door. They peeked out to see the door next to theirs was wide open. They moved down the hall to see what was going on.

"Are you sure we shouldn't stay in our room?" Nessa whispered, but she was met with silence.

Several girls were inside the room yelling at each other. From Vienna's view, one girl was singled out because she'd made herself at home on a top bunk, and a petite brunette with olive skin and red lips was saying that was her bed.

Cosima. They made eye contact, but Vienna said nothing. Her stomach turned acidic, and her heart broke for the girl Cosima screamed at. She thought about the cocoa remark from earlier and looked back up at the girl on the bunk. Vienna was filled with rage, and a zapping sound hummed in her ears. Electricity nipped at her fingers, but she closed her eyes, silencing the magic that begged to protect the girl.

"It's first come, first served," she snapped.

Vienna opened her eyes to see the targeted girl. She clenched her teeth, her cheeks pulsing as she fought with Cosima. The girl's honey eyes brightened as her face darkened with anger, and Vienna felt a strong sense of admiration for the girl—she was a fighter.

Three other girls stood beside Cosima but a foot behind, making it clear that Cosima was their leader. They swarmed around their prey like vultures. Vienna felt her insides harden as her need to protect this girl pushed all other thoughts aside, but there was no need. After Cosima used a handful of foul language, the loner grabbed her bags and flung them onto a bottom bunk. She stormed out of the room, face red and hands shaking. Vienna and her roommates looked at one another. Celine led the way as they all followed the girl to the common room.

"Sounds like it's going to be a long year," Celine said.

"Yeah, not exactly what anyone wants after coming here," the girl replied.

"I'm Iris. This is Nessa, Celine, and Vienna." She pointed to each girl.

"I'm Jayla Laveau." Defeat laced her eyes. "I can't believe I'm stuck with those three. They are so . . . I don't know." She shook her head and sat on the couch with a huff.

"We are right next to you, so if you need anything, let us know, okay?" Nessa chimed in.

Jayla smiled and relaxed. "Thanks."

"Any time you want to hang out in our room, you can. We have plenty of room," Vienna offered.

"Thanks. I'll take you up on that." Jayla smiled.

"I couldn't help but notice your amber eyes look like honey. They are beautiful, especially against your vibrant black skin. It made me look at each of us," Nessa said, looking around at each girl. We each have unique features. "Are you all from the Magic Realm?"

"I'm from the Shadow Realm," Jayla answered. "My bright eyes are rare, but they help me see in the dark, and I am also able to hunt better than most of my family. My mom has similar eyes, but they are dark amber. We joke that it's my superpower."

"That's incredible," Vienna admitted. "When I first saw you, your eyes made a huge statement. They screamed, 'Goddess'." She laughed. "My green eyes aren't common, but they're not exactly rare. Anyway"—she tossed her hand in the air—"I'm from the Human Realm. This is my first time in Magyieka."

Every girl stared at Vienna. Nervous, Vienna looked at Celine, who just shrugged. "We don't get a lot of Earth girls here. It's not something I'd announce until you're comfortable with someone," she suggested, and the rest agreed.

"Where are you from, Nessa?" Celine asked.

"I'm from the Magic Realm. I live less than an hour from Sparks," Nessa answered.

"I don't know all the realms yet, but I thought the Magic Realm would be where most of the students are from," Vienna admitted.

"That's true," Iris answered. "The Magic Realm has one of the largest populations of all the realms. It's where most Enchanters are from. I'm assuming you have a history and spells class. You'll learn a lot in there in the first week. It will help a lot."

Vienna nodded, and they headed to their room as the common area filled with other students. On the way through the hall, the three girls in Jayla's assigned room snickered and slammed their door, leaving Vienna uneasy. Closing their door, they all sat on the floor.

"Nessa, you're from the Magic Realm, and Jayla is from the Shadow Realm; what about you, Celine?" Iris asked.

"I'm part of the Magic Realm." She didn't expand, and Vienna watched as she shifted away. It was as though she was hiding part of herself.

"Iris, you haven't told us where you're from," Vienna said, shifting the topic and watching Celine relax. "Are you from the Magic Realm as well?"

"We move around a lot. I've lived in the Human Realm for a short time, but I have spent most of my time in the Magic Realm and a little time in the Shadow Realm."

All the girls looked at her, but nobody spoke. Vienna didn't know that was possible and wondered how her family was allowed to move between the realms.

"I didn't know what was possible. That's cool!" Nessa responded.

"Same." Celine blinked in shock.

"Does everyone know what their abilities are yet?" Vienna asked nervously.

"We all have some basic skills, which you'll learn in spells class. But we don't get a huge focus or deep understanding of our natural abilities or strengths until the year we graduate," Celine answered.

"Typically, anyway. Some come into their talents early. Like one girl last year who realized she could transport between realms with no portal, and two years ago, a guy tapped into his ability to walk between the realms while sleeping or focusing on the act, or something like that," Jayla said excitedly.

"What a complex world Magyieka is." Vienna didn't mean to say it out loud and blushed as all the girls laughed.

They bantered about their lives back home. It felt natural, and Vienna realized everything would be okay. Nobody's life was perfect, but they'd all had good lives. She was the only one who had no clue that magic existed until recently, which gave her a disadvantage. But these four girls helped her relax.

Before they all realized how late it was, it was dinnertime in the cafeteria, so they rushed off to find seats together.

▽ △ △ ▽ ⊕

The cafeteria was more like a five-star restaurant. Each table had a white silk tablecloth and a vase with a bouquet of carnations, and the silverware was gold and lay next to white and gold China plates. Each set had a crystal wine glass and a fresh roll.

"Are meals like this every night, or is it for special occasions?" Vienna wondered.

"I've heard it's always elegant, but it's even more so on the first night and during holidays," replied Celine.

"This is going to be hard to get used to."

They all agreed and then found a table in the middle of the room.

Over the next hour, they were served a five-course meal, ending with dessert. As the last dish was delivered, the school's dean, Ms. Maria, got up and gave a drawn-out speech emphasizing the rules and expectations of the school. Next, each teacher introduced themselves and offered stories from when they were in school. Most were humorous, some were dark, and a few were more on the creepy or romantic side. However, each professor expressed excitement for the year. The last to stand up for an introduction was Mr. Dařeek Audovera, the history professor.

"I met him earlier today," Vienna whispered to the others. "He's nice, though I'm curious about how he dresses. It's very 1800s, you know?" They all agreed, and as Vienna sat up, she spotted Mr. Audovera looking at her as if he'd heard every word. With a slight wink, he returned to finish his speech, and Vienna began feeling uneasy.

After dinner, the girls went back to their rooms, and in less than an hour, Jayla knocked on their door. "Can I please stay in here tonight?" she begged. "I can't be in that room. I'll barely take up any space, I promise."

"Of course!" they all said at once. They arranged the furniture to make a spot next to the bunk beds and helped make it as comfortable as possible.

"Thanks, guys. I was so worried I'd have to stay all night in there."

"I wonder if we could talk to the dean or a counselor about it. Maybe they would let you move over here," Nessa suggested.

Iris hummed. "I don't know about that. When they talked to us earlier, they were hell-bent on people staying in their assigned rooms."

"You'd think they would make an exception when someone's being treated poorly, though," Celine argued.

"I think it's worth a shot. I'd be willing to talk with Ms. Blight in the morning if you'd like," Vienna offered.

"I would like that very much. Anything to get me somewhere safe and comfortable."

"It's set. I'll meet you guys at breakfast first thing in the morning. Deal?"

"Deal," they said in unison.

Without warning, the light turned off for the night, and the gasps of dozens of girls could be heard throughout the wing. Vienna smiled at the sound and slowly fell asleep.

# CHAPTER
# TWENTY-ONE

"I want to help," Ms. Blight sighed, "but there's not much I can do. See, to move Jayla into another room, I'd have to file a complaint to the school board, which can take a lot of time and cause the board to look into the reasoning and create major issues with not just Jayla, but anyone else in the room. Which could come back to haunt Jayla and anyone who befriends her."

Vienna pursed her lips. "Okay, I guess." She got up to leave, but turned around. "How exactly do they sort people? You said it was based on similarities or something. I can believe it with my room, but Jayla getting placed in that room doesn't make sense."

"The system sorts based on class." Ms. Blight looked down and shook her head. "They also put in similar interests and key personality traits. If you look at your room, many of you have strong family lines, but you are also welcoming and have a strong moral compass rather than judging people based on who their family is. You also share common desires to learn and enjoy the outdoors. Many rooms have kids interested in not liking the outdoors and are cynical. While the other rooms have kids who desire the outdoors and are very intellectual and rather shy."

"I see. Guess that makes sense. Thank you!" Vienna moved toward the door.

"Wait, Vienna . . . " Ms. Blight stood up and walked to Vienna's side. She leaned down and touched Vienna's shoulder. "I can't do anything in an official capacity. However, if she were to stay in your room and *didn't get caught*, then I don't see what the problem is. Just . . . be careful." She winked at Vienna and shooed her out of her office.

As the bell rang and all the students rushed to their classes, Vienna left Ms. Blight's room, sad but hopeful. She had something to tell her roommates, even if it wasn't exactly what they'd expected.

"Okay," she whispered to herself. "First class is English, room sixty-six. Snap, I'm going to be late!" She took off running after realizing she wasn't close to the class. She'd spent the last hour talking with Ms. Blight and had no food or time to prepare for class.

Several minutes later, she found the class and rushed in, hoping the professor would be late. No such luck there.

*Crap! Crappity! Crap! What a poor way to start the day.*

"No worries, Miss Madizza-Corey," came a gentle voice. "Ms. Blight phoned and let me know you'd be late. Please take a seat." The professor, Ms. Lefèvre, looked to be in her fifties. She was short and plump, had soft round features and graying light brown hair, and wore nothing but black. She smiled at Vienna and motioned toward the last open desk in the classroom.

Vienna searched the room for a familiar face but found no one. That was disappointing. This would also be her activity and test day's homeroom, so not having friends here wouldn't be great. She did spot a girl with a long blonde braid that looked familiar, but she was busy.

"All right. Now that we're all together, let's get started." Ms. Lefèvre spoke matter-of-factly, with no more soothing laced into her voice. "Who here can tell me something they know about different writing styles used in the 1500s?" Nobody raised their hand.

"Who cares? Nobody is going to utilize styles from ancient times." Vienna looked to the back row and watched Cosima toss her dark brown hair over her shoulder in victory. *How did I miss her sitting there?*

"Awe, but it isn't ancient. Perhaps you can define ancient for us?"

Vienna looked between the two as Cosima's cheeks turned the color of a soft red rose.

"Whatever," she snarled before crossing her arms. The rest of the class giggled but was silenced as Ms. Lefèvre flicked her finger, signaling her impatience.

"Surely *somebody* knows about English from before the 21st century. In this course, you will learn English from 1500 to 1800." She paused and looked around.

"Why is it important? We don't write like they used to, do we? So why waste our time?" a small girl in the back corner of the room said bluntly.

"Great question. One I often hear. Since we access elements that grant us control of them, it's important to understand written language from past centuries. As we learn, using our ancestors' books, we must understand what they mean. This is not always an easy thing to do. Take, for example, how many people struggle to read and understand William Shakespeare's work. To fully understand messages from the past, you must understand what you are reading. We will spend time each semester reading books from each century and decipher what they're saying and how it's all being said," she concluded.

Several minutes passed before a strong voice spoke up. "Many of us have ancestors who wrote their spells down. If we try to mimic them, don't pronounce things correctly, or are confused by the message, it can backfire and cause harm or even death." Her voice was oddly familiar. Vienna looked. It was the girl with the long blonde braid. She lifted her head. *Valda!*

Valda made brief eye contact and then looked away. Not even a smile. Vienna's face burned after flashing her broad smile and waving. What was Valda's deal?

The rest of the class passed by slowly. Ms. Lefèvre gave each student a copy of *The Discoverie of Witchcraft* by Reginald Scot from 1584 and *A Midsummer Night's Dream* by William Shakespeare, with instructions to read and compare the two books to today's literature.

"The bell will ring in less than 2 minutes. I want you to start thinking about someone to pair up with in class. There should be no more than three in a group. You will read these books together or separately at an equal pace and discuss them. At the end of the first quarter, you will present your findings. Please find a partner as quickly as possible, as a quarter moves quickly. Next quarter, we will move on to the 1600s and 1700s, and then next semester, we will cover the 1800s and 1900s. Also, note that the book by Reginald Scot will be used in your history class. So please pay special attention to it —" *Ring!!* The class all but ran out the door before she could finish.

Vienna looked back, hoping to make eye contact with Valda, but she was already gone. Vienna's arms went numb. Who else was she going to pair up with?

"Professor," she asked, "does the partner have to be in this class or someone reading the same material?"

"I'm sorry, dear, but they must be in this class. You will be creating a presentation, remember? Don't worry; you'll meet someone soon."

Vienna bit her lip as uncertainty remained.

"Best be off, or you'll be late for your next class, too. Hurry along, dear." Ms. Lefèvre dismissed Vienna by picking up a book and beginning to read.

▽△△▽✳

The day went by quickly. Most of the classes were filled with talk about how they would function. She had Celine and Iris in her history class and Jayla in her spells and astronomy class. Still, she didn't know anyone in the others. She felt oddly out of place. Most girls didn't seem as inviting as she'd hoped they would be.

Lunch was like eating breakfast for royalty. There was a little of everything, and it all looked pristine. The school had hired a talented crew to run the kitchen. Like last night, the meal was five courses. Not only was it well-balanced, but the flavor was fantastic. Vienna couldn't help but be excited to try breakfast in the morning.

Once she found the other girls, they decided on their chosen spot to work together on their assignments outside to enjoy the sunlight. As they left the building, nearly the entire school was also outside, enjoying the beautiful weather.

"I thought there would be fewer people out here since we have to sit in the grass to study," Iris chirped. "I love nature, and the grass is freshly cut."

"No need to sell it to me." Nessa nudged her, and Iris blushed.

"Same here," Celine replied, "but it looks like there are several trees to choose from, so we get some shade." She shrugged.

"How about that one?" Nessa pointed to a tree next to some running water. "I love the sound of water. It's so relaxing."

Heading in that direction and picking up their scattered debris, they were able to make the area comfortable for studying. They all chose to read material for their history class, as the homework load was heavy.

After studying for a bit, Vienna cleared her throat, breaking the silence. The group looked up in question. "Why don't we make Jayla an unofficial roommate since the school can't put her in our room."

"That's a great idea!" Jayla squealed. She moved to her knees and sat on her feet. She was glowing with excitement.

"She can share a bed with me, or we can make one for her," Nessa offered.

"I'm in," Celine agreed with a nod.

"You guys are amazing." Jayla smiled.

"Enough of this mushy stuff. Let's get back to this thrilling material," Iris teased.

Breaking the study group's groove, a shadow fell over the girls. "Hello, ladies." They all looked up to see the face that went with the snarky voice—Cosima. She was with two of her roommates.

"Cosima. Remi. Yasmin," Jayla hissed.

Cosima placed her hand on her hip with a tight smile and sneered down at them. "It appears you found our favorite study spot. If you'd like, we can show you a few other options. I mean . . . you didn't think the spot was open because nobody else wanted it, did you?" Remi and Yasmin giggled.

"Right, that was the VIP sign we tossed into the trash," Nessa deadpanned.

"We can move," Iris whispered, but Jayla nudged her. Iris blinked, but remained silent.

"Look," Cosima continued, "we asked nicely. You don't want to get on our bad side. Like, seriously . . . do *not* piss us off," she emphasized.

"Likewise." Vienna stood up and matched Cosima's domineering stance.

"Do we have a problem here?" Both groups turned to find Mr. Audovera standing with his hands behind his back.

Cosima glared at Vienna before giving Mr. Audovera a sweet smile. "Of course not," she answered. "We were welcoming Vienna to the school. We know she's a bit behind and all. So, we wanted to make her feel welcome. Weren't we, girls?" she asked her minions, who smiled in agreement. "See? No trouble at all." She glanced back at Vienna, eyes still smoldering.

"Actually," Vienna added, "they were letting us know that we can keep this spot from now on to make sure I feel at home."

"You little . . . " Cosima caught herself and cleared her throat. She fluttered her lashes at the professor, glared at Vienna again, and walked away, minions in tow.

"Well played." Mr. Audovera smirked before turning and walking away.

"Oh . . . my . . . *gosh*! That was brilliant!" Nessa squealed.

"Where did that come from?" asked Iris.

Vienna shrugged and leaned back on her hands. "If she wants to play unfairly, I will too."

"I'm impressed," Celine added. "What a great way to call dibs on this sweet spot."

"We only have a few minutes of study hall left. What do you guys want to do for the next hour?" Jayla asked. She stretched and yawned, but she didn't look tired. "We don't have dinner until six."

"What options do we have?" Vienna asked.

"There is quite a bit we can do," Celine added. "We can find a sport to play, go back to our room and chill out, go for a walk, explore the school, or even volunteer to help in the kitchen for dinner."

They sat silently until the bell rang, then quickly gathered their stuff. "I say we go back to the room for now and help Jayla feel a little more at home," offered Iris. They all agreed and headed to their room.

The door was ajar. They looked at one another and hesitantly pushed the door open. Someone had tossed everything in the room: emptying bags, scattering clothes, and throwing books all over the floor.

"This had to be Cosima and them, right?" Nessa guessed.

"I don't know. I wouldn't think anyone would do this . . . would they?" Celine asked.

Just then, Cosima walked by with Remi and Yasmin right behind.

Vienna looked at the other girls and turned back to Cosima. She couldn't tell whether Cosima was genuinely shocked by the mess. Either way, Cosima snickered as if she knew something would happen.

"We need to report this, don't we?" Iris asked.

Vienna nodded. "I think we should. I'll go down to Ms. Blight and talk to her."

Celine started grabbing clothes. "We can stay here and start cleaning up. Right, guys?" In agreement, they began cleaning up.

"Okay, I'll be back soon to help."

$$\triangledown \,\, \triangle\!\!\!\triangle \,\, \triangle \,\, \triangledown \,\, \circledast$$

"I wish I could help you more." Ms. Blight walked Vienna to the door. They had come up with no leads during their hour-long discussion. Cosima's group had been in the study hall the entire hour, and there were no security cameras in the wings to help identify the culprits.

"Thanks for trying." Vienna left without saying more. She was too busy thinking. Who would ransack their room, and why? It didn't make sense. She left the office, ready to fill in the girls with what she found out, but she didn't make it far.

Outside the office door, she hit something and lost her balance. She grunted as she fell to the ground.

"Easy. Has anyone ever told you to keep your eyes forward when you walk?" A girl laughed.

Looking up, Valda smiled down at her. Valda reached her arm out and helped Vienna to her feet.

"Thanks." Vienna patted down her pants, and dust from the unkempt floor drifted around her. She felt herself turn red and stared at Valda. "I thought you were perturbed at me, but I couldn't think of anything you'd be mad at me about. What's going on?"

Valda squinted her eyes and had a far-off look, but she didn't reply.

Vienna, eyes wide with annoyance, snapped her fingers and looked directly into Valda's eyes. "Anyone home?" She snapped again.

Valda blinked, then took a step back. "No, I wasn't angry."

"What is your deal? Your mood swings are giving me whiplash." Vienna stared at Valda, trying to sort through her feelings. She settled on hurt, confused, and upset. After several moments without a response, Vienna started to walk away.

She felt a vice-like grip on her forearm before getting too far. She swung around to see Valda's deadpan face seconds before she pulled her in the other direction.

Stumbling, Vienna balanced herself as Valda moved them quickly to the bathroom. Inside, Valda slammed her hip against the sink, placing both hands behind her. She held the counter and bowed her head. Her eyes were closed, and Vienna could see the anxiety. Valda inhaled deeply and quietly exhaled.

"You are seriously freaking me out, Valda. What is going on?"

"Look." She opened her eyes and met Vienna's. "I can't tell you too much, but please know I am . . . " She looked to the ceiling, and a single tear slid down her cheek. "I'm in the middle of something, and I'm torn on what to do. I can't be your friend here. It's complicated." She met Vienna's eyes with her own, and Vienna knew she was telling the truth.

"That doesn't make sense. What's going on?" She shifted toward Valda, but as soon as her back left the wall, Valda moved sideways to extend the gap between them.

"I can't talk about it. Remember that when others are around, I can't acknowledge you. I wish I could. But I can't. Not right now." Shame crossed her features as she shook her head in sorrow.

This wasn't a choice. Valda was fighting something deep inside. Vienna sighed. "Okay, I trust you." They stood in silence for several minutes. "So . . . when *can* we spend time together?"

"Any time outside school, beyond the walls, or even like this."

"What if someone walks in?"

"Then we act like we're leaving the bathroom. That's not likely, though. The professors are sticklers on keeping kids in class."

"I didn't think you would be able to come. Did you know you would be coming?"

"It was a last-minute thing. Took some convincing. My . . . guardian needed some persuasion."

"Who's your guardian?"

"My mom. We aren't close, so I devised a better name." She shrugged like it was nothing. Vienna's heart sank. She couldn't imagine not being close to her mom.

Before she could reply, the bathroom door opened.

Valda jumped, grabbed some paper towels as if she had just washed her hands, and left the bathroom in less time than the girl entered a stall.

Vienna stood there with a million questions. Why couldn't they be seen as friends? How could they meet outside the walls when the other lands and surrounding areas were off-limits?

# CHAPTER TWENTY-TWO

When her friends had fallen asleep, Vienna laid there, still as the night sky, and was emotionally drained. After all the lights were turned off, she used what was left of her energy and rolled over.

As her body relaxed, she got the faintest whiff of smoke. Energized with fear that sent shockwaves down her limbs, she bolted upright. She looked around the room, frantic, and found the other girls were sound asleep. Fearful of waking them for no reason, she crept to the door, gently turned the knob, and quietly closed the door behind her.

Down the hall, a faint glow illuminated the far wall. Quiet chanting echoed toward her, and she realized the person . . . no, *persons*, were chanting in Latin.

*De profundis serpant.*
*Metum ex alto.*
*Introeant, custodiant.*

*Caecus ad visum,*
*niger ut nox.*

They repeated it several times before there was a pause. Then, the chanting rose again. With her curiosity piqued, she crept closer. A light showed under the door of Cosima's room. Before she reached the door, she was grabbed from behind, a hand tight over her mouth.

"Shh . . . don't make a sound," a deep baritone commanded. Her heart skipped a beat, and her body tensed. She was frozen with fear and unable to move.

Vienna shivered as cold air surrounded her. She gasped, looking around; she had just been standing in the hallway! Now, she stood in the middle of a beautiful cave with glowing moths the color of sapphires and rubies. Their wings twitched and released golden dust that drifted to the ground. She followed the gold trail of dust, resembling golden sand. It twinkled from the glow of the moths' bodies.

"Beautiful," she whispered, so quiet that she barely heard the words herself.

She turned to find who had captured her, but no one was there.

Her heart pounded in her chest. "Who's there?" she hollered into the cave. How could she have been so foolish and unaware? *Stupid moths*, she thought.

A well-toned chest appeared several seconds later, but the face was hidden in the shadows.

"Who are you?" she demanded.

"Give me one second, V."

"Logan?" she screeched. Reprieve won against the shock, and without thinking, she ran toward the figure, wrapping her arms and legs around him. She slid her head onto his neck and began to sob.

Thick biceps squeezed her waist, holding her firm against his body. There were no words, only a warm embrace. He pulled her hair across her face, exposing her damp lashes.

"Foolish girl. What if it hadn't been me?" His words rattled his chest, but the emotion seemed empty.

"I knew it was you. I can feel you, Logan." The words came out without thought. She flushed. As she pulled her head back, she felt the flesh of his stomach against her thighs. Surprised, she looked down.

*Sweat. Where did the sweat come from?* she thought.

"Why are you so sweaty?"

"I ran here. I had no other way to reach you without being caught or detected. I wasn't supposed to contact you, but this was too important."

"Wait, what do you mean you ran? We're in the middle of nowhere." She waved her arms to make her point.

"Where in a land of magic, V. Anything's possible." He smiled.

She knew he was hiding something, but she didn't want to spoil this time.

"Where's your shirt?" The words were airy and faint. "And why are your shorts shredded?"

She tried to drop to the ground, but he didn't release her. Instead, he placed his forehead to hers, his breath quick and shallow.

"V." His voice trembled, and he pulled her body tight to his chest.

Vienna bit her lip; warmth spread across her stomach and traveled down her legs. She shivered, desire rising.

Logan shifted his head, allowing his lips to brush hers, then licked the corner of her mouth, requesting entrance. She withheld, unsure of the emotions overcoming her. He ran his tongue across her bottom lip, and Vienna froze. She closed her eyes as he pulled her lip into his mouth. The heat burst from her chest, replacing the night chill she once felt.

His heart matched hers, then grew hotter until waves of steam covered his skin and moistened Vienna's clothes. Without returning his kiss, she broke away.

"You're hot." She gasped as she pulled back, tracing the steam from his body with her hand.

"You make me feel alive, V." He moved in, his eyes locked on her lips.

Her heart fluttered, but she pushed away thoughts of giving in to her desire. Squashing the warmth, she sighed and unwrapped her legs, placing them back into the cold dirt.

"Why are you here?" she squeaked. "I thought you couldn't come this way." She stepped back, instantly missing his body pressing against her own.

"I shouldn't be here, but I had no choice." He growled, taking a step toward her.

"What do you mean, you had no choice?"

"Can you listen for once?" he snarled.

Irritated, she took a step forward, matching his determination. "Maybe if you didn't take so long to—"

"I don't have time to explain everything." His features darkened, and his pupils covered his irises.

"Okay." This was no time for sarcasm, she realized. A chill sank into her bones. She shivered from a mixture of fear and anticipation. *What could be vital enough that this visit isn't a friendly one?*

As if reading her mind, Logan began. "There have been whispers of an ancient evil roaming the area. Darkness has started to cover the hills earlier each day. No one knows where it comes from, but . . . " He paused and started to pace.

"But what, Logan?" She watched his muscles spasm, fighting the rage he was holding back.

"The whispers say it's because the Quintessence has awoken." He turned toward her, no longer pacing. Shocked, her mind searched for a response. *The Quintessence. It can't be.*

"What is the darkness that looms?" she blurted out. "Wait, I heard chanting tonight when you grabbed me. Was that part of it? A summoning?"

"It could be. We aren't sure who all is in on it." Frustrated, his pace quickened. Vienna watched as his features hardened. Deep in thought, he stared at the ground.

"So, what is the darkness?" she asked again. "And what does it mean?"

Logan stopped pacing. "It means you're a target for those threatened by your potential. It means you need protection," he hesitated, and pain laced his features. "Protection I can't provide," he grumbled as he shot his hand through his sweat-drenched hair.

"What do you mean, my potential?"

"You're powerful, and maybe more powerful than we realized," Logan said.

"Do you think I might be the Quintessence as well?" Vienna raised her eyebrow and waited. Logan stopped, but didn't answer.

"Why aren't you answering me?"

"Because I don't know what I believe about Spirit and Quintessence, and my focus is your safety, not your importance," Logan snapped.

"Message received," Vienna whispered.

"Look, all I can tell you is that over the next several months, you'll learn a lot of information that will shock you. You must be careful whom you trust, V. Not everyone you *believe* has your back." He moved forward and held her shoulder, his eyes drilling into her soul. At that moment, she realized he was afraid for her beyond what she'd understood before. Her heart sank, the weight hitting her stomach and souring.

"How will I know who to trust?" Her heart sank as a wall of emotions hit her.

"Trust your instincts. Too many people talk themselves out of what their gut is telling them." He placed his forehead on hers, and warmth flooded over her body.

"Okay," she whispered, overcome by the fluttering of her heart.

She caressed his face with her palm. A blue glow illuminated, enhancing his stunning features. She rubbed her thumb over his lip. He stiffened, and she felt the muscles in his jaw pulse, clenching, then relaxing. He looked down into her eyes, and she inhaled at the sight of his eyes. They were inhuman; black 1 minute, brown the next. His breathing deepened, and he closed his eyes and leaned into her caress. He reached up and clasped her hand in his. Vienna smiled, proud she wasn't terrified of his eyes changing. This time, the change held a comfort to her, and she realized it was part of him.

"I've missed you," she said with a sigh.

"I can smell your emotions." His growl vibrated his chest.

Her breath became deep and shallow, and her voice was squeaky. "Sometimes when your eyes go black, I can't help but wonder if you're dangerous. It doesn't matter how my heart feels, because thoughts of Demons and Werewolves take over, and I want to run."

"V, never forget how much you mean to me. I'll never harm you. Deep down, I think you know that. Why is it so hard for you to admit you have feelings for me?" he asked.

"You have hurt me. Even if your eyes didn't shift, how do I know you won't abandon me again?"

"I've always been with you, V. Some souls can't be separated," Logan growled.

Vienna's heart paused at his words, and her heartbeat sped up. Logan pulled her closer. She heard him smell her hair and felt the rumble in his chest before a feline vibration escaped his throat.

"Wha—" A loud snap cut her off. She turned toward the sound and saw nothing. Embarrassed, she turned to Logan, but he was gone.

"Logan?" She ran to where he had hidden, but he wasn't there. The moths that earlier illuminated Logan's soft features now stormed in frantic circles around the cave, mimicking startled bats.

She ran to the cave entrance and saw lightning hitting the trees around her. There was no sign of Logan. All she saw was a large eight-foot feline body with blackened navy hair that lay on black roots. The creature had a thick lion's mane, and the massive muscles from its four limbs rippled as it moved. Seconds before it took off into the forest, it looked back, and Vienna took a step back. Between its sharply pointed black ears protruded ebony horns, resembling those of an elk, and scars of blue showed imperfection in the antlers. The moonlight lit up its face, and the blackened navy hair brightened across the lion's wide snout and radiated the golden eyes that stared at her. The creature roared, sending birds fluttering into the sky. As it turned, she realized the tail was like a panther.

"What are you, you majestic cat?" Vienna watched as the creature disappeared into the night. "Like a black panther with blue hair and the body and face of a lion, but elk antlers." She wondered if this was Logan's Shifter form or the reason he left.

Vienna backed into the cave as the wind picked up and rain began to pour. Lightning continued to strike around the cave, blocking the way out. Thunder crackled, and Vienna's body broke out into goosebumps.

"Where did you go?" she yelled. Part of her hoped he was near and would hear her, but she knew better. He was gone, but how? *How did he disappear? And how could she be calm when frenzied moths swarmed around her head?*

"Focus. Breathe." She tried to soothe herself, inhaling through her nose and exhaling through her mouth. She focused on the gold dust falling off the moths and how it slowly drifted to the ground.

Several moments later, she walked back to the cave's entrance. The lightning was gone. She closed her eyes and, gathering all her courage, she headed into the pouring rain—clueless about where to go or where she was. But she was determined to make it back to Sparks. She couldn't wait any longer.

▽ ⟁ △ ▽ ✳

Vienna wandered for hours, not failing to note that she had made a wrong turn and passed the same tree several times. "Damn it." Pulling from her childhood, Vienna found pebbles to drop behind her as she tried again to make it back to Sparks.

She was drenched, but the rain had finally stopped, and now the sun was peeking over the mountains. The trail had been easy, and the view was gorgeous. Several minutes into the walk, she realized she felt more at peace out here than she'd felt in years. Everything was tranquil. The birds chirped, the wind rustled the tree leaves, and the flower petals glistened in the sun that lit the path.

There had been no sign of Logan or anyone else since the loud noise back at the cave. But she'd seen one moth periodically during her walk. At least, she thought it was a moth. Sometimes, it looked human. Vienna talked to the moth when she got nervous. It was grounding, and she enjoyed having someone . . . something on this journey.

"Look there, Tabetha. Or should I call you Tabbie for short?" She looked at the moth, which appeared to be listening. When she talked, the moth trembled, shooting turquoise sparkles and leaving a trail behind them. It made Vienna feel safe, knowing she could find her way back to the cave.

"No, I like Tabetha. Tabbie's too simple for your beauty, isn't it?" She sighed. "I hope you'll stick around when we get to the school. It'd be nice to have another friend."

Vienna spotted Sparks Boarding School. Exhausted, she laughed loudly, throwing her head back. Filled with joy, she spun in a circle, arms flowing free.

"We found it, Tab . . . " But Tabetha was gone. "Tabetha?" She peeked under a few bushes, but there was no trace of her. Vienna's heart sank.

"If I was a flying cutie, where would I hide?" she thought aloud. She leaned down and looked under a flower petal.

"There you are! You had us worried," came a soft voice. Vienna pivoted in surprise.

Celine, Nessa, Iris, and Jayla rushed to Vienna. She closed the distance and hugged each of them.

"Oh my gosh! What happened to you?" Nessa walked around Vienna, taking in the muddy nightgown.

"It looks like you took a mud bath." Jayla picked up a strand of Vienna's dirty hair and cringed.

"I fell a few times coming down the last hill," Vienna explained. She looked at her pajamas and touched her hair.

Iris stared. "We woke to lightning, and when you weren't there . . . We've been out looking everywhere for you! Where have you been?" She huffed.

"It's hard to explain," Vienna answered, feeling guilty. "Some of it, I don't know if I *can* explain."

"Can't? Or won't?" Celine criticized. "We were worried sick, and now . . . now we're all truant!" She threw her hands in the air and stomped her feet, splashing mud over them.

The shock was instant. Celine's face reddened as mud speckled her face.

"I'm so sorry, I . . . " But before she could finish, all the girls were laughing. They stomped in the mud and splashed back at Celine. Their laughter filled the hill and echoed happiness. Each face sprouted a smile.

Drenched in mud, they all walked back to the school, talking about the joy of a mud fight, the blessing of good friends, and their dread about what lay ahead. More than anything, they spoke of feeling closer to each other than they ever had—that maybe truancy could be a blessing . . . in the right situation.

Vienna glanced back again, hoping to spot Tabetha, but there wasn't even a sparkle to indicate she ever existed.

# CHAPTER TWENTY-THREE

"Are you ready to tell us why we found you wandering the woods miles from the school?" Iris asked as she pulled on her jeans and snapped the top button. Vienna and Iris showered and prepared quickly; the other girls were still preparing for the day.

"All I remember is walking down the hall. I heard someone talking . . . well . . . " She thought for a minute. "I heard people *chanting*. I went to see who it was and what they were saying, but the next thing I knew, I was in a cave."

"A cave?" Iris moved toward Vienna's bed and sat down. "How far did you walk before we found you?"

"I'm not sure," Vienna admitted. "I started when it was pitch black, maybe 10 minutes after the rain started."

Iris gasped. "Vienna, it started raining around midnight. We found you just before dawn. Did you take breaks?"

"No, Tabetha and I kept a steady pace." Vienna flinched. She hadn't wanted to tell anyone about the moth. She hoped Iris didn't noticed her slip. "I followed the best trails I could see."

"Who is Tabetha?" Nessa asked.

Vienna turned to see the other three girls staring at her. She blushed. "Uh . . . " She cleared her throat. "A moth that kept me company."

The girls looked at one another and then back at Vienna. They blinked rapidly, confused.

"I think you caught a fever." Celine placed the back of her hand on Vienna's forehead.

"I'm not crazy, you guys. The moths were beautiful, and one followed me." She shrugged, acting like it was no big deal. "I named her Tabetha. I didn't want to call her 'moth' when I spoke to her. She kept me from being afraid."

"So, you spoke with this moth . . . Did she," Iris hesitated, "did she answer you?"

"Don't look at me like I'm crazy," she chastised. "You don't understand how terrifying it was out there."

"You were alone in the dark and needed someone. That's understandable," Nessa validated Vienna, and she was grateful.

"Thank you, Nessa." Vienna looked at the other girls, waiting for a reply.

"How did you know it was a girl moth?" Iris asked with curiosity.

"Her sparkles were turquoise," Vienna muttered nervously as she brushed her hair. She didn't know how to help her friends understand everything that happened last night or if she should tell them.

*Trust your gut,* Logan's words echoed. She felt so many things in her gut. Like she knew the moth was female and there to support her.

"Sparkles?" Celine asked, perking up. "Can you explain what this moth looked like besides the sparkles?"

Vienna watched Celine, taking in her features and noting her body language. With her neutral tone and sparkling eyes, she decided Celine was genuinely curious. Vienna opened up and told them about the cave and the moths; how they illuminated the cave and its surroundings, and how it felt like Tabetha was genuinely listening.

She didn't mention Logan transporting her to the cave. Whenever someone asked how she got there, she said she didn't know exactly, which wasn't a lie. The deceit consumed her. Still, she couldn't help feeling it was dangerous to tell anyone about Logan and how he had come to warn her. She also didn't mention the darkness Logan talked about. She decided to learn as much as she could about that independently.

▽△△▽✴

Ms. Blight visited and allowed the girls to take the day off. She knew Vienna had been missing that morning and suspected her roommates had gone in search of her. She covered them all by saying they were ill. Vienna didn't know why the counselor would protect them, but she decided not to question it. She and her friends talked all day about what Vienna had experienced until they passed out near midnight. Finally, Vienna was alone and looked forward to thinking about the previous night's adventures.

Instead of sleeping, she left the room and turned on the common room's electric fireplace. She stood at the window, warmed by the fire, staring into the darkness. She couldn't shut her mind off. She thought about Logan and his disappearing, odd behavior; black then brown irises. He was like an animal. Then he took off like lightning, as if he was afraid of something or someone. She would have never guessed he would leave her alone in such a vulnerable situation, which meant whatever the reason for his disappearance, it had to be a good one.

Mid-thought, she spotted what looked like glitter dashing around the garden. It had to be Tabetha. Excitement flowed through her. Thrilled to enter nature and investigate the sparkles, she rushed to her room, grabbed a night robe, and dashed down the stairs. Halfway down, her heart thudded with excitement, and the whooshing sound of blood flooded her ears. She hit the downstairs floor, balanced, and then ran to the exit.

*Ooof!*

She sat on the floor, dazed. The door was locked, and she had run into it with full force. She stood, closed her eyes until the dizziness faded, then shook the door. Someone had locked them in for the night. She didn't remember feeling imprisoned until she thought about not being able to reach Tabetha.

Vienna turned, rushing back to her room and searching for the spell book she had checked out of the library. Sure enough, at the back of the book was a spell to open any locked door, if it was locked by key and not by supernatural powers. She dashed back to the door and confidently chanted, "*Clausum ab homine, clausum amplius . . . Libera me per portam hanc!*" As she finished, the door popped open with a screech—triumph!

She snapped the book shut and ran out to the garden. The cool air nipped at her skin when she exited the warm building. Her robe was not enough to fight the chill, but her adrenaline was too high to be bothered.

"Tabetha," she quietly called into the night. "Is that you?" She walked the paths peeking around trees, seats, and rocks. Defeated, she sat on a bench, wondering if she had imagined the whole thing.

"Tabetha?" She gave one last call before giving up. She stared into the night. "I truly thought you were more than a figment of my imagination." She inhaled the air with closed eyes, noticing the peacefulness it gave. Still, she was lonely after expecting the company of a sparkling moth.

Leaves rustled behind her as a tear cascaded down her cheek. She hopped up and spotted something glowing behind a big leaf in the tree she was next to. "Tabetha, is that you?" She was about to climb the tree, but the moth appeared before she reached the first branch.

Tabetha zipped toward her forehead and collided with her. Vienna lost her grip and fell. Air rushed out of her lungs and her sight went fuzzy. All she could see was a mess of turquoise and white sparkles falling onto her lap.

"What was that for?" she slurred out before she fell asleep. The last thing she saw was a human's cute face attached to the fluffy white wings she was searching for.

▽△△▽✳

"Person!" An excited high-pitched treble assaulted Vienna's ears.

Vienna roused, the disorienting fog clearing from her head. Nausea rose as the world spun.

"Hi, person!" The small, high-pitched voice attacked Vienna's ears again. She sat up and searched for the source. Her head spun, and she blinked rapidly to clear the foggy vision.

"Person," came the voice again. This time with more annoyance than care, causing Vienna to flinch.

Peering around, she couldn't find who spoke to her. Her belly shuddered when she realized the voice was close . . . very close. She looked down to find Tabetha standing on her stomach. Stern fuzzy features turned cheerful as Tabetha's arms, four fuzzy extensions of her peculiar body, clapped excitedly; hopping up and down, cheering.

Vienna stared transfixed at the wondrous creature, taking in each delicate feature. Fluffy white voluminous wings attached to a petite Human form. Fighting the urge to touch the thick wings, she looked on, mesmerized.

Tabetha wiggled in excitement, sending a waterfall of sparkles to cascade onto Vienna's robe—turquoise and silver shimmering against the material. Vienna shook her head and rubbed her eyes, yet the creature remained in place, staring up at her. She imagined puckered lips to match the creature's obvious annoyance. Thin hairs danced across the snowy wings, like a breeze across grass, as the tiny creature slammed her hands against her hips, silently screaming for attention.

"What's going on . . . What do you want?" Her voice cracked. "What are you?"

The creature gasped. "Rude . . . We don't do rude!" chimed the small voice, shaking her finger in Vienna's face. "We are friends. Last night we stayed together. Now I am yours." With her head clearing, the voice reminded Vienna of a soft bell. Vienna sat back with fleeting relief that the creature was real. Processing what stood on her, the relief faded, confusion taking its place.

Fascinated by the big tempered bug, she looked at each detail: the white moth wings, large white antennae, four fluffy white arms attached to what appeared to be a little body—her skin a blinding gold that illuminated several inches around the creature, preventing Vienna from focusing on any single feature. All Vienna could think about was how much Tabetha resembled a fairy.

"You're staring . . . ahhh . . . *rude*," Tabetha said as she shifted her head for effect.

"Uhm mm . . . I, ahhh . . . I'm, well, I'm sorry." She shook her head, feeling awful for making her companion uncomfortable. "I just haven't seen anything like you before. And you *talk!*" Vienna exclaimed.

Tabetha giggled. "Of course, I talk." She began to pace across Vienna's stomach.

"Are you a sprite?" she asked innocently.

"Are. You. Kidding." About the size of a two-pound kitten, her abrupt halt sent Vienna's belly into a somersault. "FAIRY!" she said with repulsion. "FAIRY, not a sprite. Do I look like I'd bite you?"

"I'm sorry. I'm still learning a lot of this stuff. Okay, you're a fairy. But why do you look bigger than last night? I don't remember you being this big."

"Silly girl. We aren't in your realm. This is my true size. Not the size of a human moth."

"That's so . . . " Vienna paused, thinking of the right word—nothing seemed right.

"Anyway," Tabetha interrupted, "I have business with you."

"Oh?" Vienna watched the creature. She shifted her head and tried to catch every feature as Tabetha passed by—still pacing. Vienna was still in awe of her majestic beauty.

"Yes." Tabetha either didn't notice or ignored Vienna's behavior.

"First, I like the name Tabetha." She gave a quick nod. "Next, we need to discuss why you wandered the woods by yourself last night. That's not safe, not safe at all." She fluttered up and stood on Vienna's head, looking down at her—fear lacing her features.

"Wait," Vienna interrupted, "can I ask some questions first?"

Tabetha rolled her eyes, gave a dramatic sigh, then crossed her fuzzy arms across her body. "I'll give you three, and then it's my turn again," Tabetha answered, nose in the air.

"Fine. First—"

"Don't be mean." Tabetha's voice quaked, and her wings drooped. "*Fine* is such a mean word." Her little arms wrapped around her knees.

"I'm sorry. I didn't mean to be rude. I promise."

Tabetha shook her head and gestured for Vienna to continue as she sat on Vienna's stomach.

"Okay"—Vienna cleared her throat— "so you're a fairy?"

"Yes. I am a fairy." She beamed.

Vienna's mind went blank. A fairy . . . A real-life *fairy . . . No way!*

"You doubt?" Tabetha asked sadly.

"No, I just thought you were a myth."

"Like witches?" Tabetha countered, clearly ready to debate.

"Touché," Vienna replied with a smile. She *really* liked this moth and her attitude. "I'm sorry. I mean, I learned about the Fae or Fairy Realm, but I guess the idea of a Fae wasn't something I thought deeply about."

They moved in silence while Vienna watched her flutter around like a dancing flower petal. It was mesmerizing, and Vienna thought about all the magic and beauty she didn't know existed.

"Why are . . . well, why did you follow . . . No, that's not what I . . ."

Tabetha giggled. "Why you?" she provided.

"Yes, that's the simplest way to put it."

She shrugged her little shoulders. "You needed me."

"What do you mean?"

"Is that your final question?"

"No!" Vienna nearly yelled, afraid she would lose her next question.

Tabetha rolled over on her side, laughing and kicking her little legs. "Okay . . . " She gasped and sat back up. "We will count that as the same question."

Vienna missed her laugh instantly. It was like a jingling brass bell.

"I saw you alone by the exit of the cave. You were afraid. When I neared you, my magic coursed through you. That's when I knew you were my person. I gave you courage, and you made me feel safe. I'm usually afraid of people."

"What does it mean that I'm your person?"

"Have you ever heard those stories of people who have . . . what are they called . . . " Tabetha tapped her lips. "Ah, yes. A spirit animal?"

"I know a little about that."

"That's the best I can explain it. I'll be around whenever you need me. I'll be invisible or tiny in the Human world and look like a normal moth. Here"—she gestured around and looked into the sky with awe—"you will see the real me." She smiled at Vienna.

"This is the real you, then?"

"It is! Do you like it?" She puffed out her chest and snapped her wings open.

"I do," she said eagerly. "You're beautiful. It's strange how I can't focus on your face, though."

"Yeah, fairies are bright. Like, super bright," she said with wide eyes and outstretched arms. "No one can see us in our purest form."

"Darn . . . you're so lovely."

Tabetha did a little happy dance. "Thank you! My turn for questions!" Tabetha bounced, and turquoise sparkles flew everywhere, tickling Vienna's nose. She had to hold it closed to prevent a sneeze.

"Who was the boy?" Tabetha asked, vibrating with energy. "He was gorgeous! I mean, I wouldn't steal him from you, but you know." She hopped up and began pacing again. "He was so handsome and seemed to be defending you. So one, how did you get to the cave? And two, who is the boy?" She clapped her hands excitedly and sat down on Vienna's stomach again. She crossed her legs and patted them in anticipation.

Laughing, Vienna explained who Logan was and why he was there. Finally, she had someone she could share things with. All the things she had kept to herself.

"That's so scary. Who do you think is after you? Can you truly trust him? Oh my gosh, what about your friends and roommates? Can you trust *them*? Oh dear, maybe I should be around you more. No, I can't always be there . . . Maybe I can . . . "

She rambled too quickly for Vienna to catch everything she said. "Slow down, Tabetha!!" Vienna pleaded. "I can't make out your words."

"Oh dear, sorry." Tabetha stopped abruptly.

"It's okay. I can tell you're easily excited." Vienna chuckled. "Hey. Off-topic, but how do I return to the Human world, and how can I jump back to your world when I need to?"

"To come here, I must bring you. To return to the Magic Realm . . . " She looked at Vienna, who blushed.

"Right."

"For the Magic Realm, you ask. If I can't take you for any reason, you'd be stuck here unless you talked to the Fae Queen."

"Is the Fae Queen nice? In stories, she's very . . . " Vienna tried to think of a less abrasive way to say evil or tricky. "Well, the Fae are usually untrustworthy."

"That's true," Tabetha piped up with a sad look. "You must be very careful if you talk to most Fae. I am different, as I am yours, and you are mine. We're a team." She smiled sweetly.

It filled Vienna's heart to know this Fae was her companion. "Can I tell anyone about you?"

"Most won't believe you if you did, since most don't know about this realm. But if you have anyone you know you can trust *100 hundred percent*," she emphasized with a strong voice and pointed look, "then you can tell them," she finished calmly.

"Got it. Final question for tonight. How do I contact you if you're not around?"

"We are connected, Vienna. All you do is think of me or call my name, and I will be there. If I sense danger, I'll just come. I won't ever be too far. You are mine now."

Vienna felt safer now, but she felt a little like a possession. "What if you decide you don't want me anymore?"

"Oh, no, no, no, no," Tabetha said, body tense. "That's not at all how it works. I will always want you to be mine. But . . . " She drooped a little. "You can decide you don't want me. If that happens, you can tell me, and I will leave."

"When you leave, will our tie disappear?"

Tabetha's little arms crossed her body, and she shivered. "Yes, but because I chose you, I will perish. I chose willingly to be with you until I'm not needed, and the alternative is not to exist."

"*What?* Why would you choose that? What if I never wanted you? That . . . that could have been like suicide."

She shrugged. "It is worth the cost to be yours and help you. It is my duty, and I have no, and will never have any, regret."

"What about when I die?"

"I will be passed down to either a descendant or a close family member, or if there's no one like that, I'll perish with you."

Vienna shook her head in disbelief. "Note to self: have kids before I die," she joked.

"Please do!" Tabetha jumped up and down, clapping all four hands. "Kids are charming!"

"You're too cute, Tabetha," Vienna said with a yawn. "Once you meet my brothers, you might change your mind."

"I doubt it. But you're tired. I'll send you back now. Would you like to wake up where you left or in your bed?"

"You can do that?"

As Tabetha saluted, Vienna realized she was no longer cold. She looked around and smiled when she realized she was in her bed.

Before another word could be said, Vienna laid down with Tabetha next to her and fell fast asleep, curled up and hidden under a mound of blankets, snug as a bug.

# CHAPTER TWENTY-FOUR

## Vienna & Logan's POV

Vienna's favorite class quickly became spells, and she shifted in her chair as she anticipated today's lesson. During the last few days, she learned about the complexity of all the realms in Magyieka. Mrs. Jaheem was thorough with each discussion, and today's topic focused on each realm and the central spells.

The board had a list of realms, and Vienna chuckled at the Fairy/Fae Realm. She looked at Tabetha, who slept on her lap as though she were a cat. She tucked her fluffy moth wings around her Human body, allowing only her illuminating head and fluffy white antennas to show. Vienna still couldn't make out her features with her light lower than usual when she slept, but she could sense her comfort as they grew closer.

"Today, we deep-dive into the realms of our world. Many of you know someone from each of these, so what we learn may be your knowledge. However"—she paced the front of the class, her black robe hugging her curves—"some people are learning this for the first time, so I expect patience as we learn. In the next class, we will assess how much is remembered, as the details of the realms and their spells and unique creatures are important."

The word "creatures" caught Vienna off guard, and she looked around the room. Everyone focused on Mrs. Jaheem as though they knew that different creatures were in each realm. She focused on what Mrs. Jaheem was writing on the board.

"Why do you wear a robe?" someone in the room asked before the first sentence was finished.

Mrs. Jaheem turned stoically and looked at the student. Vienna followed her stare and spotted an unfamiliar face—a small blonde sat in the corner of the room. Vienna hadn't recalled seeing her before and made a mental note to learn who she was.

"It represents my position on the Council," Mrs. Jaheem answered flatly.

"What are the colors for?" The blonde pointed to the gold lines on the corner of the robe.

"It's the color of the Magic Realm, which I represent on the Council."

Blocking any other questions, Mrs. Jaheem turned to the board and wrote in fancy letters. With each swish of the final letter of a word, she read it to the class. Although the details about the magic and the creatures of each realm were written, Vienna couldn't help but focus on the different realms and the fact she was just now learning about them.

Vienna looked at the words: Shadow, Magic, Dream, Nether, and Fae Realm, and she wondered how different each must be to have its own magic use. Broken from her thoughts, she looked at Mrs. Jaheem, who was still talking.

"Each of these realms is represented on the Council and will be the focus of our class today. If any of this information is new to you, I suggest you find a peer to learn from or dive deep. We will not go into the history of each, but we will learn magic that aligns with each realm." Mrs. Jaheem pointed out the pages in our text that went with each of the realm's magic and sat at her desk.

Vienna flipped through her book to find the details of each realm:

Shadow Realm is the continent Nocshedu. It hosts the capital for Shifters and holds Onyx Hall, where the Council gathers when needed. Their school focuses on training Shifters to harness their power; though Watchers are rare creatures, they are sent to Nocshedu's southern town, Tamuk, where they train in combat and learn about their life mission.

The Magic Realm is home to Sparks Boarding School for girls and Domar's Boarding School for boys. It is an entry school for magic wielders. Enchanters access magic by tapping into their element in the physical world, creating powerful spells.

Dream Realm is beyond the Human plane and is only accessible by Dreamwalkers.

The Nether Realm is a realm between all others, which has been described as a void. To access this plane, one must be a Dreamwalker, Watcher, Enlitner, or hold the power of Spirit.

Fae Realm includes two sectors known as the Seelie and Unseelie Courts, and each section is ruled by its royal families. All Fae have access to some degree of widespread magic, which can be harnessed through elements and animals but is harnessed supernaturally.

"I don't get it, Tabetha," Vienna whispered. "There is good information here, but I know it's leaving a lot out. How do I find out more?"

"Look in the back," Tabetha sang as she vibrated, walking circles on the desk.

Vienna jotted down Watcher and Enlitner and flipped to the back of the book, looking up the differences along with how Spirit was classified, but the end of the book failed to provide more information. Frustrated, she snapped the book closed, gaining the attention of Mrs. Jaheem, who frowned as though she knew Vienna sought more answers.

The class studied in silence for the rest of the hour, but Vienna couldn't focus on the spells and types of magic each realm had.

Instead, she talked with Tabetha about the different realms and their differences.

When the bell rang, Vienna groaned. She didn't want to attend combat class but knew she had to fight through it before study hall, so she gathered her books and went to the locker room.

After she changed, she arrived in class to see extra students in uniform. Once everyone had arrived, Mr. Malkayz motioned for Vienna. She looked around the class as everyone watched her. Pushing down the urge to run, she walked with her chin held high until she stood in front of Mr. Malkayz.

"Today, we see what skills you have as I pair you off with someone who tested as an equivalent during my one-on-one with you. There will be no magic used, and no weapons are available. The goal is to block and take down your opponent without drawing blood or knocking them out." His voice echoed, and Vienna heard her peers cheer. She looked behind her to see Ms. Blight assisting in pairing the students.

"You," Mr. Malkayz said softly, "will start with me to demonstrate what is expected today, and then you will be paired with your equivalent."

"Who is?" Vienna's voice trembled.

"Cosima." Vienna's eyes widened, and she looked back to find Cosima standing next to Ms. Blight.

"There has to be a mistake?" Vienna gasped.

"You two are strong opponents. This isn't a discussion. Let's start." Vienna's thoughts detached from her body as she walked through Mr. Malkayz's motions to the class. When they were finished, Cosima walked toward them.

"Ready when you are." Cosima smiled.

▽△△▽✳

Exhausted and emotionally taxed, Vienna walked to the fountain where her roommates waited. They headed toward a shaded area, and she crumpled to the ground, her limbs heavy and aching.

"Long day?" Jayla gave her a half smile.

Vienna nodded, unable to form words. She listened as the girls talked about their day and organized their tasks for their study hall. Once they were settled, Vienna sat up and looked at them, pulling out her own books.

"I have a girl in my class who just blurted out a question. I don't remember seeing her before. She almost looks young or has more boyish features. I couldn't figure out which," Vienna said.

"Ahh, that's Fenella O'Cain. She's from the Fairy Realm," Celine spit out before looking up. She blushed. "I'm sorry, you didn't ask that. I was distracted."

"You know there are Fae?" Vienna asked.

"Of course. Everyone knows that," Jayla answered.

The girls looked at Vienna in curiosity as she warmed in embarrassment. "I didn't until recently," she admitted.

"I'm sorry," Nessa said. "I guess we all assumed that since we have been here a while, we know all the realms. Do you have any other questions?"

"No." Vienna flinched at her own venom. She knew it wasn't fair to take her anger out on them. "Actually, yes. You all know what realm I'm from. But how many do we have here from the Fairy Realm?" Vienna fidgeted with her sleeve as Tabetha paced in front of her.

"Not a lot. Honestly, they don't typically come here. Fenella is here because her magic isn't active, and the Fae world sees her as unfit to practice in their realm. I heard her talking about it before. But sometimes people choose to come because they want to learn more about this realm and leave the Fae Realm." Iris shrugged as though it was nothing.

"We learned about the different realms and their magic sources, which was fascinating. I didn't know the World of Magic was so complex. Does anyone live in the Nether Realm or Dream Realm?"

"No, but there are people assigned to guard it and be the spokesperson for the rules and laws set. They sit on the Council, and you'll probably learn more about that if you study independently than you will in class," Jayla admitted.

"She's right. The people of Magyieka aren't always transparent," Nessa agreed.

Vienna was curious as she watched her roommates talking about the different realms and how much they didn't know until they started at Sparks. Not much was disclosed she didn't already know.

"By the way, in combat class, I was paired with Cosima." Vienna watched the girls in curiosity. Celine gasped, grabbing her chest.

"That's absurd. With your history, you must protest," Celine said dramatically.

"She's right," Jayla agreed, and the other nodded.

"I thought so at first, too, but I think I want to prove to Cosima that I can take her." They nodded at her, but Vienna saw the uncertainty in their eyes. She struggled and pulled out her paperwork, ready to move on from the awkward conversation.

## LOGAN

"She's acclimating well, and her studying is solid. She has undoubtedly made friendships with her roommates and is growing closer to them all, especially Iris." Logan filled the Council in on his progress after watching Vienna during her first week at Sparks. "Though she does seem to be speaking to herself a lot lately." He scrunched his eyebrows. He had noticed this odd behavior since the night he appeared in the cave to ensure she was safe.

"Vienna has a Fae that has claimed her. Only other Fae can see her, but she is present, and they talk constantly," Ms. Blight admitted.

The Council looked at her in surprise. This was a rare situation, and it was uncommon for a Fae to attach to an Enchanter, especially one raised in the Human Realm.

"How did this happen?" Mr. Humphrey asked.

"She snuck out and wandered to a cave. She was lost and frightened on her way back, and the Fae has claimed Vienna and is watching over her." Ms. Blight looked around.

"Isn't it dangerous for a Fae to claim an Enchanter?" Mrs. Jaheem asked.

"Not in this instance. This is more like an imprint. This Fae will protect Vienna with her life. It is a positive thing for Vienna, but a life sentence for the Fae, as her immortality will suffer." Ms. Blight wiped a tear from her cheek.

Nobody said a word, and Logan thought back on his history lessons; he'd never heard of this type of bond, let alone a Human-raised Enchanter having an Enlitner and two Watchers charged as Protectors. With each passing moon, he leaned increasingly into believing Vienna was the Quintessence and the one spoken of in the ancient Prophecy as the magic being who would unite all the realms through a catastrophic war. When he thought about the pigtailed girl he'd grown up with, he couldn't imagine her leading an army into a war that would endanger Humans, all magic beings, and each realm to bring peace. Yet when he thought about the fire in her that allowed her to enter the World of Magyieka as the youngest Enchanter raised in the Human Realm, he decided against underestimating her.

"Logan"—the Seelie Queen's sharp voice pulled him from his thoughts—"could you check in on her during the weirdness for a while as we work through some of the information we have been given?"

Logan nodded as he looked across the table. The Ovr'seer

watched him intently as the others talked. Logan made out scrambled words that he couldn't comprehend until he heard "StagAri". He turned toward Mr. Audovera and cocked his head, waiting to hear more, but the room fell into silence. Logan waited, looking at each member intently. He studied each of their robes and the striped color representing their realm before looking back to the Ovr'seer.

"How much do you know about the Prophecy, Logan?" Mr. Ozul asked flatly.

Logan turned to the stenographer, unwilling to speak in front of Cosima's mom despite her mind being wiped. Catching onto his fear, Mrs. Jaheem walked toward Agnes and dismissed her from the room before pouring herself a tall glass of water and taking her place back at the table.

"We aren't taught much, but I have learned a lot in Shadow Realm and among the Shifters. Recent talk from the Watchers and Enlitners has also filled in some gaps, but even combining this all, there are gaps in the story." Logan admitted his limitations without judgment.

"Do you believe that Ms. Madizza-Corey could be the Quintessence the Prophecy speaks of?" Mrs. Jaheem whispered.

Laughter erupted from Logan, and he fell back, crashing out of his chair. After several minutes of satisfying himself, he crawled to his seat and swatted at the tears of laughter that trailed down his face. "Have you met Vienna? She's a hotheaded mess. There is no way she's the Quintessence. If anyone is, it's Valda or Celine. I could see her as an asset to the Quintessence, but there is no way Vienna has the talents or backbone to fulfill such a profound prophecy."

Mr. Humphrey's face was purple. Logan watched his eyes fill with rage from being mocked. "Look, boy. Those others have no qualities the Prophecy speaks of. Vienna is the only option. Perhaps you are blinded by your affection for her."

Logan snapped his mouth shut. He struck a chord intentionally but wasn't prepared to be targeted for it. "Perhaps. Or maybe the Quintessence hasn't been revealed yet."

"That could be," Ms. Blight agreed. "Until we know for sure, I would like you to continue watching her."

Logan nodded. "Can you tell me all the reasons you think she could be the one?" he asked Mr. Humphrey, hoping to repair the rift he had caused.

The Seelie Queen slid a book across the table. It stopped in front of Logan, and he picked it up. The leather binding was thick, and the gold around the pages was old and worn. He watched the Council as he opened the first page, then froze as a chill crept up his neck. In his hand was the collection of stories passed down from several realms. He'd just been given the *Pufurate,* the book of the future.

# CHAPTER
# TWENTY-FIVE

With each passing week over the next two months, Vienna became close to the other girls. For the first time, she felt at home in this new realm. It was as though she had gained the sister she had always wanted. Imagine they came in a pack. *How lucky could a girl be?* She gazed at Nessa, Jayla, Iris, and then Celine. Happiness filled her heart, and she relaxed, sitting back to take in the beauty of life. The only thing that could make it better was to have her family here, too.

Shaking her head, she brought herself back to the present. The girls were talking about school, which reminded her of their studies.

"Hey, what do you guys think of *The Discoverie of Witchcraft* and *A Midsummer Night's Dream*?" Her voice squeaked with her excitement. Vienna had a newfound interest in the mesmerizing land crafted by William Shakespeare in his play.

"It's almost as though Shakespeare knew, ya know?" Nessa jumped up and sat next to Vienna. "When he talked about the fields, I couldn't help but think he was one of us."

Tabetha, still invisible to everyone else, had been sitting on Vienna's shoulder. The moment Nessa spoke, she jumped and started pacing excitedly. Vienna looked at her with curiosity. *Were they on to something?* she thought.

"That makes a lot of sense," Jayla said as she blinked rapidly. "That hadn't crossed my mind." She tapped her finger on her lips, thinking, while the rest continued the discussion.

"Nessa, do you really think he could be one of us?" Iris knitted her brows as she pondered this question. "I can totally see it," she whispered, shaking her head.

"You might be on to something," Vienna added. "The fact he used potions, fairies." She looked at Tabitha, who was inspired by their insight and paced around, thinking about the conversation and ideas.

"Oh, and the charmed flower." Iris' eyes widened. "Holy crap!"

As they continued discussing the possibility, they began to talk over each other. Before long, the conversation switched to *The Discoverie of Witchcraft*. The discussion was shallow and didn't last long; none enjoyed the old-fashioned reading and lack of fluidity.

"I'm glad I'm not the only one fascinated by all of it," Vienna continued. "What about your other classes? How are they going?"

"I really enjoy history and astronomy," Nessa answered.

"Me too," Iris agreed. "Though they are both REALLY heavy with homework. And I wonder if astronomy will get harder now that we have snow in the forecast."

"Professor Markeive says winters are mild, and the sky is seldom overcast here," Vienna said. "So, I'm sure it'll be just fine."

"That makes sense," Celine jumped in. "We are technically in a different realm. Why would they make it a miserable winter if they didn't need to?"

"Speaking of winter," Jayla piped up, "did you guys hear about the Winter Ball that we'll have near Christmas time for the Winter Solstice?"

"No!" all the girls said at once. Vienna could feel the excitement coming off each girl and couldn't help but get excited herself.

"The Winter Solstice is only a couple of weeks away. That's so little time!" Nessa said, as she twisted her hands.

"Why haven't we heard about it yet?" Vienna wondered.

"Maybe it will be in the December announcement. We technically have almost a month left. Next week is Thanksgiving," Iris offered.

"That makes sense," Celine stated. "We don't need an entire month preparing to celebrate."

"Are you sure you don't, Celine? You do take a while to get ready," Jayla teased. All the girls laughed. All except Iris.

"I do take a long time," she moaned, eyes wide. "I don't have *anything*. Can we find a date? Who would we dance with?" She turned to Jayla. "What do you know? Tell us everything!"

"Well, I heard Domar's Boarding School will be there!" Jayla practically screamed at the end of her statement.

"No freaking way!" Celine giggled with joy. "Now we *really* need to start getting ready!" She looked at Iris, who started to turn pink.

"Are you okay, Iris?" Vienna asked as she touched Iris' arm.

"Um . . . yes. But I never really learned how to dance. Do we need to know how?"

"Oh, I saw in our newsletter this month that one of our study hours will be for dancing," Vienna said with a grin. "We'll be okay."

They all murmured their excitement and made their way to their classes.

▽ ☖ △ ▽ ✳

Domar's leader, Principal Cozbi, came to the cafeteria that afternoon to make an announcement with Ms. Blight during lunch. "Many of you have learned that we will have a winter formal with the boys from Domar's Boarding School. Attendance is not mandatory, but those not attending must be checked into their rooms at the normal time. As for general rules, no narcotics will be allowed on campus, and *no alcohol*."

"Now," Ms. Blight said sternly, "modest dress will be required. Dresses must touch the knees, no bare shoulders, and no belly shirts. We will have more details in the December newsletter." As she continued to speak, the entire room buzzed with excitement.

Vienna wanted to contact her mom so badly, but the technology was limited during the school year. She pondered how past generations waited for traditional letters to arrive on horseback through the mail without going insane.

"Finally"—Vienna realized she'd stopped listening to Ms. Blight, and she brought her attention back—"next week, we will head out for Thanksgiving. Anyone not going home will need to check in with their counselor. Please remember to leave all your books here and enjoy the break. Now, finish lunch and hurry on with your day." With that, both principals left the cafeteria, and the girls' excitement continued to explode.

"So much for waiting for the newsletter," Jayla giggled. "Good news travels too fast."

"Is everyone going home next week?" Iris asked timidly.

"I am!" Vienna said. "What about you all?"

All the girls, except Iris, stated they would be going home. Iris said, barely above a whisper, "Actually, I found out my family will be gone all week. I can't go home because no one will be there."

"Come home with me, then!" Vienna offered. A second later, she realized she hadn't thought about what her family would think.

"Really?" Iris was wide-eyed and delighted.

Vienna pushed aside her worry. "Absolutely! I'm sure my family would love to get to know you." She started planning for Iris to come home with her, realizing she was more excited about being away from school knowing she wasn't going home alone.

"Everyone in on studying for our astronomy quiz tonight? It's supposed to be clear." Iris switched topics as she squirmed.

All the girls agreed to meet after dinner to study. Vienna loved seeing the stars from the top of the hills, but she didn't know if she could convince all the girls to go beyond the garden. To have the rest of them explore the area and see the cave would be worth the time to convince them. They could practice their magic, learn to work together . . . find out what else is out there. She had a plan, though; if she was lucky, she would get them not just there but to the cave.

▽△△▽✴

That night, as Vienna and the girls prepared to head out, Vienna packed extra drinks and snacks. She knew it would be hard to convince them to hike with her, but she was determined after Tabetha excitedly talked about a midnight stroll.

They quietly snuck to the doors to exit the building. Vienna kneeled and pulled out two pins as she started to pick the lock, fearful to use her magic without her spell book.

"Wait"—Iris sat next to Vienna—"I want to try magic. I've been practicing small things." Vienna nodded and moved.

Iris began to chant and moved her hands in motions Vienna didn't understand. Several attempts later, Iris sat back. "Maybe we should all try. Follow my lead."

"Heck ya," Nessa said, as she moved beside Iris. Vienna shrugged and stepped in line with them.

"We're already sneaking out. This is pushing the limits." Celine crossed her arms.

"We can't sneak out if we can't get out. At this point, we'll get caught, anyway. Are you going to help?" Jayla smiled and nudged Celine with her shoulder.

After a big sigh, Celine begrudgingly moved forward, standing next to Jayla. All in a circle, they followed after Iris. On the second attempt, the door opened.

"Awesome!" Nessa squealed. All the girls high-fived each other and talked over one another about the success of picking the lock. "Now, wasn't that worth it?" she asked Celine.

"I guess. Let's go." Celine opened the door, holding it for each of them.

After exiting the school, Vienna smiled at Tabetha, and she received an encouraging nod. She turned to the girls. "What would you guys think about going to the cave I found?"

The girls looked at each other, uneasy.

"Hiking is so dirty! Why would we want to do that?" Celine snarked.

"There's a lot to see there, putting us several hundred feet closer to the stars. It's a beautiful area, too." Vienna rambled on about the majestic beauty of the place before the girls finally agreed. Smiling, she handed each girl the water she had packed for them, and they were on their way.

Tabatha rode on Vienna's shoulder, vibrating with excitement. For days she had been talking about visiting nature that wasn't manmade.

"Shh, calm down, my friend," Vienna whispered, lightly patting Tabetha's head. "I know you're excited. We'll be there soon."

"Are you talking to me?" Nessa asked, one eyebrow raised.

"No, just to myself." Vienna blushed and looked at Tabetha, who giggled.

After an hour, Celine continued complaining, and the other girls started to moan in boredom. Even Vienna was beginning to feel cold and achy.

Suddenly, she could smell something faintly musky. The trees were also taller. Vienna took in the deep greens and the dark cotton candy sky that shifted slowly to deep orange. The warm colors high-lighted the hills, shooting warm streaks of deep golden rays across the landscape.

"This really is a beautiful walk," Nessa said, as she touched one of the large green leaves of a nearby bush.

"Look at these flowers," Jayla pointed out. "They are huge and bright. How are they alive this time of year?"

"Our alchemy creates wonder in our lands," Celine said.

"Is that the entrance?" Nessa pointed toward a dark hole in the side of a hill.

"That's it!" Vienna squealed.

"Let's go. I could use a break." Celine led the way after an exasperated sigh. "We still have to get back *down*," she mumbled.

All the girls groaned, except for Vienna, who was too excited for her friends to see and feel the cave's charm.

Once inside, they gasped at the glowing creatures. Vienna stood, smiling and reveling in her victory. She knew they'd love it.

"It's beautiful, isn't it?"

"V," Nessa said, turning to her, "it's otherworldly! Look at the color of the moths! And the glitter falling from their wings. I've never heard of something like this."

"Why isn't this in our books?" Iris inquired. "You'd think something so marvelous would be known."

"Yeah. But think about what would happen if the wrong people discovered this place and these creatures," Jayla reminded them.

"You're right. Which is why I think we need to keep this place to ourselves," Vienna stated firmly, leaving no room for argument. They all agreed, regardless.

Nessa started building a fire.

"Smart to bring supplies, Nessa," Jayla said. "It'll keep us warm while we explore."

Nessa nodded in agreement.

"*Explore?* I thought we were taking a break?" Celine whined.

"You can watch the fire," Jayla offered. "Let's each go get a few big rocks to keep the fire contained."

Celine stayed inside as the rest of the group gathered some rocks and formed a circle around the fire. They then sat back and relaxed for several moments before Nessa encouraged them to explore.

The cave had several tunnels, so they chose to take the one that didn't seem as dark initially. It quickly shrunk enough that they had to crawl before they contemplated returning.

"How far are we going?" Iris whined.

"Nessa, what's the plan? I don't think we can even go backward at this point." Vienna panted. Under Vienna, Tabetha walked around, just below her chest. She didn't look afraid, so Vienna felt they were safe. "I think we're okay for now, though. My intuition isn't screaming for me to run . . . yet." She wished she could say why.

"*Ouch!*" Nessa screamed in pain.

"What happened?" Jayla said, voice trembling.

"Just the wall, or ceiling, or whatever. It scratched my back."

"I smell blood." Tabetha's small voice quivered.

"I bet it's Nessa's back," Vienna whispered.

"What did you say?" Nessa asked.

"Nothing. How much farther?" Vienna needed to work on talking to Tabetha quieter or not out loud at all.

Vienna was sweaty and exhausted by the time they found the exit of the tunnel. They army-crawled the last bit, and Vienna's butt almost didn't make it through the exit.

"Good . . . grief," Iris said between pants. "I . . . . didn't think . . . we were . . . going to make . . . it."

"I second that." Jayla lay flat on her back, eyes closed.

"Wow," Nessa breathed, and Vienna turned to look up at her.

"What is it?" She couldn't find the energy to roll over.

"It's beautiful . . . Check this out, guys." Iris and Jayla looked at Vienna and, with a mutual groan, they all crawled to their knees.

Several gasps echoed off the walls of the room. It was round, but there were five distinct corners. The room was maybe ten feet wide and fifty feet high. On the walls hung five candles in tarnished silver candle holders.

Vienna was speechless. The other girls talked, but she didn't pay attention. *What is this place?*

Tabetha fluttered next to her face, and the breeze from her wings brought Vienna back to awareness. "It's for rituals," Tabetha said.

"Did I . . . "

"No. You thought it." Tabetha brightened.

Vienna smiled at Tabetha, realizing that the other three girls were looking at her. Several moments went by before anyone spoke. They just stared in wonder at the cave, and then they stared back at Vienna.

"Is this why you brought us here?" Jayla placed her hand on her hip, then gagged as she felt mud slide down her hand. "Yuck."

"I didn't know about this place, actually."

"It looks like it's for rituals," Iris offered. "I've seen these in our history book. Just not this type of style. If you go to the book's last two chapters, you'll see all kinds of ritual designs, temples, and even natural temples set up for solstice worship."

"Wait, you're done with the book?" Jayla gasped.

"I get bored." Iris shrugged.

"What are the candle holders for?" Nessa asked.

"I believe you light them before the ritual. See how there are five? That means it would take five people to light them, which is odd. All the circles I've seen in the book had four. North, East, South, and West." She mumbled to herself, "It doesn't make sense."

"Vienna, have you ever seen anything like this?" Jayla asked.

"Why would I know?"

"I don't know . . . Sometimes you just know things." Jayla shrugged, and the girls agreed.

"Not this time, but I want to find out." Vienna's stomach tightened, fearful she'd let these girls get too close. She reached for her stubborn streak and refused to put her wall back up.

Vienna looked at Tabetha for a clue, but she said nothing.

It was cold inside the cave but quickly warmed due to the lack of exits and the four girls' body heat. They stood in wonder for several minutes before they agreed to get back to Celine.

"Wait, I think I need to go . . . well, not last." Vienna blushed.

"Why?" Nessa inquired.

"Well, my butt barely made it through the exit." Vienna bit her lip and looked at her friends sideways.

For a moment, there was nothing but silence. Then Jayla began to laugh hysterically. Within seconds, they were all laughing.

"Mine was tight too," Jayla chuckled after she caught her breath, "so I was wondering how you did."

"Thanks, Jayla." Vienna joked, "I've got some junk in my trunk. What can I say?"

"Nothing wrong with that!" Nessa jumped in on the fun with, "I have no butt, so you make up for what I lack." They all laughed again.

"Okay, Nessa should go first again since she is our little girl scout. Then you go ahead, V. I'll help if your rear needs assistance." Jayla winked. "Iris can go last. Unless you want me to go last." She turned to Iris.

"No, you go ahead, Jayla. I'm okay going last."

After Nessa disappeared, Vienna got down to the army crawl position. Sure enough, Jayla needed to help her with a slight push. They were all giggling like elementary school girls. Vienna knew she had curves, but this was a first. She started scooting through the cave when her butt finally made it through. She was relieved once she could move to her hands and knees.

Thankfully, the way back felt quicker. Vienna exited the tunnel. Jayla and Iris popped out right behind her.

"It's about time," Celine snarked. "I was starting to get worried."

"You won't believe what we found!" Nessa chirped. "It was a room with five candles on the wall—"

"You shouldn't have left me alone! If I'd known you were going to be gone that long . . . Wait . . . did you say there is a room in there? There is no way." She shook her head with a sigh and looked at her friends sternly.

"She's serious," Iris replied. "It looks like a ritual room created for five people."

"That doesn't make sense. Rituals are typically even numbers. Aren't they? At least, that's what I thought."

"Me too. I'm honestly not sure how to explain it."

"Do you want to go see it?" Nessa asked.

"Heck no!" Celine barked. "Have you lost your mind? It's dark and creepy in there."

"It's not creepy," Vienna said.

"It was actually stunning," Jayla added.

Celine paused. "Maybe another time," she finally replied.

"Fine by me. The fire is almost out," Vienna pointed out. "Should we add more wood or call it a night? How long has it been?"

"2 hours," Celine spat.

"*What?!*" the other girls exclaimed.

"Why do you think I was mad? I was alone for 2 *hours* and didn't know how to find you." Celine lifted her eyebrows and pursed her lips.

"It seemed like just a couple of minutes." Iris paused. "The tunnel must have been longer than we realized."

"Could the room have a different timeline than we do? Maybe time pauses or slows while we are in there?" Jayla asked.

"That would make sense. I know it doesn't feel like it's been 2 hours. Not even close," Vienna admitted.

"I thought maybe 20 minutes had passed," Nessa added.

"That means there's no time for homework, but I think it was worth it." Vienna sighed. The others agreed.

They put out the fire and headed out. Vienna took in the glowing creatures on the ceiling and the last few smoking embers one more time. The embers' glow matched the beauty of the ceiling, but in a darker, more dangerous way.

▽△△▽✳

The walk home was long and full of talk about the mysterious room, the upcoming winter formal, and the boys attending. Chatter finally died down when they arrived at campus. Sneaking back into their room went smoother than anticipated.

Hair raised on the back of her neck as they entered the building. Vienna looked around, feeling watched. *Do you feel that?* she thought, hoping Tabetha would hear.

"I do. Somebody is watching." Tabetha quivered. She scanned the area as Vienna opened the door to the west wing. The other girls headed straight for the bedroom, but Vienna stayed behind.

"I think I'm going to hit the restrooms," Vienna told the others.

"What? Why not use the one in Winderaia?" Iris asked. She cocked her head.

"What if the noise wakes someone?"

"Why would it?" Nessa asked. "You're acting intense all of a sudden."

"I just need some downtime . . . alone. I won't be long." Vienna watched Celine shrug and walk away, and the others followed. Once alone, Vienna decided to find out who was watching them.

# CHAPTER TWENTY-SIX

Tabetha clung to Vienna's back as she walked down the hall, peeking around each corner. The hall was quiet and eerie, and each of her footsteps, even as she tiptoed, created a muffled echo.

She made her way to the east wing. Chills ran down her back. With hair on end, she continued to explore the school. Her heart raced . . . *thump* . . . *thump* . . . *thump*. Perspiration dampened her hairline and back.

"Someone's watching us." Tabetha's voice trembled, and she pulled her body closer to Vienna's back.

"I know . . . but I can't find anyone. Can you sense where they are?"

"N . . . n . . . no . . . but it's not a good feeling." Her light faded, and Vienna wondered if negative emotions dampened a Fae's light. Before she could ask, she heard something behind her. She froze.

She spun as fast as she could, but like each corner of the building, she found nothing. The moonlight shined through in the west window as she made her way back. As she entered the west wing, a note taped to the door was addressed to her.

She glanced around, then looked at Tabetha for several moments before she pulled the note from the door. There was a short message in fancy cursive.

## Transporto Spelunca Quinque Puncta

She looked at Tabetha before asking, "Do you know what *transporto spelunca quinque puncta* mea . . . " Before she could finish, the floor dropped from under her feet, and she fell.

"Don't you know not to say Latin out loud?" came a small voice.

Vienna's eyes opened but slammed back shut as bright light assaulted her pupils. "Tabetha . . . ugh, that hurts."

"I'm sorry . . . " Vienna heard fluttering, and a weight lifted from her chest. "What did you say about Latin?" She covered her eyes with her palms, waiting for the pounding of her head to stop.

"You . . . you spoke Latin out loud," Tabetha whispered with a quiver. "That can be da . . . dangerous. We are okay this time. Next time might not be the same."

"Why would it be dangerous to say out loud?" Vienna was confused. "We don't use Latin in the Human Realm, but some people study it, and it doesn't hold importance."

"There is a power in it. You must know exactly what you mean and what to say. Otherwise, a small slip of Latin out loud can cause mass destruction." Tabatha continued to quiver.

"Wait, what?" It took Vienna a second to understand what Tabetha was saying. They had been transported, but where?

Tabetha repeated herself telepathically, and Vienna understood, noting to be cautious of using Latin in the future.

Forcing her mind from the pain, she pried open her eyes. The room was fuzzy, and she blinked several times. As her vision cleared, brown walls came into view. There was a musky smell, and she felt rocks and dirt under her hands.

"Are we back in the cave?" she asked as she sat up with a groan. "Ohhh . . . my head." The room spun, and she slowly laid back down.

"You hit the ground very hard. Yes, we are in the cave. The one with five candles. They are lit this time." Her words shuddered with hesitation.

"Why did you hesitate?" Vienna asked as she cracked one eye open. She tried to sit up again and felt a little better, but she still couldn't sit up all the way.

"Soon, you will feel better and be able to see for yourself," Tabetha said with trepidation.

After several minutes, Vienna was able to sit up and look around. Each candle was lit, but they appeared dim. Looking closer, she noticed they were pitch black in the center, so black she couldn't see a wick. Where luminous yellow should be present, it was different for each candle. One was blue, another dark orange, and the third was green. Rising closer, she saw that the fourth was pink, and the final resembled the dancing colors of an opal.

"These are astonishing," Tabetha whispered.

"Look closely. The inner glow is lighter than the outer glow. Each flame goes from black to a light color to a deep color. I've never seen anything like it. Have you?"

"Nope. Never."

"I wonder what they all mean. Why are each different?"

"I don't know. If you think about it, it's like Earth, Air, Fire, and Water. But what about this one? The colors change."

Vienna reached out to touch the opalescent flame. "There's no heat," she said, puzzled.

Tabetha landed on her shoulder and stared into the light. "I see pink, blue, green, orange, and . . . is that clear? It's more than transparent, though. It's shiny."

"Similar to a diamond. It's a mixture of the other colors—like looking into a transparent opal. It's stunning." Vienna looked around. "Who else has been here? We didn't leave that long ago. And the wax isn't melting." Vienna looked at Tabetha.

The little fairy was shaking. "I don't think we should stay."

"Agreed." Vienna headed for the tunnel she had crawled through earlier that night. It was a tight squeeze, but she got down and crawled. Tabetha led the way and illuminated the tunnel with a brilliant turquoise light. Neither spoke a word as they worked their way through.

"Wait. Do you see that?" Vienna asked. "It's glowing right ahead of you."

"I see it. It's a crystal. But it's not glowing."

"It *is* glowing. Keep moving forward so I can get to it."

Tabetha flittered two feet forward, and Vienna was able to rise to hands and knees. She moved forward and started to dig where the light beamed. After several inches, the glow dimmed, then it disappeared. She continued to dig, and her fingers slid across something smooth. She carved it out of the ground but couldn't see anything.

"Tabetha, come here!" she yelled. Tabetha came and glowed brightly.

The stone was nearly all white, but the tip was dark. It was almost perfectly round and unpolished. Flakes of black and gray were speckled throughout the stone.

"It's a moonstone," Tabetha gasped.

"I've never heard of a moonstone before. What is it?"

"Oh, dear! Never?" She shook her head in shock. "I don't know how it found you, but it is a natural crystal that harvests the moon's energy. Tonight is a full moon, which may be why it is glowing . . . or because of you." Tabatha quivered.

"How does it harvest the moon's energy when it's in a cave?"

"I don't know all the details. Maybe a professor will know? I do know it enhances intuition and is found in very few areas. If you look closer, you can see some tiny green, pink, yellow, orange, and blue specks. Not just gray and black."

"I can't see any of those colors."

"Maybe with help?" Before Vienna could answer, Tabetha connected with Vienna's head.

This time, Vienna didn't pass out. But she was in the Fae Realm. Everything was so bright she couldn't make out shapes or colors. She groaned, trying to clear her head, but the illuminating lights from the realm caused an instant pain in her eyes each time she peeked through her lashes.

"Thanks for the warning. The pain is unbearable," Vienna cried.

"Sorry," Tabetha giggled.

Vienna felt a firm pressure against her temple, then a tickling sensation danced down the back of her head. The pain began to fade as she fought the urge to curl into a ball and hide.

"Better?" Tabetha asked, still quivering.

"I don't know." Vienna grabbed her head, afraid to try again.

"*Look!*" Tabetha demanded as excitement spilled over.

Sure enough, as Vienna saw the stone in the Fae Realm, there were slight hints of the other colors. Colors that were invisible to the naked Human eye.

"Wow. It's incredible." Vienna stared in shock as the brightness faded and deep, vibrant colors began to show.

"It's known for healing and balancing and enhancing intuition. It is rare and represents feminine energy, balancing emotions. It speaks volumes that it found you."

"Did you notice, or is it just me?" She looked at Tabetha with wide eyes as her voice shook. "It's like the colorful flame in the cave."

"Yes . . . it has to mean something. We must find out what!" Before Vienna could reply, Tabetha transported her.

Once she balanced herself, Vienna was not in her room as she had expected. She was in a glade surrounded by willow trees. The trees were in shades of yellow, gold, and brown. But in the center of the glade stood a sizable pink willow with a white throne carved into the trunk. At a closer look, the entire trunk was white and shiny, almost metallic.

"What is this place?" The glade was full of fine, pale green grass with a path of pink ornamental grass that looked like cotton candy. "I've never seen such a clear sky, one so black. There's no blue," she gasped as she noticed no signs of clouds, the Milky Way, or anything else. The sky was pitch black, with stars scattered everywhere, like a canvas. To the west was a white and gray planet with what appeared to be three rings, slowly moving vertically.

"Is that Saturn?"

"No, it is Zaldun Zuria. It's the language of the Fae. It means 'white knight'. It is the moon to this realm."

"What is this realm?"

"It is still part of the Fae Realm. You may know the different Fae houses, such as the Seelie or Summer Court. I have brought you to seek answers. But beware—though they are benevolent, they are still dangerous."

"Wait, what?" Vienna was trembling. "How are they dangerous?" She started to feel faint and closed her eyes. Bending and placing her hands on her knees, she inhaled and focused on steadying her heart.

"Each Court is unique, let me teach . . . " Before she could finish, a powerful voice interrupted.

"The Rogue Fae. How interesting! Are you back from the Magic Realm? After so many centuries?" The voice commanded attention and obedience.

Tabetha trembled in fear. "Yes, Banrigh Gheal." She bowed.

Unsure how to proceed, Vienna bowed too.

"Who is this?" Vienna felt fingers slide through her hair. "A Human . . . no, power courses through her." Banrigh Gheal cocked her head at Vienna. "What is your purpose here?"

"Shall I introduce you two . . . " Tabetha asked, still trembling.

"Please do," the voice beckoned.

"Banrigh Gheal, I'd like to introduce Vienna Madizza-Corey, from the Italian Madizzas."

With that, Vienna's chin throbbed under the cold, bony hand that demanded her attention. As her head was lifted, she saw the face that belonged to the commanding voice. The woman's features were sharp, and her piercing, icy blue eyes sent a shiver down Vienna's spine. Her skin was like porcelain, and a hint of peach shadowed her cheeks. It suited the strawberry-blonde hair that cascaded the length of her body. She wore a leafy gold tiara entwined with thin branches and petite pink and orange flowers. The same flowers were strategically placed in her hair. She was stunning. Her bold, delicate curves and full lips caused Vienna to ponder if she stood before a goddess.

"This plain girl is what the world has been waiting for?" She peered at Vienna with narrowed eyes. With a snap of the woman's fingers, Vienna laid at the base of the white throne. With no control of her body, she stared at the grass beneath her hands and watched as the tips of pointed white cloth shoes lifted Vienna's chin. Their eyes locked.

"Welcome to the Seelie Court, Quintessence. As Queen of the Summer Court, I say we have much to discuss."

# CHAPTER TWENTY-SEVEN

Heart pounding, Vienna's ears swished as her irritation grew. Again, Quintessence defined *who* she may be to someone she didn't know. But how did this queen, the ruler of another realm, know about her and the Quintessence?

She learned she was to call the White Queen "Banrigh Gheal", which meant "Queen of the House." She was a force of power and confidence. From there, the conversation became more structured.

"Sit up, child," demanded the White Queen.

Vienna straightened like a puppet.

Under the planet's glow, the White Queen's icy white silk dress took on a light shade of blue, making her eyes appear even icier. Yet Vienna noticed warmth behind the cold mask and stern features.

"Ask your questions," she commanded with an uplifted eyebrow. "I see you have many."

"How do you know me? You used two names that are to be important." Vienna sat on her legs, staring at the beautiful Fae.

"Hmm . . ." She peered at Vienna, then looked at Tabetha. "Do you know how unique it is for a Human not just to see a Fae, but to have one bound to them?"

Anger swelled as the Queen dodged her question. "No. But Tabetha has told me it's not unique," she spat.

"Tabetha"—the White Queen pursed her lips—"I like it." She moved closer to Vienna and extended her hand. "Come with me. We shall discuss some important matters before you leave. I see your strain as you've avoided the question. I have many of my own. We shall walk among the fall colors as we speak. Know that we are safe here, and no other will hear."

Vienna pondered the truth of her statement and doubted its validity after Tabetha's warning of the Fae. She thought about the consequences of disclosing too much and wondered if this Seelie Queen meant her harm.

After a slight hesitation, Vienna took her hand and rose. Tabetha flittered up, leaving a stream of unusually thick sparkles, before landing on Vienna's shoulder.

"Speak with caution and clarity, Vienna. Fae will use your words as they see fit," Tabetha trembled.

Vienna nodded, and the two strode to the woods with the White Queen, hoping to gain answers to questions that would help lay the ground for Vienna's future.

"To be fair, we shall take turns asking questions. Since you are my guest here, you are welcome to start," the Queen snarked.

"Why did you refer to me as Madizza-Corey the Quintessence?"

"Ahhh, we shall get along just fine. I would rather be direct." She turned to Vienna, and her face softened. "I assume you have heard of the Witch Trials that led so many to America and how the Magic Realm was formed to create safety, especially for schools."

Vienna nodded.

"Good . . . " The White Queen placed her hands behind her back as she passed rows of golden willows. "After the realm was created, Beatrice Sparks remembered rumors of a prophecy before the witches fled to America from other parts of the world. It was the

Prophecy of one child, destined to create peace between all the realms."

"All realms?" Vienna interrupted.

"Tsk, tsk. That's question number two."

*Damn it*, Vienna chastised herself.

"Little was known about the child except that her presence would come before the War of the Realms, a war that would change all we know today. Though we were uncertain of when or who this Prophecy spoke of, those who deciphered the writings pulled hints from each passage. These hints tell us that two pure bloodlines will unite to create a powerful being, who blooms early with unique abilities.

"Granted, there was no talk about what these abilities were," she continued. "The only clue was that one family name would be Italian." She glanced at Vienna, who was deep in thought about her own unique abilities. "It is also prophesied that this . . . chosen one could walk between planes."

The quiet enveloped Vienna, and she looked up at the White Queen, who wore a defiant smile.

"If this is your question, I will answer it," Vienna said.

"Ahhh, you are wise."

"That wasn't an answer. If that is your question, I shall answer." Vienna chose her words carefully, being sure not to ask a question.

The White Queen's smile vanished. "It is."

They had made it back to the center of the glade, and she sat back on her throne. Vienna sat in front of her with crossed legs. Tabetha curled up between her legs and quickly fell asleep.

"I am a Dreamwalker," she said flatly, hiding all emotion from the clever queen.

"Yet you deny this gift," the White Queen stated.

Vienna could hear the shock in the Queen's voice. The White Queen had not asked a question and allowed her emotion to slip through.

Vienna would not offer the Queen any more kindness than she

herself received. She stepped forward, features confident as her chin tilted up. "Is this your final question?" Vienna countered.

With a smirk, the White Queen rose. "You are wise, young one. But note, I will not be challenged in my court."

"I merely ask for equal rights," Vienna whispered as she bowed.

"Finish the question, and we will move forward."

Before Vienna could respond, Tabetha shook her head. Upon seeing her wide eyes, Vienna decided to hold this error for future use if needed.

"I do not deny this gift. But I don't seek it, either." She hoped that offering extra information would create a connection and garner admiration from the Queen.

"These experiences can be terrifying. The dream I experienced was, anyway. Then the Ovr'seer used my power to gather info just to find out it was me who could walk between planes. He warned me of others taking advantage of my powers. So I stopped them. I focused on Logan's training with hand-to-hand combat and forgot the rest." Vienna hadn't admitted any of this to anyone, or herself. She hadn't even thought about that night until now.

"Ovr'seer? What do you know of this person you are referencing?"

"Again, you're asking multiple questions."

"Do not challenge me, girl . . . You will meet your doom." Her body shook with rage, and the ground trembled. Annoyed, Vienna refused to back down.

"I will answer your questions," she assured the White Queen. "In exchange for additional questions of my own."

Pain gripped her stomach, and she fell to her knees.

"Apologize!" Tabetha shrieked. "Apologize before she kills you!"

"Let me rephrase this for you . . . Tell me who the Ovr'seer is. Question revoked." Vienna hadn't noticed the White Queen's hand clenched until the pain was released.

She gasped for air and pulled herself into a fetal position as Tabetha rubbed her back.

"I . . . I don't . . . know." Vienna gasped for more air as the pain slowly subsided. "Why?"

The White Queen smiled in victory, and a cruel smile spread across her features.

"For the Chosen One shall be sought out by the Ovr'seer, and the powers will become dormant until the Opal Moon awakens them once more. There is no doubt about it, Vienna. You are the Chosen One. Your powers became dormant, not of your fear but because the Ovr'seer was testing you. Then, that stone in your pocket landed you here. That Opal Moonstone." She stared at Vienna with wild eyes.

Vienna's mind was racing. She had never mentioned the stone. They hadn't gotten that far. In fact, she had forgotten about it until now. Opal Moon. The moonstone looked like an opal. The candle looked like an opal as well. Could it be? Could she really be destined to create peace in the realms and rule them? No . . . she wasn't the ruling type.

"I don't know if I can believe all this. I am just a girl who inherited powers from my parents, and now . . . now I just want to go to the winter dance. I want to meet a cute boy and fall in love. I want to go to law school or study something fun, like music. I can't be this person."

"I'm sure it's hard. But there is no doubt about it. You are The Chosen One," the Queen said tenderly.

"What about the Ovr'seer's warning? He said something about trials and people testing me or . . . what was it . . . " She jumped up and paced with both hands behind her head. She couldn't recall exactly what his warning was.

"The Chosen One shall experience trials that test her power, alliance, will, and intuition. Those she trusts shall fall, and if the Chosen One chooses the wrong alliance or fails to win against the Nemesis, the Magic Realm shall cease to exist."

Stunned, she realized this queen, the White Queen of the Summer Court, had just summarized what the Ovr'seer had disclosed. Was it possible that they were right? What were the odds that they were wrong? These two people whom she had met at different times in her life had exposed the same prophecy.

"Can you tell me . . . What are all the qualifications that prove I can be this . . . this Chosen One?" She caressed Tabetha's wings, watching them lift and drop with each breath. Even in her sleep, her body shined brightly, and her white wings dropped glitter with each movement.

"You will have lineage from two original and powerful families. You will be able to move between planes. You will come to power early with no knowledge of who you truly are. The Ovr'seer will find you and silence your powers. This power will be restored at the arrival of the Opal Moon. You will be beautiful for the Human world, but plain for the Fae."

Vienna tensed at the last criteria. She had always been beautiful, but since arriving at Sparks Boarding School, she realized she didn't hold a candle to some girls. "How many others could this be?" She looked up as she asked.

The Queen's face became stern and cold. "You cannot deny this destiny. If you fail, we shall all cease to exist, child. If you trust the wrong person, the same shall come to be, as you heard from the Ovr'seer. Perhaps your focus should be not on denial, but on how to hone in and use your powers once they reawaken.

"For now, the time has come for you to go home. Your school awakens, and you will be no help if you lose your position at Sparks Boarding School. Dive in, Chosen One. Learn all you can, harness your strength, and may you save us all."

At that, Vienna looked up. The White Queen smiled, a smile that failed to reach her eyes. She snapped her fingers once, and Vienna was gone.

▽△△▽✳

Vienna woke to her alarm. Remembering the night before, she bolted out of bed and looked around. The others finished adding powder to their nose or grabbed their books. Tabetha laid at her side, fast asleep. She felt something in her hand. Curious, she opened her palm. Inside was the moonstone. She held it up; the light hit it just right, illuminating hidden colors.

"You better get ready, V. Classes start in 10 minutes," Celine said. She paused. "You look like you didn't sleep a wink last night."

"I didn't," Vienna admitted.

"Why are there leaves in your hair?" Celine walked over, plucked two orange leaves from Vienna's hair, and crunched them. "I haven't seen those leaves around here. Did you leave again?" she accused.

"They're just leaves. Probably half-dead from me rolling on them all night," Vienna deflected.

Celine squinted her eyes, but she didn't dispute it. Instead, she went back to getting ready for class.

Vienna rushed to get ready. She wanted to talk to some of her professors to learn more about prophecies and moonstones.

Each class left her disappointed. None of the books in the room appeared to have any information. She decided to go to the library during lunch to research.

She found several books in the library related to the history of the Magic Realm. She found a quiet corner where she would be free of distractions and dove in.

"Should you not be in class, Ms. Madizza-Corey?"

She looked up, knowing Professor Audovera would be standing with arms straight behind his back. She smiled when she, indeed, looked up and found him, exactly like she expected. His 1800s clothes were still perfectly pressed, even at midday.

"I figured lunch break was a good time to do some personal research," she replied confidently.

"The hour is fifteen hundred," he replied skeptically.

"What?" The clock confirmed the time. "Oh, no," she groaned. Her forehead hit the table. "How stupid!" she exclaimed.

"It appears your discoveries are not just time-consuming, but enjoyable. You seemed pleased but frustrated when I arrived. May I sit?" He gestured to the seat across from her.

"Of course," she replied in surprise. She wondered how he always seemed to appear when she was in need, but dismissed the thought and leaned into the comfort of his presence.

"I have a sense you are on a mission. Based on the material, you are seeking answers on the Prophecy," he stated.

"How do you know about the Prophecy?" she asked, her brows knit and her shoulders rigid.

"Ah." He smiled. "I have been around for many centuries and know much about it. In fact, I believe the question is, how do *you* know about the Prophecy?"

# CHAPTER TWENTY-EIGHT

## Vienna & Logan's
## POV

Vienna spent the afternoon discussing the basics of how she knew about the Prophecy. She disclosed her findings at home regarding certain powers to be used to help the realm, but she left out any more important information. She wasn't sure if she could trust Professor Audovera, but his knowledge as a history teacher who had been around for decades could prove priceless.

After the bell for dinner, they parted ways but agreed to connect again after Thanksgiving break once he explored the topic more to discuss any critical information.

"There you are." Iris giggled. "Were you here with Professor Audovera?"

"Yeah, he was helping me with some history research," she answered as she packed books into her bags.

"Want me to carry some? There are too many for one person," Iris offered.

"No, but thanks. Most will be returned. The librarian said to leave them here, and she'd gather them later. How about we head to dinner?"

"Yes! I'm starving. I heard we're having spaghetti and meatballs. The others will already be there."

"Why didn't they come with you?" Unfortunately, Vienna was unsure who she could trust. She felt a little guarded after realizing that if the Prophecy was correct and she was the Chosen One, not everyone would be on her side. The Ovr'seer and the White Queen warned of deceit.

"They were talking about Thanksgiving with their families. We leave soon, and I wanted to make sure you talked to your parents about me going with you. I was also hoping we could go dress shopping for the winter formal," she stated in a wavering voice.

"I don't see why not. I'm sure my mom will want to go with me. She won't want to miss helping me find my first fancy dress." She laughed.

"Sweet." Iris looked and sounded sad. "I wish I could celebrate and shop with my family, but I'm sure yours will be amazing." She smiled.

Vienna matched her smile, and as they walked into the dining hall, the exciting chatter revolved around the upcoming break and the dance that followed. The winter formal would fall on the solstice, which many speculated was a coincidence. Vienna assumed it was done to celebrate the solstice, but she didn't state her opinion.

"There you guys are. We have your food." Jayla ushered them over to the table occupied by Celine and Nessa. Right behind them were Cosima and her minions.

"How did we end up so close to them?" Iris asked Jayla.

"Oddly," Jayla whispered, "they sat behind us as soon as we chose our seats. They've been rather quiet, too."

The girls all sat, and Cosima glared as Vienna settled directly behind her. Ignoring Cosima's petty behavior, Vienna concentrated on eating and answering all her friends' questions about where she'd been, why she missed her last classes, and why Professor Audovera was there. She evaded most of the questions, but feeling someone watching, she turned to see Cosima eavesdropping. She instantly wondered if she was one of the people she needed to be careful not to trust.

"Are you okay, V?" Nessa looked concerned at Vienna's distance, and the others exchanged looks that indicated they were all concerned. "You've been a bit off since this morning."

"I didn't sleep well," she replied with little conviction. "I think I should turn in early tonight."

"What about fight practice? It's only been two weeks, and you're ditching? It was your idea to try and learn extra."

"Actually," Celine jumped in, "the announcement at breakfast yesterday—the one you all missed after our hike—stated that no extracurricular activities can take place without prior authorization from our counselor. The school has too many people creating clubs, and grades are dropping in many classes."

Vienna relaxed; grateful one thing was taken off her plate. The magic and physical defense she learned in her weight and sports class was plenty, let alone when they were practicing their homework during study hall.

"More time for exploring then," Vienna offered.

"I actually would like that," Jayla exclaimed.

"Me too," Nessa and Iris echoed.

"Um, is this mandatory?" Celine asked.

They all ignored Celine and discussed places to explore. The conversation shifted to going back to the cave to explore more before Thanksgiving.

## LOGAN

"Vienna was in the Fae Realm," the Seelie Queen began. "She was accompanied by Tabetha at the Seelie Court. I held my disguise, and no one would know I sat on the Council as I played the Fae game well. But it shows her power is growing. Even with a Fae's help, she should not have been able to enter."

"She also inquired about the Prophecy this afternoon and gave me information regarding her knowledge that came from various sources but is limited," Mr. Audovera added. "During her training this summer, her parents dropped her hints along with Valda, but overall, she only knows the basics to which all people from the World of Magyieka are privy."

"There is no doubt, with everything beginning to line up, she must be the Quintessence. With her powers growing, I'm afraid the Prophecy is unfolding." Ms. Blight clasped her hands as she shook her head.

Logan placed *Pufurate,* the book of the future, on the table. The Council waited as he gathered his thoughts. He stood and looked around. "I was told by my father as a child that the one prophesied to unite our lands would come from the Human Realm and access her magic early, but I didn't know much more. As I watched Vienna train with Valda and as I've worked with the Council, I have gathered bits and pieces that have added to this knowledge." Logan stared at the book and laid his hand on it. "Now that I have read these pages, I don't know how we could deny it is her. Even though we are missing some information"—he flipped to the pages that had been removed and to the chapters that jumped, showing some realms hadn't added information—"she fits all of it. The only thing I don't understand is the meaning of the twin flame at the end of the book."

"What is the twin flame you speak of?" Mr. Ozul grabbed the book and looked at the page. "This page is empty."

"No, it's not. There are daggers on there. They are drawn in detail." Logan pointed to the page, then looked at the Ovr'seer.

The Seelie Queen stood gracefully and walked toward Mr. Ozul. She swung her hand over the book, whispering so quietly Logan couldn't make out the words. As her hand passed over the page, two images flickered and a set of daggers appeared.

"Look at that," Mr. Humphrey gasped. "The details are uncanny."

"What are the stones?" Mrs. Jaheem asked.

Mr. Ozul handed the book to Ms. Blight and pointed to the stones secured in the metal. The drawing was detailed with various smeared dark splotches of different intensities through the light stone. Ms. Blight took the book and turned it, looking at the daggers and the stone intently.

"It's a moonstone with prominent coloring that resembles an opal." She looked at the Ovr'seer. "A moonstone has the shimmer of different colors, unlike an opal with distinguishable colored specks. A moonstone pressed into a dagger with this many colors is rare. Its meaning is complex, and different versions of the moonstone can alter its energy."

Ms. Blight handed the book to the Ovr'seer and quieted as he flipped through the pages behind it. "What would be your guess as to the meaning of the diverse coloring?"

"A moonstone always represents clarity, new beginnings or change, and the connection to femininity such as softness, intuition, and fertility. It's also known for its healing properties. With the increased coloring, I'd wager this stone is what awakens the Quintessence and her powers while providing emotional balance and psychic protection. It also symbolizes intuition and connection to the other elements, such as Earth, Air, Fire, and Water, clearly represented, meaning they symbolize someone who is Spirit," Ms. Blight said, her eyes unfocused.

Logan gulped as he recalled Vienna's obsession with daggers, but he quickly pushed the thought away, as the ones she used did not have stones. "How do we proceed?" he asked flatly.

"When Vienna appeared in the Fae Realm, she held a moonstone," the Seelie Queen said softly. "There were no daggers, but with what Ms. Blight shared, it is time to increase Valda, Elric, and Logan's orders."

"Vienna and Iris leave for the Human Realm for Thanksgiving," Ms. Blight reminded them.

"That's right." Mr. Humphrey rubbed his strained forehead. "If time allows, please ensure Elric will be on watch while they are in the Human Realm. It may be wise to also notify the staff at Sparks to increase their watches over the next few weeks. There is increased movement in the Shadow Realm, and we have yet to find the source."

"If granted permission"—Professor Audovera stood—"as we move toward the break, I can increase studies with Vienna and reduce the time she has to sneak out of the school."

The room filled with murmurs as the Council considered this. Knowledge of the built rapport with Vienna would help in reducing suspicion.

"Next week, our studies will include facts about spells and their origin and prophecies. I will be sure to briefly mention of The Prophecy. I would wager this will send her back to you for insight before we leave for break," Mrs. Jaheem said.

Each member nodded in agreement and then moved on to discuss theories of what was happening in the Shadow Realm.

# CHAPTER TWENTY-NINE

Vienna had the desire to learn as much as she could before she left for Thanksgiving break. Each day she woke with new questions to ask Professor Audovera. After discussing her desire to find answers, Professor Audovera agreed to meet a few times before break. Each moment she had outside of class and practice with her roommates, she'd meet with him, and he'd assist in her research. Though they'd dug, they had not found many answers, but she had learned more about philosophy and the history of how philosophy came about. She was excited to share the information before she realized there was nobody to discuss it with. She was keeping another secret from her family and friends. Her friends continued to ask questions about her spare time spent with professors and how she seemed to have little time for them. She was unsure how much longer she could keep up the charade.

Balancing everything, time flashed by and before she knew it, the weekend before Thanksgiving had arrived. Exhaustion flooded

Vienna, and she smiled weakly, trying to hide her lack of energy as she entered the room and flopped on her bed.

"Hey stranger," Iris greeted Vienna.

"Were you with Professor Audovera again?" Celine asked.

Vienna nodded, closing her eyes briefly.

"What are you hoping to learn from him, anyway?" Iris probed again.

"Just a deeper understanding of our history. I keep telling you this. Why can't you accept the answer?" she snapped.

"Sorry, it just seems . . . odd," Nessa said with a shrug.

"Are you jealous because you find the professor attractive, Nessa?" Jayla accused.

"As if!" Nessa huffed.

"How about we forget about it? When she's ready to share more, she will," Celine offered.

*"Let me help,"* Tabetha told Vienna, and Vienna nodded.

Tabetha fluttered between the girls as they talked, hoping her Fae energy could calm them. Knowing they would go home in two days had them all on edge. Most were excited to go, but there was the stress of getting things ready for the winter formal. The fact that winter was coming meant holidays and the pressures of living up to family expectations were coming too. Vienna felt lucky to not have those pressures; her family was pretty laid back. Sure, they had their problems, but nothing like many others. At least not her immediate family.

Vienna watched Tabetha flutter around and thought about Celine. She was talking about the extravagant parties her family hosted and the importance of her regal appearance. Then she thought about Jayla's excitement about going home, but how little she actually shared. She just said her family was excited to have her home and that the holidays were celebrated with a focus on family connection and the importance of tradition. Nessa said there wasn't a focus on tradition, but more on bonding and fun in nature. Vienna imagined their families and smiled.

"Are you ready?"

Vienna looked around; the other girls looked ready to go. "Crap." Vienna rushed around, gathering her things. She'd almost forgot they were heading to the cave. "Ready, let's go."

▽△△▽✳

"We're here!" Iris exclaimed.

Vienna smiled. They were all thrilled to have the opportunity to explore the cave again. Even Celine had dressed to be able to explore the tunnel and the ritual circle they'd found.

Entering the cave, Vienna felt a rush of excitement. They had brought enough supplies to stay most of the night. She had also brought a book to help them light the candles. She hadn't told the rest about the book, but they had discussed practicing magic to light the candles.

"Who wants to go first?" Celine asked with a quivering voice.

"Follow me, Celine," Iris chirped. "One of the others will jump in the right behind you. You'll be safe and secure."

"Okay, I'm okay with that. Yep. Okay." Celine nodded several times.

They all began to crawl, and Vienna wished they could see Tabetha's glow. It made the crawl easier, especially when they started the army crawl. Halfway through the tunnel, Celine gasped in pain.

"Ouch, what was that?" They all stopped. She told the others something poked her, and she unburied the sharp item.

A few minutes passed until they found their way to the open room. Celine gasped and remarked on the room's beauty and how much she wished she hadn't missed it last time.

"It's okay. You're here now," Jayla said soothingly. "And look what you found!"

They all gathered to see Celine's stone. She had found a Ceylon sapphire. It looked like a deep blue diamond.

"I've seen that in my book," Vienna exclaimed. "Look." She dug through her sack and pulled out the ritual book. She flipped to the pages of crystals and pointed out the sapphire. "It states it's a powerful amulet that will protect against envy, create the desire for knowledge and inspiration, and protect the wearer. It represents purity and will bring the owner prudence."

The others gathered around the book.

"How did the gems get here?" Celine asked.

Vienna flipped through the book, finding no answers. She looked at Tabetha.

"They are transported here and embedded into the soil after the previous owners pass. Stories have been told of the owner's soul bringing their stone here to bury it with a spell of protection until the next rightful owner finds it." Tabetha nodded smugly. Vienna giggled at her pride.

After Vienna shared the story, they sat there in wonder. No words were spoken as they each contemplated the meaning of being chosen by those before them.

Celine looked at her sapphire with admiration. "I feel so much pride and peace," she whispered.

Vienna smiled and then flipped through the pages. Seconds later, a gem jumped out to Jayla.

"What about this one?" Jayla pulled out a ruby crystal set on a chain around her neck. "I found it the last time we were here. It was almost like it found me."

Iris gasped and pulled out a similar necklace, but it appeared to be two stones mixed. "I found mine the same day Jayla did. Why does mine have two stones?"

Everyone looked at Nessa expectantly. She shook her head as if to say, "I don't have one."

"Let's look up the others." Vienna flipped through the pages. "Here, Jayla. Yours is a ruby, which we knew. Helps to overcome darkness and fear and can glow in the face of danger. It also protects from malicious evil, spirits, and being charmed. It can also restore forces and awaken passion."

"Ew!" All the girls sang in a teasing tone.

"Very funny." Jayla blushed.

"Iris, let's look at yours." Vienna flipped several pages and couldn't find any mixed stones. "There's no mixture, so we'll look up the two individually."

"I don't see what else we could do," Iris said, leaning over to look.

"One stone is zircon, like a brown or blush pink. It brings energy, strength, and confidence. It also helps to uncover lies and deception. They will cultivate truth while also having improved memory and intellectual abilities."

"Oh no," Celine commented. "That's all we need. She already knows everything before we do."

They all laughed, even Iris.

"Okay, the other one, the one wrapped around it like a wire or lightning . . . that's jasper, the stone of happiness. Worn as a pendant, like you are, it can protect you from evil spirits. It also helps with courage and removes negative energy, replacing it with tranquility."

"Wow," Iris whispered. "It's like it knew what I needed."

"Or what you are inside," Nessa offered, as she looked up. Her focus diverted, and she turned. When Vienna looked, she saw something odd in a small puddle of water.

Nessa walked over. "Check it out!" she squealed. "There's a stone down here." She started digging it out with her fingers, but after a moment, she slowed down. "Anyone have a pen or pencil?" she asked.

"I do." Vienna tossed over her thick metal pen she had brought with the book.

"Thanks. I think this may be my stone!" Several minutes later, with the girls standing behind, Nessa pulled out her own stone. It was packed with dirt, so they used bottled water to clean it.

"It's beautiful," Nessa breathed.

"It's so green!" Iris pointed out while looking over Nessa's shoulder.

Nessa turned to show the others. Like Iris said, it was bright emerald green.

"Find out what it means!" She hopped up and down and then ran to Vienna's side.

"All right," Vienna laughed. It only took her a couple of seconds to find the suitable stone. "It's an emerald. Emeralds have spiritual benefits to increase meditation ability, insightfulness, and your ability to read the motives of others. It can also help to neutralize negative influences, and goes on about snakes and protection. It says it helps to learn secrets and penetrate the future, too . . . That's intense," she said, looking at Nessa.

"What about you, V? Did you find a stone?" Nessa asked.

After realizing she hadn't told them about her stone, Vienna smiled and pulled it out. "It's a moonstone. It heals, balances, and enhances intuition. It also helps to become connected to one's own subconscious."

"Why do we all have one?" Jayla asked.

"And why here?" Nessa added.

"I was looking more into the ritual setup here . . . " Vienna pointed around the room. "See all the candles? Each one is a little different. People used setups like these to practice their skills, especially before schools were designed to help. Maybe the stones and the candles together mean something."

"That makes sense," Iris said.

"But how do we find out what it means?" Celine shuffled her feet and played with her sapphire.

"Well," Vienna said with a grin, "we have the next 6 hours to figure it out."

They decided to try to find the candle that matched their stones. Vienna knew which one was hers. As she walked up to it, the candle lit with a flame that shot a foot up, and sparks flew everywhere.

"Yikes!" Nessa screamed and jumped backward. The sparks fizzled out before dropping below the candle. "Magnificent!" she said, gaping.

"That was incredible," Jayla gasped.

"Keep walking in front of the candles. Maybe they will all do the same thing," Vienna suggested.

They continued walking in front of the candles. One by one, they found their candles, each lighting and shooting into the air. Each candle's flame matched the color of its stone. Iris' was salmon, Celine's was blue, Jayla's was red, and Nessa's was green. From the side, Vienna affirmed that there must be a connection. But why did the stones empower the candle?

"V, your candle . . . Well, it's unique. Why is that?" Celine asked with curiosity.

"I don't know." Vienna shrugged like it was no big deal. "Each of ours is unique."

"Yeah, but yours has multiple colors," Jayla pointed out, and all the girls began to talk about its uniqueness: the variety of colors that matched each element; the way it sparkled multiple colors at once; how bold the sparkles were; what it could mean as a stone; what it could mean for the finder . . . for Vienna.

"Anyway," Vienna sighed, wanting to avoid the topic. "What are we supposed to do with the candles and stones?" She tapped her chin while staring at her candle.

"Maybe your book will have something?" Celine suggested.

"Right." Vienna nodded.

They all gathered in the room and settled on the cold ground. The candles continued to glow if they sat directly in front of them, of which Vienna took silent note. Vienna skimmed through the book but found nothing. She remembered another book she had checked out regarding rituals of the 1800s.

"This is exciting," Tabetha said in a singsong voice. She glowed brightly from all the excitement.

Vienna smiled at her and pressed her cheek against the Fae's fluffy wing. Tabetha quivered in delight. Then, they both turned their attention back to the group.

"Jayla, would you mind grabbing my bag, please?" Vienna asked.

Jayla nodded and set her ruby on the ground before grabbing the bag. As Jayla broke the line to her candle, it faded out. Vienna squinted her eyes. Then, as Jayla came back between her candle and her stone, the candle lit again. That answered Vienna's question; to create power, the person *and* stone must be aligned with the correct candle.

Flipping through the new book, Vienna landed on a picture of a candle, stone, and room with four points. Not five, but it was close enough.

"Look," she pointed out excitedly. "It says that for the candles to alight, they must align with an Enchanter and their given stone." She looked up at the girls and continued, "That must mean stones chosen by whatever power, right?"

"I'd think so. Like nature, our natural power helps the correct stone find us?" Iris offered. The other girls nodded, so Vienna decided to continue.

"'The alignment of all four elements allows Enchanters to create rituals that will harness the energy of the given element to create magic with tenfold the power of an individual.' I guess that means we are stronger together, but can tap into our power individually, just on a smaller scale."

"That's how I perceive it," Nessa said.

"Me too," Iris agreed.

The others nodded, and Vienna continued. By the time they had finished the chapter, they had learned that with the right group and spells, they could create a large variety of power. From something small, like making flowers grow, becoming invisible to others, or even filling cups with water, or as a group, they could also create large-scale spells, like creating tornados or other storms, summoning people, or even transporting themselves or another person.

"How is this possible?" Celine asked with a trembling voice. "I mean, this seems impossible. That's a lot of power. Why us? And why now? What makes us so special? Why hasn't, or have others . . . well, wouldn't we know?"

"Slow down, Celine. You're not making sense." Nessa touched her arm.

"I'm sorry. There is just so much information, and it all seems impossible. I mean, summoning people? And transporting them? Creating major storms? We barely learn about the small things we can do, like moving objects. And none of us have even learned how. We are learning about it and the witch world before modern times."

"It does seem impossible," Iris agreed.

"Let's try some," Jayla offered.

The cave became cold with the tension. They stared at one another for several minutes before they all nodded.

Just then, Tabetha zipped over. "Wait, weren't you warned that one of these girls would betray you? Are you ready?" she asked as the girls trembled in fear.

Vienna paused. Tabetha's fears made sense, but Vienna felt okay so far. *Calm down, Tabetha. We're only doing a minor spell. It'll be okay.* She smiled, stroking the Fae's wing and tapped her head.

Tabetha let out a string of high-pitched cusses before sitting on Vienna's shoulder. "If I can't convince you to wait, I will not leave you." She nodded with a heavy sigh.

Vienna smiled without turning to her, and her heart warmed. She always felt safe when Tabetha refused to leave her.

"What spells do you have, Vienna?" Jayla asked, bouncing slightly. She didn't seem to be as worried as the other girls.

Vienna was still stuck on the circle of four expressed in the book compared to the circle of five that they had. Her color and stone weren't mentioned in the book, and she felt unsettled about them. What did that mean—they had extra power with a fifth person? Could they do more? Was there a particular meaning? Should she ask her friends or keep it to herself? She decided it wasn't the time when some of the girls already felt unsettled.

"Sorry, what do we want to try? Some are as simple as creating wind, or we could do something more complex, like creating a lightning storm. Ooh, or we could create grass and flowers in the cave?"

She looked up with excitement. It would be nice for the room to be more than musky dirt.

"Ooh . . . that one!" Iris jumped up and clapped her hands.

Jayla responded with a laugh. "Of course you like that one. Your stone is Earth! What about you, Nessa and Celine? Do we want something special for your element? Nessa is Water, and Celine is Air. I'm Fire," she pointed out. "We could do one thing of each . . ." She broke off and looked at Vienna. "Wait. What is yours?" she asked with knitted brows.

They all turned to her with curious looks on their faces.

"I'm . . . I'm not sure," Vienna stammered.

"Go back to the first book," Jayla demanded as she tossed it to her. "What does it say?"

Vienna flipped through but found nothing. She asked for her bag again and pulled out an old journal instead, one bound on pages that looked like flesh. She flipped through until she found information on a fifth element: Spirit.

"Um . . . maybe Spirit?" She held the journal up and pointed at the top of the page.

"I haven't heard of that," Celine said, eyebrows low. "What does it mean?"

"Well, it looks like there's only one page about it, but it refers to a second journal with more information." Vienna looked back up and noticed each girl glancing at one another, then back at her like she was a freak. She waited for them to attack her with insults.

"No way!" Iris' eyes grew large. "So you're saying the books had nothing, but this journal expresses very little? Where did you get the journal?"

"I found it in bed with me last week. I don't know where it came from," Vienna answered honestly.

"Why didn't you tell us?" Celine demanded.

"I was afraid you'd think I was a freak." Vienna closed her eyes.

"We all are." Nessa grabbed Vienna's hand and held it. "But we are a team, Vienna. That means we're in it together." All the girls agreed.

All Vienna could think about was her warnings regarding not being able to trust someone. The real reason she didn't tell anyone. How silly was that? "You're right," she admitted. Remembering her conversation with Valda, she focused on each girl as she tried to tap into her telepathy. *Who can I trust?* The air paused as she looked at each girl, determined to align with them completely.

Celine's crystal eyes sparkled, and Vienna sensed purity. Her body eased, and she instantly felt a gentle breeze circling her—aligned and at peace. There was no doubt she could trust Celine with her life and all her secrets. She looked at Nessa, soaking in her fiery hair. Waves of cool drizzles washed over her stomach and crept across her skin—her moist skin shivered as whispering waves of healing filled her. She felt like a piece of her childhood was given back to her. Next, she looked at Jayla. Her honey eyes soothed her soul, and she felt a warm embrace wrapping around her as though a wall of fire protected her from any outside force. Enveloped in impenetrable protection, Vienna gasped. Finally, she looked at Iris, excited about what gift she would sense from her. At first it was silent, then she heard a faint whisper. *We are all here for you, Vienna. To protect and shelter you from any storm that comes to you.* Vienna looked at Iris and was met with a nod of solidarity.

All doubt vanished. The girls were gifted by the universe. Her circle and tribe—the family she chose. Vienna smiled, and the air began to flow naturally again, the slow mode no longer controlling the cave.

"Well," Jayla exclaimed, "what information do we have about Spirit?"

"Let's see." Vienna flipped to the first page. "It says, 'Spirit is the connection to the universe, infinite time, a veil, and a guide for here and other plains.'" She looked up at them.

"Wow!" Nessa exclaimed. "That sounds badass." The others muttered agreement.

"Go on," Jayla prodded.

"'The Spirit is white, which in terms of light is a mix of all colors, meaning Spirit can control all elements to some degree.'"

They all looked at Vienna's candle, embodying several colors.

Vienna was encouraged to continue with several nods. "'The Spirit symbol is a spiral of stars, as it is endless and holds the power of the universe. With a Spirit person in a circle, increased power moves from twofold to five.'" Her eyes widened, and they all gasped and looked at one another.

"'The downfall is that without guidance and a pure heart, a Spirit-wielder can become poisoned and cause chaos or even genocide. Moving to the dark side is the biggest danger a Spirit person and those in his or her world can experience, as it means complete destruction and an end to all that is known.'" Vienna's stomach turned, and she dropped the journal.

Iris grabbed it and continued to read. "'*But*,'" she emphasized, "'if the Spirit-wielder remains pure, he or she is destined to create peace and unity in his or her world in measures unknown before that time. A rare gift indeed, a Spirit only comes when the world requires change and a savior.'"

"No pressure," Jayla squeaked as she looked sympathetically at Vienna.

Iris continued, "'With a trusted circle of the Earth, Air, Fire, and Water users, the Spirit user's odds of success rise. Should the group fall, it could mean the end of life as they know it, or"—she looked into Vienna's eyes—"the destruction of the entire universe."

Vienna sat there frozen in fear for several minutes before she heard her friends call her.

"I know this is intimidating," Celine said, voice quiet. "But I would like to still try something small. What are your thoughts?"

"Yeah," Vienna responded weakly. She went back to her books and found an easy spell. "How about we start with trying to grow a flower?"

They all agreed, and Vienna showed them the words. They

discussed how it would work and stood in their spots, keeping their stones close.

"You're sure about this?" Tabetha asked, voice shaking. Vienna merely nodded before turning to the girls.

On Vienna's mark, they all began to chant:

*Flos crescunt*
*Flos floris*
*A terra descensus*
*Viribus floreat;*
*Florescant cum amore*
*Flos floris*
*Flos crescunt.*

They continued to chant until air tossed their hair, pulling it upward, so it swayed freely above their heads. Tabetha held on to Vienna's shoulder with strong, vice-like fingers and pulled her wings as close to her body as possible. The girls reached for each other's hands on the final chant. As they commanded the final word, their arms stretched toward the ceiling, hands still latched. All at once, the air stilled, and the girls fell to their knees. Vienna was exhausted, and as her eyes closed, she noticed everyone else looked as tired as she felt. As she opened her eyes again, so did everyone else. They glanced at one another before they found a large pink flower in the circle's center.

They all squealed and jumped around.

"That was incredible!" Jayla shrieked with a huge smile.

"Let's try something harder," Celine suggested.

In agreement, they decided to try to create a storm. Vienna found a spell, and they all memorized it.

"Since that one was pretty easy—" Iris began.

"And almost natural," Nessa interrupted.

"Right," Iris continued with a glare, "this shouldn't be too hard."

"Vienna . . . please try some more small ones first," Tabetha whispered, voice shaking again.

Vienna could feel the fear rolling off her and nodded in agreement. "Let's try two more small ones real quick," Vienna countered.

"Thank you," Tabetha squeaked.

After adding some grass, a small stream, and warm air, they decided they were ready to try a storm. The storm would be rain and thunder, but nothing more. Feeling confident after several practices, they all got into position and began to chant:

*Tempestas medicandi*
*Tempestas in viribus*
*Incipe imber*
*rugiet . . .*
*Tempestas cum fortitudine*
*Tempestas pernoctabit*
*Reperio potestatem*
*Retine lucem.*

On their third chant, Vienna felt sweat run down her brow.

"Please stop. It's too strong. You'll be hurt."

Vienna ignored Tabetha, afraid to break the connection with the others. Air flew in a frenzy, and their bodies shook. Fatigue set in on the fifth chant, and lightning struck the middle of the circle, sending electricity toward each girl.

At once, they shot back against the wall. A bright white light surrounded them. Flickers of electricity bounced around the dome. Then, all went black as her eyes drifted shut. The last thing Vienna saw was Tabetha standing by her with drooping wings.

▽△△▽✳

Red rocks and black sand covered everything as far as Vienna could see. Above was deep gray, but it didn't look like a sky or the top of a cave; it was nothingness. She felt void of emotion and feeling. Cool air nipped at her skin. Wearing a simple embroidered white cloth dress with a corset bodice, she shivered, feeling vulnerable and out of place. The bottom of the dress flowed over her bare feet. Moving her toes, she smiled as sand filtered between her toes.

"Welcome to the Nether Realm," came a strong feminine voice.

Valda stood a foot away, staring at Vienna's surprised features.

"I'm sure you have many questions, so let's begin. This is what many call the Dream Realm."

Vienna nodded, but remained quiet.

"Good. Less to explain." She circled Vienna and stopped when she closed the circle. "Although this place seems unreal, what happens here bleeds into reality. Most of us Dreamwalkers use this place for safety, though. We come here to hide, gather, or even just find a calm place . . . to be." She shrugged. "Normally, people come alone or spend much time wandering to find who, or what, they are looking for." Her hand remained behind her back in a formal stance, which made Vienna uneasy. Valda was cold and distant.

"Then are we here together?" Vienna asked.

"Good question," Valda replied with a lifted brow. She was dressed in a leather suit that hugged every curve. She also had two daggers on each hip and swords crossed behind her back. *The exact opposite of my appearance.* "I was in the cave watching you guys. You knocked us both out, so here we are." She gestured to the red rocks to the north.

"Wait"—Vienna turned to her—"why were you watching?"

"I can't tell you too much. But I was afraid. How do we know who to trust?"

"You're the one sneaking around all the time." Then it dawned on her. "Were you the one I could feel watching me the other night at the school?" She cocked her head, shocked she hadn't connected it to Valda before.

Dropping her head, Valda nodded.

"Why?"

"I told you before, my guardian won't let me near you. So, I have to watch from a distance." There was no conviction in her voice.

"I'm starting to get nervous, Valda. You have so many secrets." Vienna paced. "You always appear when there's chaos. I don't know how I'm supposed to trust *you*," she shouted.

"I get that. And I'm sorry."

"Never mind. We'll deal with that later. How do we get out of here?"

"You don't like it here? I always find it peaceful."

"I read you can get trapped in the Nether Realm in the journal I was just reading."

"We won't get trapped. And we will be able to leave when you wake up."

"Like, we just won't be here anymore?" Vienna asked with confusion. "Can't I wake myself up now? I was in the middle of something."

"Or you'll find your orb, which will take you out of here." Valda shrugged like it was simple.

"So I have my own orb?"

"We all do. For some, it's a door, others a gateway or black hole."

"Once I find that, I can go through and wake up where I fell asleep?" she asked.

"Sometimes. Or you'll wander endlessly and end up lost. But that can create chaos. The goal is always to get back where you started."

"What is the main purpose of this place?" Vienna motioned her arms around, taking in the massive scene.

"We can walk in someone else's dream to communicate with them like we are now. You can also observe or control others. You can even go to other realms."

"Other realms? Like the Fae Realm, without the Fae's help?"

Before Vienna could ask another question, everything began to get blurry. "Wait, I have more questions!" she exclaimed.

"See you back at school, Vienna. Write the questions down. We'll have time to go over them in the future." She walked away, vanishing mid-stride.

Vienna drifted into blackness.

▽ △ △ ▽ ✳

"*Finally!*" Tabetha's high-pitched voice increased the pounding in Vienna's head. "We thought we lost you. It's been hours."

"Welcome back, sleepyhead," Jayla teased.

"You realize it's been like . . . " Iris checked her watch. " . . . 4 hours."

"A few more minutes, and we would have had to get help. What happened?" Nessa asked.

"Nothing. It just wiped me out," Vienna lied. "Let's get back to campus, or we'll be late for lockdown."

"*Pfgh,*" Jayla teased. "We can always just use magic to pick the lock." They all laughed before helping Vienna to her feet and gathering all their stuff. Once they had everything ready, they started the hike back to campus.

# CHAPTER THIRTY

Everyone slept after their long day, but Vienna laid awake, her mind racing as she picked apart all the day's events. The school year was over after the Winter Solstice, and she would be home for Thanksgiving in just a few days. Yet she felt as though things had just started to make sense. She thumbed Tabetha's wing. She was the first to fall asleep, and a small wheeze escaped her. Vienna longed to explore the Nether Realm, but she didn't know how to get there on command. Finally, she decided the only thing she could do was try and hope it was a success.

Defeated, she opened her eyes. Instead of lying in a dark room, she stood before Valda. Vienna smiled with pride.

"Long time," Valda joked, as she walked toward Vienna. "Looks like your powers are awakening more each day. Welcome to my dream." Valda motioned to the surrounding area, filled with mountains, open fields, and forest animals. Instead of her Nether Realm gear, she wore red combat boots, skinny white jeans, and a lavender belly shirt. Her hair ran freely down her back, and she wore just a touch of natural makeup.

"You look so different here," Vienna commented.

"It's the one place I can be the true me. Not what others expect or what duty requires." She began to walk to the stream, and Vienna followed. Once they had arrived, Valda removed her boots and placed her feet in the water, sitting on a large rock.

Vienna admired this side of the girl she'd known for several months. She seemed content instead of ready to fight. "I guess that means we are safest in our dreams?"

"Mostly," Valda whispered as she looked up to Vienna. "There are other Dreamwalkers. But unless they have a cause, they don't bother people in their Dream Realm. If anything, they would challenge them by summoning them to the Nether Realm."

"I see." Vienna crouched down next to Valda. "I have many questions, as you probably could assume. Can I trust you to answer them?"

Valda nodded.

"I know I'm called Madizza-Corey due to the strong lineage I hold and that I have developed my skills young. But I'm confused. Why am I the Spirit? And why do we have to keep our friendship secret? Back home, you seemed so relaxed around my family. Now, I feel like I can't even mention you." Her words were pressured and gained speed as she continued. "I know you said it's to keep us safe, so your guardian won't know. But I can't help but feel like there's something you're leaving out. You're my most trusted friend, but you're hesitant to trust me."

"You're right," Valda muttered with a hung head. "I can't tell you yet, though. I must have your complete trust first. Something is coming, and I wish to achieve success, which requires you to be on my side. There must be no wavering doubt in your heart," she whispered as a blue bird landed on her lap. She ran her finger down the bird's back as it chirped.

"When will I get to know more?" Vienna's voice wavered.

"Soon. For now, keep practicing. I know Iris is going home with you for Thanksgiving. Maybe the two of you can practice your skills and get stronger," she offered with a faint smile. "Either way, our time is up. The bell to be dismissed for break will ring soon."

Without another word, all the colors in Valda's world blurred. With eyes open, Vienna laid on her bed, staring at the ceiling. Tabetha remained sound asleep at her side, and she could hear the girls' deep breathing in the stillness of the night.

▽△△▽✳

"I am *so* excited to be going home with you," Iris squealed. She had spent hours trying to find clothes she felt would impress the Corey family.

"My family is going to love you. You don't need to try so hard." Vienna giggled as she continued packing.

Iris sat on her bed and looked at her reflection in the mirror. Her dark hair was in a high ponytail, and her dark brown eyes appeared to have less spark. Vienna could understand Iris was sad to be missing a holiday with her family. Still, she was grateful for the opportunity to go home with Vienna. This would be their first try at teleporting themselves to Station Isle, and it helped keep Iris' sadness away.

"She looks sad." Tabetha's soft voice brought Vienna back to awareness. "Do you have plans for her while you're home?"

*I'm not sure what we'll do. Will you be coming, though?* Vienna looked down at the Fae curled up in her lap and stared at Iris.

"Of course! I only won't be with you when you are in the Nether Realm or when you demand."

Vienna realized that her companion's body dimmed when she was tired. Still, she never completely stopped shedding glitter or sparkles. *Dust. I think it's dust,* she thought.

"I heard that, and yes, it's dust that sparkles," she answered weakly. "When do we leave?"

*About 20 minutes. We'll meet by the fire at the entrance of the west wing. They'll help us transport from there.*

"I see. Maybe," Tabetha suggested, looking at Iris, "you should talk with Iris. She looks anxious."

*You're right, Tabetha.* Vienna walked closer to Iris. "Is there anything I can help you pack?"

"I have everything. Do you think Ms. Blight will let us go early?" Iris asked quickly.

Laughing, Vienna shook her head. "You need to relax. But yes, we can go and see if we have to wait much longer."

"Great! Let's go." Iris grabbed her bags and headed to the front room.

The room was full of hustle and bustle as all the girls from the west wing gathered early in hopes of departing. Vienna and Iris looked at one another with disappointment and then flopped onto the couch. They watched the girls transport one by one. They said their goodbyes and gave hugs to their roommates before they left. Soon, it was down to just them.

"Iris, your turn." Ms. Blight nodded.

Iris gathered her stuff and turned back to Vienna. "See you on the other side," she squealed. Before Iris said another word, she was gone.

"Ms. Corey." Ms. Blight motioned for her.

Vienna approached, grinning.

"Who is this?" Ms. Blight asked, nodding toward Tabetha with a grin.

Vienna gasped. "You can see her?" She looked at her Fae and then back at Ms. Blight.

"I can," she answered. "I, too, am in tune with the Fae. May I ask how you came to be her person?"

"I was lost, and she found me," she answered hurriedly.

"I see," she said as she walked toward Tabetha. "Was this the night you disappeared to the cave, and Mr. Artrusha . . . Logan helped you?"

"How do you know about that?" Vienna knitted her brows and pursed her lips. She hadn't told anyone any details about that night.

"Ah! Yes, I forgot to mention that I know Mr. Artrusha well. He has reported back to me on your progress for some time. He has taken a liking to you, my dear. Don't worry. Nothing was put into your paperwork."

Vienna nodded, but didn't know how to respond. Why hadn't either of them mentioned the other? And why had Logan been reporting on her? She had many questions.

"Ask your questions. I've frozen time in this realm to give us ample time to discuss things."

"Oh. Um. Well, the first thing I'm curious about is how many of us are in touch with the Fae Realm?" She asked something basic to feel the temperature of the discussion.

"Less than five percent. The Fae Realm is not fond of most of us. Many are cruel and seek to gain power."

"Wow, that's awful." She reached out and touched Tabetha's wing, smiling at her. "What about Logan? Why was he reporting on me?"

"Mr. Artrusha works with recruitment at his school. However, he knew you, and he came to me when he noticed your name pop up as an early comer." She was standing with her hands behind her and was, as usual, very proper. She looked at Tabetha as much as she made eye contact with Vienna. "He wanted the opportunity to help you since he had gone through some transitions and understood how hard it could be to change realms." She smiled at Vienna as the heat rose up Vienna's neck and onto her cheeks.

"I didn't know that. I was pretty harsh on Logan when he was training me. I felt jaded for not knowing anything." Vienna's cheeks flushed, more from the memory of their practices.

"That's understandable. No reason to feel ashamed." Ms. Blight reached out and used one finger to shift Vienna's chin back up. "Any other questions?"

"Yes. What does it mean if I am the Sp—"

"Shh," Ms. Blight whispered as she placed four fingers on Vienna's lips. "You must not discuss that here," she said as she looked around. "Should you want to explore that, you know the safest way to talk to me about it." She winked at her, and before Vienna could ask anything else, Ms. Blight snapped her fingers, and Vienna was gone.

▽△△▽✳

Vienna wobbled as she landed at Station Isle. She was disappointed that she didn't get to try the transportation spell and frustrated that she had been shushed.

"There you are!" Iris grabbed her arms and pulled her into a hug. "I am SO excited. How did you transport? Was it easy? I couldn't believe how easy it was."

"I have never seen you so talkative before." Vienna laughed.

"I'm proud," Iris said with a singsong voice.

"You should be! Now let's go," Vienna insisted with a wide grin.

The portal glowed as they stood in Station Isle. They walked to the portal in silence and saw Mr. Audovera standing next to the purple swirl that was the size of a door. He looked official, with 1800s clothing and a serious demeanor.

"Hi, Mr. Audovera. Are you here to help us transport?" Iris asked as she bounced on the heels of her feet, impatient.

"Yes, ma'am," he said with a nod. "It's quite simple. Please repeat these words." He handed them each a slip of paper. "The Coreys will be waiting on the other side to pick you up. Kindly have a joyous holiday." With a nod, he stepped sideways, placed his hands behind his back, and stood on guard.

The girls looked at one another and, at the same time, read the paper that would transport them back to Oregon.

*Oregon oram de Magia Regno*
*Transporte nos illuc nullis ambages*
*Cum imus, claude ostium*

*Serva nos incolumes in itineribus nostris domum*

Iris fell to her knees, puke erupting onto the ground. Vienna reached down to hold her hair. "That was rough?" Vienna laughed.

"First . . . " Iris gasped " . . . time . . . " she whispered, "riding . . . with . . . someone."

"I'm sorry. I've heard it can be rough." She kneeled and rubbed Iris' back with her free hand.

"It didn't bother you?" Iris choked out.

"Guess not."

Tabetha jumped off Vienna's shoulder and landed on Iris' back. Her glow intensified until Vienna had to look away.

*What are you doing?* Vienna asked.

"Taking the sickness away. Iris should be fine soon," Tabetha answered softly with a rush of air. "It's a little straining. I shall not talk until I'm done."

She continued for a split second before Iris sat up on her heels, wiped her mouth with her sleeve, and looked up to the sky.

"Better?" Vienna asked.

"Much. I feel like I've been reset," Iris said with a big smile. "Though I could use a drink." After a couple of gulps of water, she grabbed her gear and stood up.

Tabetha beamed brightly, and her turquoise sparkles were thicker than ever.

Vienna smiled at Tabetha and thanked her with a nod.

Tabetha fluttered back to Vienna's shoulder. She nuzzled tight against her neck, and before she relaxed to recharge, all Vienna could hear was, "Welcome, my person."

Just then, Vienna heard branches snap and turned to see her parents. She hadn't seen such a beautiful sight. Her eyes teared up instantly, and she ran to embrace them.

Iris walked up behind them after several minutes of endless questions and answers. Her mom reached out and pulled Iris into a hug.

"Welcome to the family, Iris. We're thrilled you'll be spending the holiday with us."

"Thanks, Mrs. Corey . . . "

"Please call me Grace," she requested.

"Thank you, Grace! I'm excited to spend the holiday with you. Vienna has told me all about your food and cooking. She also said you have some great ideas for dress shopping. Can you believe the end of the year will be here in a month and that we end it with a *formal dance*?" Iris rambled.

Her mom laughed so hard that she threw her head back. "You're going to fit in perfectly here." With that, they all headed down the road to the car.

▽△△▽✸

"Hi, Ms. Blight." Vienna took the opportunity in the car to snooze and try walking into Ms. Blight's dream. It was the only thing she could assume she meant by them talking in a safe location.

"You did understand my comment," Ms. Blight responded, obviously pleased.

"I hope I'm not intruding."

"Never. Let's walk, and I will show you my dreamscape," Ms. Blight answered firmly and led the way.

They walked across an aqua-colored path that resembled clouds. Rows of pink cherry trees ran along the pebble stone path, with gardens beyond them spanning as far as the eyes could see. A bright blue waterfall cascaded down light tan and black rocks. There was no top in sight. At the bottom was a pool of water that looked heavenly. Vienna hoped secretly she would get to touch it.

"This place is stunning!" Vienna gasped.

"Thank you! You'll learn to create yours as you see fit in time." She smiled. "We'll walk to the pool so you can see it up close. It's one of my favorite creations." She beamed.

"Deal! While we walk, can you tell me about the power of Spirit and how it relates to the Quintessence?"

"I see you've had many discoveries over the school year. That's good." As usual, she walked with her hands clasped in front of her hips. "Tell me first what you've discovered."

Vienna told her what she knew of Spirit and Quintessence, and how her parents had explained it. "But I feel like they are the same thing, with the Quintessence being more advanced, which I don't think is right," she concluded.

"It sounds like there's some confusion. Spirit and Quintessence can be similar. However, the Spirit is a gift, an element. Like your father told you, there have been some before you. However, the Quintessence is prophesied as the highest of all Spirits to walk the Realms. An entire prophecy was written about this. It is said that when the Quintessence comes to be, things will change. There is no proof that the Quintessence walks among us today."

"Most prophecies have signs and elements to them that make it clear they are the one," Vienna states.

"There are many aspects, criteria if you will, that must be met to be the prophesied Quintessence. It is a long list, but the most commonly known is early access of powers, a family of pure lineage, and ability to access multiple elements." Ms. Blight looked at Vienna, her eyes soft.

"Sound like a powerful woman." Vienna mentally checked off the criteria, straining herself to be still, giving no energy to the fear growing within her.

"Indeed. When we compare this to you, there is much missing. You have the lineage and you developed early, but other than that, I am unsure if you are. Only time will tell." They made it to the pool, and Ms. Blight sat beside the water.

Vienna sat next to her on a rock that was as comfortable as a cotton cushion. As she leaned back, a backrest appeared. "Eek!" she gasped in surprise. She shook it off quickly. "Can you tell me exactly what to look for to know whether I am the Quintessence?"

"Many have this misconception. Few know of the Prophecy, as it could bring chaos to the world and all its realms. Which no one can become aware of," Ms. Blight scolded. "But no, I cannot tell you anything I know, as it could interfere with the Prophecy."

"I can see that," Vienna responded flatly as her heart raced. She looked from Ms. Blight to the pond. "What about the ability of Spirit?"

"You know much about that. But some more details would help." Ms. Blight nodded. "First, the Spirit is like the glue of a group. The Earth, Air, Fire, and Water you connect with will hold extra strength, so you must choose wisely. Sometimes nature does not choose right, but sometimes it does," Ms. Blight explained. "You bring extra power, but you also have an extra ability. Not only can you bend or use each element, but you can also use your power to strengthen others when they are harnessing theirs. Or you can split it and use some of your power to do what you want while fueling all the others or just one or two. On top of the extra power you provide, you will again heighten what they are currently creating."

"That sounds like a lot of power," Vienna squeaked out—her mind could barely wrap around it.

"It is, and unlike many others, you don't need a group or circle to cast major spells, though adding others can create more stability. You can also pull power from your group members no matter where they are to gain more strength, but you must do so carefully, as it could drain them."

"Would it drain them completely?"

"Yes, or it could kill them," she warned.

Vienna's stomach turned at the thought of hurting a friend.

"What about the warning I keep getting about someone breaking my trust?"

"Ahh, yes! *If*," Ms. Blight emphasized, "you are indeed the Quintessence, then someone you trust completely will cross you."

"When will I find out if I am?" Before she got an answer, Vienna looked into Ms. Blight's eyes. "Do you believe I am?"

"The question is, do *you*"—Ms. Blight moved a strand of Vienna's hair from her face and lifted her chin back up—"believe you are she?"

"How could I . . . " Before Vienna could finish, all the colors of the dreamscape began to blur.

"Be safe, child, and trust your heart."

Those were the last words she heard before opening her eyes and finding herself back in the car.

▽△△▽✳

"We're home!" her dad cheered. All the kids were asleep except Vienna.

"That went fast," Vienna replied as she stretched.

"We'll get the boys to their rooms. Why don't you get Iris situated?" her mom suggested.

Several minutes later, with Iris comfortable in her bedroom, Vienna hopped down the stairs, hoping to get time with her parents. She turned into the kitchen to find them sitting at the table. A steaming cup of hot chocolate with a peppermint stick sat in her spot, and both parents smiled at her.

"That smells delicious," Tabetha chirped.

*It really is. Try some,* Vienna offered. Tabetha sipped some and trembled with delight. Vienna giggled. Her parents looked at her like she'd gone insane.

"I haven't had this in a while," she responded, hoping to cover her mistake. They just smiled.

They talked for hours about how school was going, and Vienna filled them in on what she had learned about the Quintessence and Spirit and how they were different. Her dad's downcast eyes spoke volumes.

"You knew there was a difference? You had said, before I went to Sparks, they were pretty much the same." She shook her head, processing the change.

"We knew there was a slight difference, but not the full extent.

Most of us have basic knowledge of the Prophecy," her dad admitted. "I can't believe how different the two are, but it makes sense."

"Why didn't you guys just say there was a difference?" Vienna asked.

"We were afraid if we told you too much, you'd go seeking answers," her mom admitted.

"I can see that. But now that we know about the Quintessence and what it truly is, how do I know if it's me?"

"Time," her mom replied. She took her daughter's hand in hers. "We pray you're not, because we have heard great challenges exist. But we also hope you are, as the changes prophesied are needed, and you have the heart needed to make it happen."

The silence grew heavy, and Vienna's exhaustion increased.

"I'm going to turn it in; I'll see you guys in the morning." Vienna stood, moving into a big stretch.

"Would you girls like to go dress shopping while you are home?" her mom asked, walking toward her.

"Hell ya." She blushed. "Yes. We were hoping we could find time for that."

Her mom nodded and kissed Vienna on the forehead. "Get some sleep."

She hugged her dad, then she and Tabetha headed to bed.

"We've learned so much today," Tabetha yawned.

"Too much," Vienna snarked. "What am I supposed to do with all this information?"

"We'll figure it out. But, for now, let's help Iris have a great fall break. Then, when we get back, we can figure out the rest."

"Such a wise little Fae you are." She leaned her head against Tabetha, who curled into Vienna's neck.

"Thank you, person," she whispered as she beamed with pride. Her light brightened, she quivered, and then she nuzzled into Vienna.

# CHAPTER THIRTY-ONE

"It's perfect!" Vienna exclaimed as Iris walked down the little runway of the dress shop and turned around in front of the six mirrors surrounding them. Iris was trying on a black and copper-brown dress. It hugged her curves and made her naturally olive skin, dark hair, and eyes pop.

"Isn't it? I like that the front comes to the knees, but the back has a train. And this tapered waist! It's gorgeous. Looking closely, you can see some orange snowflake designs on it. I felt it was ideal for a winter formal." She laughed. "Colors of the earth and snowflakes. How odd but perfect!" She was correct; it was perfect for her.

Now to find something for Vienna. She'd tried several dresses on and couldn't seem to find the right one.

"Are you done too?" Iris asked Vienna.

"Nope, she's only tried on most of the store," her mom teased.

"I can't find the right one," Vienna whined as she collapsed on a chair.

"Maybe I can help," offered a middle-aged clerk. "We have some inventory in the back. It's stuff out of season or special orders that weren't picked up."

"Worth a try," her mom responded. "What do you think, V? Want to look at a few more?"

"I guess." Vienna shook her head. "Do you want to come or change?" she asked Iris.

"I'll wait here," Iris said as she twirled in the mirror. "I need to think about shoes, anyway."

The back of the store had fewer than a dozen dresses, but one stood out instantly. "This one," Tabetha squealed as she landed on a white dress.

Vienna pulled it off the shelf and decided to give it a try. In the dressing room, Tabetha buzzed around with excitement. "Calm down, Tabetha! It's just a dress."

"Just a dress? *Just a dress?*" Tabetha chided. "It's the most perfect Vienna dress I've ever seen."

Vienna rolled her eyes and slipped out of her clothes. As she pulled up the dress, it felt . . . right. Each area hugged her perfectly, and she looked stunning. The dress was a short home-coming style with a tulle skirt that tiered to the waist. From there, it was a strapless bodice with a sweetheart neckline. The neckline and the base of the bodice glistened with rhinestones that sparkled blue, pink, and silver. The bodice had sweeps of white embroidery and a touch of silver sequins. It screamed power.

Vienna left the changing room to show the others what she had found and how well it fit her. Walking down the small stage, she heard her mom gasp and Iris whistle.

"A wonderful choice," the clerk stood. "We've had that one for quite some time. I've never understood why it's been overlooked by so many." She smiled at Vienna and then checked the dress to ensure nothing needed to be altered. "A perfect fit, indeed!" she said with a half-sigh.

"I'll take it!" Vienna declared.

As they waited for their dresses to be rung up and bagged, the girls chatted about the upcoming dance and the supplies they still needed: shoes, tiaras, jewelry, and maybe even new makeup. Tabetha shook her head at mentioning the makeup, and Vienna chuckled before patting her wing.

Vienna watched as Iris shifted nervously.

"Are you okay?" Vienna asked Iris.

"I don't know how I'm going to pay," Iris whispered. "I usually just put everything I buy on credit, like most people in the Magic Realm. We just put it under our family name." Vienna watched Iris as she looked between the cashier and Grace.

"I'm sure my mom is going to get it all. I told you: this trip is our treat." Vienna smiled and touched Iris' arm.

"All right! We're ready to go," her mom said, handing the girls their bags and heading out of the store and across the street to the local shoe store. The girls followed, excited to continue being spoiled.

"I'm beat," her mom announced as they sat down for dinner that night. Her dad had cooked a nice dinner, and the boys were scarfing down their food.

"How was shopping today?" her dad asked.

"Amazing, Dad. I found the perfect dress. So did Iris." Vienna beamed.

"Glad to hear it. It's only a couple more days before Thanksgiving. Hopefully, it will be all hands on deck. What else would you girls like to do while you're home?"

"Honestly, I'd love to explore the area," Iris began. "I've never seen so many trees; they're so lush and green. It's beautiful."

"Sounds like some hiking and exploring is in the future," he responded.

"I think that's a great idea," Vienna agreed.

"When do we start cooking?" Iris asked.

"Tomorrow. Some of the food has to sit a day or two to be its best," Vienna informed her. "Do you know much about cooking?"

"Nope, but I'll admit, I'm excited to learn after hearing about the feast your family creates," she admitted.

The Coreys all laughed. They couldn't deny they always over-cooked and used too much sugar during the holidays.

The rest of the night was filled with games and movies, talking about school, and catching up on what Vienna had missed while she was gone. Her heart was filled with joy by the end of the night. She couldn't wait to explore the mountains with her friend and show her how unique the area was.

▽△△▽✸

The break flew by, and before they knew it, it was time to return to the school. The girls had spent an entire day hiking; the next, they spent cooking for an army. Iris was astonished at how much food was prepared, but after trying it, she realized it wouldn't last long. The vacation brought the two girls closer together, making it hard for them both to leave the Coreys' home.

"We'll be at the portal in a few minutes," her dad informed them while they talked about the upcoming dance.

"I really appreciate you having me for the week, Mr. and Mrs. Corey. I had a wonderful time," Iris admitted.

"It was a pleasure having you. You're welcome anytime, okay, dear?" Vienna's mom assured her.

"Thanks." Iris smiled, and her eyes welled with tears. "I don't think I've ever felt this loved. Not even by my own family."

Before anyone knew it, they were at the portal, giving everyone hugs and saying their goodbyes. All the girls held back streams of tears, wiping the few that escaped as quickly as possible. Even Tabetha snif-fled here and there, and her body buzzed while making a high-pitched sound. It made it hard for Vienna to hold her emotions back.

Transporting didn't make Iris sick this time. She stumbled a little, but that was it.

"Good to have your back," stated a strong voice.

"Thanks, Nessa. How was your week?" Vienna asked.

"It was nice. Didn't last long enough, but I enjoyed it. Did you guys get dresses?" Nessa asked, wide-eyed and bouncing.

"Yes!" They all squealed, and Vienna was excited to see the different dresses they found.

▽ △ △ ▽ ✳

The days blended as the girls studied for their finals, which were just a week away. They studied diligently to ensure they passed and could attend the Winter Ball. Each weekend, they hiked to the cave to practice casting together, improving their skills each week. Finally, they went back to the basics and worked their way up to intermediate, spending 12 to 24 hours together. They unified in a way that made them feel like family. Trust was built with each gathering, and a successful spell left their bond deeper.

Finals week flew by; not only did they all pass, but they also hit top marks in each class. Studying together was a great choice. They had spent the week quizzing each other and taking several practice tests. The news of passing with high ranks thrilled them. To celebrate, they decided to spend the night in their cave.

The trek to the cave was quick and the banter light. The girls talked about hopes for the ball and their growth as students and friends. Tabetha fluttered nearby, creating a calm as Vienna observed the still night sky.

As they entered the cave, the air died down and the musky cave was comforting. Vienna smiled, looking at each of the girls to see how they responded. Like her, they looked at ease as they glanced around the cavern walls. The sparkling lights from the creatures clinging to the dirt walls lit the way to the crawl hole.

"Let's go." Nessa led the way to the tunnel. Without stopping, she crawled through, and each of the girls followed. Within minutes, they all emerged in the cavern room. Each girl lit their candle without effort, the merits of their practice paying off.

"It's incredible how easy it is to light the candles and do simple spells now." Jayla snapped her fingers and ignited a flame on the tip of her index finger. She blew it, sending an extra light to the candle. The flame grew momentarily, then shrank back to normal.

"During break, I went to a waterfall and practiced playing with my magic," Nessa admitted. "I'm able to intensify rainstorms and manipulate water." Vienna watched as she opened a bottle of water and sat in the middle of the circle they made. She motioned upward and watched as drops of water rose from the bottle, then floated to the sky. Nessa closed her hand, and the droplets gathered above them. Then she opened her hand and wiggled her fingers. Small drops of rain fell onto the dirt in front of them.

"That's incredible!" Iris gasped.

"Isn't it?" Nessa giggled. "Have you guys been practicing?"

Eager nods reassured Vienna as she watched her friends glow with pride.

"We've seen Jayla and Nessa do a cool trick. Maybe the rest of us could share something we've learned." Vienna nodded to Celine.

Celine closed her eyes and lifted her face to the roof of the cave. She lifted her arms, and a breeze moved slowly around the cave; gentle enough the dirt barely shifted. When she was done, she lowered her hands, and the breeze stopped.

"That was incredible control," Jayla admitted.

Vienna noticed beads of sweat on Celine's forehead from keeping the wind at bay. She thought about the first time they practiced and how chaotic it was. This time, they all showed improvement and pristine control.

"Iris, do you want to try?" Vienna asked. Iris nodded.

Vienna watched as Iris stood. Jayla and Nessa looked at Vienna, then back at Iris, but Celine kept her eyes on Iris. Iris twisted her hand slowly at first, then picked up the speed. A small dirt devil formed, and Iris used her other hand as a cup beside her finger. All extra dirt from the dirt devil moved closer to the tunnel, no grains of sand drifting from it. Iris moved her hands upward, and the formation lengthened as rocks gathered into the funnel. The dirt devil thinned out and reached to the top of the cave. No wind escaped the inner circle until Iris removed her cupped hand slightly and a few grains of sand pelted Celine and Vienna before Iris clapped her hands and the dirt devil vanished.

"Holy shit!" Nessa stood. "How did you learn how to control that so well?"

Celine blinked rapidly, not saying a word as Iris looked at each of them. "I was bored and practiced." She laughed. "What about you, Vienna? What have you learned?"

"Right." Vienna shook her head in shock. She hadn't realized how much control and precision could be displayed while creating a twister from dirt. "I don't know if I can come close to that, or what you guys have done." She laughed off her nerves.

Vienna focused on her cupped hands. She calmly chanted soft words to invoke Spirit. A transparent formation, like a waving body of mist, appeared above her hands. From the side of her eye, Vienna watched the girls look at one another with confusion. She smiled, knowing they weren't aware of her ability to create a mirror and place them all within it.

"Each of you harness your energy and focus on the magic you just did. Use the symbol of your element and hold it in your palm." As requested, they opened their hands, their palms facing up. In Jayla's palm, a flame danced. On Iris' palm, a stone laid with dirt surrounding it. A small puddle of water covered Nessa's palm, and in Celine's, a small, gray tornado moved around her hand. Vienna smiled at their shocked expressions but remained focused. One at a time, she called their elements to join her. As each element moved around the mirror that stood in her hand, she focused on merging the elements.

A storm within her hands began. Dark rain clouds formed a foot above Vienna's hands and lightning and thunder danced across her palms. Small flowers sprouted on her hands as raindrops fell onto the mud that now covered her hands. Each element was represented, but to make it more exciting, Vienna struck the flowers with lightning and a fire sparked. She let it grow before increasing the pressure of the rain that doused the fire and sent the mud sliding off her hands onto the floor of the cave. One by one, the elements disappeared, leaving nothing but empty palms washed clean from the rain.

Vienna smiled and looked up at her friends, who stared wide-eyed back at her. On her shoulder, Tabetha giggled.

*"They didn't know you could increase their powers like that."*

Vienna smiled at Tabetha, then looked back at her friends. "I think we make one hell of a team. What do you guys think?"

Iris looked at Vienna without saying a word. For a brief second, she thought she saw fear in her eyes, but it quickly faded. "I've never seen anything like that. It's incredible. I see why people say a circle of five is so powerful. You just enhanced our powers and used them in a way I don't think has ever been done."

"I agree. There is something unique about what you just did. It's beyond being Spirit," Celine added.

They talked about each of their powers and how Vienna was able to use them on her own as long as they were present. "So you can't access them when we aren't here?" Nessa asked.

"No, I tried before. I could see it, but I couldn't actually access anything. Just the vision of what I could do appeared. So I practiced as though I had access to it hoping it would work when we all got together."

"That's awesome," Jayla admitted. "Why didn't you say anything before?"

"I wanted to make sure I really could do it." Vienna shrugged.

"Well, I'm impressed with all of our growth," Celine added. "We've done well this year and we have just begun."

They chatted for a while as they listened to the weather outside. But as the night went on, they talked less and one by one, each girl fell asleep.

The night was gloomy, and the wind howled outside. Vienna laid there with Tabetha, staring at the cave's roof, thinking about the last few months. Tabetha's breaths were shallow as she rested in the nook of Vienna's neck.

*"What are your thoughts?"* she asked Vienna.

*"The Winter Solstice. It's only a week away, and the closer it gets, the more anxious I feel,"* she admitted.

They both knew there would be changes. They could feel a shift in the air as the time closed in. Neither could explain why or verbalize the emotions being experienced. They just sat there in comfortable silence until they both fell asleep, hopefully to get a few hours' rest before they had to head back to Sparks to prepare for the day.

▽△△▽✸

"I think we should try to portal back to our room," Vienna suggested.

After they all agreed, they worked together and summoned a portal. It opened in the middle of the room, right above the first flower they had created together. They looked at one another with pride and beaming smiles.

"We rock," Celine stated with her hands on her hips. Then, without another word, they all entered the portal.

Celine and Iris landed in their dorm room on their knees, Nessa on her stomach, Jayla on her butt, and Vienna on her back.

"Ooh," Iris groaned. "That was a bit rough. We need more practice."

"Guess we need to start transporting *to* the cave," Jayla offered.

"Right. But for now, I want to relax in bed until morning."

After all the girls were in bed and sound asleep, Vienna wondered if she should try to find Valda in her dreamscape or the Nether Realm. Finally, she decided on Valda's dreamscape, hoping she wouldn't cross any boundaries.

"Here goes nothing," she told Tabetha, who nodded and curled into her armpit with covers over her body. "Right," she laughed. "I'll see you again in a few hours."

▽△△▽✳

"Hello, V," Valda greeted. "It's nice to see you. It's been a while. Come and sit." She gestured to the golden throne. As she looked around, Vienna realized Valda's dreamscape changed and was now a tranquil glade. The throne room was made of gold metal and light gray stones.

"I'll never get over how different each person's dreamscape is," Vienna told her friend.

"It's a great way to learn about people," Valda pointed out. "Come sit with me." She gestured to the throne next to hers.

"But how do people change their own dreamscape?" Vienna asked.

"As we change, so do the things that make us comfortable." Valda shrugged.

Vienna studied Valda's formal dress and crown. Vienna thought she looked like a young queen in her royal blue dress, or a queen from the 1400s.

"So, what does this place tell me about you?" Vienna prodded.

"Of what benefit would it be to tell you? You must learn to decipher things on your own." Valda cocked her head sideways in a challenge.

"I see." Vienna nodded. "You desire to rule your own realm," she guessed.

"Not bad. Yes, I would love to have my own kingdom. But my deepest desire is to be part of a society ruled by a kind and gracious ruler." Valda switched gears. "What brings you here, Vienna?"

"I haven't seen you in school much and was worried."

"My class schedule was switched," she explained. "We no longer have classes together."

"Why was it changed?"

"My guardian felt we were getting too close. Odd since I didn't know she even realized I was communicating with you. Clearly, someone saw us at some point."

"Are you ready to tell me who your guardian is yet?"

"No," she muttered and hung her head.

"Fair enough. Are you going to be at the Winter Ball this Sunday?"

"I won't," she answered with a quivering voice. "I wish I could be, but I have prior arrangements."

"Will this be the last time I see you before the break?"

"Perhaps. But I can't make that a guarantee. Sometimes, my guardian changes her mind. If the meeting I have to attend ends sooner, I'll be able to go."

"I hope it does. I'd enjoy seeing you there. I hope that in the future we'll be able to be friends in a way others can know. You had become my best friend throughout training, and it sucks we can't hang out more."

Valda stayed silent, staring at Vienna for a moment before saying, "It's time for you to go."

They hugged, and Vienna left Valda's dreamscape and returned to her own.

▽ △ △ ▽ ✴

The weekend passed quickly, and soon the day of the Winter Solstice was upon them. The entire school rushed around, getting ready for the ball, which would start in just a few hours. The girls helped each other do their hair with elegant designs. Some wore fresh flowers; others went more natural. Vienna had diamonds scattered throughout the top half of her hair, which was half-up in a bridal updo. The rest was pulled to the right, cascading over her shoulder. She couldn't help but wonder how much better the diamonds would look if her hair was a darker brown, but they looked good enough.

"You look like a princess," Tabetha cheered as she fluttered around Vienna.

*Thank you.* Vienna blushed. She never believed she could look this beautiful. Her makeup was natural, minus some thick mascara and sparkly lip gloss. As a result, her cheeks and nose had a little extra shine.

"I feel like a celebrity," Iris said as she walked in. She stopped halfway across the room and gasped. "You look phenomenal. Guys," she hollered at the other girls, "come look at the final result."

They all rushed in and gasped, giving one another compliments.

"Look at your colors! They almost match your elements," Vienna pointed out.

The girls buzzed with this realization. Although they had helped one another get ready, they hadn't seen each other's dresses, except for Iris and Vienna.

Iris wore her black and copper dress that resembled earth.

Celine wore a long baby blue dress with spaghetti straps that crossed the back and left a pucker of the material above her chest. It had a slit up to her left leg and was polished off with a sash and shawl that changed colors, mimicking an opal.

Jayla wore a bright gold pencil dress that shined yellow.

Nessa wore a long turquoise ball gown that reached the floor and was shaped like a bell. The top was heart-shaped, but the chest, neck, and arms were covered with sheer mesh.

"You all look otherworldly," Vienna exclaimed.

"Did you all purposefully choose colors to match your elements?" Tabetha asked as she made herself comfortable on Vienna's shoulder.

"Um . . . " She looked at Tabetha and then back to all her friends. "How did you guys pick your dresses?"

"Mine just popped out, and I couldn't resist," Jayla shrugged. They all had a similar story.

"That's odd. That's how I ended up with my dress, too," Vienna admitted.

After a pause, Iris said, "One hour left before we head down. Should we go see if we can help?"

"I say we go watch for the boys," Nessa countered.

"I'm with Nessa," Celine giggled.

"Me too," Jayla added.

"Fine. I'll meet you guys at the ball," Iris said as she headed out the door.

Vienna hugged each of the girls and then rushed to Iris' side. "I'm with you." She squeezed her hand. "Let's go see how we can help."

# CHAPTER THIRTY-TWO

The shortest day followed by the longest night meant the Winter Ball would be long and filled with excitement—Enchanters celebrated by spending time with loved ones during festivals filled with singing, dancing, and fires. Sparks Boarding School did not hold back on the celebration.

By the time Vienna and Iris had finished helping, the gymnasium looked like a winter wonderland, with a white and blue fire in the middle of the floor. Snowflakes fell periodically, but they weren't cold and never melted. Food lined the north wall, and the drinks were on the east. Servers prepared food trays and filled trays with white and rosé wine, which would be served throughout the night regardless of students' ages. The servers themselves dressed in silver tuxedos with opal-inspired ties and masks.

Vienna waved away several waiters who offered her a drink. She was focused on the students piling in. She felt slightly out of place as the girls around her discussed which wine they would try first. Vienna longed to try some, but she feared losing control when so many events continued to confuse her. But part of her wondered if she'd enjoy it.

Jayla and Nessa grabbed sparkling cider, and Vienna exhaled in relief. Celine and Iris each grabbed a glass of wine and sipped it like it wasn't their first time. Vienna realized it probably wasn't, as their families were higher class and probably offered wine at each meal. She asked the girls about it, the answers to which confirmed her suspicions.

"It's weird how different our families are," Jayla admitted.

"At our home, once you turn sixteen, you can drink one glass of wine with your family. Much like the United Kingdom in your realm, Vienna," Celine explained.

"That makes sense. It's a cultural experience," Iris agreed.

Vienna dazed out as the other girls talked. Most of the girls who were drinking wine rather than cider were from the Magic Realm. She wondered if her opinion would be different had she been raised like those in this realm. Or if she wasn't afraid of an enemy taking advantage of the new experience.

"You're deep in thought," Ms. Blight said. Startled, Vienna dropped her cup. Ms. Blight caught it mid-air. "Easy. Are you okay?" she asked with concern. "I didn't mean to scare you."

"I feel on edge. I don't know why. My heart's been racing, and I feel like I'm being watched," Vienna whispered. She wondered if Valda was nearby. On her shoulder, Tabetha nodded in agreement. Ms. Blight looked around the room.

"I don't see anyone, but I'm glad to hear you've learned how important it is to focus on your instincts this year. You've made great progress, Vienna. You should be proud of yourself. Not only are you the youngest in your class, but you have top marks. You hold great potential. Be sure to listen and always heed your intuition, Vienna. One day, it may save your life."

Before Vienna responded, Ms. Blight turned to one of the other professors and walked away.

"What was that about?" Iris probed.

"She congratulated me for not completely sucking as a student," Vienna joked. Jayla and Celine laughed, but Iris stared at her unamused.

"I hardly think . . . " Iris was cut off.

Ms. Blight tapped on the microphone, sending an ear-assaulting screech across the room. Everyone covered their ears as she motioned for it to be turned up.

"Welcome, everyone!" Ms. Blight greeted the girls. "Domar's Boarding School students will arrive in the next few minutes." She looked around the room, waiting for the excited chatter to stop. When she had everyone's attention again, she continued. "Principal Cozbi will escort them in. We expect you to be respectful and hospitable, as we should be with all that visit." She smiled as the doors in the back swung open. "Girls of Sparks Boarding School, we present the gentlemen of Domar's Boarding School. Let the energy of the Winter Solstice flow through you as we celebrate the end of this season." As she finished, fireworks in several shades of blue, silver, and white flickered across the room.

Everyone turned around. Principal Cozbi walked toward the center of the room, followed by hundreds of boys. Vienna had to push through several groups of gossiping girls as they peeked at the boys. The harder she moved, the more aggravated she got. She harnessed some power and made an aisle through the girls. Finally cleared, she walked toward Principal Cozbi.

She was correct; it was a familiar face. Principal Cozbi was the Ovr'seer. She shook her head. *How didn't I put that together before?* She continued to move closer, but someone grabbed her elbow.

"What are you doing?" Iris asked in confusion.

"I know that guy," Vienna said without looking away. "He tested me once to ensure I was ready to attend. After that, he warned me about trusting others and told me my intuition would decide the fate of civilization."

"No pressure there," Iris teased.

"My thoughts exactly." Vienna looked at Iris and smiled. "I'm going to see if I can talk with him and find out if Logan will be here. Where will you be?"

"I'm going to find someone to dance with," Iris mused. "Jayla and Celine are already searching. They'll probably have someone before the music starts." She pointed to the other girls talking with a small group of guys.

"What about Nessa?" Vienna asked, looking around.

"She already found someone. Look at the drink table."

Sure enough, Nessa stood by a tall brunette, holding onto his elbow. They looked engrossed in a conversation.

"Dang!" Vienna said in wonder. "Girl's got game!"

"Yeah, she does. I'll see you around, okay? I see a cute redhead moving toward the back corner." Iris squeezed Vienna's arm before rushing off.

Vienna was happy for them all, but she wanted to talk with the Ovr'seer to see if she could get some more answers.

She weaved through the crowd but never found him. She asked several professors, but no one else had seen him, either. Eventually, she found an empty table in the back corner of the room and sat down, disappointed. She watched as people danced to the upbeat songs, then half the crowd disbursed during the slow songs to grab food and drinks. Several students giggled; their speech became slurred.

Vienna felt someone watching her and looked around.

"Do you feel that?" Tabetha asked. "I think you have an admirer," she chimed.

"Can you see who it is?" Vienna looked around, but nobody stood out.

"Other side of the drink table." Tabetha nodded in that direction.

Vienna turned around and spotted a young man in the shadows. She could hardly make out his silhouette in the dark corner.

"I wonder who it is," Tabetha whispered with excitement.

"I don't know. But if it's Logan, I hope he acts fast; I'm getting restless," Vienna muttered.

"Of course. It's the man's duty." Tabetha's tone was unwavering. Vienna looked at Tabetha and shook her head. "Don't shake your head. It is our culture for a man to be the one to approach the female. Or the more masculine female to approach the feminine female. Is it not like that in the Human Realm?"

"Not really, but I don't want to chance being shot down." She turned back to face the dance floor. She could see all her roommates dancing and having a wonderful time. Her heart warmed for them.

"That's why us females wait." Tabetha stuck her nose up stubbornly and flopped down.

Just behind Iris, Vienna spotted a familiar face in the middle of the crowd. A face she'd had hoped to see but doubted she would. But there he stood, in a white tuxedo and silver tie.

"Logan," she whispered.

"That's who saved you that night," Tabetha squealed.

Vienna nodded and watched as Cosima walked up to Logan. She placed a hand on his chest and secured her body to his. He narrowly moved her away from him. She stood there, arms moving dramatically. Logan ignored her and began moving to the music; Cosima walked away angrily without looking at her. Satisfied, and a little relieved, Vienna smiled.

Vienna watched as Logan danced, unfazed by the people around him. As though he felt her stare, he turned, and their eyes locked. Her cheeks reddened as an uncontrollable smile spread across her lips. His lips pulled into a wide grin and he winked before continuing to jump around and head bop to the heavy metal music blasting through the speakers.

After seeing him, she couldn't help but notice how few of the boys wore white suits. *How didn't I spot him earlier?* she thought. Most chose the traditional black, and a few wore odd colors like blue, green, red, and even yellow or orange.

"I think he likes you." Tabetha giggled.

"Not likely. We're just friends." She thought about the moment in the cave and her stomach heated. She bit her lip as she wondered if he would ever care for her more than a friend.

"If you say so."

"There you are! We've been looking everywhere for you. Where's Iris?" Nessa asked.

"Why aren't you dancing?" Jayla jumped in.

Vienna looked around, realizing Iris was missing. "I don't know. She was here a while ago."

"Oh well. I need a drink. Then, I'm heading back to the floor. Want to join us?" Nessa invited her. "I spotted several cute guys without a dance partner."

"You sound so girly," Celine said with a giggle. "I love this side of you, Nessa."

Jayla laughed. "Oh, hey! I think I see my dance partner, Azel!" She strode over, determined to reach him before someone else asked him to dance. Moving in front of him, she stopped abruptly, then took his elbow—guiding him to the drink table. She turned back long enough to blow a kiss to her friends. They laughed as they watched Jayla's cheeks redden.

One by one, each girl found someone new to dance with, except Vienna. She sat alone, watching. Part of her felt bad for herself, but the other part was thankful to relax after going nonstop for the last several weeks. Practicing magic was helpful, but also exhausting.

"Ask Logan to dance," Tabetha pressured. She sat at the table next to Vienna's cider.

Vienna ran her hand down the base of the glass and shook her head. "It would be fun, but I would rather relax. Besides, I'm having a great time watching everyone," she assured her.

"Excuse me." A deep bravado interrupted her. "Mind if I sit here?" It was the guy from the dark corner. He was stunning, with raven black hair, dark olive skin, and piercing green eyes.

"Beautiful," she whispered, then covered her mouth.

He chuckled and gestured to the chair next to her.

"Of course." She motioned for him to sit.

"Thanks. Why aren't you dancing?" he asked, unbuttoning his dress coat with one hand before sitting down.

"Why aren't you?" she shot back.

"Touché," he replied with a wide grin. He held his hand out. "I'm Elric."

"Vienna. It's nice to meet you, Elric."

"Have we met before?" Déjà vu washed over her. She tried over and over to recall why he seemed familiar, but failed.

Before he could answer, Remi, Cosima, and Yasmin walked up and snickered.

"Be careful with whom you converse. This vile twit will scar your name for life," Cosima spat as she tossed her hair over her shoulder.

"I'd be honored to have her tarnish my name," he responded without looking away from Vienna.

Vienna's heart pounded as she watched his pupils dilate. She smiled.

"Then you deserve what you get," Cosima shot back.

"Are you jealous he's talking to her instead of you?" Iris asked from behind her.

"No," Cosima snapped, face laced with disgust. "I have my choice of guys."

"Then go find them," Elric commanded, eyes locked on Vienna. "Because tonight is for celebration, not for building your ego."

"Whatever. You're not worth my time, anyway. Let's go," Cosima demanded. Remi and Yasmin followed.

"Sorry about that," Vienna muttered.

"No worries. She's been watching me all night," he admitted. "I was hoping talking with a lovely lady like yourself would help deter her." He laughed, and it was beautiful and light, like a whispering wind.

"Well, whatever the reason you came to sit by me, thanks," Vienna said with a smile. "She's been catty all year."

"I wouldn't worry about it. All schools have a group like hers."

"Even your school?" Vienna looked into the crowd.

"Even in mine," he laughed. "Look over there." He pointed to the entrance doors where four boys stood. Their shirts were unbuttoned, and they had no ties. One's hair was greasy and tousled, and the others had mullets. One of them stuck out a foot and stepped on a passing girl's dress, sending her crashing to the ground.

"Wow . . . I guess Cosima could be worse," Vienna admitted.

"They're just misunderstood and mostly harmless," he offered.

"Maybe, but they do a lot of emotional damage. It's not right."

"Agreed."

They talked mindlessly until Tabetha hopped on Vienna's glass to get her attention. She trembled, and sparkles fluttered everywhere.

"I don't trust him," Tabetha announced.

Vienna looked down at her with curiosity. *Be nice. He's the first boy to talk to us.*

Tabetha crossed her arms and thudded onto the table. "Why are you ignoring me and my intuition?" She shook, spewing glitter across the table.

Vienna thought Elric could see the glitter for a second as he wiped crumbs from the table.

"See? He's wiping my dust and not talking when I do. Something's wrong!" Tabetha insisted.

*Calm down,* Vienna told her.

"So . . . " Vienna turned her attention back to Elric. "You noticed an admirer earlier and didn't ask her to dance? Are you particular about who you socialize with?"

"Not at all. I just found you interesting."

"How so?"

"Like me, you ignored your admirer and found joy in flying solo when your friends weren't around."

"What admirer?" she questioned.

Elric gestured toward the punch bowl. "Logan has been watching you. You didn't know?"

Vienna gazed at Logan, smiling at the fun he was having. As he turned toward her, the smile she once controlled spread into a grin.

But his smile faded. Vienna followed Logan's eyes to Elric. Logan's face turned to stone.

Elric turned back to Vienna. "See? We each had someone we weren't interested in."

Vienna didn't correct him, but looked away from Logan.

"Would you like to dance?" Standing, Elric held out his hand.

*When did he move?* she wondered.

"I'd love to." She took his hand, and he guided her to the dance floor.

They danced in silence until they found each other's rhythm. Vienna felt instantly at ease with Elric's peaceful presence. They talked about their families, school, and even their hopes for the following year.

"It's a trick." Tabetha dropped to Vienna's shoulder and glared at Elric.

Vienna ignored her and continued her conversation, thrilled to have someone so open. She shook her shoulder, trying to shoo Tabetha, but she didn't budge.

"Will you be attending Sparks Boarding School next year?" Elric asked.

"I believe so. At least I haven't heard otherwise. Will you be at Domar's?"

"No. This is my final year."

"Oh. What are your plans after school?"

"I'm not sure." Elric's energy vibrated with Vienna's, and she moved closer to his body.

Looking into his eyes, she felt safe. "I swear I know you," she whispered.

His response was a smile, and he leaned in, his lips brushing the lobe of her ear. Warmth spread, and her stomach overwhelmed and pushed as heat shot between her legs, chills consuming her body.

"Where have we met?" His chest rumbled.

"In a dream?" she asked.

He answered, but Vienna didn't hear what he said.

She cocked her head at him and watched as his lips moved from her ear to her chin, where he placed the faintest kiss.

She'd spotted Logan as he walked toward her, pushing the mass of students one by one. She hadn't realized it, but she and Elric had danced to the other side of the room.

Logan's face was frantic. She'd never seen him so distraught. A cool breeze brushed across her feet. She looked from Tabetha to Elric, his full lips turning into a mischievous grin. Before she could push him away, his emerald eyes brightened, starkly contrasting with his dark olive skin and black hair.

Panicked, she tried to pull away, but his grip tightened. "Next time, take heed when your bug senses darkness," he spat.

Before he could say another word, the room blurred, and the last thing Vienna saw was Logan. Less than six feet away, he reached for her hand; his features filled with fear.

# CHAPTER THIRTY-THREE

Vienna's eyes fluttered open, but bright white assaulted her sensitive eyes. She groaned and put her arm across her face to block all traces of light.

"Wake up," a timid voice requested. "The Queen wants to see you."

"The Queen?" Vienna mumbled.

"Yes. Her Majesty has been waiting all day for you to wake."

Her eyes shot open. "All day?"

"Indeed. You have been here all day without moving."

Vienna looked up to find a little girl with long white hair and crystal blue eyes kneeling beside her. She wore a blue dress and appeared to be younger than ten.

The girl stood up. "My name is Saltriez. It's a pleasure to meet you." She bowed, and Vienna realized she wasn't wearing any shoes despite snow covering the ground.

"Aren't you freezing?" Vienna asked.

"Oh no, I am used to the cold. Hopefully, you will be warm too. The Queen placed a spell of warmth on you. Are you ready to meet her?" Saltriez held out her hand.

Vienna ignored the hand. "What time is it?"

"Here or in the Human Realm?" Saltriez asked.

"Both."

"It's been 10 minutes in your time, but almost 5 hours in ours," she said with a smile.

Vienna got up slowly, looking around for Tabetha. She couldn't see or hear her. Not knowing what else to do, she followed the child.

She looked around the area; it was like the Summer Court. Instead of flowers and colored trees, the area was covered with sparkling white snow. The trees were bare of leaves and only held a small layer of ice and powdery snow. The path she walked with Saltriez was blue ice weaving through this winter wonderland. Ahead, she saw a throne of ice. She couldn't imagine anyone sitting on it.

"We are almost there. Once we arrive, kneel at the throne, and the Shadow Queen will make herself known," Saltriez instructed.

"Thank you, Saltriez. I appreciate your help." Vienna was confused by the new queen's name, but she had suspicions about who it might be. She hesitated for a couple of seconds before asking, "Did I arrive with anyone?"

"A moth," Saltriez said with a nod. "Didn't stay, though. Maybe for a few seconds, but then it left. I am unsure where it went. You know, bugs? They wander. Is it a pet?" she asked, wide-eyed.

"Something like that."

"Hopefully, it will come back. We are here." She gestured toward the throne. Nobody had arrived, and Vienna looked around, curious about what she missed. She spotted the giant planet with the ring from the Summer Court. Why would they send a new person to get her, though? And why in the middle of a dance?

"You must be Vienna." Vienna jumped at the sound of the deep alto voice. This wasn't Banrigh Gheal, White Queen of the Summer Court. That meant one thing . . . This was the Unseelie Court.

Vienna bowed, praying for her heart to slow down. *First, she meets with the Seelie Court, now the Unseelie? How could this be?*

"Do not fear me, Quintessence. I mean you no harm."

"We don't know if I am the Quintessence yet," Vienna countered.

"Tsk, tsk, tsk." The Queen moved closer to Vienna. "Someone has been withholding the Prophecy from you. Tell me, dear"—she kneeled to Vienna's eye level—"have you heard about the Prophecy of the Highest Celestial?"

Vienna looked up to meet her gaze.

"No, of course not," the Queen sighed. She circled Vienna like a vulture.

Vienna had no knowledge of this dark, sinister queen, not even her name. She froze in fear as she compared her to the Seelie Queen, who was harsh but less terrifying.

"Let's make a deal," the Queen offered. "You have dinner with me, where we will discuss what I know, and then I'll let you go home."

*This isn't a request; it's a command.* Afraid to decline, Vienna nodded.

"Fantastic." The Queen clapped her hands. "Elric will bring you to the dining hall once Saltriez has you fixed up and appropriate for dining."

"Elric?" Vienna questioned, but the Queen disappeared into a black cloud before answering. She turned to find Elric walking toward her.

"*You!*" she screamed. "How could you bring me here? I can't believe I . . . " She stopped herself.

"What? Found me attractive? Trusted me? Both," he mused. "Or failed to heed Tabetha's warning. One should never ignore a trusted Fae's instinct. That you should have known."

She punched him in the chin, sending him flying back, landing on his back with a groan. She called to the elements and sent an ice storm at him. Placing one foot behind her for balance, she stretched both arms toward him, moving them in a circular rotation, and began muttering a spell.

The wind picked up, creating a deafening howl. Elric slid backward, his feet dragging as he tried to guard his face with both hands. As the ice started to form, she felt a backlash. Elric was countering her storm with his own. Hail began to form, knocking out each of her shards of ice. The pressure started to build, and she was pushed backward. Her firm stance was no match for the storm.

She screamed in frustration, trying to summon more power, but something blocked it.

"We felt your energy flowing, Vienna. I'm glad we came when we did, as you two were on a dangerous path." The Queen turned toward Elric and summoned him with a wiggle of her finger. "I know you're angry and confused, Vienna, but starting fights is not the way. Now clean up and join us at the dining hall."

Before Vienna could respond, everyone except Saltriez vanished.

"I'm sorry about that. She does things in her own time," the girl informed her.

"What's her name?"

"Skygge Lineal, which means Shadow Ruler. She is the Queen of the Winter Court, the Unseelie Fae, known as the Shadow Queen."

There was no response as Vienna followed the girl who would prepare her for a feast.

▽△△▽✳

It didn't take long to tidy up. Within an hour, Vienna sat at a long dining table that hosted fifty people. She had been the first to arrive, so she chose a seat next to where Saltriez said the Shadow Queen would sit.

The realization had hit while she was getting ready. The only way to get answers was to listen to the Shadow Queen.

Several Fae filed into the dining room moments after the Shadow Queen, who entered with Elric by her side. Except for the three seats across, the table was full. Food and drinks were served, but with wine being the only option and not trusting the food provided by the Fae, Vienna sat there in silence, stomach growling. She ignored it and fixated on her heartbeat, fearful that three people would accompany them. All she could think about was the warning she had heard all year about being betrayed by those she trusted most. It could be several people.

"We shall have the plates cleared and we will talk if you're finished." The Shadow Queen ordered the table to be cleared of all food, leaving just drinks. "As you have noticed, three people are missing from the group. Before I bring them in, we have some things to discuss.

"I promised to tell you about the Prophecy of the Highest Celestial, or at least what I know about it. See, each realm was gifted a different clue to the Prophecy. The section I was given revealed two clues. First, the Quintessence will be able to access both the Seelie and Unseelie Court, which you have demonstrated. Second"—she rubbed her finger around her golden goblet, making it sing—"the Chosen One will harness power from all the elements while also wielding the Spirit." She paused and motioned for her guards to come forward.

The guards opened the doors, and Vienna stood, anticipating who would walk through the door. The moment she saw her face, Vienna fell into her seat, her heart shattered. Valda stood just behind the door, her face void of emotion. Behind her was Gwen, her mom's sister, the woman who haunted her dreams for years, who left her frozen in fear and tormented her, assuring Vienna she wouldn't win. Vienna felt sick. They hadn't been dreams. She tried her hardest to move . . . to speak, but she couldn't. Instead, she felt a fire burning in her gut as anger grew.

The Shadow Queen stood and welcomed Valda and Gwen by

kissing each of their cheeks. After they sat, The Shadow Queen flicked her wrist, and suddenly Vienna was sitting.

She felt her throat relax. She tried to speak. "Valda." She teared up at the name. "I thought I could trust you." She looked down. Her anger turned to pain. This girl she considered her best friend, the girl she had confided everything to, had been the one to betray her. Not one of the girls in her circle like she thought.

"I . . ."

"Silence," Gwen hissed at Valda.

Valda closed her mouth, looking away from Vienna.

"Now," the Shadow Queen started, "down to business. We have gathered because we believe you are to be the Quintessence. But it is prophesied that the one to take the life of the Quintessence during a one-on-one battle can wield power. So, since you have less knowledge, training, support, well . . . everything, it makes sense for the power to be transferred to Valda."

Vienna sat for several minutes, thinking about what she had just been told. She couldn't understand it or determine why they would want that.

"That doesn't make any sense," Vienna finally responded.

"Sure, it does. Let me explain," Gwen snapped. "The power will transfer to someone worthy of it." She sneered without looking at Vienna. "I believe you received this power in error, as my daughter"—she brushed Valda's cheek—"is also of royal lineage on both sides."

Vienna watched Valda's body as it shuddered under Gwen's touch.

"But can she enter both realms?" Vienna asked.

"Once she wields your power, she will," Elric said.

She couldn't make sense of it, no matter how hard she tried. But she decided it would be best to remain silent.

"A couple more things." The Shadow Queen motioned to her guards. Vienna couldn't speak; all she could move was her head. She watched as another familiar face walked in.

Logan.

He entered with Tabetha, who was locked in a cage. Tears flowed over in streams as she realized the two people she'd trusted most had betrayed her. Vienna's heart shattered.

"Why am I carrying this cage?" Logan held it up.

"Ah yes, you cannot see, nor can most. But a Fae sits inside. She is sworn to Vienna, meaning she will lay down her life to protect her. Therefore, she must remain caged during the battle."

"Battle?" Logan's eyes widened, and he took a step back. "What battle?"

"Valda and Vienna will be dueling to determine if Vienna is strong enough to be named the Quintessence." The Queen's face shifted into a cold, menacing smile.

"There is no doubt that Valda will prevail. Vienna has barely begun training, and there is nothing special about her," Gwen hissed.

"You're wrong!" Tabetha screamed as she slammed her body against the bars of the cage. It fell on deaf ears, as only Vienna and the Queen could hear her. But the determination in Tabetha's words brought hope to Vienna, and she harnessed it.

"I was under the impression that the Quintessence was born and not created. If the power can be transferred, how could it be a prophecy?" Logan asked.

"Many believe that the ability to transfer power is valid. However, Valda holds the same qualities as Vienna. As Gwen has told me over the years, she believes Valda is the true Quintessence. Their duel will prove to us who really is." The Shadow Queen looked at Logan, who nodded and sat directly across from Vienna.

"When will this duel begin?" he asked.

"Once the Winter Solstice ends," Gwen answered with a smirk. "Less than an hour to go."

▽△△▽✷

Time dragged by as Vienna listened to the members at the table. They discussed what they wanted from the Prophecy: how life would change after and who the onlookers believed would win. They all agreed it would be Valda. She had the skills, experience, and heart for it. Vienna was the underdog.

Vienna watched Valda's confidence grow as they talked about her skills. She avoided looking at Vienna but smugly looked at the others around them. Logan, on the other hand, was unnerved. He was hiding it well, but Vienna knew his tells. He shook his legs anxiously and his eyes darted across the table to each person that spoke.

Her chance of survival soured her stomach as she took in each perspective. It was clear she was the underdog. Vienna agreed. From all their practices, there was seldom a time she got a good hit in that wasn't due to Valda slipping up or allowing her to get the hit to boost her confidence.

"5 minutes to go," Logan announced. "Where will this take place? Here?" he guessed.

"No," the Shadow Queen answered. "They will transport to the Nether Realm. Which means very few people will be able to attend."

"I see. Who will go?" he asked.

"Valda, Vienna, and I are Dreamwalkers and can go between realms. Can anyone else here transport you to the Nether Realm?" the Queen asked. Everyone shook their heads. "Then there will be few to worry about. Let's get ready."

Valda and the Shadow Queen moved to Vienna and made a circle. They grasped her hands—she still had no control over her body. Vienna felt numb, with no ability or desire to fight. She looked into Valda's eyes as tears burned her own. She thought she saw regret on Valda's face for the briefest moment, but she couldn't be sure.

The dining hall began to turn faster and faster, and all the colors blurred together. The wind tossed Vienna's hair. She looked up to see Valda watching her. They locked eyes, and Vienna fought the urge to scream. It was as though her body was vibrating between realms, pulling her soul from her body—but she fought the detachment and stayed whole.

Within seconds, the three of them stood in the Nether Realm.

The landscape was the same, as was Valda's black leather outfit, but Vienna's was different from the last time she was here. Instead of a cotton dress, her outfit matched Valda's, but with white leather instead of black. She also had two daggers at her side and two swords across her back. Her hair was in a slicked-back, high ponytail.

They were both ready for battle.

# CHAPTER THIRTY-FOUR

There was a slight breeze in the Nether Realm, which wasn't there before. Vienna believed it was due to the chaos the three brought to this silent land.

The Shadow Queen walked a circle around the two girls and chanted words Vienna couldn't understand.

"Are we really doing this?" Vienna whispered.

Valda disregarded her, turning her face toward the Shadow Queen.

"I can't believe this. You were like a sister to me." Vienna batted away an angry tear.

"We haven't known each other that long, V," Valda countered. "It's been less than a year. How can you say we're that close?"

"It feels like we've known each other longer," Vienna murmured. "I know you feel the same way . . . or I thought you did. You were always there for me. Or was it all an act?"

"It doesn't matter what it was. What matters is where we are now. Only one of us can win." She turned her back on Vienna.

"I disagree . . ."

"Enough!" the Shadow Queen screamed. "We have thirty seconds to go. Find your stance."

Valda pulled out her two daggers and twirled them. Vienna felt a pull, and when she looked in the direction it was coming from, she saw two blades in the middle of the Nether Realm—directly between her and Valda. She focused on them, thinking about her last battle with Valda. Vienna had little hope of victory—she was beaten more than she won against Valda. *How can I find the courage to win, especially against this girl I feel so close to?* she thought.

"Remember, there are no rules," the Shadow Queen declared. "Magic, weapons, words, nature; you can use anything that will name you the victor. Do you understand?"

Vienna stared at the daggers blankly; from her peripheral vision, she saw Valda nod.

"Good. I'll be waiting to announce the true Quintessence—you have five seconds to prepare." She walked away and stood on a nearby mound of dirt.

As Valda began to move counterclockwise, she continued nodding at Vienna to arm herself. Vienna pulled out one dagger, but the second caught and dropped to the ground.

"This will be easier than I expected," the Shadow Queen proclaimed. "Don't hold back, Valda."

Vienna heard a high-pitched whistle. The Winter Solstice had ended, and as the last echo of the whistle faded into the night, her blood slowed to a crawl. Fear gripped her heart.

Ignoring the fear coursing through her was only possible when she saw Valda moving forward. Blood rushed to Vienna's head, and she scrambled toward her weapon. She shuffled on her hands and knees and finally made it to the dagger. Picking it up, she paused, along with everything around her. She looked down, stunned—electricity shocked her. Adrenaline shot from her fingertips to her heart; power radiated from her hand. Confused, she looked at her hand as it gripped the dagger's hilt. The pommel held a shining moonstone that beamed like an opal of all the elemental colors. Vienna searched for her knowledge and recalled the opal represented telepathy. It could be used to influence others to create compassion and confidence. It also allowed foresight.

Her mind whirled: *Is this a sign? To find courage, to know I have the strength. How did someone get this here? It has to be a gift.* She looked around, but it was still just the three of them. As she gripped the daggers tighter, she felt grounded.

Valda started charging, both daggers held tight. She tucked and rolled left just in time to avoid a blade slicing her arm.

Vienna jumped to her feet and ran, praying she could escape. As she picked up speed, she hit an invisible wall, sending a slicing pain through her head. She landed on her back and slid several feet. The Shadow Queen croaked out an evil laugh. Vienna felt foolish; she hadn't realized the Shadow Queen was putting up a barrier. She couldn't afford to keep making these mistakes.

"Fight me!" Valda commanded, as she rushed toward Vienna. She came down upon Vienna with both daggers, but missed her by inches as Vienna rolled right and jumped to her feet. She adjusted her stance and realized she was missing one weapon. Her eyes searched the area frantically. Finally, she spotted it several feet away, next to the invisible wall she'd just hit. Vienna scrambled forward, grabbing the blade. Before she could turn around, a sharp pain penetrated her spine and tingled down her back.

She screamed and slowly fell to her knees. She dropped to the ground and increased the grip on each dagger, then rolled to her back and kicked Valda in the stomach, launching her several feet backward.

Valda landed with a hard thud but was back on her feet before Vienna could reach her knees. Valda waited for her to stand before transporting behind her and hitting her again. This time, she stuck her blade straight through her left shoulder.

Vienna pulled away, screaming in agony, and sliced Valda's bicep. She would need to fight back, not just play defense, to live.

"I didn't want it to come to this," she told Valda, as rage filled her chest.

"Nor did I . . . but here we are," Valda hissed, arms open wide.

Valda ducked as Vienna slashed at her stomach, and then Valda tackled Vienna, hitting her in the chest and taking her down. Vienna lost all her wind and began to see stars. Valda sat on her and stuck her blade through the same hole in her left shoulder. Vienna screamed and writhed in pain.

"Don't go for deadly blows," Valda hissed. "You need to fight back, but don't go for the kill. Aim for the arms, legs, anything that will show we're battling." She jumped up and began to walk in a circle around Vienna.

Angry and ready to avoid pain, Vienna focused on transporting in front of Valda. She successfully slashed Valda across her left cheek, then stuck her second dagger into Valda's foot, pinning her to the ground. Valda let out an earth-shattering scream.

As Vienna pulled the sword from her back, she spotted the Shadow Queen's smile. She was enjoying this.

A flickering light danced behind the Shadow Queen, and Vienna stared in confusion. Valda's screaming faded to the background as Vienna walked toward the Shadow Queen. She had to know what that light was.

"Finish her!" the Shadow Queen raged.

As Vienna inched closer, Logan appeared. A moment later, a sword slid out of the Shadow Queen's stomach. Her eyes widened and turned black, but before anything else happened, she disappeared.

Vienna stood confused as Logan held the sword that had just been in the Shadow Queen. "How did you get here?"

"I'm a Dreamwalker," he admitted. "I'd kept it secret, as I was unsure who would try to use it." He nodded to Valda. "Like they used her."

"Used her? She lied to me. She stabbed me, and she broke my trust."

"But she had no option, V."

"Everyone has a choice," Vienna murmured.

"Not always . . . Death isn't a choice for most people," he pointed out. She couldn't object.

Vienna turned back to Valda, who was trying to remove the dagger from her foot and groaning in pain. Unsure what to do, Vienna walked back to Valda and pulled the dagger out.

"Why didn't you fight me? You could've done more damage instead of letting me hurt you," Valda accused.

"I didn't want to fight you," Vienna hissed through gritted teeth. "This is all outrageous. I trusted you, Valda. You were my friend."

"I *am* your friend. Otherwise, I would have killed you while you stood there like an idiot instead of fighting me," she yelled back.

"An idiot. Seriously . . ."

"Valda is on our side," Logan interrupted. "But she couldn't let the Shadow Queen or her mom know. Otherwise, they would have killed her for betrayal."

"And what about you, Logan? What's your excuse?" She turned on him. Anger continued to boil through her, and she didn't know how to stop it.

He shook his head and averted his eyes. "When I first met Valda, I knew there was a story." He looked at Valda with what seemed like sympathy. "I tortured her for days before she told me what she was doing. How her mom was Grace's twin, and she was your cousin. How her mom and the Shadow Queen were working together to train her to kill you and steal your power . . . something I don't believe would work, I might add."

Valda nodded in agreement.

"We formed a plan to keep you protected." He reached out to touch Vienna's cheek, but she took a step back. He dropped his hand and nodded.

"If this is all true, then . . . what now?" Vienna asked.

"We need to summon the rest of your circle here to transport

Gwen and track her in the Nether Realm. It's the only thing we could conclude would keep you and our world safe," Valda answered.

"She's your mom," Vienna pointed out. "Are you sure you can do that?"

"She's only my mom by blood," Valda began. "She has tortured me emotionally, physically, and mentally my whole life. I am nothing but a tool to her. I love her because she's my mom. But she is also a monster that can't be trusted. She needs to be put somewhere safe, somewhere she can't hurt others."

"Then why not kill her?" Vienna asked.

"Because," Valda hesitated, looked down at her hands, and whispered, "she's my mom. I can't bear the thought of her being murdered."

"I'm sorry," Vienna whispered as she walked toward Valda. "You went hard on me to make it look like you were fulfilling your role. Is that to ensure the Shadow Queen believes you aren't a traitor?"

"Yes, just in case we need her insight again."

"I see," Vienna admitted. She looked at her shoulder and watched as blood dripped down her arm, turning the white leather pink everywhere it touched. "Anyone able to heal?"

"I can," Valda said. She walked over, placed her hand on Vienna's shoulder, and light flowed through her hand.

Vienna watched as her skin slowly closed. "How is that possible?" she asked in shock.

"I am a Dreamwalker, but my element is Earth. We are made of the earth, which means I can heal people. You can, too, V. You can control all the elements to some level, just more with someone in your circle. You need to practice."

"Wait, how do you know about my circle?" Vienna asked.

"I think she needs to know before we summon them," Valda said.

"You're right, because the others can't know or may not trust us to complete the ritual," Logan answered.

Vienna looked between the two of them. She watched as Logan

handed Valda a vial of yellow liquid. Valda took it and popped off the lid.

"Trust and forgive me, V." She hugged Vienna, then drank the vial in one gulp. The wind around her began to spin. The black dust from the ground stirred, and Vienna had to cover her eyes. She could feel her hair whipping around, then nothing. Everything went still. She uncovered her eyes, and when she looked down, Iris laid on the ground, wearing the black leather suit Valda had worn just minutes before.

Vienna gasped as she took a step back. She looked at Logan, who nodded. "Is this why you said I couldn't trust someone? Why you both did?" she asked, clenching her fists.

"No." Logan gripped his hair in frustration. "Kind of." He stopped and moved back toward Vienna. "I didn't know about this"—he gestured to Iris' motionless body—"until last week when I walked in on Valda . . . changing." His brows furrowed and he looked up at Vienna with desperation. His eyes filled with trepidation.

"Then who were you warning me about?" she spat, moving closer to him. Her arms were locked at her sides, fists clenched. Logan took a step back, looking at her like his heart's been crushed.

"Everyone. We knew there would be spies, but we weren't sure who they were. The Shadow Queen uses spies on anyone of interest."

"Tabetha?" she asked, suddenly terrified. Had Tabetha been the one to report back . . . Was she the one who couldn't be trusted? Her heart broke as she thought of her loyal companion, who felt like part of her soul. *Could she have betrayed me?*

"No, not her," Logan reassured her and stepped forward. Vienna's nostrils flared, eyes squinted, and she stepped back. Logan closed his eyes. "Tabetha is clear and trustworthy. I can feel her energy. Whoever the spy is," he admitted, "I don't know her or who she is, I should say." He stared at Vienna and shook his head, defeated. He'd broken her trust, and her pain oozed from every pore.

"How do you know it's a she, then?" she asked in confusion.

"We found out last week that Valda's guardian . . . Gwen had sent a spy. Unfortunately, neither Valda or I have been able to discover who it is. It will take time before we know for sure. But she referred to her as she. Which helps eliminate some . . . "

"How?" Vienna interrupted. "We are in an all-girls school with few males. That doesn't really help us much."

"Right." His lips went taunt. "My best guess is Cosima."

"I would believe that," Vienna seethed through gritted teeth.

Vienna heard groaning and looked over to see Iris waking up. She sat up, holding her head, and Vienna struggled between feeling bad and enjoying the pain she was experiencing.

Vienna's heart hurt—she'd been betrayed. She had trusted Iris, taken her home, and introduced her to her family. Now, she knew that she had taken Valda home, and that Iris was just a character created to gain her trust. She was a weapon to gather information for Valda's guardian. A weapon designed to infringe on Vienna's family —a weapon to deceive her whole family, to gain their trust, and to find their weakness.

Vienna couldn't help but wonder, though: *Did I actually share much? Did Valda do all this to betray her mom and the Shadow Queen? Or was that her explanation for continuing to deceive us?* Even if it was done to betray others, it didn't resolve Vienna's trust issues. Vienna felt violated. Washing that feeling away would take a long time.

Iris or . . . Valda . . . looked up at Vienna; eyes filled with shame. "I'm sorry, but right now, we need to summon the rest of the circle to banish Gwen before she and the Shadow Queen decide to try something else. You can ask questions later."

"She's right," Logan agreed.

"How do we do it?" Vienna asked.

"We will join hands, and the two of us will call them. Then, when they feel us, they will naturally relax and be transported here."

Vienna took Iris' hands and paused. "Do I call you Iris or Valda?" she asked bluntly.

"For now, call me who I look like; we need the others to maintain trust." She couldn't look Vienna in the eyes—instead, she stared at the ground with shame.

Logan put a hand on Vienna's shoulder. "We need to transport your circle here to help you banish Gwen now."

The urgency in his voice caused Vienna to pause. She centered her emotions. Breathing deeply, she released her negative energy. Once she felt a sense of calm flow through her veins, she nodded and, together, they closed their eyes. In unison, they said their names one by one: "Jayla, Nessa, Celine, come. Come and give us aid." Then, with voices that crescendoed, they repeated this chant until the wind turned around them.

The earth trembled. In the distance, rocks rolled down from the hills. They broadened their stance for balance and chanted louder until everything stilled. Several seconds passed, and they opened their eyes. Jayla, Nessa, and Celine stood with their mouths agape.

"What . . . just . . . happened?" Celine choked with a shaking voice.

"We transported you here, to the Nether Realm, because we need your help," Vienna answered.

"Where now?" Jayla asked, looking around the landscape.

Vienna filled them in as quickly as she could. The only thing she left out was that Iris was actually Valda, and she was the one who had wounded her. She told them of her dreams before entering Magyieka and about her Aunt Gwen's desire to take her life, partially as a way to get back at her parents.

"I don't know what to say," Celine admitted.

"You don't need to say anything," Iris assured. "But we do need your help, and we need it now. We can't wait."

Without question, the girls formed a circle. Logan disappeared and then reappeared with their candles from the cave. Vienna smiled at him while the rest of the girls looked at him with uncertainty on their faces.

"This is Logan. He is a good friend. He is one that we can trust," Vienna reassured them.

"Ah, this is the kid you grew up with. The one you told us stories about?" Nessa teased.

The others smiled as Vienna blushed, but she ignored them. With that, the girls didn't hesitate to take their candles and light them. They each placed their candle behind them and then grabbed hands.

"We need to chant in unison. I will start, and then we'll all repeat it together," Iris said. She took a deep breath and then began chanting loud enough to reach the sky. "Earth, Air, Fire, Water, Spirit. We summon thee."

*Profer eam unum mentitum*
*Qui decepit*
*et numquam exclamavit*
*Educ ad poenam vicium*
*In terra longinqua sola per omne tempus*

After Iris said it a second time, the rest of the group jumped in, chanting louder with time. As they continued, their hands tightened, and their arms rose. Each time they finished the chant, the ground rumbled with increased intensity. On the fifth time through, the entire landscape shook, nearly sending Vienna to the ground. She repositioned and bent her knees, watching as the rest of the group did the same. She spotted Logan from the corner of her eye as she stood there on guard, waiting to protect them should danger arise.

Vienna's chest filled with power, and on the seventh chant, her eyes flew open. She saw the other girls do the same. Their eyes shifted to the color of their stones and they looked up to the sky. A deep humming filled her ears as Vienna focused on remaining upright. Fatigue assaulted her muscles and Vienna breathed deeply.

Exhausted, they all dropped their arms, and in the middle of the circle Gwen laid, curled in a fetal position, naked. The girls looked at one another, unsure of what to do next.

Before the recognition of success hit, Nessa crumbled to the ground, blood oozing from her nose. Vienna rushed to her and kneeled. She placed Nessa's head in her lap and pushed her hair out of her face.

"Nessa . . . " She shook her lightly. "She's not breathing!" Vienna yelled at Logan. "Help!"

Iris, Logan, and Celine rushed over. They tried everything they could—slapping, tugging, poking—but Nessa remained motionless. Iris began CPR, but it failed to work.

Jayla laid dazed, unable to help. But she didn't look injured. "Are you okay, Jayla?" Vienna shouted. Jayla nodded, so everyone she turned her focus back to Nessa.

Logan looked at the candle behind Nessa. "She needs water. That's her element, and she's drained," Logan said. "V, you can summon all elements. Can you pull some water to her?"

"I can try," Vienna said with determination. She closed her eyes and focused on pulling any liquid to her. Then she opened her eyes to see three drops of water hovering in front of her. She gasped, looking at Logan for guidance.

"Put them in her mouth," he demanded.

Vienna moved her hands slowly, guiding the droplets to Nessa's mouth. She placed them on her lips, one by one. When the third drop rolled into her mouth, Nessa moaned.

"We need to get her to bed," Iris said.

"Send me with her," Jayla offered.

"You're up!" Vienna said in surprise.

"I'm kind of a badass," Jayla teased. "Send me with her."

Iris, Celine, and Vienna worked together, chanting. It took them several rounds, but then Jayla and Nessa were gone.

"Is this her?" Celine asked, nodding toward Gwen's still form.

"Yes," Iris answered solemnly. "We need to leave her here."

"Do we have clothes for her?" Celine questioned—her voice filled with empathy.

"No, she will not need them here. She is not of this land. She will walk it as if a ghost," Iris answered, a sob causing her voice to become pitchy at the end.

Logan laid a hand on Iris' shoulder. "The only way she can leave is with Vienna's help. The one who needed her cast here is the only one who can decide to let her leave."

"Can I ask what she did?" Celine asked.

"She tried to kill Vienna. She sought her power, and there was no deterring her," Iris explained flatly.

"I'm sorry, V." Celine placed her hand on Vienna's back for support. Vienna patted her and then turned to Iris.

Empathy filled Vienna's heart as she watched Iris, who looked up to the sky, trying to keep tears from falling down her face. In that instant, Vienna completely forgave her friend . . . her cousin.

"We need to get back to our realm," Logan insisted.

"How do we leave?" Celine asked.

"Think of home, or the school, to be more accurate," he answered. "As long as you all imagine yourself there while standing in your circle, you'll get there."

"Can we come back to this place?" Celine asked. "I've never seen a place like this. I've only heard of it through our teachings at schools."

"Not without being summoned here by a Dreamwalker, like Vienna."

Celine twisted her lips and nodded once, letting them know she understood.

"Let's form a circle to get you home," Iris said, grasping Celine's hand. Iris took her stance first. Seconds passed, and not only did Celine disappear, but so did all the candles.

Once Celine was gone, Iris pulled out a vial and drank it. She shook for several seconds and fell to the ground, writhing. Vienna held her until she stopped.

Valda curled into Vienna, crying and begging Vienna for forgiveness. "I'm sorry. I'm so sorry . . ." She hugged Vienna and kept apologizing for all she had done.

Vienna's heart broke as she watched Valda tremble; she felt Valda's anger, fear, loss, and pain as if it were her own. Finally, she pulled Valda into her and kissed her forehead. "Come home with me," she offered. "My family would welcome you."

"After all I have done," she sobbed, "how could they?"

"Because you're my family, and you saved my life today. You made a mistake, but haven't we all? In the end, you saved me . . ." She paused, smiling. "In the end, you chose me. You chose love. You're sacrificing your guardian to save our world—all the realms . . . really. There is nothing more selfless."

Valda nodded, but didn't speak as tears poured down her cheeks. Her body shook, overcome with emotions. *Breathe*, Vienna thought, sending calming energy to Valda. *Just breathe.* Their connections united, and Vienna watched as a wave of energy washed over Valda's body. Valda inhaled deeply, lifting her entire chest. Head turned back to the sky, she inhaled through her nose, slow and steady. She breathed out, grounding herself, then looked over at the woman who raised her.

Vienna followed Valda's stare and looked at Gwen—the aunt she had never known existed until recently, the woman she learned tormented her mother. Red. The woman who had haunted her dreams laid lifeless for several minutes before Vienna spotted her chest rising. Laying on her side, she breathed shallowly.

"I'm sorry, Valda. I wish . . . " Valda vanished before Vienna could finish her thought. Vienna looked around, confused, before meeting Logan's eyes. He blinked, letting her know Valda was home safe.

Vienna and Logan stood there in silence. They stared at Gwen; she looked helpless, but her features were peaceful. Vienna's heart ached seeing someone so damn vulnerable and unconscious; no matter how much wrong she'd done, nobody deserved that—not a second passed when a red cotton dress materialized on her.

"Nobody should have to roam this plain naked," she whispered. Logan nodded in understanding. He reached out, took her hand in his, and they turned their backs on the heartless, once mighty, now powerless, sorcerer.

Hands intertwined, they transported back to Sparks Boarding School.

# CHAPTER THIRTY-FIVE

## Vienna & Logan's
## POV

Vienna couldn't bear to leave Logan yet or to be inside. So, they sat on a bench outside the school in silence. Vienna laid her head on Logan's shoulder for comfort. She was exhausted emotionally and physically. She felt guilty for all the times she doubted Logan but brushed them off as her thoughts roamed to Valda and Iris: how she had lost Iris, but she still had part of her. She also thought about Gwen. Could Gwen find a way to harm them? Of course, they knew she'd wake and be trapped. But what if the Shadow Queen discovered what happened to Gwen? There was so much to consider.

"What happens now?" she asked Logan.

"I don't know. I guess we finish the school year and go home." He wasn't very convincing.

"Home . . . that sounds nice." But she wasn't sure if it really did. The words were more reflex than anything.

"Are you really going to take Valda home with you?"

"I am. I worry about explaining Iris to my parents. I'm not sure how much to tell and what to leave out," she admitted.

"Your parents are amazing. They'll understand. The more you tell them, the more they'll be able to help you both. Valda's going to need all the love and support she can get. She's had a messed-up life." He laid his head on top of hers.

"You're right. I don't have time to warn them before we go, so it'll definitely be a surprise. I mean, I could also have her show up as Iris initially." They laughed at that, and Vienna started feeling a little better.

"Oh, I almost forgot." He reached behind him and pulled out a cage. "The Ovr'seer sent this with me."

It was the small cage she had seen when they were in the Winter Court.

"Tabetha! I thought I lost you," she squealed. "How did you get her?"

"I can't see it, but I know it's important to you." He shrugged. "I left it with the Ovr'seer while I was getting ready to join you in the Nether Realm. And he just sent it over. He wanted you to know he is still on your side."

"I keep hearing that from people, but I'm struggling to believe it now." Saying it aloud made her feel vulnerable. "Anyway, this is a Fae . . ."

"Do you trust this Fae?" He gave the cage a light shake.

Tabetha gasped. "Who wouldn't trust me?"

"It's okay. He doesn't know better, and he doesn't know you." Vienna opened the cage and let her out. "Don't worry, she's a good Fae, and I trust her with my life. Maybe she will show herself to you? What do you think, Tabetha? Help him see the good that can come from the Fae Realm?" Vienna smiled with encouragement.

Tabetha nodded, and Vienna summoned enough energy to calm Logan. Tabetha fluttered in between them, waiting.

"Holy crap!" He blinked. "I expected something," he pondered for a second, "less cute." He moved around Tabetha, inspecting every inch of her. "Its wings are easy to see. So is the dusty, sparkly stuff.

But its body is too bright. It's like a florescent body with . . . with moth wings?" he said hesitantly.

"*She*," Vienna corrected him. "This is Tabetha, and she found me the night you saved me in the cave and helped me get home. She calls me her person now. Have you ever read about people who have a spirit animal?"

"Yes," he said while continuing to inspect Tabetha.

"The bond is a lot like that. She protects me, keeps me company, and even entertains me." She laughed to herself.

"She talks to you?" Logan asked.

"She does."

"You said Tabetha earlier. Is that her name?"

"What else would it be?" Tabetha said, huffing. "He's a bright one."

"Be nice," Vienna warned her. "He's our friend."

"Tabetha, you're beautiful," he said as he moved closer to look at the back of her wings. Then, his look of wonder shifted to confusion. "That jingling . . . is that her voice?"

"For those who can't actually talk to her, yes. To me, she sounds just like a Human."

"She looks like a moth, but more beautiful." He smiled.

Vienna nodded, then remembered something that had been bothering her for months. "Logan, can you tell me about your eyes?"

He sighed. "You noticed them."

"It was hard not to," she admitted. She looked at him, and he took her hand.

"I'm a Shifter, Vienna. That's why I was able to move so fast. The Ovr'seer has been teaching me how to harness my shifting. How to control it."

"When you shift, what do you become?" She pictured him as a tall werewolf who walked on two legs and had very little hair.

"I become . . . "

"Logan!" a loud bellow rang out. It was the Ovr'seer. "Good to see you again, Ms. Corey." He nodded. "But we must go."

"We'll talk next time we meet, okay?" He placed a lingering kiss on her forehead before he walked away.

She chased after him, grabbed his arm, and turned him around. "Thank you," she whispered before kissing him with all the emotion she had left. He smiled, touching her hips, and then she let him go. Before she could wave, he and the Ovr'seer disappeared.

▽△△▽✳

Breakfast was filled with animated discussions about the dance, but Ms. Blight's arrival brought an immediate end to the lively conversation. She walked to the front of the room and let out a resounding whistle.

"Although this is your last meal at Sparks Boarding School for this year, we hope you find happiness as you recall your time here," she said, her commanding voice filling the empty space. "Many of you built lifelong friendships, and many more have learned who you are and what you are capable of." She glanced at Vienna before she returned her gaze to the rest of the group. "For those returning next year, we look forward to your continued growth. For those graduating next week, know you will always have a place here. We are not just part of your journey, but a resource as you walk through life. The staff of Sparks Boarding School wishes you all a safe and relaxing break." With a final bow, she brought her hands together, causing confetti to shower down and fill the room with bursts of vibrant colors.

Students cheered and hugged one another as it sank in that the end was official, and they had successfully made it through another year.

Vienna and her friends sat at their table, waiting until it was time to leave. She was exhausted after spending the morning explaining to her roommates who Valda was and what had happened to Iris. They immediately noticed the new face in Iris' bed, and the discussion was inevitable. She realized the truth was far better than continuing to lie to them. After the conversation ended, the girls' moods had been sullen. Trust disappeared, and they refused to accept Valda's apology. Even now, they sat on the other side of the table, and Vienna brainstormed ways to help them mend the cracked relationship. Vienna knew Valda felt awful, but they both understood why the others couldn't forgive Valda. Not yet, anyway.

As they sat in silence, Vienna felt a tap on her shoulder. She began to turn as she was handed a note. Opening the thin paper, she scanned it briefly; she had been asked to report to Ms. Blight with Valda before she left. Deciding this was as good an excuse to leave as any, Vienna showed Valda the note, and they agreed to head out. Vienna gave Celine, Jayla, and Nessa each a long hug. They held back tears until they couldn't hold them any longer. Vienna gave in first, and Celine wiped the tear from Vienna's cheek, smiling at her.

"We'll be back together before you know it, V," she whispered as she embraced her in one last hug. "Be safe, my friend."

Feeling better about the situation and knowing her friends would leave soon, Vienna took Valda's hand and headed to Ms. Blight's room.

They waited for Ms. Blight to arrive for nearly an hour. They sat silently, enjoying the downtime after such a chaotic final semester.

"Good morning, you two." Ms. Blight walked in with a bright smile. She squeezed and rubbed Vienna's back as she walked by, then took her place behind the desk. "I heard you will be going home with Vienna?" she asked Valda.

Valda nodded.

"Why?"

Vienna explained the situation about Iris and Valda, Valda's mom, and the Shadow Queen, and even disclosed how they had learned they were related. Ms. Blight nodded, pausing to take in the information.

"Thank you for such a detailed summary." She sat forward in her chair. "I am well aware of what happened in the Nether Realm," she admitted. "And that Iris and Valda were one and the same."

"What?" Valda asked, leaning back.

"Why didn't you say anything?" Vienna asked.

"It wouldn't have done any good. However, the purpose behind the deceit was valid, and what I knew of both Iris and Valda led me to believe she would choose the right side. See, as Quintessence, you can go dark or stay light. And those you surround yourself with can influence where you end up."

"What about the others? Did they know?" Valda asked. "They seemed shocked when we talked to them."

"No," Ms. Blight whispered as she shook her head. "They didn't know any of it. As we speak, Jayla, Celine, Nessa, and anyone else who met Iris are being taken to a holding center. There, they will have their memories altered to erase Iris and replace her with Valda."

"But why?" Valda asked, her voice hoarse.

"Because next year is your final year here," she answered. "You will find that the journey of the Quintessence is just beginning. She is prophesied to create a much-needed change in all the realms, one that will unite all the realms in a way that has never happened before. Or, if she were to go dark, she would create a dangerous rift between the realms." She looked at Vienna pointedly.

"Wait . . . I thought I was done after the Nether Realm," Vienna admitted.

"No. You have only fulfilled *part* of the Prophecy. You ended the reign of an unworthy royal, your Aunt Gwen. You still need to gather information from the other realms to understand your full destiny, Vienna. The journey will be a little easier with Valda by your side."

"What realms are you referring to when discussing uniting them?" Valda asked.

"All of them." Ms. Blight sat at the desk in front of them. "More details will come as needed," Ms. Blight continued. "For now, you will continue your studies and become stronger. You won't become the Dark Quintessence; you have already chosen the light."

"What about the next few weeks before school starts up again? What should I be focusing on?"

"You will work together and study the Prophecy and the other realms. Your books will be sent after you arrive. Logan will help along the way."

"Me, Valda, and Logan, huh? What about the other three that complete my circle?"

"They will be there when you need them. For now, educate yourself about the realms you're prophesied to align. You will need their help to get their prophecy sections," Ms. Blight explained.

"This seems unreasonable or impossible," Valda admitted.

"Nothing is impossible. You must find faith, friendship, and trust in yourself. With those three things, anything is possible." Ms. Blight smiled down at the girls. "It's time for you to go. I will see you after the break."

As the girls walked toward the door, Vienna turned back. "Ms. Blight?"

"Yes?"

"What if I fail?"

"Believe you won't, then you won't," she answered. "Take care, Vienna. And may your strength and faith guide you." With a snap of Ms. Blight's fingers, Vienna and Valda blinked from Ms. Blight's room.

## **LOGAN**

Logan felt an urge to find Vienna. He'd been sparring with the other Watchers when he was hit with a strong sense of danger, and the vision of Vienna and Valda in combat flooded his mind. He'd taken several blows to the head before his partner stopped and asked him what was happening.

"I need to get to my Ward. Where is the Ovr'seer?"

"He's not returned from the last council meeting, but Mr. Humphrey is at Onyx Hall." His classmate pointed in Logan's direction as if he needed it.

Disregarding regulations, Logan shifted, knowing it would save him time. His bones crunched as his body contorted. Hair raven black and deep blue sprouted from his pores, and his face broadened. Antlers cracked from his skull, touring several feet high, the pain ripping a horrifying roar from Logan's throat.

Logan's sweat dripped from the hair covering his body as it continued to shift. He watched the boy's horror in his eyes as his body grew to an enormous height, his paws the size of two grown men's feet.

With his body numb from the pain of becoming the StagAri, Logan's nostrils flared as snot shot to the ground. A deep guttural whine vibrated in his chest as he soothed himself. Transitions were like being sliced apart and then sewn back together without any numbing agent, but doing it during daylight and without the moon's blessing was indescribable.

"Can I help?" The boy's voice quivered.

Logan shook his head, his enormous antlers slicing through the air, the whooshing powerful. He grunted as he pawed at the dirt, then stomped his paw, shaking the ground, which sent the kid topping over.

No longer disoriented, Logan ground his paws and charged toward Onyx Hall. His black and blue mane flattened against his body as his speed increased beyond the average jungle king.

Trees sped by in a blur as he focused on his destination. He used his antlers to toss tree branches and leap over fallen logs. The rush filled him with freedom as he harnessed his shifter form. He swung his tail at the pesky sprites buzzing toward him and increased his speed. He knew sprites shouldn't be in the Shadow Realm or the Isle of Mist. Something was wrong, and there was no doubt that V was in danger.

*Thud.* Logan's vision went black. The last thing he saw was a small blonde with pointy ears looking down at him. Her mouth moved, but he couldn't hear a sound.

# CHAPTER THIRTY-SIX

## Vienna & Logan's POV

Vienna and Valda opened their eyes and found themselves standing on a cliff in Oregon. In front of them, the vortex that took them between the Magic and Human Realm stood ready, humming with energy. "I didn't know she could do that," Vienna gasped. "She didn't need a portal."

"She's powerful and wise. I'm not surprised." Valda looked around the area.

"I'm ready." Vienna no longer trembled, and she felt her courage growing.

"We can do this. I'm here to help however you need," Valda told her. She grabbed Vienna's hand.

"It's going to be weird not having the others with us," Vienna admitted.

As Vienna turned toward Valda, a purple and white lightning bolt caught her attention. She looked out over the Oregon landscape and spotted the bolt. It was moving toward the Earth; the color shifted to blue the closer it got to the Earth—fire burned at the tip as the speed increased, penetrating the ozone of Earth's atmosphere. Vienna's chest seized—she held her breath, paralyzed with fear. Valda followed her gaze.

Valda hesitated. "Is that . . . an . . . ? Are we . . . ?" she stammered.

"I don't know. At first, it looked like a lightning bolt, but I'm not sure." Vienna couldn't blink or move at all. All she could do was stare wide-eyed at the horizon.

From the corner of her eye, Vienna spotted the Shadow Queen standing amongst trees. Beside her stood Cosima. Her blood boiled. "Look over there," Vienna commanded. She remembered accusing Cosima of being a spy. Now she knew for certain.

"Is that the Shadow Queen and Cosima?" Valda asked.

"It must be. Why would they be here?" Vienna readied herself to run toward them but was stopped. Valda held her arm.

"This could be a trap. We can't go rushing in without knowing anything." Valda's voice was unwavering. Vienna couldn't tell whether she was stunned or truly didn't care about the Human Realm.

"What's happening, Tabetha? Tell me you know something . . ." Vienna begged.

"It's heading straight for your house!" Tabetha shrieked.

"How do you know that?" Vienna screamed. "We can't see my house."

"I can." Tabetha sobbed.

Before Vienna could respond, a raging ball of fire violently collided with the ground. The earth-shattering blast sent a bone-rattling shockwave through the air, leaving her breathless in terror. The earth beneath her shook. She fought to keep her balance, grabbing onto Valda for support as fire torched through the forest at lightning speed.

"*What do we do!*" Vienna screamed as she ran toward the impact.

A strong grip shot pain around Vienna's wrist, an inhuman strength that stopped her from moving. She swung around and stared into large emerald eyes. Blood dripped from her arm, and she peered down, taking in the ebony claws attached to thick, scaly, enormous hands. Vienna looked back to the creature, its massive body engulfing her view.

The grip on Vienna's arms tightened, the pressure searing into her skin. The world around her shifted in a blink, the air crackling with energy. Before Vienna processed what happened, she stood in the Nether Realm, the earth beneath her feet dry and solid.

"No, take me back!" she screamed. Beside her, Valda was bent over, her breakfast splattered across the copper sand.

"That I can't do," a thunderous voice answered.

Vienna pulled out her daggers and turned to an unfamiliar voice. Shocked at the sight, her daggers fell to the ground, and a hollow thud fell on deaf ears. Within reach stood an enormous, pitch-black Dragon with bright emerald eyes. Wafts of smoke exited its nostrils as its chest rose and fell as it breathed, waiting for her to respond.

Words escaped her as she stared at the mystical creature. The Dragon raised its head with pride and her eyes crossed each feature. The teardrop scales that shimmered as he moved were captivating. She reached out without thought, and the creature shifted; its rippling muscles vibrating the ground.

"Where did you come from?" She took a step back.

The creature lifted his front arms, pounding the ground. He acted . . . excited. She scrunched her features, confused by the behavior.

"Tell me what you're doing here," she commanded.

"I'm your Protector. I have watched over you since you were a young child. You know me, but we have never met while in this form."

She moved closer, looking into his blazing eyes. He kneeled, his body rumbling, tossing her off balance as he bowed at her feet. She placed her palm on his chest, where his heartbeat was strong. Images flickered through her memory: the emerald eyes, the raven black hair, and the olive skin. With a gasp, she pulled back, removing her hand from his scales.

"Elric." It wasn't a question. She knew; it suddenly made sense why he seemed so familiar, why she couldn't believe he would betray her. He was protecting her.

"But in the Winter Court," she began.

"It was the only way to gain the information needed to ensure your survival," he said softly, regret in his voice. "The Queen couldn't know why I was there."

"But you're a Shifter. How did you enter the Fae world?"

"I'm a Dragon with Fae blood. Like Tabetha, I can transform as needed."

"He's a Dragon Fairy," Tabetha trembled. "None have been trusted before; they are rare, and the Fae deceit mixed with Dragon temper . . ." she squealed.

Vienna touched his scales, and a vision of his other forms flashed through her memories. A Dragon, the size of a moth with green sparkles, drifted to the ground as she practiced in the forest with Logan. The same Dragon, half the size of Tabetha, hid in the forest as she returned to Sparks the night she met Tabetha. She stepped back and looked up at Elric. The memories of his familiarity at the dance and the dream of him introducing himself. She closed her eyes and felt soft bedding under her as she looked up to the ceiling of her childhood home. The black Dragon fluttered at the top of her ceiling, looking down at her, the green sparkles falling off him and onto her face, which caused her to sneeze. She opened her eyes and shook her head.

"You've been watching me since I was a child. Why didn't I remember?" Confused, she moved closer, demanding answers.

"I cleared your memory when my fairy dust fell upon you. It was the only way to protect you." His trunk-sized legs shifted. Vienna caught her balance and looked up at his enormous size.

"Can you be any size?" she asked.

A deep laugh escaped, and smoke bellowed from his nostrils. "Only the two sizes in Dragon form. As a Shifter, I am this size; as a

Fae, I take on the size of a small, winged fairy. In Human form, I have but one size."

Vienna opened her mouth to answer but was cut off.

"Vienna." Valda's voice was laced with concern.

A glass ball formed in front of them, and the image of the Earth, and the destruction that engulfed it, unfolded. "I can't hold it much longer," Valda groaned. Valda's outstretched arms shook, holding the sphere steady as the images of hurricanes, tornados, and fire spread across the Human Realm.

Vienna covered her mouth. Breath-hitching sobs wracked her body. The weight of the moment pressed down on her, the gravity of the situation sinking in. Closing her eyes, she prayed for a reprieve from the emotions destroying her.

Tabetha fluttered down, nuzzling Vienna's neck. The vibration eased her pain.

*Why is this happening?* she asked Tabetha.

Tabetha fluttered into the air and looked around. "I think the Shadow Queen just started the War of the Realms!" she sniffled.

"You came into your powers early," the baritone voice said. "Your element is Spirit." He moved toward her. "You walk between realms and come from a pure bloodline."

Vienna turned at the silence. Behind her stood Elric in Human form. She stared at him, pleading for it to not be so.

"You are the Quintessence. And the fate of the realms lies in your hands." There was sorrow in his eyes.

"But you have us," Tabetha said. "We will be here to help."

Vienna's head swam. *I'm the Quintessence. Blessed with the power of Spirit, I am destined to unite all the realms.*

This war, Vienna realized, would spread to all realms, destroying life as Enchanters, Shifters, Fae, and Humans—and Earth was the first target.

"I have a lot to learn, and I'm going to need as much help as we can round up." Vienna snapped her fingers, her blazing passion transforming her eyes to violet.

"You're ready." Elric touched her cheek. "Your eyes now match your soul."

"The Quintessence has woken!" Tabetha shrieked as she clapped.

"It's time to find Logan and the girls," Valda offered.

Vienna said confidently, "They'll be gathering at the Council, where the news will be presented as they form a plan."

"Then that's where we go." Elric grabbed Vienna's hand and then offered his other to Valda.

*Please find me, Logan.*

*He will,* Tabetha answered.

Linked, all three closed their eyes, and Elric transported them to Sparks, leaving the Nether Realm.

The Prophecy had begun.

## LOGAN

Fire tore through his torso as warm blood dripped from his side. A groan escaped his lips, and the murmurs of the room silenced. Logan's eyelashes fluttered. He couldn't make out the room or the people, but there were two distinct female voices.

The last thing he remembered was running through the thick mist of the Shadow Realm toward Onyx Hall, anxious to notify Mr. Humphrey and the Council that Vienna was in danger. He remembered the sprites, the speed, and the power . . . the freedom he felt. Then, all he could remember was blackness.

"He's clammy," one of them said. "If he dies, he's no good to us."

"If he dies, we'll get another hostage." The voice was familiar, but Logan couldn't make it out with the swishing in his head.

Logan screamed as a sharp object was plunged into his shoulder. Before he could catch his breath, something sliced the back of his thigh. This time, the pain was too much, and he was unable to make a sound. Instead, his body shuddered as his legs gave out. He felt his weight pull against chains that were wrapped around his wrists.

"Logan?" a small, familiar voice whispered to him.

*Who does that voice belong to?* Logan squeezed his eyes shut, blinked, and then looked around.

"My God," he croaked out. He took in the horrors of the room. His stomach turned and vomit erupted from him.

The dungeon was dark, and the smell of mold was thick. Movement from his chains echoed, bouncing across the brick walls. There were no windows, so he waited for his eyes to adjust to the black room.

In front of him, arms above their heads, with chains choking their hands, were Kreo and Vulcan. They were covered in ash and blood. Vulcan pulled at his chains animalistically. A guttural growl escaped as he pulled so hard he lifted his body so his toes no longer touched the floor. Next to him, Kreo was unconscious.

Anger and fear fought as Logan looked at the two boys he'd known since they were babies. He growled, causing the room to shake. The sorrow he felt in his chest was overwhelming.

Through gritted teeth, he sought answers. "What happened, Vulcan?"

"I . . . I don't know." Vulcan looked at Logan, fear from the growl fading as tears welled in eyes. "But I think my parents are dead." Vulcan cried as he pulled on his chains, trying to free himself.

Logan had never felt so helpless. He pictured Vulcan as a toddler begging Vienna and Logan to let him play with them. He remembered sitting at the breakfast table with Vienna's family, eating breakfast as her brothers asked him a million questions. Kreo looked lifeless with the black soot all over him, but Logan used his

Shifter senses and quickly picked up on his heartbeat and shallow breath.

Vulcan yelled, and Logan followed his eyes. Next to the entry door of the dungeon stood several figures. He blinked until the figures cleared. Huddled together, he saw Cosima and Fenella, as well as the Unseelie Queen and Mr. Humphrey, both of whom were wearing red robes.

Logan suppressed his rage as he locked eyes with Mr. Humphrey. A deceitful smile spread across Mr. Humphrey's face as he looked at Vulcan, then back at Logan. "Sometimes to change the world, sacrifices must be made." Before Logan could respond, the metal door closed, and a loud clink let him know the door had been locked.

# StagAri

## Logan's Shifter Form

# Elric's Fae Dragon

Elric's Shifter Dragon

#  INDEX

**Elite Enchantress** — Enchantress with pure lineage on both sides of her family and royalty or elite family on at least one side.

**Elite Spirit** — Enchanter with the gift of Spirit who has pure lineage and elite or royal blood.

**Enchanters** — Magic wielders in the form of Earth, Air, Fire, and Water. There are Dark and Light Enchanters.

**Enlitner** — A rare magic wielder who has extra-human strength and natural combat skills. They are able to use other Enchanter's magic to boost their own but have weak magic skills without boosting from others. They can create deep connections and read emotions due to their heightened empathy. Females are the only Enlitners known and they are a weaker Enchantress.

**Protector** — Term used when a Watcher is assigned to a Ward to watch over and protect them.

**Pure Spirit** — A light Enchanter who has the gift of Spirit.

**Quintessence** — An Enchantress who is a Pure and Elite Spirit and is destined to fulfill all or part of the Prophecy.

**Ward** — Term used for an Enchantress that a Watcher is assigned to.

**Watchers** — Trained in the Shadow Realm to become skilled soldiers with refined combat skills and the ability to mimic their assigned Enchantress' magic. They are created to be assigned to a powerful or Elite Enchantress to protect them with their life. They are a rare creature as they are created from one magic bearing parent and a Shadowwalker.

## THE WORLD OF MAGYIEKA

**Shadow Realm** — Shifter Territory

**Magic Realm** — Enchanter Territory

**Fae/Fairy Realm** — Seelie and Unseelie Court

**Dream Realm** — Dreamwalker Territory

**Nether Realm** — Territory of Eternal Void

# COUNCIL MEMBERS

**Ovr'seer** — Head of the Council and voice of Magyieka

**Silver Stripe** — Shadow Realm, Shifter Territory

Logan and Mr. Humphrey

**Gold Stripe** — Magic Realm, Enlitner Representative

Ms. Kaliese and Mrs. Laveau

**Blue Stripe** — Magic Realm, Enchanter Representative

Mrs. Jaheem and Mr. Castro

**Green Stripe** — Fae Realm, Seelie Court

White Queen and Elric

**Purple Stripe** — Dream Realm, Dreamwalker Territory

Ms. Blight and Mr. O'Cain

**Red Stripe** — Nether Realm, Territory of Eternal Void

Mr. Ozul and Mr. Audovera

# ACKNOWLEDGMENTS

Thank you to everyone who has helped me on this journey.

A special thanks goes to:

All my parents and siblings by blood and marriage, thank you for giving me courage and faith in myself to chase this dream.

My children and spouse, thank you for encouraging the journey.

Thank you, Represent Publishing and Brittany Evans. I literally wouldn't be here without your help with editing, the self-publishing process, and the book cover design.

Thank you to Kelly Scriven for line editing, and Kristin Petersen for all the guidance you provided for this book.

# ABOUT THE AUTHOR

Shabucky WinterRose was born and raised in a small valley in Wyoming and now resides in Idaho. As a child, she had her head in the clouds and loved to daydream. As a young adult, she discovered stories of the supernatural world and began creating her own worlds.

She is currently attaining her MFA in Creative Writing at Lindenwood University. During the day, Shabucky works as a clinical social worker with a focus on neurodiversity. When she's not working, you can find her enjoying nature or seeking adventure with her family and pets.